OUTSIDE ETERNITY

THREE FEET OF SKY

BOOK TWO

STEPHEN AYRES

Outside Eternity: Three Feet of Sky
© 2013 Stephen Ayres

ISBN-13: 978-1482586534
ISBN-10: 1482586533

LOOK TO THE SKY

Eight AM, like clockwork, the billions of resurrected woke up clean and refreshed in their miniaturised environments. Most enjoyed another day of carefree leisure and material self-indulgence, but Adam Eden had a different agenda. Sitting uncomfortably on a cushion at the top of the playground slide, he nonchalantly munched a chocolate Hobnob. Between bites, he stared unblinkingly at a small patch of sky just to the right of the ruined chapel. Partially obscuring the view was a stand of hawthorn trees, but Adam still scrutinized every nuance of the artificial blue. A light smattering of biscuit crumbs coated Adam's baggy grey sweat shirt and the legs of his faded blue jeans, but he was far too engrossed in the sky to notice.

Every morning for the past month, Adam followed the same routine. After slipping into his clothes, and eating a breakfast of hot buttered toast, he headed out of his small ground floor annexe, holding a cushion under his arm and clutching a paper bag in his hand. The jog up to the high meadow was always brisk, as Adam was eager to get started. Pushing through a light copse, he walked across the viro playground, climbed the ladder to the top of the tall slide, and began his daily vigil.

While watching the sky, Adam contemplated his situation. Two years after his resurrection, he still found it hard to believe that he was only an inch tall. In fact, with everything in the Viroverse built to the same 1/70 scale, everybody simply kept to their old measurements and barely acknowledged their tiny size. Therefore, despite his miniaturisation, Adam still saw himself as a little under 6 feet tall.

The environments—commonly known as viros—gave the scaled impression of being a mile square, but despite being sealed tight, they were not prisons. Anyone could travel to another viro, perhaps to visit friends or family, but it involved an unseen process that took place after midnight, when the entire population of the Viroverse were in their enforced sleep phase. You simply arranged a visit, went to sleep, and then woke up the next day at your destination, clueless as to how you got there.

Knowing how to escape from a viro, venturing outside the walls, was the closely guarded secret of a small despicable elite—even though they themselves could never leave. This was Adam's intended goal, but it meant finding a physical exit.

Seemingly impenetrable, the viro walls and ceilings used retinal projection to fool the eye, making it look as though the landscape stretched into the far distance. The walls therefore seemed invisible, making Adam's lonely vigil, staring at the fake sky, a true test of willpower and focus.

Nearly a month had passed since Adam had defeated the psychopathic glam gang in a final bloody encounter. Groover, the psychopaths' leader, and one of the first resurrected humans, had lived up to his end of the deal, telling Adam about a secret portal found in all viros. Adam sat looking for it every day, but it remained frustratingly elusive.

According to Groover, the portal was a small patch of wall membrane that could only be cut with a special metal shard. The membrane, always located to the right of the most cluttered corner of the viro, was roughly thirty feet above ground level. The problem for Adam was that the membrane had the same retinal projection qualities as the normal viro wall, making it virtually impossible to see. However, at certain times and under certain lighting conditions the keenest eye might detect a slight distortion in the sky. Groover promised that once spotted and recognised, the portal would fully reveal itself to the viewer.

"Gotta love that empty sky!" someone shouted from below.

Startled by the voice, Adam choked on his biscuit, puffing a shower of crumbs onto his already well-coated sweatshirt. He looked down, and saw Stern, the celebrity hind-reader, holding the railing at the bottom of the ladder. Impressively muscular in an eye-catching gold tracksuit, wild raven black hair barely tamed by a leather headband, the thick carpet of rubber chippings on the playground floor had muffled his approach.

"I'm meditating," said Adam, wary of his pushy neighbour's intentions, and determined not to reveal the secret. "Or at least I was until you showed up. Now, if you don't mind ...."

Ignoring Adam's wish to be left alone, Stern nimbly climbed the steps of the ladder.

"Ok, what do you want?" asked Adam, distracted from his sky gazing.

"Well now you've got the time," said Stern, reaching into the bag, "I'll join you in a snack. By the look of your clothes, they're obviously good enough to wear. Mmm, these are good. By the way, have you told your family that you murdered them?"

"I think they have a pretty good idea. Anyway, who told you?"

Stern cast a sly grin, and admitted, "You just did. I guess you didn't want them getting in the way whilst you were fighting the psycho gang, huh?"

After midnight, whilst the Viroverse slept, a number of unseen services sprang into action: healing, cleaning, travel, and if necessary, resurrection. Even though all three family members resurrected the following morning, Adam still felt a deep sense of shame. He had killed each one with the sole purpose of gaining tactical advantage over the glittering maniacs.

Ironically, now Adam's identity as Copacabana, legendary slaughterer of psychopaths, was common knowledge, both his mother and father treated him like a demi-god, constantly plying him with thoughtful presents and gushing praise. He knew their newfound affection for him was borne of a selfish desire to impress the wider family, and the tantalising prospect of entertaining celebrity guests.

Needing time alone to look for the portal, Adam told everyone he needed rest and solitude after the trauma of his psycho fighting days, and that meditating at the top of the playground slide was his chosen method of achieving inner peace. The plan had worked up until now, leaving Adam alone to watch the sky.

"Stern, what do you really want?"

"Well, another one of these for a start," said Stern, taking another biscuit, and popping it completely into his mouth. Slowly, purposefully, he ate, whilst staring straight at Adam in an unsubtle attempt at intimidation.

"And now, Adam, I would like to know what the hell has happened to our arrangement?"

"What arrangement? I made no arrangement with you."

"Remember when I got you through that day at Mama Fiestas, when people first found out that you were Copacabana? You agreed that I could act as your official agent and manager. Remember?"

"Vaguely, but you know I need some time to meditate."

"You don't fool me with this meditation shit! There's no way you're up here lookin' to find yourself. You've grown too cold and calculating for that. This is everything to do with what that psychopath told you after you killed his gang. Groover is one the originals—an experimental phase resurrected—and I'm sure he gave up some major secret knowledge. That's why you sit up here on your ass all day!"

Stern may have been fishing for information, but he was already too close to the truth for comfort. Adam decided to drop the meditation charade, but stopped short of giving away his secret.

"And what if it is? It's my business."

"You know how busy I've been on your behalf the past few weeks?" said Stern. "I've got celebrities lined up just desperate to meet the mighty Copacabana. Of course, you will need to wear that Hawaiian pink flower shirt and stuff, as you did when you fought the glam gang. But, if you wanted, in a couple of days you could be having tea and scones with Queen Victoria at the Goodwood hub. Surely you could take some time off for that, huh?"

"And what would you do while we're there? Sit under her ball gown all day, smelling her arse?"

"Hey, insult my noble profession all you want. At least no one gets killed when I perform my act. Look, muchacho, there's no way you can handle all the introductions, glad-handing, and crazy ass fans. Fame can be fleeting, my friend. Without me around to pump up the volume, your reputation might evaporate faster than spit in a dollar whore's snatch. Let me set up a few meetings, minor names at first, and if it doesn't work out then at least we gave it a shot."

Adam was about to refuse the proposal, when the appearance of a familiar figure distracted both men. Rhapsody, dressed in a simple cream cotton top, blue jeans, and light shoulder length hair, walked through the thin copse separating the playground from the surrounding fields. Smiling and waving, she hurried over to the slide. Unhappy to see the former psychopath, Stern muttered quietly to Adam, "Why is that psycho still coming here? I told you Kaylee doesn't like it. You might have murdered your parents, but that glam bitch killed my woman."

"She's harmless," whispered Adam through a ventriloquist smile. "The AI filtered out her bloodlust, and she needs a break from that damned psychoviro. It's only once a week. Manny invites her over to his place on Sundays. She killed me a few times and I have no problem with her visits."

Reaching the ladder, Rhapsody put her hands on her hips and pouted, "Oh darlings, have I got to stand down here straining my neck, or are you coming down from your little play perch?"

In swift response, Stern gave Adam a hefty push, slipping him sideways down the slide. Then, with typical macho bravado, the hind-reader leapt from the ladder, landing neatly in front of the bemused visitor.

"Hey Rhapsody, what do ya think of the costume? A little glitter and some platform heels, and I could join your gang. Perhaps you and I could go on a killing spree together. That is what you do, isn't it? You still hunt and kill innocent people in your psychoviro? You just come here for a break."

"I have no choice," pleaded Rhapsody, hurt by the comments. "If Groover finds out that I no longer have a lust for blood, then my life will be a never ending Hell. Look, I am truly sorry about Kaylee. I didn't want to kill her."

"Just following orders, eh?" snarled Stern, glad to see the woman's discomfort.

After lying stunned for a moment at the bottom of the slide, Adam achingly got to his feet, brushed the rubber chippings from his clothes, and intervened in the confrontation.

"Stern, back off! No one intimidates one of my guests. Inviting Rhapsody to the viro is my responsibility. So, if you have a problem with it, then talk to me."

Before Stern could respond, Adam turned to Rhapsody, his tone just as harsh.

"And you promised you'd stay near the Manor. I told you Robert's playground was strictly out of bounds when I'm meditating. Now, please keep your promise and get back there."

Rhapsody frowned with unmistakeable wounded affection, and left as quickly as she had arrived. Stern simply grimaced until she was out of sight. Then, without a word, Adam returned to the top of the slide.

Stern once again leapt up the ladder, and roughly grabbed Adam's shoulder.

"Don't you ignore me, you patronising little shit!" he yelled. "Even if you're gonna break our deal, you can at least tell me how long we have to put up with that killer paying us unwanted visits."

"Don't push me, Stern," said Adam, shrugging off the shoulder grip. "This is no business of yours."

"Oh, but it is … it is. When you killed that gang of psychos, Groover wasn't planning to honour his end of the deal. If I hadn't blackmailed him, then that secret knowledge would've remained secret. I put my head on the block for you."

"I know, and I can't thank you enough for doing that for me."

"I didn't do that for you," seethed Stern, losing his temper. "I did that so none of us would have to face that slaughter again. After all this time, all that blood and death might be normal for you, but we suffered. And then that murdering bitch turns up every week to rub our faces in it."

Using violence, or at least its threat, was an option, but Adam knew he was in the hind-reader's debt. Given the circumstances, throwing his insistent neighbour a proverbial bone seemed a better option.

"If it helps, the problem might soon resolve itself," he said cryptically. "Give it a little time, and I don't expect you'll be seeing any more of Rhapsody. You have my word, Stern."

Stern looked Adam in the eye, nodded, and immediately released his grip. Then, taking Adam by surprise, Stern asked offhandedly, "So once you spot the way out, you're taking her with you, eh?"

Without thinking, Adam replied, "Of course, once I see the …"

Clamming up immediately, knowing his secret was out, Adam face palmed and shook his head in disbelief. Stern beamed a triumphant smile, and smugly raised an eyebrow.

It took a matter of seconds before the mood changed, as a dark truth came to the fore. Stern's smile dropped, replaced by a sudden look of fear. Adam's expression also changed—squinting eyes, lips drawn thin, resigned to a deadly necessity. Strangely, Adam felt he was no longer in complete control of his actions. However, he knew that if he killed Stern, then the hind-reader's memories of his final few minutes would be erased. Once resurrected, Stern would no longer remember Adam's slip of the tongue. The situation gave terrifying life to the usually good-humoured saying, 'If I tell you, then I'll have to kill you.'

"I'll make this quick, my friend," said Adam, cold and emotionless, reaching out his hands towards Stern's neck.

Stern let out a frightened squawk and hurled himself off the ladder, landing flat on his back on the rubber chippings below. Oblivious to any damage or pain, he pulled himself up and began running frantically across the playground. Adam was in immediate pursuit, leaping and landing with well-practised precision, leading into a focused sprint. The outcome was inevitable. Though fit and muscular, Stern was just a pampered egocentric celebrity, hunted by Copacabana, the most famous killer in all humanity.

In his panicked state, Stern tried to run through the tyre swings but caught his arm on a chain, spinning him awkwardly off balance. Keen to avoid another apparatus mishap, he then skirted around the seesaw, but Adam vaulted powerfully over it, bringing down his screaming, golden prey in a flying tackle.

With Stern face down on the ground, his cries muffled by a mouthful of chippings, Adam placed his knee in the small of his back. After glancing at his G-Shock Mudman watch and setting the timer, Adam clutched Stern's head tightly with both hands. Obviously fighting for his life, the distraught hind-reader strained his head sideways, spat out the chippings, and pleaded with his attacker.

"For Christ's sake, don't do this, Adam! I can help you! Honestly, I can help you! I know more about this place than anyone!"

Adam leant forward, still gripping Stern's head tightly, and hissed, "I reckon I've got about three minutes before I need to kill you. I'll tell you what I'm looking for, and we'll see if you can help."

"P … Promise you won't kill me if I help?"

"You have Copacabana's word of honour, and that's a lock. Now, listen carefully or you'll run out of time."

Adam explained to Stern about the portal and its location, but as a matter of caution left out any mention of the shards. Unexpectedly, Stern started chuckling, albeit with a distinct note of fear.

"What's so funny?" Adam asked, releasing his grip.

"Ha, you've been sitting up there all this time, staring like some obsessed freak, at the wrong corner."

"But, it's the most cluttered corner. Look at all the trees, and the ruined chapel. No other corner comes close.

"Ah, but that's where my superior knowledge comes in. The chapel and half of those trees are new, installed around the same time as your parent's mansion. You should be looking elsewhere."

Taking a furtive glance at his watch, Adam helped Stern to his feet and brushed off the chippings in as friendly a manner as he could muster. Adam held up his hands in apology.

"Stern, I can only beg for your forgiveness. You were there for me at Mama Fiesta's, and you blackmailed that psycho into telling me the secret. If I can't trust you then maybe I shouldn't even trust myself. From now on I want you to remind me that I'm a human being when I start acting like a dick."

Hearing an ominous beep from his wrist, Adam looked at his watch again and grimaced.

"Damn, you lucky bugger, you beat the clock! Now I have to mean what I just said. Damn it!"

Both men just looked at each other silently, and Stern let out a relieved sigh. Adam put a supportive arm around Stern's strong, though still trembling, shoulders.

"So where should I have been looking for the past bloody month," he laughed.

"Err … still this side of the stream," said Stern, "but over in the other corner. Hmm, probably by the yew trees next to the tall hedgerow. You can't quite see them from here, but …"

"Don't worry, I know where you mean. That's brilliant. Outside, here I come!"

Once again, Adam gripped either side of Stern's head, but this time with a warm smile.

"You know, my wonderful arse-sniffing friend, I could kiss you right now!"

Relaxing a little, Stern returned the smile. He would carry this happy expression into death as Adam easily broke his neck with a sudden snapping jolt.

"And with just 20 seconds to spare," muttered Adam, looking at his watch one last time. He felt little guilt at murdering Stern. After all, the hind-reader would resurrect tomorrow morning with a brand new body. Immortality and fitness were guaranteed in the Viroverse, and you always came back looking the age you always wanted—and apart from a few exceptions that meant under the age of forty. The only downside to resurrection, and why death was still feared, was the agonising pain of the dark place, the terrifying limbo between lives as your new body was prepared.

After hoisting his dead friend onto his shoulders, like a huge golden man-scarf, Adam slowly ambled back to the slide. Sniffing the air, he picked up the agreeable waft of Stern's signature cologne, and made a mental note to find out its name. Arranging the body in a twisted pose at the bottom of the ladder, Adam carefully placed a biscuit in Stern's dead hand, plus a few crumbs in and around the mouth for authenticity.

If anybody asked, Adam would say that, 'I warned him to be careful, but Stern went for his third biscuit. As he took the first bite, he let go of the railing and began to fall. I tried to reach out but it was too late.'

As he made his way across the meadow to break the tragic news to Kaylee, Adam paused as his mind became clearer. Now back in control of his actions, he shuddered, shocked by what he had just done. Something or someone had possessed him, choosing violence over negotiation. Adam tried telling himself that it was not personal and not wrong—that it was always the mission and never the emotion that mattered. However, no matter how many times he tried to fool himself with motivational slogans from his fighting days as Copacabana, the guilt and shame kept growing.

Adam stopped by the stream to splash cool water in his face. Temporarily refreshed, he carried on, all the while humming the Copacabana song. The familiar tune raised his spirits, and for now chased away his demons.

NOW YOU SEE IT ...

A dam shuffled and shifted on the bough of a magnificent oak, not far from his parent's Georgian-style mansion. Running a hand along the grooves of the bark, appreciating the gnarly texture, he felt that this standalone tree seemed far more detailed than those in the dense woodland; much like a model railway set or miniature diorama, where eye-catching individual pieces were of superior quality than their generic background brethren.

Finally finding a comfortable seating position, Adam settled and looked over to the line of stately yews some eighty feet away. If Groover's information proved correct, then the exit portal was likely located just above the tree line. Sitting back, another sturdy branch providing a convenient backrest, Adam rebooted his lonely vigil, desperately hoping it would not take another month.

That morning, leaving a tearful Kaylee to cope with the news of the tragic playground accident, Adam had headed straight to the viro corner that Stern had pointed out. Kaylee believed every word of Adam's wicked lie. It was not that she was stupid, but that her friendliness and generosity of spirit gave her the most trusting nature. Tomorrow morning, however, with Stern having faced the intense agony of resurrection, the biscuit tale would be viewed with suspicion. At the very least, both neighbours would treat Adam as persona non grata—a status with which he was well acquainted.

Of far more concern to Adam, was the hijacking of his mind. The first signs of the problem had appeared only a few days after the defeat of the glam gang. With so much finally going right in his life, Adam entertained the idea of staying in the viro, rather than embarking on an adventure beyond the walls. Stern's management offer was tempting, and Adam relished the thought that he could lead a celebrity lifestyle, feted by the great and the good—and of course, the downright awful. However, whenever Adam came close to making the decision to stay, he became overwhelmed with a throbbing headache. The headache mysteriously subsided when he dropped the idea in favour of leaving.

Within a week, the increasing head pain had trained Adam to accept his fate. A part of his own mind was forcing him to leave, and no other option would be entertained. Stern's death starkly illustrated the power and ruthlessness of the shadowy intruder, prepared to go to any lengths to protect the mission. Now, Adam had an idea who he was dealing with. On occasion, he could hear a distant voice in his head, scolding him for taking so long to find the portal. The voice was his own, but the words belonged to Copacabana: the side of his personality that fought the psychopaths week after week for two years, suffering death and dealing it.

"Hey ya!" called a familiar voice, Adam once again distracted from his sky gazing.

Adam looked down through the criss-crossed branches, and saw Kaylee standing below holding up a small paper carrier bag.

"Thought ya might be hungry up there, so I brought you some take-out. Half pounder chilli burger and fries, with a big gulp of coke, that's ya favourite, yeah?"

"Err yeah, but … how did you know I was here and not at the playground."

Adam was surprised at Kaylee's sudden appearance, but glad of the food. In his haste to see the portal from his new perch, he forgot to bring any refreshments, and did not relish a hike back to his apartment to stock up. Possibly Adam's favourite perk of the Viroverse was that you could eat whatever you liked, and any amount you liked, without any negative consequences. Having been morbidly obese in his first-life, he always patted his rock hard abs every morning in gratitude.

"I watched you with binoculars after you left," explained Kaylee. "You can see most of the viro from our roof terrace. Don't worry none. I know you couldn't do your meditating with a dead body lying so close."

"Moving him away from the slide would be disrespectful," lied Adam, somewhat fearful that Copacabana might rise up again and deal with Kaylee. "I learnt that on the field of battle. It is only fitting that he lies where he fell until taken by night and restored by morning."

"Whatever Stern has said about you in the past, you've been a true friend today, Adam. Now, are you comin' down to get your food 'cause I sure ain't climbing up there, even if I'm not wearing ma usual heels."

"There's a rope hanging down the other side of the tree. If you can attach the bag then I'll just pull it up."

Displaying instinctive resourcefulness, Kaylee untied a red ribbon from her ponytail and tightly tied the bag's handle to the thick rope. She gave the rope a playful tug before turning to leave.

"Lunch is served," she said, taking a bow. "Enjoy it now, y'all!"

"Going so soon?" asked Adam, edging along the branch and reaching around for the rope.

"I … just … gotta go, hun."

"Oh, you're thinking about Stern."

"Yeah, that …," Kaylee sheepishly replied, "and I found three episodes of 'The Young and the Restless' that I ain't never seen before. That's four Martini's worth."

As Kaylee hurried back across the field to the parked Satan Bug—Stern's prized jet-black hunting buggy—Adam carefully pulled up the rope and eagerly untied the bag. Gingerly bumping back along the branch to his chosen comfortable place, he sat back to enjoy his meal—the bag placed securely on his lap. After quenching his thirst with a drawn-out slurp of ice-cold coke, he rummaged past the large wrapped burger and the red cardboard container of fries and collected the few loose salty fries from the bottom of the bag, greedily shoving them in his mouth all at once. Somehow, the ones that escaped always tasted the best.

Discarding the greaseproof wrapper, holding the chilli burger two-handed, Adam readied himself for the spicy, messy, and deliciously juicy first bite. As he brought the burger to his mouth, something caught his eye and he paused. A dark line, about ten feet across, level with the top of the central yew tree, appeared for a moment and then vanished; so briefly, that Adam was unsure if he had really seen something. He stared hard at the spot for a few seconds but saw nothing more.

Suddenly, the burger seemed lighter, and something bounced off his leg. Glancing down, he saw one of the burger patties falling to the grass below, the only evidence of its passing, a thick slide of chilli sauce on his jeans. Adam groaned. Losing some sauce was expected with a burger of this size, and even a slice of tomato was considered expendable. However, to lose half the meat was a severe blow to the eating experience and a huge disappointment: a catastrophe easily avoided if Kaylee had remembered the cheese—the culinary glue of the fast food world.

Reminding himself to be a cup half-full type of person, or at least a chilli burger half-full, Adam once more raised the diminished meaty treat to his lips. Again, he paused. Taking a quick look at the yew trees, Adam gasped, then cheered loudly as the portal revealed itself.

As Groover promised, the bottom edge of the portal aligned perfectly with the treetops, appearing much like a large smoke-glass square tabletop embedded in the sky, or a simple Photoshop transparency effect. As Adam gauged the size of the portal at roughly 7ft square, the second burger patty escaped from the bun, unnoticed and unlamented, joining its meaty colleague below.

Placing the spicy tomato and lettuce vegetarian bap back in the bag, Adam took out the carton of fries and munched happily and uncharacteristically slowly, all the while staring in wonder at the square in the sky. He always imagined the portal would be circular, gleaming epically like a second sun, but in truth a dull square seemed far more practical if there was a flat floor beyond, with the dark grey tones easily distinguishable from the surrounding sky.

As Adam pondered what might lie on the other side, the portal glitched and scrolled for a second. Once stable, the updated grey square displayed a vertical row of large white icons on the right-hand side, much like those found on the resurrection bracelets. On the left hand-side was an image of a smiling naked man, hands on hips.

"Oh shit! Oh no!" cried Adam, almost choking on his fries, as he recognised the photo-realistic image as himself, right down to the 'tiniest' of details.

Knowing that the portal was invisible to anyone else in the viro bought a modicum of relief, but he still found it disconcerting there was a huge grey banner in the sky featuring a smiling Adam Eden with micro-penis unveiled.

As late afternoon drifted into the dull grey-blue of early evening, the portal became less noticeable and Adam decided it was time to head home. His backside was numb from sitting on the branch for so long, and he needed another long cool drink to quench his thirst. Before rounding the corner of the mansion, Adam looked back one last time and felt relief that he could still see the portal. Groover promised that it was not a matter of 'now you see it, now you don't', but 'now you see it, now you can always see it.' Tomorrow, Adam would begin searching for the metallic shards.

***

Late afternoon, pitch black, total silence. The Terminal building fluorescents were off, and the world outside, beyond the huge viewing windows, seemed as a limitless dark void.

An eager female voice, with a pronounced Highland lilt, cut through the deathly hush.

"Captain Andrews, Adam Eden has seen the portal. Would you like me to contact the inkman?"

"That won't be necessary, Liana," said the Captain, tipping the gold embroidered peak of his pilot's cap, his voice faintly Scottish, smooth yet commanding. "I think we have a few more days before Mr Eden's departure. In addition, I am not sure that the inkman is the right choice for this one. Keep me informed of any change in the situation."

Liana smiled as she saluted her boss, and then left the office. The Captain rubbed his clean-shaven chin thoughtfully, and leant back in his executive swivel chair.

Wet 'n' Wild Bikini Girl!

If Groover was to be believed, then time was running out. After seeing the portal, Adam apparently had only five days to find the shards. Beyond that time, the shards would prove impossible to find. Since the psychopath was known to lie on occasion, usually just for fun, Adam at first decided not to take the rule too seriously.

Adam had started his first day of searching with an almost smug nonchalance. All he knew was that the shards were hidden in the oldest structure in the viro, and that they would glow if he looked in the right place. His parent's mansion and the ruined chapel were recent additions, which left only three viable choices: the cobblestone bridge, the utility cottage, and Stern's house.

Even though the bridge and utility cottage were close neighbours, Adam decided to search them separately –a whole day for each, starting with the bridge. A low humpback design, the grey cobblestone structure had a single arch crossing a rocky section of the stream. A meticulous inspection of the upper section with its low stone walls and surface of smoothly worn cobbles took an entire morning, and Adam made four detailed passes—even using a torch and magnifying glass on the final round to peer into any small cracks and hollows.

After lunch, the search resumed, this time concentrating under the arch. Fortunately, at the base of either side of the arch ran a narrow stone ledge. Adam borrowed his father's aluminium extendable ladder, and laid it ledge to ledge across the stream. Using duct tape to secure toughened glass tablemats across the ladder's rungs he created a rudimentary platform from which to work. He poked each stone block hard with an extendable paint roller pole—again borrowed from his father—but found nothing. With midnight, and its enforced sleep, only twenty minutes away, Adam finally gave up on the bridge.

Searching the utility cottage and its adjacent block of wake-up cubicles took another day, also producing no results. At lunchtime, Adam chose to eat inside the utility cottage with the ulterior motive of asking the resident androids, Amelia and Frederick, if they knew where the shards were hidden. As expected, neither offered any information and expressed total ignorance of the shard's existence. By late afternoon, Adam was ready to go home and relax. However, the increasingly dominant Copacabana side of his personality kicked in, forcing two more fruitless circuits of the building.

Adam had been so sure that the bridge or utility cottage harboured the mysterious shards that, by the third day, he approached the search of Stern's house with a growing sense of self-doubt. After the playground incident, there was little chance that Stern or Kaylee would happily open the door and let him inside, so Adam hoped that the shards could be found somewhere on the outside.

Adam was trained and experienced for stealth missions—a combination of the Sarge's tough talking instructions and months stalking his prey in Groover's psychoviro. Choosing to view the shards as an enemy gone to ground, and possibly disguised, Adam decided against his old Aloha clothing, instead choosing a lightweight mesh ghillie suit for camouflage, and a compact military grade monoscope for detailed inspection of the building.

Taking a carefully planned circuitous path, dodging from tree to bush and crawling behind a number of low stone walls, Adam settled amongst a cluster of leafy green shrubs to the rear of the house and its perfectly striped lawn. Keeping movement to a minimum, Adam set up the monoscope on a slim telescopic monopod and began his initial survey.

Whilst Adam had never set foot inside the large house, he had always admired the striking exterior design: curved granite walls, natural wood beams, and narrow tall windows contrasted with sleek terraces framed with simple cast iron balustrades. The roof terrace sported a striped canopied sun lounge and a comprehensive range of designer patio furniture. Standing on the terrace, unmistakeable in a flame red bikini, Kaylee poured a Martini from a large glass pitcher.

Kaylee relaxed into a plush cushioned lounger, with her back to Adam, and slowly sipped her drink. Adam scanned the rear of the house with the monoscope but saw no trace of the shards or any likely hiding places. Confident that he would not be seen, he broke cover and made his way across the lawn, heading for the side of the house. Taking him completely by surprise, Kaylee stood up, wheeled around, and pointed an accusing finger.

"What the Hell do ya think you're doing, creeping around on our property?"

For a moment, Adam froze, not sure of his next move.

"I know it's you Adam Eden. I saw ya reflected in the jug. Come for some more killin' no doubt. Now you stay right there, 'cause I got something to say to you."

Kaylee reached over to her side-table and picked up a pair of binoculars. As she adjusted the focus and zoom, Adam took his chance, and sprinted across the lawn. Confronted by a low hedge, he attempted a commando roll over the top –the move failed as the twigs caught in the fine mesh of the ghillie suit. Lying on his back on top of the hedge, Adam fought to free himself. Struggling only made it worse and he soon became hopelessly pinned down, even unable to move his arms or legs.

"Well, if that ain't the darnedest thing," said Kaylee, putting down the binoculars. "I'm guessin' you'll be stayin' fer a while after all."

Adam frantically looked around, desperate for a means of escape, and saw a figure standing back in the shadows on the lowest terrace.

"Hey Stern," shouted Adam. "We need to talk. You've gotta let me explain about the other day. There's a lot you don't know, and you probably think I had something to do with your death. Just help me outta this bush, and I'll come clean about everything. Please trust me on this one, old buddy."

Without a sound, the figure edged back into the room behind the terrace, pulled shut the patio doors, and rolled down the blinds.

"You aint dealin' with Stern no more, you're dealin' with me," yelled Kaylee from the roof terrace, pulling on a silver silk robe. "I tried to be understandin' when your mad bitch whore killed me; I really did. Now I'm convinced that ya murdered my man over at your stupid playground, and made me look a fool for believing all those lies. You need to know that anyone messes with my man then they're gonna pay."

Adam attempted to placate his angry neighbour, shouting, "Kaylee, you and Stern mean a lot to me! Can't we all sort this out with a drink in the cottage? A few hours and we'll all be laughing about it!"

"You aint gonna be laughin' today, Adam Eden, that's for sure. Pa always said I was quick thinkin', and I just cooked somethin' up that you aint never gonna forget. You may think dyin's a joke, but you don't know who ya dealin' with."

Kaylee disappeared out of view for a few minutes. Whilst she was gone, Adam adopted a deep stealth tactic, becoming one with his surroundings, 'You are not in the bush, you are the bush," he continually recited in his head, hoping to induce a calm meditative state. When Kaylee returned, Adam could hear her voice only as if in a faraway dream.

"Oh, don't tell me you're gonna try sleepin' through this! I'm talkin' to you, Adam Eden!"

Seconds later, Adam winced and woke from his meditation, as a sharp burning sensation flashed across his chest. Opening both eyes, he saw Kaylee on the sun terrace brandishing a hose—her face, raw malevolence.

"Fixed this baby up to our boiling water tap, and ya oughta know that it's good for a hundred gallons. Ya see, I'm not so much kick-ass as cook-ass. By the time I'm done with you, little hedge pig, you're gonna be sooo tender that the meat's gonna be fallin' clean off the bone. Sorry I aint got none of my Pa's North Carolina marinade, but you … just … don't … deserve it."

True to her word, Kaylee enacted her cruel vengeance, relentlessly maintaining a jet of boiling hot water on her helpless victim. Adam's lightweight suit offered no protection from the slow cooking, and his skin soon took on a bright pink hue. He screamed in agony as the scalding torrent savaged his face—his eyes twisting and bubbling in their sockets. At this point, Copacabana stepped in and guided Adam, using every learnt technique to block out the pain, sending him into coma-like trance. Mercifully, Adam died long before his skin rendered away from the moist meat below.

GOODBYE FAMILY, HELLO STERN

8:00 AM. Back to life, Adam sat straight up in his double bed and took in a huge gasp of air. His evolved mental defences quickly blocked out the pain of the dark place that stood between death and resurrection—a fortunate side effect of his many deaths—and mercifully, he only remembered the first blast of Kaylee's lethal water torture. Aware that time was running out, Groover's five day limit now taken very seriously, Adam jumped out of bed, threw on his clothes, chugged a cold glass of water, and left his apartment without eating breakfast.

Adam stood outside Eden Manor, his parent's capacious pillared and porticoed McMansion. After ringing the entrance bell continually for a couple of minutes, Adam let go of the iron chain-pull as one of the large oak doors creaked open.

"My goodness, it's early, Adam," said Harry, his father, tightening his blue paisley print silk robe. "If you've come to take your brother to the park, you'll have to wait a few minutes while we get him ready. He can dress himself now, but still won't run a comb through his hair."

Adam shook his head, saying, "I won't be taking Robert to the park today, Dad. What I really need is to pick your brains about the history of the viro."

"Fire away, son, although Stern's probably the one to ask. He was here years before the rest of us. I remember him telling me that when he first arrived, the Environment was just one ruddy great field with a stream running through it … and his odd looking house of course."

"So Stern's house was the first structure in the viro?"

"I'm not entirely sure," answered Harry, scratching the side of his head. "You'll have to ask Stern. Does this have something to do with your meditation? You wouldn't tell me why you needed my ladder the other day. We saw you poking around the bridge for hours. Your mother said you were probably looking for another meditation spot. I guess the sound of running water can be quite soothing."

"You're right," lied Adam, "it is linked to the meditation. It's a feng shui type of thing. Seems I need to talk to Stern."

Before Adam could thank Harry, a cheerful, make-up caked face peered around the door.

"My little Superstar!" said Edna, his mother, holding out her arms for a hug. She rudely pushed past Harry, enveloping Adam in a crushing embrace, planting a sticky lipstick kiss firmly on his cheek. Once done, she stood back, feigning love and admiration, and unexpectedly threw open her racy black gown. Adam baulked, expecting shocking maternal nakedness, but thankfully, Edna was only exposing her new hot-pink t-shirt, bearing the words in silver glitter, 'Copacabana Superstar: Official Lovin' Mother'.

"Do you like it?" Edna gushed. "I thought I could wear this if any of your famous friends come to visit."

"Absolutely love it, Mum," said Adam not knowing where to rest his gaze after noticing her nipples standing unusually erect under the thin material. "Err … if any celebrities visit the viro, then I'll tell them that Edna Eden is not only my mother but also the Head of the Official Copacabana Fan Club."

"Ooo, thank you so much, Adam!" Edna gushed. "And, you are quite welcome to use the manor to entertain your guests. We'll pretend it belongs to you, and just stay in the background. If you need to go to the loo, then I could stand in for you until you get back. I've watched enough telly to know how to parley with celebs."

"Well first, I'm going to step the meditation up a notch, and probably not leave my apartment for a few months. So, if I don't call for Robert, or you just don't see me around, don't worry. After that, it could be celebrity city almost every day."

Realising that he had no choice but to confront Stern, Adam said goodbye to his parents. As he turned to leave Harry suddenly said, "If you're going to see Stern, then please ask him what they were cooking yesterday. You see, your mother and I were walking by the stream when this wonderful waft came across the meadow. Your mother reckons it was a ham joint ..."

"A sweet-cure ham joint," added Edna, "but your stupid father thought it was cheap hotdog sausages."

"That's what it smelled like," insisted Harry.

Kaylee had obviously made good on her promise of death by boiling, and Adam, now feeling quite queasy, claimed he had to leave right away. Blatantly ignoring his request, unable to let Harry have the final word, Edna said, "It was definitely a sweet porky smell, nothing like hotdogs. Anyway, they're Americans, and I believe they call them wieners over there. I'm right aren't I, Adam? Americans cook wieners?"

Glad he decided to forgo breakfast, Adam took a couple of deep breaths and left in hurry—not looking back to see if his parents were waving. He felt an unexpected pang of sadness at the thought of never seeing his family again. For all their selfishness, simmering aggression, and hidden agendas, they were still the tiny world around which Adam maintained a lonely orbit.

Kaylee left Adam in no doubt about her feelings when he called at the Stern mansion. The large stylish front door, smooth blonde wood with delicate inlaid floral ironwork, had a small barred viewing hatch, from which Kaylee glared with venomous hatred.

"Back so soon," she spat. "Did I forget to put an apple in your mouth or are you some kind of pain freak?"

Gently laying a hand on the door, in an amateurish attempt at bonding, Adam put on his most humble voice.

"Kaylee, I deserved what happened to me. I know I pushed you into a dark place where vengeance was the only option."

"Nobody pushes me, Adam Eden, and don't ya forget it. Get back over your side of the stream and don't ya dare show your ugly lyin' face here ever again."

Adam did not leave. Instead, he pleaded with Kaylee.

"Oh Kaylee, please let me speak to Stern. I'm prepared to tell him the truth about the playground incident. I promise there'll be no more killing."

"He's not coming out and that's final. You're not hurting him again!"

As if to emphasize the point, Kaylee slammed the hatch shut, and left Adam desperately in need of an immediate Plan B. Allowing his mind to slip into Copacabana mode was always an option, but violence was probably not the best course of action given recent events. Unable to decide his next move, Adam suddenly heard Stern calling him from one of the mansion's downstairs windows.

Adam stepped off the stone tiled porch, made his way along the wood-clad front of the house, and noticed that one of the tall narrow windows was open a fraction. A figure sat on the other side, barely visible through the translucent red glass. Stern spoke first, his voice tinged with an uncharacteristic hesitance.

"Say what you have to say, but make it quick. And, please don't lie, because I know you murdered me. I remember I was about to ask you whether you were going to leave the viro. That's the secret Groover told you, and that's why you killed me."

Adam knelt on the grass outside and rested his arms on the windowsill. Telling Stern the truth was a necessity at this point, since any more lies might close the door forever on escaping the viro. Copacabana made no effort to intervene, so Adam was free to ask for the hind-reader's help.

"Stern, my friend, please accept my sincerest apologies," Adam began. "You're right about me wanting to leave, and I won't deny that I killed you for finding out. Although, please believe me when I say that it wasn't really up to me."

"Not up to you? I don't remember seeing anyone else there, unless that glam bitch came back without me knowing."

"Lately, ever since the showdown with the glam gang, I haven't always been in total control of my own mind. It's like Copacabana has become a separate person inside my head. He only comes out when he thinks the mission is threatened. He wants to leave but I…" Adam felt his head begin to throb, and so was careful with his words. "I stupidly thought of staying. Since I want to leave as well now, there's no conflict between us."

"So, now you're pleading insanity. You're saying that you're a schizoid, and that when you kill someone, like me for instance, I should be understanding rather than angry because it was your other personality's fault. Is that what you're saying, mi vecino loco?"

"I know it's a crappy excuse, but you told me not to lie to you. I admit that I didn't really come here to apologise, but to ask for your help. Call me a jerk, but I'm acting purely out of self-interest."

"Now, that's the kind of honesty I was looking for!" said Stern, his tone slightly lighter. "However, it doesn't excuse anything that you've done."

"But, are we good now?" asked Adam hopefully. "Will you help me?"

"No, Adam, we're not good, and we might never be. I believe that as long as you're here, in this viro, we're all in danger. Your murderous ways are like a virus, which is infecting us all. Thanks to you pushing her too far, Kaylee is now a murderer. And, that is why I will help you leave. I want you and your girlfriend gone." Stern clapped his hands together and exclaimed, "Now tell me what you want to know!"

With well-rehearsed efficiency, Adam told Stern everything: the portal, the shards, the time limit, even the details of the playground incident; nothing was off the table. Stern sat silently, without interrupting, carefully listening to every word. When all the information was finally out, Adam asked if he could come in and look for the shards.

Stern shook his head, saying, "Not a chance, Adam. If the shards are in the oldest structure, then they are not in this house."

"Where then?" asked Adam, not knowing where else to look.

"I'll take you there myself, but first …"

Stern stood to close and fasten the window, saying, "I'm gonna sit and chill out for an hour before we go—maybe brush up on my Vicente Fernandez. That way you won't kill me when I come out, because I'll still remember everything you've told me when I resurrect tomorrow. Taking my time is my Life Insurance Policy.

DO YOU SEE WHAT I SEE?

As the Satan Bug rushed over another rocky bump, sending it leaping into the air, Stern whooped with excitement. Adam, now firmly reacquainted with his neighbour's reckless mode of driving, sat frozen with fear in the buggy's passenger seat, tightly grasping the side rail. The sleek black buggy charged down the long meadow towards the cottage and cobblestone bridge, Stern maniacally zigzagging and skidding with ecstatic thrill seeking abandon.

"Remember your promise," shouted Adam, his words swept away by the onrush of air. "Slow down across the bridge in case someone's walking up on the other side! Slow down ..."

Stern laughed, taking a hand off the jittery steering wheel to slap Adam on the back.

"Shut your whining," he yelled, "you can see nobody's there. You killed me the other day, and in return, I get to jump the bridge one last time. I think I got the shitty end of that deal. Now hold on and scream to high heaven if you must."

Settling the wildly meandering vehicle into a straight course to the bridge, Stern floored the accelerator, and let out a mighty roar. The buggy's huge tyres and jacked up suspension made short work of the cobblestones underneath, and Adam could only manage a pathetic squeak, his face screwed up as if straining on the toilet.

The Satan Bug sped up the low hump of the bridge and shot off the crest, coursing through the air for some feet until landing with a heavy bounce— much like the feeling in Adam's stomach. Stern whooped and thrust his fist in the air, then carried on towards the solitary oak tree near the portal. Adam took a few deep breaths. Despite his legendary abilities on the field of combat, he never really enjoyed the dubious pleasures of high-speed, great heights, or the gut-wrenching jerk and jounce of the amusement park.

A few minutes later, both men stood by the oak tree, looking towards the line of yews. Stern leaned against the side of the buggy, staring hard where Adam had indicated, a furrowed brow betraying his scepticism.

"How long does this take, Adam? Is it like one of those 'magic eye' patterns? Do I have to focus in a certain way?"

"Just keep looking where I said. I don't think it matters how you focus. Remember, if you don't see the portal then you can't see where the shards are hidden."

Stern shook his head, clearly losing patience. Adam tried his best to delay any premature departure by asking, "I really liked the cologne you were wearing the other day. You wear that a lot don't you. I'm not usually one for aftershave, but I could certainly wear that. What was it, if you don't mind me asking?"

"The other day ... when you killed me? You gotta be kiddin'. Now, I'm not staying here staring at the damn sky all day, so this portal better show up soon."

Running out of ideas, Adam was going to suggest that they climb the tree for a better view, when he noticed Stern's jaw drop and his eyes widen.

"Do you see it," Adam asked excitedly.

"Big grey square ... just hovering in the sky, yeah I see it. You know, somehow I thought it would be round."

"Then we should go right away," suggested Adam.

"Whoa, slow down there, muchacho, I gotta take this in. This is like some way out freaky sci-fi shit. Those shards ain't going anywhere. Oh wait ... wait, it's changing! Yeah, there's some weird shapes appeared down the side. They look like the shapes on my resurrection wristband. Must be the language the ..."

Stern went silent, and then a broad smile crept across his face—he had obviously seen the naked image. Adam hung his head in embarrassment as

Stern put an arm around his shoulders, slowly shaking his head with incredulous enjoyment:

"Hah, that's the one you don't show your Mama. Looks like they got everything to scale, right down to my rather big ... ha-ha ... feet."

"So, the picture on the portal is you?" asked Adam, trying to hide his relief. "Right, that means anyone who sees it, sees themselves?"

Stern thought for a moment, before saying, "Did you think I could see you? Oh, pene pequeño, you may be a legend on the battlefield, but there are some challenges in life that you will never win."

UNDER THE BRIDGE

When the Satan Bug came to a dramatic skidding stop next to the cobblestone bridge, Adam wondered what was going on. Stern already knew that the bridge had been thoroughly searched, so there seemed no reason to make a stop. With a furtive grin, explaining nothing, the hind-reader jumped out of the vehicle and jogged to the middle of the bridge. Standing on the top of the low hump, he turned to face Adam, his arms outstretched.

"This is where you want to be, muchacho!" he yelled. "This bridge is the oldest structure in the viro!"

Wondering if Stern was wasting his time, taking revenge for recent events, Adam got out of the buggy. As he walked over, he glanced at the cobbles and the low stone walls, looking for anything he might have missed, questioning his previous search. There was no sign of the shards or the faintest hint of their promised glow.

"I told you I already searched the bridge," said Adam, sitting down on the wall. "I spent an entire day looking in every nook and cranny. The shards aren't here. This can't be the oldest structure."

Stern sat next to Adam, and said, "When I was resurrected, there were only fields with a stream running down the middle, and this bridge." He slapped a hand on the stone. "You know how our concierge is with her finances. My house was supposed to be waiting for my arrival, but she went for the cheaper item first. I spent months sleeping in the middle of a field."

"Did you have a tent?"

"No I did not," stated Stern pointedly. "I had a king-size bed with a silk covered duvet, three leather armchair recliners, and a working lamp—all just sitting on the grass. I even had a dispenser, standing there like a huge ATM machine. It was surreal. Thank God it never rains."

"Then explain why I didn't find the shards."

"Before we set off in the bug, I wondered if perhaps the genie had lied to you. Those originals can be difficult at the best of times. However, after seeing that portal, I'm pretty sure he was telling the truth. Ha, you probably just didn't look hard enough."

They spent the next two hours painstakingly scrutinising the upper part of the bridge, Adam on one side and Stern on the other, walking slowly sideways to ensure they were always looking straight on. It took four passes before they gave up, each time crouching lower to inspect each layer of stone separately—by the fourth pass they were sitting on the roadway, bouncing along on their backsides.

After a short break, spent sitting in the buggy, eating spicy chicken wings, and resting their sore behinds, it was time to search the underside of the bridge. Retrieving a couple of short wooden paddles with blue plastic blades from the buggy's rear lock-up, Stern asked Adam to help him unstrap the small two-man dinghy from the roof. Adam had wrongly assumed that the dinghy played no part in finding the shards, since it was almost a permanent fixture on the vehicle.

Stern pushed the dinghy into the water, and then held it steady while Adam cautiously stepped across and sat down. Without a care, Stern jumped in—the dinghy rocking precariously from side to side—and handed Adam a paddle.

Once in the water, the current was weaker than Adam had anticipated. Paddling under the bridge took very little effort.

"Now what?" asked Adam, as they floated under the arch.

The plan was to paddle the dinghy to the end of the arch then let the current slowly take it back to the other end. Whilst floating under the arch, Adam and Stern would fix their gaze on a layer of stones, looking for any sign of the shards. They would repeat the process five times, one for each layer, staring higher with each pass. As with the upper part of the bridge, they saw nothing but stones, but this time ended up with stiff necks.

"I told you they weren't here," said Adam, disappointed to be right. "Maybe the genie was lying after all. What was I expecting, putting my trust in a bloodthirsty psychopath?"

Gripping the snorkel and mask in his hand, the torch clipped to his belt, Adam slipped off the side of the dinghy into the cool stream. The water came just past his waist, and he slowly waded under the arch of the bridge. Though the water was clear, the arch blocked out much of the light, casting a large shadow over the rippling surface, hiding what lay below.

Adam stared hard at the water, hoping to catch a glimpse of a glow, but saw nothing. Fixing a clip over his nose, he pulled on the snorkel mask and blew a few breaths. Dipping his head beneath the surface, Adam switched on the torch and inspected the bridge foundations.

Expecting to spend at least the next hour swimming up and down, futilely going through the motions, Adam instead enjoyed immediate success. About two feet below the waterline a row of blue lights blinked into life, illuminating the dark water with an almost neon glow.

Adam pulled off the snorkel, and plunged down to get a closer look. Set into the sturdy stone blocks were five glowing squares. Pressing a hand gently against one of the squares caused it to slide open, revealing a small niche. Needing a gulp of air, but worried that the glowing squares might disappear at any moment, Adam quickly reached into the niche and grabbed a hard object lying inside.

"Are you OK?" called Stern from the dinghy, as Adam stood up in a wash of water.

Wading back to the dinghy, thanking Stern with every slow step, Adam held his prize aloft—a metallic blade-like shard. He climbed back into the boat, and for a few minutes both men stared in wonder at the misshapen dagger.

Their adventure brought to a successful conclusion, Stern pulled the dinghy up against the bank. Adam wondered if one shard would be enough. What if he lost this one? What if he needed to open two portals at once? More importantly, what if he and Rhapsody somehow got separated? Having a spare shard would probably be a wise move, and still left three for any future viro emergency.

"Hey Stern," he said, "I'm sorry about this, but …"

Completely without warning, Stern pulled the blue plastic blade off his paddle, revealing a sharpened end to the wood. The hind-reader lunged forward, stabbing Adam in the upper leg. Before Adam could react, the pointed paddle stabbed again, this time in the other leg. Going for a third attack, this time aimed at the head, Stern missed his target as Adam quickly leaned to the left, snatching the homemade weapon as it jabbed past.

Stern fell back, unsettling the dinghy, his face an expression of fear and confusion. Just as blood began to well up from his deep leg wounds, Adam expertly twirled the weapon and adopted a defensive posture. If Copacabana decided to intervene now, then Stern was dead. Luckily, Adam retained control, slapping a hand down firmly on one of the wounds to staunch the warm sticky flow.

"Aaagh, what was that for, you bastard?" cried Adam. "Was that revenge for the other day?"

"I … I … Thought you were gonna kill me again," Stern spluttered, eyes firmly fixed on the sharpened point wavering in front of his face. "Please don't kill me again. No way I wanna go back to the dark place!"

Adam managed a strained smile, which quickly turned into a pained grimace.

"I just wanted to get another shard," he explained, reversing the weapon and handing it back to Stern in a gesture of trust. "You know, in case Rhapsody and I needed one each."

Stern put down the paddle, and quickly stripped off his t-shirt, revealing his finely honed physique.

"We can tear this into strips and tie off the wounds."

Stern grunted and groaned as he wrestled with the garment, his arm muscles bulging with effort, but despite his efforts, the t-shirt remained intact. Panting from the exertion, Stern shook his head in dismay.

"This is premium quality 'Fruit of the Loom'," he declared, tossing the garment to Adam. "First time I've been beaten by a high thread count."

Adam reached into his pocket and pulled out a folding combat knife. A click of a button and the blade flicked open. Working quickly, mindful of the blood loss, Adam sliced through the heavy cotton as razor through paper."

"You brought a hunting knife with you?" asked Stern, somewhat in fear of the lethal weapon.

"I always carry it."

"Hmm, then that's another reason you need to leave the viro."

Adam securely tied the strips around his legs, over the wounds, and the blood began slowly saturating the fabric. For now, the makeshift bandage would have to do.

"Stabbing aside," said Stern, "with all that I've done for you today, I think you owe me a big favour."

"Well, near fatal stabbing aside," said Adam, gesturing to his bloody legs, "what do you want?"

"When you leave the viro, is there room for one more, and I don't mean me?"

"Who then?"

"Manny."

"You must be joking!"

In his first-life, Manny—Emmanuel Beaumont—had rescued Adam from a life of poverty and depression. For over a year, the devout Christian selflessly struggled to turn Adam's life around: a life scarred by divorce, unemployment, obesity, and alcoholism. The endeavour was almost successful, ending in a celebration as Adam regained visiting rights to his children, only for him to die that very same evening. In return, Adam helped Manny come to terms with his new resurrected life in the Viroverse, and introduced him to Stern's daughter, Sophia. The couple were already engaged to be married, so Stern's request was strange and unexpected.

"I wish I was joking," said Stern. "The man is driving us all totally loco. Every time he visits, he won't stop telling us that Jesus is out there somewhere, and that he wants to meet him. Don't get me wrong, I have nothing against the guy's beliefs, but I caught him crying the other day about it. He was blubbing like a spanked kid, saying how God and Jesus are waiting for him outside. It's getting so you can't stay in the same room with him."

"He's said nothing to me about this, but then again, I haven't talked to him for a few months. I know he can get over excited when it comes to religion. He lives in a follower viro remember."

"Please, please take him with you, mi amigo," begged Stern. "Just show him that Jesus isn't waiting for him out there, and then shove him straight back. If he's going to marry my daughter, he needs to get this outta his system."

Adam shook his head, worried that Manny might prove a burden.

"I don't know about this, Stern. Rhapsody and I are experienced fighters. We might stand a chance if there's any danger out there. But, Manny ... he's one for singing hymns and organising church jumble sales. Damn good jumble sales though, I might add."

"Didn't he drag you off the streets when you were down and out? That takes guts and real commitment."

"Yeah, that's true," Adam admitted, "but a kind heart rarely wields a bloody blade."

"So, your answer's no?"

"I'll ask him if he wants to join us," conceded Adam, remembering he was deeply in Stern's debt, "but I'll also make it clear that I expect him to step up to the plate if it comes to a fight—no praying, no turning the other cheek, and no fainting at the first sight of blood. If he doesn't agree, then he's not coming. That good enough for you?"

"Yeah, that's fine," said Stern, shaking Adam's hand, "but don't tell him about our little conversation. Just ask him along for the ride."

An hour later, with Stern's help, Adam was lying comfortably on the sofa in his apartment—his legs properly bandaged—sipping a bottle of ice-cold Mexican beer. On the coffee table, snug on a purple velvet cushion, lay the coveted shards, now cleaned and gleaming like pure silver.

TERMINAL

Captain Andrews sat silently in the darkness as the data filtered through– Adam Eden had acquired a portal shard. Sliding open the wide drawer on his executive oak desk, he took out a large bunch of keys, and promptly left his office. As expected, Liana was waiting outside, ready to break the news that he already possessed.

"Adam Eden has a portal shard," Liana announced, smoothing down the dress of her powder blue hostess uniform.

"Thank you, Liana. I shall block off the south-side of the hall as soon as possible."

"Should I send for the inkman?"

"I still believe our colourful friend is wrong for this particular job. He is too eccentric."

"He always gets the job done," said Liana.

"Send for John Down."

"John Down is not reliable."

"Liana, you know I have a soft spot for humans. Their belief in second chances is fascinating and often admirable."

"But Sir, John Down has failed us on at least three occasions. You are giving him a fourth chance. Is that a human trait?"

Captain Andrews straightened his cap, and fastened a gold wing-shaped clip to his dark blue tie.

"Send for John Down. My word is final."

"Of course, Sir."

"And tell the rest of the staff that I will be addressing them in 20 minutes outside the VIP Lounge. I want the terminal running every day from now on, even at weekends, whether we have visitors or not."

"Even at night, Sir?"

Even though his android brain instantly made the decision, Andrews hesitated and rubbed his chin, as if pondering the matter—another human trait he enjoyed.

"No, there is no point in staying open during the human sleep phase. I think it best we save those resources."

After Liana left, Captain Andrews unlocked a large switchbox, and flicked every switch. In human fashion, he nodded his approval as the overhead fluorescents sputtered into life. Outside, beyond the Terminal windows, bright daylight had replaced the ebon void, revealing the three huge passenger jets parked in parallel on the tarmac below, and a Boeing 747, bound for Zurich, taxiing onto the nearby runway.

The whirring and clicking of the many vending machines, and the distant din of over thirty games booting up in the Terminal's video arcade, broke the interior silence. A few seconds later and the smooth tones of airport muzak filled the entire building with its soft saccharine sedation.

"Hmm, 'Will You Still Love Me Tomorrow' indeed, mused Captain Andrews, hands in his pockets, and he made his way to the meeting.

THROUGH THE PORTAL

Five days after the discovery of the shards, the disparate group gathered below the portal. Using Stern's buggy as a base, a ladder extended above the yew trees and leant against the grey square in the sky. Luckily, for all concerned, the portal did not display the violent bounce back qualities of the viro wall, yet had a similar springy feel.

Three days previously, with Reverend Calvin Steven's permission, Adam had personally travelled to Manny's religious viro, and made his pitch. To Adam's surprise, Manny asked very few questions and eagerly accepted his chance at escape, even agreeing to step up if required. Given Manny's obsessive nature—sometimes verging on Asperger's—Adam had expected a far more difficult confrontation. However, Adam really knew that Manny's swift acceptance not only borne of trust, mutual respect, and pure friendship, but also perhaps the deep human desire for adventure.

Adam helped Stern secure the ladder to the top struts of the buggy, before a final check on equipment and provisions. Adam, Rhapsody, and Manny all had backpacks with built-in water bladders. The backpacks also contained a number of useful items: multipurpose tools, sunscreen, sunglasses, a cup, and a variety of medical dressings, plus three weeks supply of Hooah! US Marine ration bars. Adam prayed that a reliable water source lay outside the viro, or the whole escapade would be over in a matter of days.

Stern scratched his head, bemused at Adam's choice of attire.

"Are you sure wearing your Aloha get-up is the right way to go?" he asked, referring to the pink hibiscus shirt, white jeans, and blue deck shoes. "Unless you know something I don't, I reckon the chance of a Hawaiian beach barbeque waiting for you on the other side is less than nada."

"Well, I've got a jacket in the buggy. Remember, these are my fighting clothes. The shirt may look flimsy, but you feel the material."

Stern obliged, and was astonished at the strength and texture.

"Feels like toughened leather. How's the hell is that possible?"

Adam explained how his clothing had mysteriously evolved during his two years fighting the glam gang. Without the armoured clothing, he could never have defeated the psychos. Rhapsody was decked out in her flouncy glam finery: turquoise silk trouser-suit and a matching bandana. She also saw her flamboyant ensemble as her fighting clothes, having worn them for over ten hunts, but admitted that her platform shoes were lower than usual.

Ironically, to the uninitiated eye, Manny seemed best dressed for the occasion. Instead of his usual clothing choice of unfashionable jeans, sensible shoes, and Christian volunteer sweatshirt, Manny now looked like an extra from a jungle warfare movie. With high-laced black leather combat boots, camouflage fatigues, and a rough leather headband, he looked ready for action. Smears of black face paint completed the tough-guy impression—a sharp contrast to his notoriously finicky manner.

"Adam, there doesn't seem to be any toilet roll in here," he fretted, rummaging around in his backpack. "What if there isn't any outside? What will we do? I mean, do we use leaves ..."

"Rolls take up too much room," Adam explained. "There's a pouch of dry tissues and a pouch of wet-wipes. Should last us a while if we don't waste them."

Adam turned to Rhapsody, and said, "Right, weapons check. I'm carrying a machete and combat blade on my belt, plus a spare blade in the backpack."

"Two blades, one on the belt and one in the backpack," replied Rhapsody, "plus a compact foldable crossbow with 20 lightweight aluminium bolts. Easily take down a human or any other large game."

"Great stuff! And, you Manny?" Adam asked, with a tinge of apprehension.

Manny reached in his pocket and proudly pulled out a chunky though small metallic object with red sides.

"Swiss army knife with over 21 functions!"

"But, we've got multi-tools in the bags," said Adam. "I told you to bring a weapon."

Manny defended his choice, "It has a fold out knife which I am sure will prove useful should we run into any nefarious characters. Err, now which one is it … no that's the corkscrew …"

"Well, if we ever devise a battle plan that involves removing a cork from someone's butt, then I'll know who to call."

Sucking up his pride, blushing red under the war-paint, Manny offered to run back to the wake-up cubicle and pick up a better weapon. Pressed for time, Adam told him not to bother. He wanted to be out of the viro before his parents finished their breakfast and early morning argument. If Manny needed a weapon then he could borrow one of the spare blades.

With the shard safely holstered in his belt, Adam pulled his grey lightweight bomber jacket from the buggy's storage compartment, and climbed onto the roof of the buggy. As he zipped up the lightweight garment, Stern tugged his trouser leg.

"What's up?" asked Adam.

"That cologne you were asking about the other day, muchacho, is Bois du Portugal. A bit old school perhaps, but a real man's scent. If you ever wanna smell like me, then check it out."

"Hmm, Bois du Portugal; I'll remember it."

Stern stepped up onto the buggy. Lowering his voice so the others could not hear, he said, "Hey, one last thing. It concerns Rhapsody."

"This better not be some last minute insult."

"No, no, just I hope you realise that the girl totally loves you. I mean, not a simple crush, but the real deal. I see it whenever you two are together."

"I … can't say I haven't noticed."

"Then do something about it, Adam, 'cause I don't need to read your damned ass to know it's mutual. You may have an eternity to waste, but don't wait too long."

"Only a few days ago, you called her a 'psychopathic bitch."

"Then you'll make the perfect couple."

With an extra firm handshake, Adam thanked Stern for all his help, and began ascending the ladder. The climb was brisk, Adam's usual fear of heights subverted by an intense anticipation of what lay ahead. Once at the top, he wasted no time in employing the shard, and carefully cut a long slit in the grey membrane—the silver blade slicing cleanly, like an oversize scalpel through thick skin. As Adam holstered the shard, he noticed the slit was slowly shrinking, as if repairing itself. Setting fear aside, Adam pushed through the tight rubbery orifice, experiencing a sensation similar to being born, though without the blood and screaming.

Skin Deep

O n the other side of the portal, Adam flopped onto a cold stone-like surface, and was confronted by total darkness. The membrane slit was too tight to allow light to filter through, so he retrieved a torch from the backpack. Before he had even switched it on, the room automatically lit up, the translucent white ceiling offering a uniform luminosity. Adam stood up. The room was roughly twice as wide as the portal and about twice the length –the walls were the same mica-flecked stone as the floor. Two rows of cushioned benches stood along each of the sidewalls. Catching Adam's interest at the far side of the room was a sliding double door.

After putting the torch back in the backpack, Adam inspected the door. A glasslike palm-panel complete with sci-fi trope etched hand design, gave an obvious clue as to the door's operation, although Adam erred on the side of caution and fought the temptation to try it out.

Next to the door was another metallic panel, which Adam recognized immediately as a dispenser. This viro 'reception room' could prove useful if supplies began to dwindle. They could come back for more provisions without having to return to the viro—and face a bone breaking 30ft drop or a dangerous leap into the yew trees. Better still, if they encountered other viros along the way, and had access to similar reception rooms, then food and drink would not be a problem. For a moment, Adam considered ditching some of the ration bars, but decided that it was far too early to take such a risk.

The slit in the portal was already healed shut, so Adam made a long fresh slice with the shard. Sticking his head through the opening, he shouted down below:

"Time to go, my friends! It's not the outside, but I think it might be a decent first step!"

Rhapsody hurried up the ladder, and shouted up to Adam, "What's in there: a nuclear wasteland, giant spiders?"

"Nothing to worry about! Just get up here!"

Once at the top of the ladder, Adam helped pull Rhapsody through the tight membrane, and then beckoned for Manny to follow. Taking protracted quivering steps, Manny very slowly made his way up the ladder, eyes squeezed shut, fingers white with tension as he laboured from rung to rung. As soon as Manny was within grabbing distance, Adam took firm hold of his arm and heaved him into the room.

With the slit almost closed, Adam risked another minute for one last duty.

"Hey Stern," he called, "do you want to come with us?"

Stern shook his head, and replied, "Of course I'd like to know what's out there, but I'm happy where I am. With you and Rhapsody outta the way, Kaylee and I can get back to enjoying our lives. Hey muchacho, I don't hate you, it's just you're a loose cannon. The Viroverse is about eternal life and leisure, and somehow the death you bring to it doesn't fit in. If ever you lose the killer instinct then be sure to come back and visit."

"I'll look forward to that day!"

"Oh, and remember what I said about Rhapsody! Everybody needs somebody to love, muchacho!"

"You're full of love and romance today, aren't you?" laughed Adam.

"I'm a lover not a fighter. You also know I spent years secretly reading historical romances. The stuff's ingrained in the brain."

After a brief exchange of goodbye nods, Adam popped his head back through the portal, and turned to Rhapsody and Manny. Then the screaming started.

Adam was shocked as both friends backed away from him, pointing in panic, fear in their faces. Thinking something terrifying was behind him, Adam quickly swung around, but saw nothing out of the ordinary.

"Your face, your face," wailed Rhapsody, "what the Hell's happened to your face?"

Manny, already hard up against the far door, hid behind his female teammate, and spoke haltingly, as if finding it hard to breath.

"Who ... are ... you?" he wheezed. "What have you ... done with Adam?"

Taking a small step forward, Adam provoked further screams, and Rhapsody unsheathed her combat knife—her expression was humourless, grim, with the determined eyes of a desperate killer. Desperate to avoid a violent confrontation with his friends, Adam held out his hands beseechingly and noticed something odd. Both hands were almost featureless, as if clad in grey skin-tight rubber. Breaking out in a fearful sweat, Adam took of his jacket, only to find his arms had also changed. Finally, he unbuttoned his Aloha shirt.

"Oh shit, what's happened?" he cried. "This is my skin! It feels normal ...but look at it!"

Rhapsody wielded the blade in warning.

"Don't take another step, rubberboy, or I'll stick you!"

"Yes, you just do as she says," wittered Manny, brandishing the Swiss Army Knife, "or you'll get some of this!"

Adam stepped back, draining some of the tension from the situation, and said, "Manny, that's the can opener attachment. And, both of you, I swear this is me, Adam Eden. Back there in the viro, I looked normal, didn't I?"

"That may be true," said Rhapsody, "but it doesn't explain why Manny and I are unaffected? You were in here for quite some time before you called us up."

Manny excitedly raised his hand, as if in a classroom.

"Ooh, ooh, I know, I know. Adam's an undesirable. Maybe undesirables have different bodies."

"Hmm, I think you might be onto something," agreed Rhapsody. "Our darling Adam probably has the budget version; looks normal in the viro, but outside he's a creepy doll."

Rhapsody lowered her weapon and operated the dispenser, quickly obtaining a small ornate gilt framed mirror. With Manny close behind, still armed with his can opener, Rhapsody cautiously handed the mirror to Adam. Resigned to the horror of the reflection, Adam raised the mirror to his face. He gasped at the featureless skin, unrealistic doll-like hair, and white Ping-Pong ball eyes. Adam half expected the mirror to shatter.

"Oh God," he muttered, "I look like a shop window dummy. Wait, wait, I need to test this."

For Adam this was just another in a long line of embarrassing problems. It seemed that wherever he went, and whatever he did, life would always find another way to kick him hard in the balls. Needing further confirmation, Adam once more sliced an opening in the portal membrane. Removing his shirt, he pushed through the slit, right up to his waist. Quickly inspecting his hands and arms, he was relieved to see his usual detailed pinkish skin. Stern was still below, fixing the compacted ladder onto the buggy's roof.

"Hey, Stern!" called Adam.

Stern looked up and grinned.

"Long time no see," he yelled. "Bet you had some awesome adventures out there."

"Stern, do I seem normal to you? Look carefully before you answer."

"If normal means hanging out of my dick, then yeah, you look normal."

"What's that supposed to mean? I'm trying to be serious here."

"Well amigo, instead of that gorgeous picture of myself on the portal, I've got a naked Adam Eden hanging out where my dick should be. Other than that disturbing image, which would send most people into therapy, you look pretty normal to me."

"What about my skin?"

"You have beautiful skin," gushed Stern, mockingly batting his eyelids. "Have you recently switched to using Shea butter wet-wipes?"

"Knock it off, Stern! Tell me, do I look like a creepy waxwork?"

Perhaps reading the earnestness in Adam's voice, Stern dropped the humour.

"No, you look like you always do. Have you run into trouble out there? I know I said I wanted you outta the viro, but if you're in real danger I'm sure we can work something out."

It took a few minutes to convince Stern that everything was fine. Then, after yet another round of manly nods, substituting for goodbyes, Adam eased back through the closing portal.

Rhapsody and Manny still stood back by the door, weapons held at the ready. Adam unclipped his belt, threw it to the floor, and walked forward, arms outstretched.

"You want to kill me? Well, here I am, unarmed, in the flesh—freakin' creepy flesh. Come on! Make up your mind! Will you trust me or will you kill me?"

Rhapsody sheathed her dagger and slow clapped her hands in mock applause.

"Oh, you are such a drama queen," she laughed, stepping up and placing a soft kiss on Adam's cheek. "Just promise you'll cover up those scary undead eyes."

"And, what about you?" Adam asked Manny, arms still outstretched. "You still wanna use that can opener, go right ahead. I'm yours for the opening."

Manny flipped shut the can opener, pocketed the Swiss Army Knife, and said, "I promised I'd step up if we were in danger, but not to murder my best friend. If we are setting foot outside that door, we do it together. Nevertheless, Rhapsody is right. You do need to cover up those eyes."

Twenty minutes later, all three stood facing the door, mentally preparing for what might lay outside. Adam wore black wraparound sunglasses, coolly complementing his Hawaiian ensemble, and kept one hand close to his machete. The dull grey bomber jacket lay discarded and unwanted on one of the benches. It was the legend of Copacabana that brought Adam to this moment and no way was he covering up his trademark pink hibiscus shirt.

Adam paused before he pressed his hand against the palm panel.

"Anyone care to speculate what's out there?" he asked. "I mean, we all look normal size, but if the concierges are to be believed, we're only an inch tall. If that's the case, then there might be some humungous future city populated by giants. We'll be lucky not to get stepped on."

"Oh Adam, haven't you seen any science fiction films?" said Rhapsody. "There's bound to be an apocalyptic wasteland with filthy survivors living off the ruins of the old world. Probably a few mutants and barbaric biker gangs as well. Seeing as we're only an inch tall, we'll probably end up as a snack for a mutant rat."

Manny, looking more thoughtful than usual, offered, "My pet theory is that the Viroverse is a vast spaceship. This room could be an airlock. Once you open that door, then phfut, we'll be sucked out into space and our heads will pop like bloody balloons."

Adam and Rhapsody gulped, and cast a slightly perturbed look at one another.

"Thanks for that, Manny," said Adam, wondering if the dispensers provided spacesuits. "You never know, Jesus might be waiting outside with all his disciples."

Manny grinned, and said, "Now you're just being silly. I'm sure if Jesus is out there, he'll be by himself."

Taking a deep breath, Adam pressed his hand firmly against the panel. Nothing happened, and the door remained closed. After waiting for a few seconds, just in case there was a delayed reaction, he tried again, but again the door stayed shut. Rhapsody nudged Adam aside and placed her hand on the panel, which instantly lit up.

"You obviously haven't got the 'desirable' touch, rubberboy."

With a soft hiss, the door slid open.

HALL TROUBLE

G iven the frightening expectations, the anti-climax that followed was somewhat welcome. The door automatically closed behind the wary adventurers as they stepped into a wide corridor, similar in materials and design to the reception room. Over thirty feet across, the perfectly straight corridor stretched far into the distance in either direction, as if infinite in length. Set into the light grey floor, ten white lines, each about a foot in width, seemed like tracks on an endless roadway. The corridor was a silent, soulless, monotony—at once echoing the sterile thoroughfares of a modern hospital and the cold marble hush of a public mausoleum.

Adam was ready to toss a coin to decide whether to go left or right, but then a nosebleed intervened. Viewing the coin toss as gambling, and therefore a sin, Manny pointed to the right, and confidently strolled away. He only got a few feet before painfully colliding with an invisible barrier. The impact sent him slumping to the floor, blood streaming from his nose. Rhapsody rushed to help, proffering tissues and some soothing words, whilst Adam inspected the unseen obstacle. Running his hands across the invisible wall, Adam quickly surmised that it was some sort of toughened glass completely blocking off the corridor.

With an arm outstretched in front of him, Adam cautiously walked along the corridor in the other direction. If there was a barrier also blocking off this side, then the whole adventure might suffer a premature end. After nearly 200 yards, he decided to return, by which time Manny was back on his feet, two twists of tissue protruding from his nostrils.

"Try this," said Manny in a low nasal drone, handing Adam the Swiss Army Knife. "It's a glass cutter; got a diamond head."

Adam knelt down and pressed the tool hard against the glass. With a firm downward motion, he attempted to mark the transparent material, yet achieved nothing but an irritating high-pitched 'nails on a chalkboard' noise. Using a shard produced a similar noise, but again the glass remained unmarked.

Handing back the tool to Manny, Adam suggested that they head along the corridor—although he was secretly concerned that the barrier was a means to shepherd them to a predetermined destination.

After half a mile's brisk walking, and Manny's increasing insistence that he needed the toilet, they found an identical door to the one they had exited, although set into the opposite wall.

"I guess this leads to our neighbours across the hall," smiled Adam. "Anyone think we should pay a visit?"

Manny, worried as usual, said, "I'm not so sure that's a good idea, Adam. There could be people from any time or any place living in there. What if they're Ancient Romans? If they discover my beliefs, I could end up being crucified."

"So, you stay in the reception room," said Adam. "Rhapsody and I will check out the viro. If it's safe, we'll come back and get you."

"And what if you don't come back?"

"Then you can join us and suffer whatever we've suffered, or head back to my viro and go back to your normal life."

A loud human scream, accompanied by a whooshing sound, broke Adam and Manny from their conversation. All heads turned as a figure whizzed into view, surfing along one of the white lines on a small rectangular board. Some ten feet away from the group, the stranger executed a perfect high-speed power slide, stopping the board dead.

Up close, it was evident that, apart from a pair of tight leather shorts covered in steel rings, he was naked, but completely covered in tattoos. Unlike the temporary rub on tattoos available in the Viroverse, these were the real deal: vibrant, defined, not faded with age, but freshly needled and seepingly bloody. The only piece of skin not inked was a round shaved patch on his head, from which sprouted a golden blonde ponytail. Kicking up the board and tucking it under an arm, he grinned a mouth of sharpened teeth, and pointed a spiked knuckle-ringed finger directly at Adam.

"Ahaha, you're on your own!" he shouted, betraying a distinct Australian accent. "I knew Down wouldn't show up, I knew it! Sensitive bugger's probably too busy reading poetry to his wife. The Captain should've sent me! I've got a 100 per cent success rate ... 100 per cent, and he goes and picks John Down! And you know what, because of that, you're all probably going to die!"

"Err, we mean no harm," said Adam, his machete already unsheathed. "I'm Adam Eden, and these ..."

"Shut up, I know who you are!" the inkman shrieked. "And don't think your fame means anything out here! Out here you .... Oh, gross, what's up with your skin, mate? For goodness sake, cover up! Nobody wants to see that!"

Taking swift control of his mind, Copacabana pushed Adam into the background and went into action. Clipping the machete back in its sheath, he raced towards the inkman, determined to incapacitate, capture, and interrogate.

The inkman laughed, casually throwing the board back onto the line, and said, "Haha, I didn't come to fight you, you bastard, I just came to gloat."

Before Copacabana reached his target, the inkman jumped onto the board, crouched in a dynamic surfing pose, and shot off back down the corridor, laughing maniacally all the while. Within seconds, he was out of sight.

The target lost, Copacabana relinquished control to Adam and slunk off into the mental shadows. For a few minutes afterwards, all discussion focused on the inkman's sudden appearance, and what he meant by, 'you're all probably going to die.' Adam asked Manny and Rhapsody if they still wished to continue, and although they had understandable misgivings, they decided it was far too early to turn back. It was then that Rhapsody noticed a large wet patch on the wall, close to where Manny had been standing.

"Feeling better now?" she asked. "Pissing in the street is so much easier for you boys."

Manny was aghast with horror and the accusation.

"No, no, no, I did no such thing," he stuttered. "No way was that me. I ... I am not, and have never been, a public urinator. Tell her, Adam. I am holding it in as we speak, and it is exceedingly uncomfortable."

"It's no big deal," said Adam, giving Manny a friendly punch on the arm. "If you gotta go, you gotta go. There doesn't seem to be any toilets around here, so you did the best you could."

Manny simply stared at Adam, and then at Rhapsody before sucking in a big breath.

"Ok, not only have you both accused me of a most heinous act," he said, turning his back and standing by a dry section of wall, "but you have also called my honesty into question. Well, if proving I am not from the gutter means descending into the gutter, then so be it. If I had just relieved myself then could I do this?"

Adam and Rhapsody were not sure where to look as Manny began peeing against the wall, nervously humming 'The Dance of the Sugar Plum Fairy'. The urine slipped down the wall without the slightest sign of a stain, and pooled around the thick soles of his combat boots.

After an inordinate amount of time, Manny finished and zipped up.

"Do you believe me now?" he said, expecting an apology.

Ignoring Manny, Rhapsody once more pointed out the wet patch on the wall, which was now about five feet tall and disturbingly thicker. It appeared as if translucent green mucus was oozing out. Bubbling and sputtering, the almost fluorescent slimy blob gradually fattened, taking on a roughly human form. With a pronounced slurping sound, the featureless jelly-like figure plopped away from the wall, and took a few faltering sticky steps towards the group.

Swiftly concluding that the jellyman was a threat, Adam moved to confront the approaching menace, and advised the others to stand back. Once within striking distance, the green jellyman lunged forward, taking a slow swipe with a fingerless glob of a hand. Adam weaved around and swung his machete into the creature's neck. The razor sharp blade barely dug in an inch and sent painful quivering ripples up Adam's arm. Ducking down, as the jellyman launched another punch, Adam pulled hard but could not retrieve the machete—the blade stuck fast in the translucent goo.

"Rhapsody, I think it's time for a headshot," cried Adam, backing off, leaving his weapon lodged in the jellyman's neck.

Rhapsody had her crossbow at the ready, and aimed squarely at the creature's forehead. Her aim was true, but the aluminium tipped hunting bolt stopped inside the green quivering head, as if trapped in a bowl of lime jelly.

"Damn," swore Adam as the jellyman slopped and wobbled closer. "Manny, if you've got a spoon attachment, now's the time to use it."

"Oh my God, there's more of them," warned Rhapsody, as two more wet patches appeared and began oozing slime. Unlike the first jellyman, these two, one orange and one blue, were forming very rapidly.

Within seconds, the additional jellymen were free of the wall, and slowly making their way over to assist their verdant brother.

"I think we should open that door and hide in the reception room," suggested Adam, grabbing Rhapsody by the arm.

Adam and Rhapsody headed straight for the door, but Manny paused, obviously worried about what lay on the other side. His hesitation proved a dangerous mistake as the jellyman's sticky green handmade slight contact with the side of his face. Letting out a startled yelp, Manny pulled away, but the jellyman remained attached by a long gummy strand.

With haste, Rhapsody slammed her hand on the door's palm panel. Adam turning his attention to Manny, whipped out his combat knife, and severed the thin gummy link with one slice. The door slid open, and all three bundled inside.

The door took a moment to close, but the jellymen did not attempt to follow. With a soft hiss, the door finally slid shut, and everyone breathed a deep sigh of relief.

CHUCKLEHEADS

Sitting quietly on a bench in the reception room, Manny meticulously thumbed through a hefty medical encyclopaedia that Rhapsody had obtained from the dispenser. His face, mirroring the symptom of a stroke victim, had slumped on the side where the jelly man made contact, and he wanted answers. Though clearly shaken by the experience, he insisted that he felt nothing, claiming that the area was completely numb.

"There you go," said Adam, pulling the crusty tissue twists from Manny's nostrils. "At least your nosebleed's cleared up."

"Do you think this is permanent?" dribbled Manny, a low sucking sound issuing from the fallen side of his mouth.

"I have no idea, but it doesn't seem to be getting any worse. We'll watch it for another hour and see what happens."

Once the hour was up, Adam saw no deterioration in Manny's condition, and so busied himself with the portal. Having made a small cut in the portal membrane, he pulled the sides apart, and peered through.

The view was partially obscured by a tall coniferous tree, a mature Ponderosa Pine, part of a thick forest that covered the rocky foothills of a large valley. Using his monoscope to glimpse through the gaps in the dense foliage, Adam spied a fast flowing river, about twice as wide as the stream back home, carving its course through the rough landscape. In the distance, the imposing snow-capped mountains were certainly viro wall fakery. Beyond the veil of twigs, branches and needle-like leaves, Adam caught a glimpse of what may have been a wooden bridge crossing the river, but he could not be sure.

"What's out there?" asked Rhapsody, as Adam crossed the room and began operating the dispenser.

"Well, it's hard to see because there's a ruddy great tree just outside the portal, but I reckon we can use that to get in and out. Trouble is it's one of those trees without any branches near the bottom, so we're going to need some rope and tough gloves. And, Rhapsody, you need to get some more appropriate footwear. The ground is sloped and pretty rocky, so those platforms will be lethal."

"What about me?" said Manny.

"Well, I didn't spot any Romans, but you should stay here. For now, I think you need to rest."

Adam and Rhapsody leapt from the portal to the nearest branch of the Ponderosa Pine without incident, and since the tree was artificial, there was little chance of the branch breaking. Climbing down through the prickly foliage proved a harder task, and by the time they reached the lower branches, Rhapsody had grazed her cheek and ripped her turquoise silk trouser-suit in a number of places. At least her hiking boots were up to the job, offering plenty of protection and grip. Working quickly, Adam tied the rope securely to a branch facing away from the valley, and close to the trunk, making it less conspicuous should one of the locals happen past.

Once on the ground, Rhapsody caught Adam by the arm. Before he could register any complaint or question, she hugged him close and kissed him full on the mouth. Adam was still wide-eyed with shock as her moist lips left his and her large-lashed eyes fluttered open, and even more surprised when she started laughing.

"Oh, you poor baby, you look absolutely terrified. Were you really married or was that some story you made up?"

"I ... err ... just wasn't expecting that."

"Well, I got tired waiting for you to do something, so I thought I'd move things along. With your priggish friend out of the way, it seemed the perfect moment. Plus, you look normal in here. The rubber boy thing still freaks me out."

"I was never good at making the first move," confessed Adam, not sure whether to feel exhilarated or emasculated. "That's unless I was drunk of course, which I usually was."

"Then I'll leave the next move up to you, whatever and whenever that may be."

"Could it wait until we're out of here? I'm not really an outdoors type of guy."

"Hmm, now you're just teasing."

Clambering down the gentle wooded slope, taking advantage of a couple of flat trails, they soon reached the banks of the river. The wild water, rushing and bubbling around rocky outcrops, appeared refreshing and inviting. Adam knelt down and drank a few handfuls.

"Oh God, that's good mountain water. Nice and cold, plus you can taste the minerals."

Rhapsody had climbed onto one of the huge riverside boulders. She turned and said, "You do know that the mountains aren't real. The water probably recycles in a loop."

"I know that, but the AI has got the taste spot-on. Come back down and try some."

"You might be more interested in what's upstream. I can see that bridge you were talking about. Looks quite a walk from here. Rickety looking thing."

Adam climbed up and sat next to Rhapsody. Using the monoscope, he scanned the area around the bridge. Immediately catching his attention was a substantial whitewashed house: two storeys, clapboard sidings, with simple lattice windows. Given the central location alongside the bridge, and the house's size, Adam assumed that this was the viro's utility building.

A cluster of small clapboard cabins spread out beyond the bridge, with a modest log cabin chapel, and a communal well completing the rugged rural idyll. Adam spied a couple of locals, both women, going about their daily business. Their clothes, plain cotton bonnets, full-length skirts, and high-necked blouses, perhaps identified the viro's inhabitants as originating in the USA in the late 19th century.

The whole scene seemed peaceful and unthreatening, so Adam and Rhapsody decided to take a closer look. Shuffling back down the boulder to fetch his backpack, Adam was surprised to find someone standing there.

A muscular man of medium height, profusely whiskered, eyed the couple suspiciously. His attire matched the assumed era: bowler hat, white shirt and grey waistcoat, sturdy denim work trousers, and metal toe-capped boots. With casual skill, he spat a gob of brown tobacco juice sideways into the river:

"You wouldn't be thinkin' o' going o'er there, would yer?" he drawled, pointing toward the village. "People roun' here have got mighty unfriendly of late, and they mightn't take too kindly to strangers rollin' in dressed like a couple o' chuckleheaded clowns."

The man leant down and picked up the backpack. Apparently not interested in its contents, he threw it over to Adam, who caught it with both hands. Rhapsody slid down the smooth rock, joining her partner.

"Looks like yer had a rough ride there, Missee," said the man, referring to Rhapsody's torn clothing. "These hills ain't the best place to be wearin' yer finest Chinese silk pyjamas."

Adam walked up and extended a hand of friendship, judging the man as being in his early thirties.

"My name is Adam Eden. We are just visiting an old friend. Err ... they invited us over for their birthday. Thought we'd go for a walk through the woods and take in the scenery."

"Is that so? Well, my name is Ellison Hobbs, but folks roun' here calls me Tombstone, on account of me out livin' an' buryin' the rest o' them."

Tombstone spat another gob of juice, which landed just short of Adam's feet:

"An' I don't care to be lied to, 'specially in ma own home."

Before Adam could spin another lie, Tombstone beckoned them to follow him:

"Yer can both explain yerselves later. If yer want to avoid any trouble, I advise yer follow me. Ma house is jus' behind that low rise across the river. It's a fair distance out o' the village and away from pryin' eyes. There's a place nearby yer can cross the river without usin' the bridge."

"There's a shallow ford in my viro as well," said Adam.

Tombstone laughed throatily, brown spittle dribbling down his chin.

"There ain't no darn' shallow ford along this river. Let's just say, where we're goin', if yer get wet then yer dead."

Further downstream, well away from the village, Tombstone headed up a steep rocky escarpment, which Adam guessed was very close to the viro wall. Once at the top it was clear that this was the beginning of a narrow ravine, the river channelled into a wild foaming rage between treacherously smooth walls of rock. After walking another few feet, Tombstone stopped and stamped the ground with his heavy hobnailed boot:

"This here's the narrowest part o' the ravine. I'm guessing it's only 'bout 10ft to the other side. It might look narrower further up, but that's beyond the viro wall, so ain't an option."

Adam took a quick look over the edge at the furious aqua-violence far below, and gulped.

"Are you saying we have to jump?"

"Yer got a decent run up before the gap. I suggest yer throw yer bags over first to lose some weight."

As Adam mulled over the terrifying prospect of leaping across the space, Rhapsody took off her backpack and walked back a few feet to take a running jump.

"Are you sure about this?" said Adam, as Rhapsody began her sprint.

Without reply, she powered past both men. Her turquoise trouser-suit billowed as she soared gracefully through the air, landing on the other side with the solidity of a perfect gymnastic dismount.

"I'm guessin' that where yer come from it's the done thing for the woman to take the lead," said Tombstone with a wry smile.

Adam picked up the backpacks and threw them over to Rhapsody. Wishing that Copacabana take control of his mind and jump the ravine, Adam took a few steps back and then sprinted towards the edge. Any worries that he may have held were quashed as his training—both at the playground and with the Sarge—made light work of the jump and landing, although the impressive commando roll at the end was probably unnecessary.

"Ma cabin's easy to spot. It's the one with 'Tombstone' carved in the door. Stay low roun' the back an' don't make a sound. I'll be with yer shortly."

"But … aren't you jumping," asked Adam, as Tombstone gingerly made his way back down the escarpment.

"I ain't no fool!" he yelled. "I'm headin' fer the bridge! You's the first chuckleheads crazy enough to jump the gap!"

GIRL OUT OF TIME

The wood cabin was surprisingly small, given the material generosity of the Viroverse, comprising one large room with a curtained off sleeping area. Adam and Tombstone sat on hard-seated chairs at a rustic pine dining table, whilst Rhapsody enjoyed the relative comfort of a cushioned rocking chair by the fake log fire.

Casting his gaze across the room, Adam appreciated the unsophisticated décor: a glass-fronted cabinet with medals and commemorative coins, and an abundance of railroad memorabilia. One item in particular caught Adam's eye, a seven-inch gold spike on a shelf above the fireplace.

"I'm guessing you worked on the railways," said Adam.

"Darn sure I did. After the war, I worked for Union Pacific on the Transcontinental railroad. I supervised a trouble shootin' gang. We was the ones who went in when there was a problem along the line. Could be anythin' from unexploded dynamite to fixin' a run o' spikes. I remember one time we was even called in to help defend a labour camp from injun attacks. Lost two of the boys that day."

"So, what's the gold spike about?"

"That's the solid gold, final spike in the railroad, joining us to the Central Pacific's line. Naturally, they replaced it with a regular iron spike, so as no-one could go an' steal it. When I came here, I thought 'Hell' if I don't deserve one o' ma own. I know it's just a copy, but I earned it. All the boys have got one."

Tombstone went on to explain that all the men in the viro were former members of his rail gang, and that after the Transcontinental was finished, they were employed upgrading and repairing the important rail link. Over the years, Tombstone arranged and attended the funeral of each and every one of his men. The women in the viro were an assortment of wives and girlfriends, many of whom also worked the line in a number of capacities.

Rhapsody left the comfort of the rocking chair, and joined the men at the table.

"Did you choose this house?" she asked, with a slight note of scorn.

"Nah, when I first arrived, the Boss man told me this AI feller chose it. S'pposed to be ma perfect home. Anyhow, what's yer point, Missee? Something wrong with ma house?"

"Nothing, if you like this type of thing, but I'm sure the Concierge … err Boss man could have offered you something a little larger."

"I don't know what castle you live in, but heck, this is better than I ever had on the line. We used to sleep 10 in a tent and two in a cot. Yer imagine 10 men, with the sweat o' the day dried on, trying to sleep together. Ma best friend, Lao Han, used to shift farts like the Devil's own breath. Sharin' a cot with him for four years gave yer two choices: slit yer throat or learn to love the stink like it's yer own. What I'm tryin' to say is that this house is ma home, an' I like it."

Tombstone spat a swift gob of juice into a spittoon on the floor.

"See that there spittoon?" he said. "That's gold plated. Now tell me if I don't live like a goddamn King. Only thing missin' is ma wife, Mapiya, on account o' her not being resurrected yet."

"Mapiya?" asked Adam. "Is that a Native American name?"

"If by that yer mean Injun, then sure. She's a Lakota, used to hawk cheap tobacco by the line. Mapiya took a shine to me right away, got me hooked on the chaw. I mean, she ain't no looker, got a bit o' a mean squint, but she knows how to treat a man right, 'specially with the cheap tobacco an' all. I don't know how or when Mapiya died, on account o' me goin' first. I got me the mouth cancer in 87."

Tombstone seriously chewed on his tobacco for a moment, then continued, "Well, I don't think Mapiya's coming back any time soon. Yer see, things have been getting' mighty strange roun' here. Few weeks back, Dan Duffy slipped off a ledge onto some rocks an' cracked his skull clean open—died right there an' then. Next day, his stinkin' corpse was still lyin' where he fell, but he weren't resurrected the next day and still ain't."

"That sounds serious," said Adam, having never heard of such a problem before. "Did you talk to the Boss man about it?"

"Can't see the Boss man no more. We's all tried, but nobody's seen him fer weeks. Maybe he's takin' a break, or maybe he jus' up an' left us fer good. Worse than that, we can't go visiting other viros, and no one can visit us."

Tombstone got out of his chair and went over to a rectangular iron plate set in the wall, with what looked like a postal slot, and a wire basket below.

"Yer see, I write out an' invitation and post it in here. Usually I gets a reply the same day. If someone's inviting me, then a letter drops in the basket. I ain't got nothin' in weeks."

"I wish we could help," offered Adam, surreptitiously nudging Rhapsody under the table, "but we should really get going. We've got someone waiting for us."

Tombstone slammed a fist on the table and looked Adam straight in the eye.

"Like I jus' said, there ain't no visiting. Therefore, I'd be mighty curious to hear how both o' yer got in here. An' before you start lyin' again, I'm also fairly certain that yer that Copacabana feller that everyone's always jawin' about."

Literally laying his hands on the table, Adam decided that telling some of the truth was the best course of action. Even though they had just met, Tombstone seemed genuine, and someone who could be trusted.

"I'll be honest with you Ellison," began Adam.

"I prefer Tombstone."

"Ok, Tombstone, it's true. I am the one they call Copacabana. However, I prefer Adam. We got in here through a special kind of … opening, and to be honest, we want to be out of here before midnight."

"I ain't never seen no opening, an' I reckon I've covered every darn inch of this square mile. Where is it?"

"Please trust me when say that I really really can't share that information with you. You seem like an honest man, and we would be grateful if you would let us be on our way, and not breathe a word of our visit to anybody."

Tombstone took a pocket watch out of his waistcoat pocket and looked at the time. He tugged lightly at his whiskers for a few seconds before making his decision:

"Don't you worry about that. I ain't gonna poke yer fer any more information. I'm gonna let yer go back to wherever it is yer came from, and not tell a soul about all this. However, in return fer ma silence, yer gotta do me a favour, and there ain't no negotiatin' on that."

Adam thought for a moment, drumming his fingers on the table, making a dark decision of his own. Tombstone leant back in his chair.

"They say Buffalo Bill hiself stopped by our camp one day, stocking up on provisions. Now, he weren't famous then so he was just another man in the saddle, but now darn it if I don't have a live goddamn hero sitting at ma table. I prayed fer an answer to ma problem and it looks like God was listenin' after all."

Tombstone's words took Adam by surprise. He had never thought of himself as a hero—one of the good guys. His two years fighting the psychopaths was a purely selfish endeavour, which ultimately involved killing his own parents, and more recently, Stern. Gossip and rumour created the hero, but to Adam there was only bloody death and the promise of escape. In fact, he was not deciding whether to help Tombstone with his problem, but whether he should break the man's neck before finding out what the favour entailed. If it was true that the resurrection process was broken here, then the old adage applied that 'dead men tell no tales'.

Adam realised that he and Rhapsody were foolish to have entered the viro, especially dressed the way they were, and decided that their host should not pay for their mistake with his life. Hoping he could perhaps play the good guy for once, Adam agreed to help.

Tombstone let out a whoop, slapped his thigh, and exclaimed, "Time's a wastin', so best we be gettin' on. What I gotta show yer is jus' a little ways up the track. Hey Missee, do you want a fresh set o' clothes. Pretty sure yours ain't from ma time, so you better work the provider."

"You can call me Rhapsody."

"With respect, Missee, I won't call you that. Only gal I knew with a name like that was one who entertained the men on the line, if you catch ma drift. I gets all sweaty and horny thinkin' about her. Brings back a few memories."

"Fair enough," said Rhapsody, quite amused at how Tombstone was blushing. "Now show me how this provider works. In my viro, we call them dispensers."

Next to the fireplace was a large bulbous black iron cylinder that both Adam and Rhapsody had mistaken for a large oven. Tombstone explained that you pulled an iron lever and said what you wanted. Once you heard a bell chime, you simply opened the provider door and took out your goods.

As soon as Rhapsody obtained her new set of clothes, she went behind the bedroom curtain.

"I'll change in here if you don't mind, darlings," she purred coquettishly. "Little Miss Rhapsody don't wanna bring on no unnecessary horniness."

By the time they left Tombstone's cabin, darkness had descended on the viro. Taking a quick glance at his watch, Adam confirmed that it was nearly eight in the evening. The track wound its way deep into the majestic columned forest. They carried lanterns with artificial flickering flames, lighting their way and casting eerie shadows into the silent woodland. Adam began to feel the fatigue of the day—ladder climbing, rubber boy, inkman, jellymen, and rugged terrain had tested his endurance to the limit.

A bright play of lights through the trees indicated a nearby dwelling just around the next bend. Neither Adam nor Rhapsody expected what lay ahead. The track ended in a clearing, just large enough to accommodate a gleaming white mobile home that seemed plucked from a late 20th century trailer park. From the chrome metal handrails on the doorsteps, to the grooved plastic tops of the steps themselves, the whole structure was out of place in this late Victorian frontier community. Tombstone stepped up and rang the door buzzer.

"This turned up 'bout the same time that everything else went bust. Most folks roun' here think it cursed us all, but I don't believe that fer a second."

A beautiful, dark-haired woman opened the door, apparently in her mid-twenties, who lunged forward and hugged Tombstone enthusiastically.

"Oh Grandpa, I thought you weren't coming," she cried, kissing his whiskered cheek. "You said you'd be over after lunch."

"Sorry about that, Kim, but I been entertaining a couple o' important guests. Kimberley, these fine folks are Adam Eden and ... hmmph ... Rhapsody. They's come to help us out. Adam and Rhapsody, this is my Great, Great, Great, Great ... aw Hell, my Granddaughter Kimberly Hobbs."

The mobile home, a cheap mass-production of cream vinyl-wrap and gaudy cushioning, appeared fresh from the dealership. A compact galley kitchen with a marble-style worktop had all the usual appliances including a cordless jug kettle, and digital microwave, starkly evidencing the time anomaly. Kimberly rushed over to the dispenser—a white plastic wall unit with chrome knobs—whilst Tombstone ushered the others to sit at a foldout table with plump cushioned seating either side. Excited and eager to please, Kimberly handed Tombstone a large strawberry thick shake in a typical fast-food drink container, complete with stripy straw:

"Don't forget our guests, Kim," said Tombstone, before taking a hard suck. "I'm sure they would like one o' these."

Adam and Rhapsody both chose vanilla, and Kimberly once again gleefully rushed over to the dispenser. Tombstone put down his drink.

"Can't get enough o' these cold cream cups. Kim says they come from some upscale eating 'stablishment called McDonnell's Duck or something like that. Very popular in her day, apparently."

"And ours," said Adam. "This is late 20th century or very early 21th century. The old-style chunky TV suggests 1990s. Now, unless you all lived to be 150 years old, she's not supposed to be here. Something's seriously wrong with this viro."

The conversation was interrupted as Kimberly accidently dropped the milkshakes. The creamy contents emptied over her t-shirt and jeans, and splashed all over the floor. Clapping her hands to her cheeks in horror, tears welled up in the young woman's eyes, and she was soon screaming, bawling, and stomping her feet up and down. Tombstone leapt from his seat to console Kimberly, leaving Adam and Rhapsody to ponder the situation.

"She's a child," whispered Adam. "Just like that first time I fought in the psychoviro when I met Joshua. It always creeps me out that they resurrect children in adult bodies."

"We should have stayed in the reception room," said Rhapsody. "This is all getting a little bit strange, even for my taste."

Leaving the mess to be mopped up later, or cleaned by the mysterious post-midnight services, Tombstone told Kimberly to change into fresh clothes. Once she was out of the way, he joined the others at the table.

"So, you see what we're dealin' with. Kim may look like a full-grown woman, but inside her head she's an eight-year-old girl. As long as she is livin' in this viro, her life is in danger, so I want you to get her outta here. That there's the favour I'm askin'."

Adam was very reluctant to add another member to the group, especially one who required nannying. Perhaps it was finally time to break Tombstone's neck, and live with the guilt. As if reading Adam's thoughts, Rhapsody asked for more information.

"That's a huge favour considering what's through the special door. My mothering instinct is as strong as any woman, but I'm not sure we could cope. Just what do you mean by her life being in danger? Is it the viro breaking down, or is there something more to this?"

"Well, there were some mutterin' about killin her as a sacrifice to whoever runs this place, but I hope it don't come to that. Ma main concern is Conall Finn, a young strong-arm Irishman who died in a dynamite explosion before ever havin' a woman. He wants Kimberly fer his wife. His blood is up so he don't see her as a child, but only as a good-looking woman with curves in all the right places. Normally I wouldn't worry none, 'cause people used to be calm roun' these parts. I been keepin' him at bay so far, but I'm fast losin' support. Yer see, fer the past few weeks emotions have been running high; even ma own. Can't explain it, but then again, there ain't much I can explain about this new world o' ours."

Rhapsody was incensed.

"Adam, we've got get her out of here."

"Are you crazy?" said Adam. "You've seen what's out there. How are we going to manage with a kid slowing us down? Maybe it is safer to leave her here."

"So, you approve of paedophilia, do you?"

"Hey, I didn't say that!"

Adam knew that the cause of the high emotion in the viro was probably due to the absence of after midnight sedation. Almost all inhabitants of the Viroverse were secretly protected from hot-headedness by a sedative administered whilst they slept—Adam found this out when he blackmailed his own concierge. Without the sedative, a viro could quickly descend into chaos.

Weighing up the pros and cons of taking Kimberly out of the viro, Adam was offered some chilling advice from an unexpected quarter. Wading in from the mental shadows, Copacabana suggested that another member to the group might be beneficial; that if needed, Kimberly could be used as a human shield or cannon fodder.

Given the cold hearted advice, Adam hoped he was acting purely out of human compassion when he said, "Kimberly can come with us. As soon as she's finished getting ready, we'll go."

The door buzzer sounded, making everyone jump. Adam and Rhapsody hid in the cramped shower room, and Tombstone opened the door.

"Lao Han, ma friend, what can I do fer yer at this late hour."

Panting from exertion and panic, Lao anxiously replied:

"You must get Kim away. Ciara Dunn saw you leave house with two strangers. She tell everyone in the Saloon. Said they dressed in colourful clothing—like Chinese circus. Conall was there with some of the boys. They been drinking and get all riled up. They all armed, and on way here."

SHOWDOWN

There was no time for long introductions or social pleasantries. Tombstone directed Rhapsody to a narrow trail behind the mobile home, which led down to the river. Once they got there, it was up to Rhapsody and Kimberly to decide whether to head downstream to the ravine or upstream to the bridge. Rhapsody refused to leave the viro without Adam, and said she would wait by the rocky outcrop where they first met Tombstone.

Once the two women were on their way, Tombstone had a quiet word with Lao Han. After less than a minute, the diminutive Chinaman, dressed in a blue button-down tunic, and holding a straw coolie hat, went into Kimberly's bedroom and shut the door.

"What's he doing?" asked Adam.

"Han's gonna buy the ladies some time, should everythin' go to Hell. I advise you wear something less ladylike than that pretty pink shirt, or at least cover it up. We don't want folks thinkin' I'm consorting with a fancy-nancy."

"Thought you said everyone's been jawin' about me. Wouldn't they recognise me? They might back off if they know who I am."

"Yer smarter than yer look," said Tombstone with a grin, "and that's ma real plan. I thought yer could reveal yerself if I can't talk them down. Keep you in reserve 'til the time's right. However, jus' so yer know, Conall's no coward, nor someone who yer can easily reason with."

Adam got a denim jacket from the dispenser and wore it over the shirt. Outside, a grumbling of angry voices indicated the arrival of the gang. Calmly putting on his bowler hat, Tombstone tidied the hang of his watch chain, and went out to confront the unwanted visitors. Adam stood silently in the doorway behind the brave railroad man, avoiding the limelight, ready to jump in should the situation get out of hand.

Though relieved that the gang consisted of just Conall and two drinking buddies—plus a couple of women standing behind—Adam realised that this would not be a pushover. Standing a little over six foot tall with hard knotty muscles and a confident gait, Conall Finn swaggered up to Tombstone and stared him straight in the eye. The young hardy Irishman, rugged in denim, and a partially unbuttoned shirt, twitched his impressive handlebar moustache. Unfazed by Conall's intimidating stare, Tombstone tipped his bowler in greeting.

"To what do I owe the pleasure o' yer bourbon breath, Conall?"

"I'll be bringing ye no pleasure on this night, Hobbs," said Conall, slapping a hand on Tombstone's shoulder. "Once I have me darlin' Kim, the pleasure will be all mine."

"Yer should show some respect," said Tombstone shrugging off the hand. "I buried yer myself, remember. Yer have no right to the girl, and they call me Tombstone."

"Is that so, Hobbs? Well, maybe I don't take too kindly to being buried in the same box as a Chinaman. Ye see it offends me Catholic upbringing."

"Hell, I didn't know there was three boxes of dynamite on the supply wagon. If I did, then I wouldn't have sent yerself and Han to put out the fire. Truth is, after the explosion, there was so many pieces, yer only looked fit fer a stew. We jus' gathered the meat best we could and got yer both in a box before yer started stinkin'."

"And there I was, a young buck fresh off the boat, workin' me first line, and then boom I'm dead. I never even got to dip me cock, let alone see the last railroad spike go in. So, you'll be handin' over the woman, and then you won't be havin' no trouble."

"She's a child," insisted Tombstone. "Everyone gets a grown up body, but she's still a little girl. I won't let you take her."

"That's grand, because me and the boys were hopin' for a bit of action. I heard you had a couple of odd visitors. Now, with all that's been going wrong lately, I be figuring that they might be here to hide Kim, or somehow take her away. We're here to stop that happening."

Tombstone coldly stared at Conall, as if studying every nuance of his expression, and then spat a gob of chaw on the collar his shirt:

"Hah, sorry 'bout that. I was aimin' fer yer face. Now, you jus' get on home, and we'll discuss this tomorrow."

Conall and his cronies laughed, pouring scorn on Tombstone's attempt to defuse the situation. Conall, still laughing, unexpectedly drew a golden railroad spike from his trouser pocket and thrust it deep into Tombstone's stomach. Adam watched in horror as his whiskered friend fell back onto the steps of the mobile home, crying with pain—the head of the spike still protruding from his bloody belly.

"You're going to be Ok," said Adam, kneeling down next to Tombstone. "As long as you keep some pressure on the spike and don't pull it out, you should make it to midnight. You'll wake up tomorrow right as rain. I know the resurrection's broke in this viro, but the after midnight healing still works, yeah?"

Amid halting gasps, Tombstone whispered, "Sure does, but remember to go easy on the boys. I don't care so much for Conall, but his friends, Shamus and Patrick are good at heart. They's jus' a couple o' hotheads when Conall's aroun'. Spare them if yer can."

Adam squared up to the gang, who were all still laughing and slapping their thighs. Though youthful and unblemished, their faces had the rugged quality of those who had faced intense hardship in their lives.

"Here's the deal," commanded Adam, hoping to dictate terms. "I take on all three of you, and if I win, you leave the girl alone. If I lose, well there's not much I can do to stop you. And, since we can't resurrect, I propose we don't use blades. Do we have a deal?"

Conall looked Adam up and down, raising an eyebrow at the white trousers and blue deck shoes:

"And who are you to be making deals? By the looks of yer fancy rags and yer accent, I'd say you were a British sailor boy. It would bring shame on me drunken wretch of a father's name to do a deal with the likes of you. We never be using blades anyhow, so don't you be worrying your sad little self about that."

From seemingly out of nowhere, Conall produced a hefty length of steel chain and whipped it towards Adam's head. Having no time for a smart manoeuvre, Adam held up an arm, only for the chain to snake around his wrist. Conall's knotty muscles offered quick response, snapping back the deadly metal coil with such force that Adam somersaulted over, landing hard on his back.

The chain sliced through the air for another attack, but slapped harmlessly against the ground as Adam rolled sideways, leaping to his feet with catlike agility—Copacabana was now fully in control.

Grabbing the chain as it swung towards him, Adam anticipated another vicious pull back. As expected, Conall heaved the chain, hoping to throw his enemy to the floor once more, but Adam matched the motion and feinted to the left. Conall let out a pained cry, as Adam twisted his arm roughly behind his back and deftly wound the chain around his strong neck.

Patrick Sweeney, a redheaded whippet of a man, charged into the fray wielding an iron crowbar. In a high-pitched voice, he yapped Gaelic expletives, before brutally latching the claw end of the weapon into Adam's shoulder.

It was Adam's turn to scream as Patrick heaved at the crowbar, dragging him away from Conall. Still clutching the chain in one hand, Adam swung around, and managed to punch Patrick full in the face with the other. Staggering back, stunned by the impact, Patrick let go of the crowbar, which still hung from Adam's shoulder, deeply embedded in the flesh.

Conall, taking his chance, yanked the chain away from Adam and stood back, whistling for his other friend to join in. As if part of a tag team, Shamus, a brooding darkness with slick black hair and a thin waxed moustache, slowly approached with a billy club in hand and a malicious grin on his face. Conall threw the chain over to Patrick, who nodded appreciatively as he felt the heft of the metal.

Adam gritted his teeth and tore the crowbar from his shoulder—a chunk of bloody flesh remaining wedged in the claw. Trying to look confident, he held the crowbar in a menacing forward stance, waving it from side to side.

Without breaking stride, Shamus attacked first, his club clashing hard against the crowbar. Adam retaliated immediately, and cracked the iron bar hard against the side of Shamus's head. The blow wiped the grin from the man's face and sent him reeling sideways, tripping over his own feet as he sought to maintain his balance. A swift kick to the leg sent Shamus to the ground. As he fell, he stabbed out wildly with the billy club, driving it painfully into Adam's groin.

Seeing his foe doubled up in agony, Patrick lashed out once more with the chain. Through exhaustion and the pain of his injuries, Adam made an unconvincing grab for the snaking metal and caught one of his fingers in a link. With a loud whoop of joy, Patrick gave a sharp tug, tearing the trapped digit away from its horrified owner. Now facing certain defeat, and probably death, Adam stumbled back to the steps of the mobile home as Conall began dancing an Irish jig.

It was time to get serious. These tough railroad men were experienced brawlers, and as tight a team as the glam gang ever were. With no resurrection, it was kill or be killed, and Adam needed to bring his blade skills to bear. Discarding the blue jacket, he stood with his blood-soaked pink hibiscus shirt on full display, and machete raised. Now these laughing clowns would face the wrath of Copacabana.

"Recognise me," Adam yelled, "I'm the one they call Copacabana! Yes, the legendary killer of psychopaths! I've gone easy on you so far because of the resurrection breakdown, but now, unless you boys hightail it outta here, it's time for you to taste my steel and meet your maker ... argh ... argh!"

Adam felt a sharp sting in his side, and then another. Dropping the machete, he turned as a slender stiletto blade stabbed again. Behind him were the two women, demurely attired in bonnets and white linen, but with fury in their eyes. He had no time to react as the base of a heavy iron skillet swung towards his face.

Everything went black.

So Close to Midnight

C old. Death? Liquid. Cool liquid. Rivulets of liquid ran down his face. Was he alive? Returning to consciousness, Adam dared to open his eyes. A gauzelike blur quickly sharpened to a hazy focus, and a face filled his vision. Adam blinked as cold water ran into his eyes, and coughed as he tried to talk. The water changed its course, a soothing wash across his scalp. His vision became sharper still, and the face was male, moustachioed, with a gentle smile.

"Tombstone?" croaked Adam, regaining a semblance of speech.

"My name is Jed Wilkes," came the firm yet friendly reply. "You've been out cold for nearly two hours."

Adam was lying on rocky ground next to the river, a folded coat or jacket under his head serving as a rudimentary pillow. The soothing sound of the rushing water close by did nothing to mitigate a dull headache– as if pounded by a rubber-headed hammer. Jed Wilkes slowly wrung a water soaked rag over Adam's mouth, and encouraged him to drink.

Still groggy, Adam managed to sit up, and surveyed his surroundings. He was next to the rocky outcrop where he was to meet Rhapsody, but there was no sign of her or Kimberly.

"I … I was meant to meet people here," said Adam, placing his trust in theman.

"Don't worry. Tombstone told me everything before he died. Kim and your woman have gone on ahead."

"What, Tombstone's dead? He was alive before that witch knocked me out. Did they finish him off?"

"According to Tombstone, as soon as you hit the floor, Lao Han dashed out of that odd silver shed, wearing Kimberly's clothes. Conall and his boys fell for it, and chased him into the forest. Tombstone waited until they were gone, and came down to the village to get me. My old friend died in my arms, but not before he ordered me to help you out. You know, if he'd stayed put, he probably would've made it."

"Damn, damn, I can't believe he gave his life for me. I only met him a few hours ago."

"He didn't do it for you," said Jed, helping Adam to his feet, "he did it for Kimberly, his kin. Now, I patched you up as best I could, so you should make it to midnight. I was an assistant surgeon in the war, but afterwards the whisky took hold of me and I ended up working on the railroad. I was the gang's unofficial doctor."

A large figure appeared from the darkness, wearing denim dungarees, a woollen cap, and sporting the ubiquitous full moustache. Adam moved away as the new arrival approached.

"Don't worry about Thomas, he's a friend," said Jed. "The big lunk's going to carry you to wherever you need to go. Tombstone told me not to ask questions so whatever secret you're carrying, it's safe with us."

"I can walk," said Adam, stoically. "I've suffered worse injuries than this."

"That may be so, but in my esteemed medical opinion, you won't get very far in your condition. Trust me on that, Copacabana."

"There was a trail, edged with railway sleepers. Get me there, and I can make it the rest of the way on my own."

Sucking up his injured pride, Adam suffered the indignity of being hoisted onto Thomas's broad shoulders, piggyback style. With Jed leading the way with a lantern, their path only faintly illuminated by its dimmed flickering flame, they headed up the gentle slope and into the pine forest. Thomas made easy work of the rough uneven terrain, treating his wounded charge to a peaceful ride. The quiet man's lumbering stride, combined with the day's exertions, almost sent Adam to sleep.

"Hey Jed, so much for the legend of Copacabana," yawned Adam, blinking to keep his eyes open.

Jed allowed himself a small chuckle:

"I guess most legends don't hold up to close scrutiny. Just like lies, they grow with the telling. Then again, friend, you stood up against Conall Finn and his boys. So, I reckon there's a whole heap of truth in your legend."

"It wasn't Conall and his boys that floored me."

Thomas broke his silence, in a voice far deeper than Adam expected:

"Ain't no shame in gettin' done in by Hetty and Lara. Afore they came here, they was both genuine ladies o' the line. They were sweeter than apple pie if you had the coin, but cross them an' ya better run fer ya life, 'cause they's both tough as an iron spike and meaner than the fire that forged it. If ya still got ya balls then they was in a good mood."

As they carefully wound their way through the maze of trees and rocky levels, Adam's encounter with the tough 'ladies of the line' made him question his relationship with Rhapsody. Hetty and Lara's viciousness was probably the result of a life of brutal hardship and exploitation, whereas with Rhapsody it had been part of her nature. Could he ever be sure that the AI had filtered out her psychopathic tendencies, or would they one-day re-emerge with deadly consequences?

Adam had no time to finish his thoughts on the matter as they reached the relatively even ground of the 'sleeper trail'. They walked along the rutted track for another few minutes before Adam recognised a route through the trees that he had taken earlier. Thomas bent down at the knees, allowing his passenger to safely disembark, and Jed handed Adam the lantern.

"Here, take this. Thomas and I won't need it. The trail leads straight down to the bridge, and we have a half-moon lighting our way. Up there, in the thick of the woods, you're going to need the light."

Adam thanked the kindly railroad men, and made his way into the forest, heading in the direction of the portal. Without stopping, he checked the time on his Mudman watch, which had remained remarkably unscathed given the violence of the day. It read 23:22PM. Adam picked up the pace, grimacing through the pain of his injuries.

Just as he thought he would never make it, Adam glimpsed busy shafts of torchlight up ahead through the trees. He paused for a moment to catch his breath, when suddenly from behind, an unseen attacker threw a chain over his head, and pulled it tightly around his neck. Unable to speak, Adam choked as the chain links began crushing his windpipe, his eyes bulging with the pressure.

"Oh but it looks like yer little plan didn't work," said Conall in a lyrical tone, maliciously loosening and tightening the chain. "What made you think you could outsmart Conall Finn?"

Adam tried to elbow his assailant in the ribs, but only managed a feeble nudge as his energy levels let him down. Conall responded by kneeing Adam in the back of the leg.

"Right away I knew it was the Chinaman running into the woods, on account of his bony little arse. Ye see, me darlin' Kim is far more shapely than that, so I wasn't fooled for a moment. Keeping me distance, I followed Tombstone, then Wilkes, then yerself. Once I've put ye down, I'll be collecting what's mine. I might even have me way with yer woman before I kill her."

For the briefest moment, the chain tightened again, and then went totally limp. Hearing a stifled gasp and a thud from behind, Adam dared to look round. Conall was lying twitching on the ground, his eyes a fixed startled stare. Manny drew his Swiss Army Knife away from Conall's ear, and wiped the blood from the screwdriver attachment on the sleeve of his combat jacket.

"You cut that a bit fine," wheezed Adam, rubbing his sore neck.

"Yes, sorry about that," fussed Manny. "I couldn't decide whether to use a flathead or a Philips. I ended up going for the flathead."

"It did the job. Now let's get to the portal before midnight. I'll need your help; I'm a bit worse for wear."

Manny shone his torch at Adam, and gasped:

"Oh my goodness! Your face is all swollen and your nose … it's bent sideways! And, all that blood!"

"Calm down. Anyway, you can't see the worst of it because someone dressed my wounds. I'll be totally healed when I wake up tomorrow."

Manny shouldered his weary friend to the towering Ponderosa pine, standing silently alongside the portal like a brooding sentinel. Rhapsody and Kimberly were already up on the high branches, waiting to leave, and they waved and cheered when they saw Adam way down below. Since Adam was in no fit condition to climb, he secured the rope to his belt with a snapgate carabiner and asked the others to haul him up. Before climbing the tree to help take the strain, Manny patted Adam on his good shoulder:

"I promised I would step-up if necessary. Taking a life under any circumstances is abhorrent to my Christian beliefs, but since this place always brings us back from the dead, I decided to exercise a certain degree of latitude."

"Your conscience is clear Manny," Adam lied, "and thank you."

Ascending into the woody boughs, Adam dangled helplessly like an old puppet down to its last string. He swayed softly as he buffeted against the branches, realising that he was now the burden of the group. During his two years of fighting the glam gang, he only had himself to rely on, and death was just a temporary hitch. Today, when Adam had been found wanting, it was the trusting good nature of strangers and the love and loyalty of friends that rescued him from failure and death. Perhaps now it should be about teamwork and mutual res ...

Copacabana sparked into mind and mentally head-butted Adam out of his serene contemplation. With bellowing rage, his voice echoed inside Adam's head, "Wake up, you fucking moron! These losers don't matter! Tomorrow, you will continue the mission! If you don't, then I will take control!"

HERDED

As the first of the jellymen broke free of the wall, the group picked themselves up for the thirteenth time that day. Adam handed Kimberly her rucksack. The frightened girl, still scared of Adam's grey mannequin skin, quickly snatched the bag and ran to hold Rhapsody's hand.

Tomorrow, there was no taking control, but the nightmare continued. They had woken up in the reception room that morning in a terrible state. Everybody had the exact same clothes as the previous evening and were terrorised by an unholy underarm stink—waking up fresh and clean every morning was something all viro dwellers took for granted, so rampant B.O was an unwelcome surprise. On Adam's advice, wet-wipes and deodorant took care of the smell, and everyone got a new set of clothes from the dispenser.

More seriously, Adam's wounds were unhealed and already showing signs of infection. After removing the crusty 19th century field dressings, he obtained 21st century equivalents, along with strong antiseptics and a local-anaesthetic cream. Without the sleep-time healing, his chances of surviving his injuries were minimal.

Another unusual phenomenon was that everyone had mild stomach pains, hunger pangs, and a touch of dizziness. Drinking copious amounts of water and eating a hearty breakfast only partially alleviated the problem, but it was enough to allow them to continue.

Leaving the reception room was a one-way trip, as Manny discovered when he once again walked straight into another invisible barrier, blocking their way back to Adam's viro. Re-entering the railroader's viro was also impossible, as the palm pad no longer opened the reception room door. It was as if someone or something was closing down their options. With a damp patch already forming on the corridor wall, Adam advised they make their way to wherever the unseen hands were herding them.

Every viro was supposedly a mile wide in their relative world, a figure borne out by the groups' digital pedometers, plus an extra four yards for walls and whatever else lay between. They tried to open every door they encountered but all remained shut. After every ten viros, there was a four-way intersection, a crossroads, complete with a dispenser, and six tube-like columns at each corner. The glassy tubes, within which coursed a bubbling brown liquid, ran from floor to ceiling, and looked to have a diameter of over 5ft. Adam pondered whether these tubes were the transportation conduits that took people from one viro to another during sleep—Gloop style.

Disturbingly, at each crossroads, invisible barriers always blocked two of the four ways—further evidence of the herding theory. With little choice, they followed the only route left to them.

Mercifully, the jellymen were easy to avoid. There were never more than three at a time, and a leisurely walking speed could outpace them thanks to their slow wobbling gait. Once you were a few yards away, the sticky ghouls simply slopped back into the wall, but should you stop, they reappeared after exactly eight minutes. Mindful of the eight-minute constraint, the group stopped once per hour. They relaxed as best they could, lying flat-out on the corridor floor, but never near the walls.

The exertion took its toll on Adam's already depleted constitution. Dazed and heavily fatigued, he fell to the floor on two occasions and had to be helped back to his feet. A long drink of water cleared his cloudy head, and so he stumbled on. If they ran into serious trouble, Adam doubted he could help.

By 11:57pm, they had passed forty-four doors, all locked, and had reached door forty-five. Fear set in with the realisation that come midnight, and unavoidable sleep, there would be no safe haven from the quivering jellyman touch.

"It won't open for me either," groaned Manny, taking his hand off the palm panel. "It's three minutes until midnight. We'll never make it to the next door."

Rhapsody sat down on the floor and removed her rucksack.

"Even if we could make it, the damned door would be locked. Darlings, I suggest we stop here and prepare for sleep. Kim, you come nestle with me."

Kimberly slumped next to her newly adopted mother, and sobbed quietly. Adam and Manny joined them, and they all huddled together as the seconds ticked by.

"I'm so scared," said Kimberly, clutching Adam's arm, tears rolling down her face. "I should've stayed in the valley. There were no nasty jellymen in the valley. Look, look, the wall's all wet over there."

Adam wanted to reassure the frightened girl, but the right words eluded him. With Conall dead, perhaps they could have left Kimberly with the railroaders. However, with their viro fast losing vital services, the beautiful river valley might have become her tomb.

All along, Adam hoped the herding would lead them to some safe destination, where they would finally meet the person or persons who set the route. Now Adam feared that the barriers were placed to create a trap, where exhaustion or sleep would leave them as easy prey for the jellymen. If a numbing death awaited them, then tomorrow they would resurrect and wake up back in their own beds, except perhaps Kimberly. With resurrection unavailable in her viro, what would be her fate?

Twenty seconds before midnight, and the group nuzzled closely together, forced by their Viroverse minds to seek the best sleeping position.

"Close your eyes," mumbled Adam under a drowsy fog of inescapable sleep, "and goodnight."

"Goodnight," everyone mumbled in reply.

As the final second slipped away, they all heard the ominous sucking sound of a jellyman peeling away from the wall.

SAFE HARBOUR?

A dam blinked open his eyes, and sat up. He was alive. Around him, the others roused from their enforced slumber with expressions of worry giving way to relief. There were no signs of the jellymen, and nobody was suffering from their paralysing touch. Perhaps the jellymen shut down during the human sleep phase or could only engage fully conscious subjects.

Just like the previous morning, no automatic cleaning had taken place, and their stink was far worse than expected after only eight hours sleep. More importantly, the hunger pangs were greater and the stomach pains agonisingly pronounced.

"I don't know why those monsters left us alone while we slept," said Adam, between swigs of water, "but I suggest we don't hang around. Forget about washing and clean clothes for now. We all reek to high Heaven, so nobody should feel embarrassed. Best we drink some water and get some food inside of us."

"I have a theory," said Manny, standing up and stretching. "You said the portal was a redundant feature. Well maybe these corridors and dispensers are also redundant, and rarely used. It could be that over time the food in here has lost its nutritional value."

Adam nodded in agreement, saying, "Then from now on we stick to our original plan and only eat the ration bars we brought with us."

Adam got to his feet unaided. Though he was still sore and very weak, the new dressings seemed to be working, and the pain from his injuries had eased. Without waiting for a wet patch to form on the wall, the group made their way along the seemingly never-ending corridor, glad to be alive and hoping to find a door that opened.

By midday, everyone was fatigued; their pace slowed to little more than a forward stumble. It was then that Kimberly first noticed a glint of metal in the distance. Adam used his monoscope to get a better look and saw what looked like a shard lying on the floor next to a viro door. Their hopes raised by the unexpected object, the group hurried on leaden legs to check the palm panel.

With Adam holding the shard, all waited with baited breath as Rhapsody placed her slender hand on the panel. The panel lit up and the door hissed open, prompting a communal sigh of relief. Before they entered the reception room, Adam wanted to test a theory.

"Manny, can you walk a bit further down the corridor," he asked. "Slowly now, and hold your hand in front of you. We don't want another nose incident."

Manny took a few careful steps before encountering another invisible barrier. Adam now believed that this viro was the chosen destination, and that whoever placed the shard and the barrier was likely waiting on the other side of the portal.

Once inside the reception room, Adam headed straight for the portal and sliced an opening with the shard. He surveyed the new viro, first with the naked eye and then with the aid of the monoscope. Meanwhile, the others relaxed on the reception room floor, lounging on a number of puffy quilts and overstuffed cushions that Rhapsody had obtained from the dispenser.

"So, what's out there?" asked Rhapsody, as Adam left the portal and settled beside her. "Not more tree climbing I hope."

Addressing the whole group, Adam said, "The best way to describe it is a traditional Cornish fishing village, probably Victorian but could be earlier. Looks to be highly populated given the number of buildings."

"What's Cornish?" asked Kimberly naively. "Is it something to do with corn chips?"

"No my dear," Rhapsody corrected. "Cornish means from Cornwall: a county in the South-West of England. If there's odd going on with this viro, then this should be a nice place to visit. My parents took me on holiday there when I was your age."

"Did you see many people about," asked Manny.

Adam frowned.

"The odd thing is that I didn't see anyone. I could see plenty of cobbled streets and slate roofed houses, even a couple of boats in the harbour, but no people."

Oh, that's easily explained," said Manny, shrugging off any worrying implications. "It's lunchtime, and they're all indoors eating their meals. People were far more regular in their habits in Victorian times. Everything had a proper time and a proper place. In another hour or two, the streets will be thronging with locals out for a lovely afternoon stroll."

"If you're right, then now would be the perfect time to get in without being seen."

"Wait just a moment," said Rhapsody. "Are we going in wearing these smelly clothes or should we dress for the viro? I guess it's bearded fishermen or Cornish pasty makers."

"No, we go in as we are. I think I spotted a couple of large utility buildings by the harbour. If we can get there without being seen, then we can hide inside and change into clean clothes."

"Kimberly should stay here until we know it's safe," said Rhapsody.

"Normally I would agree," replied Adam, "but I believe that we have been brought here for a reason, and it's best we stick together. Whoever blocked off the corridor might not want someone hanging back. I have a strong instinct about this, so trust me."

With no more questions and no objections, Adam cut a long slit in the portal membrane. The flat pitch roof of a huge three-storey building stood about four feet from the portal, an empty gap between. Since the roof was about three feet lower than the portal, a death-defying leap across was a possibility, but Adam had another idea.

"Slide that big-arse plank over here," he told Manny.

Adam noticed the plank lying behind a bench when they first entered the reception room. Once he had looked into the viro, he was sure it was meant as a makeshift bridge to the flat roof of the building—perhaps placed by the mysterious herder. The wooden plank was seven feet long and thankfully wide enough so as not to require the poise and balance of a professional tightrope walker.

Adam and Manny carefully pushed and dropped the plank into place, and after summoning the courage, they cautiously crossed onto the roof. Rhapsody held onto Kimberly, offering reassurance as the plank creaked and bowed. When everyone was safely across, Adam and Manny heaved the plank onto the roof, since the closing membrane might otherwise crush the other end.

"So how do we get back?" Manny asked, peering across the gap.

"We'll work that one out later if we have to," said Adam. "I'm hoping we'll meet someone here who can help us; give us a few answers."

"You think they might know about the outside, and how to get there."

"That's right. And, fingers crossed, Manny, we'll get you some info on the holy one."

Crouching on the other side of the roof, the group looked out over the viro, taking in its simple beauty. The quaint village, set next to a sheltered bay, was a tightly packed rambling crescent of whitewashed terraced houses and dark alleyways, with two main cobbled streets leading down to the narrow granite harbour. The tide, if there was one, was in, and a couple of vibrantly painted fishing boats sat anchored in the sparkling azure water, secured by sturdy ropes to black iron bollards.

A hedge-rowed country lane wound its way around the bay, through woods, scrub, and grassy meadows, leading to a string of slate roofed waterside cottages and a colourful row of ramp-moored rowing boats. Farther still was a bleak distant headland with a lonely lighthouse, standing ready for its night-time duties. The headland was too far away to be real– a virtual extension on the viro wall.

"Reminds me of Polperro," sighed Rhapsody, enjoying a fond childhood memory. "I had the biggest Knickerbocker Glory in one of the seafront cafes. Lovely ice cream and jelly, but I hated the bones."

"Bones?" asked Adam.

"Ha, that's what I used to call tinned fruit cocktail when I was a girl. I think some of the little grapes still had their stems. Bones!"

Adam found it hard to smile at the light-hearted recollection, imagining the bloody broken bones of Rhapsody's many victims—including his own.

"Hmm, looks more like Tenby to me," mused Manny, "but that's in south Wales."

Aware of the time, Adam wrapped up the sentimentality, saying, "Well either way, we've got to find a way off this roof before the locals finish their Cornish pasties … or their last slice of Bara brith.

Searching the expansive roof, Adam was about to inspect a corner strewn with boxes, when Manny waved him over. Running down the back of the building was a robust iron drainpipe, emanating Victorian strength and reliability. The securing brackets were large enough to serve as footholds, promising an easy ladder-like descent.

Apparently unnoticed by the locals, they made their way to the harbour, cautiously peering around each alley before crossing, and careful to duck under any low windows. The soft soles of their footwear made little sound on the hard cobbles, highlighting the general eerie silence. Without incident, the weary adventurers slipped inside one of the seafront utility buildings, keen to get out of their dirty clothes and enjoy a few bites of 'fresh' dispenser food.

Twenty minutes later, sullen and disappointed, and still clad in their stinking garments, the group stepped back out onto the cold grey granite of the harbour. The utility building's elegant dispensers –pearl ceramic buttons and gleaming brass –had not responded to the usual gestures, words, or even a prolonged bout of frustrated thumping and kicking. In the bar area, behind the polished mahogany counter, the serving androids stood motionless. No matter how hard Adam punched and prodded the aproned smiling mannequins, they remained inanimate and unresponsive. It seemed that like the railroader's viro, this place was also suffering from a serious breakdown. If so, then where were the inhabitants, and why the silence?

"I've had enough of this," said Adam, as they walked back to the cobbled street. "If this viro is broken down, then why were we brought here? Why isn't someone here to meet us?"

Holding his hands either side of his mouth, Adam shouted at the top of his voice, "Hello!"

He waited a few seconds, watching and listening for any sign of life, before shouting again, "Hello!"

Manny called out, "Is anyone there?"

A low grumbling hum caught their attention. The sound, which grew with each passing second, seemed at first unplaceable, resonating throughout the village. Adam and Manny backed away as the noise quickly evolved into a chilling discordance of terrifying howls and high-pitched shrieks, screaming out from every house.

Following the cries, thin naked figures began staggering out of the doorways. Painfully emaciated and hairless, they slowly stumbled along the uneven cobbles towards the harbour, arms outstretched. Adam baulked at the sight of the approaching horrors: spiky grabbing hands, sallow skin sucked tight around bones, and cracked lips drawn up into a toothy rictus. Soon the whole street was crowded, as every house discharged its ghastly cargo.

"What the hell are they?" shouted Adam, competing against the ear-slitting noise, and about to make a dash for the nearest fishing boat.

"Zombies," shouted Manny, "they're most certainly zombies, although they don't seem to have any bits missing!"

"Don't be stupid, the dead don't come back to life!"

"We did, didn't we?" said Manny, his voice shaking with fear. "But, don't worry, because these are the classic Romero-type zombies! They're very slow, and only dangerous if we are careless, weak, or if they are in large numbers!"

"Then we're lunch three times over! They're after our brains, yeah?"

"Umm, that's a different movie franchise," Manny corrected, displaying an uncharacteristic knowledge of the genre. "These zombies will probably eat everything but the bones."

Too late, Rhapsody tried to shield Kimberly from the sight of the oncoming horde. The young girl was both terrified and fascinated.

"The Cornish people are all naked and scary! Is that normal?"

"Err … it's an old Cornish tradition! And, we're supposed to … run for the boats!"

The wailing locals reached the harbour as Rhapsody and Kimberly pushed the heavy rope off the bollard, and Adam and Manny heaved the boat close up against the harbour wall with along mooring hook. Another large crowd of the creatures staggered around the corner of the other utility building, meaning both main streets were off limits. The group were about to climb onto the boat when a loud amplified voice, forceful yet urbane, caught their attention.

"Stay away from the fishing vessel! I repeat, stay away from the fishing vessel! You cannot stay out at sea forever, and these poor souls will simply await your inevitable return."

Standing by the roof edge of the utility building, white megaphone held aloft in a white gloved hand a well-dressed man with impressive muttonchops, leaning on a silver-topped ebony cane. He was every inch the

Victorian gentleman: long velvet frock coat, crisply creased black trousers, and a black top hat.

"Proceed with haste to the entrance of this building," he ordered, "and take the stairs to the roof terrace! Do not let them get too close! They become rather fleet of foot if they catch your odour!"

Leaving the boat, Adam and his band hurried into the utility building as the screaming mob, now moving quite rapidly, closed in.

John Down

A stark crack of light invaded the bottom of the dark stairwell as the door shuddered open a fraction. Struggling to shoulder it shut—Aloha shirt drenched in sweat—Adam put his trust in fear and stubborn determination as the crowd outside kept pushing. His straining muscles ached with an unknown fatigue, the rubber soles of his deck shoes squeaking against the tiled floor under the inexorable pressure. Buying his friends some time, he had elected to hold the door for as long as possible.

From the top of the stairwell, a sharp female voice shouted down, "Adam, get up here, pronto! There's an easy way off the roof!"

Defiantly, Adam gave the door a final heave and then scrambled up the first flight of stairs. The walls quickly became a frightening confusion of fast moving shadows as the crowd surged into the building, hungrily, relentlessly, following their prey.

Staggering awkwardly on leaden legs, Adam rounded the first floor landing, but tripped on the next step. His weary arms did nothing to break the fall, his head thudding heavily on a hard edge. Some feet behind, the echoing clatter of haphazard footsteps and an unholy cacophony of rasping howls brought alarming motivation. Adam reached out an arm, grabbed the iron bannister, and heaved himself to his feet. Summoning up the insubstantial dregs of a final reserve, he resumed his ascent, cursing between gritted teeth.

Under less dangerous circumstances, Adam would have appreciated the sumptuous loungers and gaily coloured parasols on the roof terrace, offering a comfortable view over the tranquil bay, but now they were just annoying obstacles. To the rear of the terrace, Rhapsody crouched, her crossbow held at the ready. Next to her, the mysterious stranger urged Adam over to a narrow plank that crossed the adjoining alley to a steep slate roof. Manny was climbing a rope ladder that hung from the roof's ridge, and promptly disappeared over the top.

"The roof is double hipped," said the stranger, as Adam tottered across the plank and began climbing the rope ladder. "There is a drainage gulley between the two roofs in which we can hide."

As a torrent of screaming ghouls spilled out of the stairwell, soon filling the roof terrace, Rhapsody and the stranger also climbed the ladder.

"We should've pulled the damn plank!" said Adam, sitting astride the roof ridge.

Once also settled on the ridge, Rhapsody raised her crossbow with the intention of picking off any that dared to cross. Calmly, the stranger pressed his hand down over the top of the weapon.

"Young lady, please lower your weapon. We are safe here."

Keeping a grip on the trigger, Rhapsody kept her eyes trained on the most likely targets. The stranger spoke again.

"Fear not, these creatures are wiser than you think. They will not attempt to cross the gap. Many of them are my friends and family, and very dear to me. I understand that you are a woman of violence, but I beseech you, lower your weapon."

"Do as he says, Rhapsody," said Adam. "I think it best we trust this man. And, look, none of the zombies are getting near the roof edge. If anything, they look scared."

Rhapsody grunted disapprovingly, lowered the crossbow, and slid down the other side of the roof into the drainage gully. Adam and the stranger did likewise. Losing sight of their prize, the terrible howls of the creatures quickly died down to a mournful whimper.

Sitting uncomfortably in the gully between the two grey-slated roofs, the group thanked the stranger for his timely intervention.

"My name is John Down," the man announced with an unexpectedly cold demeanour. "Please excuse my tardiness, as I intended to meet you on the roof by the portal. You arrived somewhat earlier than expected."

"Well, thank you for saving us from those zombies," said Adam, proffering a handshake.

John pointedly ignored the gesture, and said, "Even though I have heard them called that on a number of occasions, they are not zombies, and most certainly do not eat human flesh. In the Viroverse, these poor creatures are commonly known as husks; a fate that might befall all of you if you do not soon receive real nourishment."

John's portentous words, spoken with an unsettling calm sophistication, sent a palpable shudder through the group. Adam admitted that they all were suffering from weakness and dizziness, but added that they had eaten from hall and reception room dispensers as well as from that of his own viro. Maintaining the same stony expression, John explained the problem.

"The food from what you call the dispensers is fake. It may have the same taste, texture, and aroma as real food, but it provides no nutrition whatsoever. So clever is the imitation that it even breaks down into a close representation of faecal matter."

John put his hand to his mouth in alarm and said, "Oh dear. I may have overstepped the mark with that defecatory comment. Whilst my dear wife and I are of liberal mind, I often forget that others, especially a young lady like yourself," he nodded at Kimberly, "might take umbrage. Please accept my humblest apology if this is so."

"Kim doesn't know what you're talking about," explained Adam. "She's a minor in an adult's body. And, as for the defecatory comment, it's something all humans deal with on a daily basis, so no-one here's going to be offended."

"She's a child?" said John. "In that case I shall choose my words more wisely, and avoid even the mildest profanity. As far as the nutrition matter is concerned, you should understand that we are all fed after midnight, during sleep. We are supposed to receive a personally optimized amount of sustenance, but as evidenced by the husks, this is not always the case."

"But we did sleep," protested Manny.

"Mr Beaumont, the feeding only takes place in a functioning viro, not in the halls or portal rooms. However, in a few viros, such as this one, where many of the services have disappeared or are functioning on a paltry level, the feeding is woefully inadequate. The reason these poor starving souls are not dead, is that the meagre morsels they receive are only enough to maintain what the Captain describes as 'a failsafe husk mode' built in to our miniaturised design. They exist in a continual dazed hunger, one step from death."

"But they won't eat us?" asked Rhapsody, folding the compact crossbow, and clipping it to her belt. "Because, it really felt like they wanted to eat us."

John shook his head, and explained, "Husks seek human vitality. They wish to touch you, to embrace you. When they do this, they absorb a small amount of your energy. One husk is a trifling inconvenience, but a large group can be very dangerous. Suffer the hugs of the many and you will undoubtedly join their ranks."

"But don't they touch each other to gain extra energy?" asked Rhapsody.

"Their own levels of energy are not enough to rouse the hunger. But, enough of this talk!"

John stood, brushed the creases out his jacket, and rapped the slate with his cane.

"If you are all rested, it is time for us to leave. We need to get to my wife's house whilst the husks are still by the harbour. If we dally here too long, then they will be trundling back to their homes, blocking our route."

Fearful of running into the husks, they helped each other to their feet. John began climbing the rope ladder on the second roof.

"On the other side is a rope leading to a first floor bedroom. Follow me!"

The bedroom was an ornate empty shell, lacking furniture and ornaments, though richly decorated with heavy crimson drapes and arabesque carpets, complementing dusky-rose flock wallpaper. John Down waited by the closed door, his hand on the brass handle.

"This room is kept clear to facilitate an uncluttered passage to the roof. It is useful if being pursued by husks. When I open this door, we will proceed along the landing, down the stairs. Once I am certain the street outside is clear, we shall run across to the side street opposite. At the sound of a bell, rung by me, a door shall open some ten yards yonder, and you will run straight in. Do you understand?"

Everyone did, and so John opened the door and cautiously peered out onto the landing. Sure there were no lurking husks, he ushered the group to follow him. As they crept to the top of the stairs, a disquieting problem presented itself. Stumbling around, moaning quietly in the hall below was a female husk. The starving creature was not yet aware of the energy-loaded treats watching her from above. John whispered instructions to the others.

"I'm afraid it's Murphy's Law that our way is obstructed by this lazy straggler. And, please, no weapons," he said, noticing Rhapsody's hand on her crossbow. "Remember, I told you that one husk is merely an inconvenience. I could confront her myself, and let her take a portion of my energy. Once sated, she will be in an intoxicated state for a few minutes and pose no further problem. Better still, if we hold each other's hands during the confrontation, the small energy drain will be shared between us."

"We're pretty weak already," said Adam.

"No problem," said John, taking a firm grip of Adam's hand. "That is why I will be in front. I shall withstand the worst of the energy loss. On my mark, we must move swiftly down the stairs. If we dawdle, she will see us and start that abominable howling. Now, all join hands …. and go!"

After rushing down the stairs in single file, the group moved across the hall. Before impact, the husk managed to turn and let out a single delighted shriek as she lunged and held onto John. It took only three seconds before she let go, gurgling contentedly, and promptly collapsed to the floor. Adam felt little changed, but could see that John was slightly doddery on his feet.

John looked out into the street.

"Oh, what a calamity," he whispered. "There are three husks loitering by the side street. Let me think …."

A deafening scream shocked the group as another husk appeared behind them. John Down sprinted into the street alone, heading straight for the three husks.

"With haste, follow me!" he shouted.

John raced over the hard cobbles and crashed headlong into the unsuspecting creatures, who swiftly absorbed their precious bounty. Meanwhile, Adam and the others charged out the front door of the house, keen to avoid the pursuing husk. Once outside, Adam slammed the door hard in the creature's face, knocking it back across the hall.

When they reached John, he was still on his feet but swaying ominously, as if his legs were about to buckle. The three husks lay on the ground around him, moaning contentedly. Adam and Manny each took an arm and shouldered the depleted hero awkwardly down the side street. Rhapsody ran alongside, dragging a terrified Kimberly with her. Grabbing the brass bell from John's hand, Rhapsody rang it loudly, hoping for an open door, but worried that it might attract the harbour-side mob.

Up ahead, a door was flung open, and a woman's voice cried out, "In here!"

OASIS

M ary Down, a quiet contented woman, handed Adam a steaming hot bowl of beef stew and dumplings. Sitting comfortably in a plumply upholstered armchair, he thanked his kindly host and blew a cooling breath over the first spoonful before eating. To his left, on a large button-back sofa, Manny and Kimberly were already tucking in to the hearty fare, whilst Rhapsody took a hot bath upstairs in Mary Down's luxury slipper bath. The house, a modest two-story fisherman's cottage, seemed as a warm oasis in this hostile viro: plush furnishings, Turkish rugs, and shelves heavy with books, porcelain figurines, and all manner of exotic trinkets.

John Down, reclining on a chaise longue pulled close to the glowing coal fire, took another glass of water as his attentive wife mopped his brow with a cold damp flannel. He was much recovered from his energy-sapping ordeal, and by the time Adam finished his meal, was able to stand. Mary collected the bowls and spoons and disappeared into the tiny kitchen nook.

John leant on his cane for support, and said, "Kimberly, if I had known a child was accompanying these murderous people, I would have escorted you safely through the halls."

"So, you're the person that tattoo freak was talking about," said Adam. "You were supposed to meet us—something about a Captain."

"My outlandish colleague spoke the truth. I had instructions from the Captain to provide you safe escort to the Terminal."

"So why didn't …"

"Mr Eden, you and your lady friend are killers. I decided to spend time with my wife rather than ease your passage. Once the Captain discovered I had reneged on my orders, he gave me another chance. He steered you to this viro, and I was meant to meet you by the portal. For missing that appointment, I have already apologised."

"What about me?" complained Manny. "I'm not a killer, and one of those jellymen nearly got me."

John pointed his cane at Manny, and spoke with a withering tone, "People who choose to associate with killers must suffer the consequences!"

Mary called from the kitchen and gently admonished her husband.

"John, where are your manners?" she said. "Because of these good people, I do not have a husk for a spouse. They could have left you lying in the street but they chose instead to help you."

Muttering a vague apology, John sat back down on the chaise longue. They all sat in silence for a few minutes until Adam asked, "Who is this Captain you work for? Is he the local strongman or something?"

"You will no doubt find the answers to your questions when you meet him. What I can say is that I am in his employ and greatly in his debt. The Captain has the ability to solve problems, but there is always a price to pay."

"And he solved a problem for you?" asked Adam.

"This is not my viro. I was resurrected in a collector's viro. Normally, people are assigned viro's by date and family connections, but some concierges wield significant power and are able to bend the rules. This particular concierge, an insidious fiend in my opinion, collected people who gave their names to maladies, such as … err … Ricketts, Hodgkin, Alzheimer, myself, and many many others." John shook his weary head, remembering those dark days. "There were nearly a hundred of us in that infernal place, and mostly men I might add. To this day, I do not know why I was chosen, but the Captain used his influence to set me free. I now have my own personal viro, but it is very far from here."

"What price did you pay?" asked Adam.

John frowned and wrung his hands together, as if dredging up more painful memories.

"The Captain was never specific about the price," he explained, "but I am expected to run various errands, some of which sour my moral fortitude and quite frankly sicken me to the stomach. I also believe that he saved Mary from the corruption of this viro, and the price she pays is that she must stay here. So many times, I have desired to take her through the portal to live with me, but we fear a calamity might follow. My sons live in this viro also, as husks, so my wife dares not leave."

Adam wondered if meeting the Captain was a good idea. What price would he extract in exchange for a glimpse of the outside world?

"You're the 'Down's Syndrome man', aren't you?" exclaimed Manny, clapping his hands together.

Mary came from the kitchen nook carrying a tray of tea and biscuits.

"He certainly is," she said proudly, pouring a cup of the steaming hot beverage for Manny. "Sometimes, I call him' my dear little syndrome'."

"I wish you wouldn't," John snorted, reaching for a biscuit.

Adam walked over and again attempted to shake John's hand.

"Very proud to have met you. I had a second cousin with Down's Syndrome, although I never met her."

Yet again declining Adam's handshake, John said, "Your murderous notoriety precedes you, Mr Eden. You may be a legend to some deluded fools, but it irks me that killers such as yourself and your lady friend are allowed back into this world, whilst those cheery innocents, blessed by the malady that bears my name, are classed as undesirables and therefore refused resurrection."

"I was brought back by accident," said Adam defensively. "I'm an undesirable too."

"You certainly are, Mr Eden. You certainly are."

CRAZY KIND O' LOVE

Leaving Manny to cope with John Down's simmering hostility, Adam went upstairs to check on Rhapsody. He stopped a moment outside the bedroom door as a once familiar tension gripped him. Standing silently on the small oak landing, he experienced the awakening of a deep dormant need. Worries about his sexual shortcomings and the ever-present spectre of humiliation were pushed aside by a single-minded physical desire. Copacabana's ruthlessness was not required for this particular indulgence. Spurred on by the pent-up passion of many sexless centuries, Adam knocked at the door, and placed his hand firmly on the handle.

"It's ok, I'm decent," came the brisk reply.

Adam immediately opened the door and stepped inside—the whole motion perhaps too fast, too eager, betraying a fervent mixture of stress and rising lust.

"Not too decent, I hope," he said coolly, successfully suppressing a nervous warble.

Rhapsody stood by the slipper bath in the far corner of the simple bedroom. She had a large towel wrapped around her body, her cleavage tantalisingly visible above the hem. Casting a knowing smile at Adam, she busily rubbed her hair dry with a smaller towel. Adam approached confidently, wondering how some people managed to wear a towel without it springing open. It was a skill he never possessed, but then again, he had been a first-life fatty and it only took the slightest wobble or belching belly expansion to loosen even the largest bath-sheet.

"Come, sit here," said Rhapsody, directing Adam to a wooden stool next to the bath, "and take off your top."

Rhapsody's words instantly shook Adam from his bath linen musings, and he hurriedly fumbled with the buttons on his Aloha shirt. He carefully folded the dirty garment, placed it on a dark oak dresser, then sat on the stool. Rhapsody dipped a sponge into the bath's soapy water, and moved up close behind Adam. She 'inadvertently' brushed her towelled breasts against his head, and gently drew the wet sponge around his neck.

The sponge slipped seductively across Adam's shoulders and chest, avoiding contact with his many wounds and dressings. He stifled a contented groan, enjoying the sensual friction of the wet caress and the soft warmth of Rhapsody's breath against his ear.

She sponged lower, snaking around the muscular contours of his abdomen before washing provocatively just above the beltline. Though not creating even the slightest crease to the front of his trousers, Adam was already erect, and confident he could maintain his diminutive rampancy. When flaccid, Adam's micro penis was an object of derision, shock, and often laughter, but when erect, like a turtle straining its neck up to the sky, he might get away with a sigh of mild disappointment.

To Adam's dismay, Rhapsody stopped sponging.

"I can smell your sweaty genitals from here," she said, ruining the moment. "I've just had a bath and am feeling fresh as a summer breeze, so I think it's time you took over. That brass panel over there with the levers is a dispenser. I'd advise you get some fresh clothes."

Confused, frustrated, and feeling let down, Adam took the sponge. Rhapsody giggled, skipped over to the bed, and slid under the colourful tapestry quilt.

"Clean up well, Adam, but please don't take all day; if you want sex that is."

Betraying his shyness, Adam pulled the curtain across the bath area. Safe from prying eyes, he took off his trousers and underwear, and then commenced sponging—paying special attention to his groin in the hope of reigniting his now limp member.

Five minutes later, Adam emerged, a towel wrapped around his waist, but clutching it tight for fear of the inevitable 'spring open'. He laid a neatly folded pile of new clothes on the stool. Still wearing the towel, he got under the quilt with Rhapsody, who was now totally naked.

Sympathetic of Adam's injuries, they embraced gently and kissed passionately, enjoying the taste of each other's mouth and the sensual flicking of tongues. Rhapsody lightly scratched her fingernails around Adam's chest, whilst he squeezed one of her breasts. He kissed and softly gnawed along her neck, his tongue heading slowly south towards the ultimate mammary goal.

Their passion became ever more intense as Adam kissed and nibbled around Rhapsody's areola, whilst she slipped her hand under the towel and pinched and massaged teasingly close to his relatively rampant member.

"It's been so long," whispered Rhapsody, cupping Adam's testicles, playfully tugging at his pubic hair. "The last time I had sex was just before I split my husband's skull open with the bedside lamp."

Adam froze, biting his tongue in response to the shocking words, and let out a lisping raspberry. Rhapsody sensed her lover's surprise.

"Err … don't worry, I didn't kill him because of the sex. He was great in bed: inventive, great stamina, and very well endowed."

At that moment, Rhapsody moved her hand to clutch Adam's penis, but found nothing there. She frantically groped around, eventually finding a tiny limp nub.

"Oh my God, Adam!" she gasped, removing her hand from under the towel. "You don't have a dick! What happened to your dick?"

Suffering an emotional confusion of embarrassment and fear, Adam could only manage a feeble mumble.

"You scared it away. Those things you said … Those things."

Throwing off the quilt, Adam got up and sat silently on the edge of the bed, his back to Rhapsody. He shuddered as she knelt behind him and began massaging his shoulders.

"Let's try again," she said. "You don't have to be shy about your little man. I'm sure I can coax him back out to play."

"It's nothing to do with my 'little man' as you call him. I just didn't know you studied the Jack the Ripper guide to sex-talk. If it's all right by you, I think I'll get dressed and go back downstairs."

Massaging more firmly, quite close to Adam's shoulder wound, Rhapsody put her mouth close to Adam's ear. With a hot breath of a whisper she said,

"Oh no, Adam, it's not all right by me. You need to sit and listen to what I have to say. If our relationship is going to work, then you need to know who I used to be."

Adam tensed up as he imagined Rhapsody snapping into psycho mode, ripping off his shoulder dressing, and plunging her sharp nailed fingers deep into the scabby gouge. He now wished he had stayed downstairs and endured John Down's hostility. With a dull, almost emotionless tone, Rhapsody began her tale.

"I always wanted to kill anyone who upset me. It was my nature. Trouble was, whether I showed it or not, I was so easily upset. It wasn't a matter of hate, but simply a belief that no one should bring even a moments darkness into my life. Remember I told you about Polperro and the Knickerbocker glory? Remember I told you that I didn't like the bones? Well, I imagined pushing the waiter through the plate glass window and then running out to roll him into the sea to watch him drown. I even imagined smashing my parent's heads in with the dessert glass for finding my 'bones' comment so amusing. Those murderous thoughts cheered me up and I soon forgot about the disgusting tinned fruit."

"I think I should go," said Adam.

"Shhhh," whispered Rhapsody, gliding a finger nonchalantly across the wound. "I'm far from finished.

"At school, I always maintained a distance. Sooner or later, every single teacher did something or said something to upset me, and I chewed on my pencil or pen, dreaming of the perfect way to kill them. Who knows, perhaps the time spent on those thoughts prevented me from achieving academic success. For me, the worst teachers were those that showed true commitment to helping the children. They tried to connect with me, believing they could bring out my true potential. In a way, they were right. I spent far longer planning their deaths than any of their boring colleagues. By the time I left school, at the age of sixteen, I had three exercise books full of highly detailed murders. 'One day', I vowed to myself, I would track them all down and take great pleasure in carrying out my plans."

A moment of potent silence, and Adam could sense Rhapsody's eyes burning a hole in the back of his head. Did the windows to her soul reveal a vulnerable woman desperately needing to unburden her sins, or did they herald the rebirth of the psychopath? Betraying neither, Rhapsody continued.

"I was a secretary before I got married. My boss was a kind man: understanding, generous, and always fun to be around. I think it was those qualities that made me want to stick his executive fountain pen in his eyes and then crush his skull with his precious art-deco marble paperweight. I was let go after I twice spilled boiling hot coffee over him. There were rumours that I did it on purpose, but they were both just clumsy accidents … honest.

"Five years later and there I was, sweaty from sex, lying next to my husband, Clive. My lovely daughter, Jade, was fast asleep in the box-room, no doubt dreaming of the presents Father Christmas would bring in a few days' time. The newspapers and TV told lies. They said I snapped due to low self-esteem. They said it was to do with my feelings towards my daughter. I never snapped and I always loved my daughter, no matter what.

"Oh Adam, shrugging off the pretence was as smooth as easing into a nice hot bath. You see, acting on my murderous impulses was my long-term ambition, and laying there next to Clive, I knew it was time to start my new life. By the time the police caught me, I had killed my husband with a lamp, stabbed my daughter, and set fire to those bloody noisy neighbours. My dear uncle Ken lived in a village nearby, and the police drew up as I was closing the front gate after a job well done. Again, the papers lied and printed that I was screaming like a goddam lunatic. Truth was that I sat silently in the police car feeling perfectly serene. Never had I felt so happy, so liberated. I was absolutely beaming. It was a feeling that stayed with me right up until a prison inmate gutted me, and sawed my head off with a steak knife."

Adam needed to leave the room. Whether Rhapsody was still a psychopath or not, the whole situation was too unnerving. He fetched his clothes from the stool and began dressing. Rhapsody stood by the bed, and started crying.

"You don't get it do you?" she bawled. "I am no longer that awful monster. The things I did horrify me, but I still have the memories. Every minute detail of every murder is scarred into my brain. Worse still, is that I remember the sheer ecstasy I felt as I took each life. Adam, these memories will never leave me. If we're here for eternity, then these bloody beasts will stalk my mind forever, like a pack of laughing hyenas."

"What the Hell has this to do with the crazy sex-talk, huh?" asked Adam, putting on his shoes, and heading towards the door.

Rhapsody threw herself on the bed and half buried her head in the pillow. With a muffled sob she explained, "I can't help it. Being normal was something I pretended to be. Now, I'm not sure what to do or say. I worry if I'm just pretending again. I need help, Adam."

Feeling a pang of sympathy as he opened the door, Adam adopted a conciliatory tone.

"We're getting out of here tonight, Rhapsody. John's got a route across the rooftops that takes us near the portal. He says there's a safe viro nearby where we can heal up and get fed overnight. Oh yes, and it turns out that John is actually something of a celebrity."

"I know who he is," Rhapsody whimpered. "He's John Langdon Down, the man they named Down's Syndrome after."

"Well, you're quite the encyclopaedia," joked Adam, forcing a smile.

Rhapsody looked at Adam, her expression haunted, eyes brimming with tears, voice trembling.

"I … I … read about him in one of the booklets they gave me when my daughter was born."

Unable to take any more, Adam left the room and stood on the small landing. His hand was still on the handle as he pondered on whether to go back in. Second chances were something in which he had always believed, and he fought to make sense of his companion's tragedy. With both head and heart suffering from a sense of helplessness and cowardly guilt, Adam took his hand off the handle and went downstairs to join the others.

NIGHTFALL

Adam stood on the roof ridge of Mary's house, leaning against a tall chimneystack. His eyes gradually adjusted to the dark as he looked out across the sheltered bay, where rippling ridges of dark water glimmered under the moonlight, and the distant lighthouse cast a repeated arc of yellow light from its lonely promontory.

The fishing village lay under the grey pall of night, a miserly run of gaslights barely affecting the gloom. In the narrow streets, the diffuse light created eerie islands of soft shadows and half-glimpsed shapes amid cavernous voids of pitch black. To Adam, the elevated rooftops seemed otherworldly: an expressionist landscape of slate-tiled planes and chimney silhouettes.

Before the group left through an upstairs window, Mary had extolled the lost virtues of the viro—a once peaceful haven of good neighbours, colourful regattas, fetes, and glorious scenery. She desperately hoped it would return to its former state, fearing an eternity imprisoned within her small cottage and the dreadful degradation of close friends and family.

Over the years, following the collapse of the viro, John Down had linked the rooftops with planks, ropes, and ladders, creating a network of safe elevated pathways. Normally, such alterations would be gone by morning, but here they remained intact.

Rhapsody nimbly skipped across the first plank onto the adjoining roof. Stepping aside, she leaned back against the steep roof and crossed her arms, booted feet braced in the strong iron gutter. She cast a combative stare at Adam. The glowering eyes were not daring him to cross, but instead daring him to accept or reject her. Adam walked across the plank, his face turned away from Rhapsody. He knew that she had bared her soul to him, but he was in no fit state to make any decision on the future of their relationship.

A few planks and ladders later, only a few buildings away from the portal, the group rested on a roof ridge. So far, the evening had proved uneventful with neither sight nor sound of the husks that stalked the streets below.

"Where are they?" asked Adam, staring hard at a dark spindly figure before realising it was the shadow of an ornate iron gate.

"Having very little energy to begin with," explained John, "by the evening they are almost spent. They are inside the houses, resting on beds and in chairs. Some simply flop on the nearest rug for whatever comfort that may provide."

"So why are we up here? If we're quiet, couldn't we just walk down the street?"

"I dare say we could, but why take unnecessary risks?" John looked at his watch—surprisingly, a 21st century digital—and slid down the roof to the next plank. "It is time we were going. The midnight hour is close."

Without incident, they crossed a couple more roofs and climbed down a drainpipe to a gloomy cobbled street. Opposite stood the flat roofed building next to the portal.

"We're safe now," announced John, shining a torch along the alley, revealing a crudely constructed brick wall. "The gap across the alley is a little too wide for a simple plank, especially since the portal house has an extra floor, so I built the wall to keep the husks out. I did contemplate a trussed wooden bridge from roof to roof, butalas, my carpentry skills are even worse than my masonry ones. The other end of the alley is the viro wall so no danger there."

With just over an hour before midnight, they entered the building and headed up a dimly lit staircase, illuminated by gaslight diffused through a bottle-glass window. They gathered at the top of the stairs and John slid open the sash window. He reached for a rope that dangled outside and pulled it in.

"This rope leads to the roof," he said. "I know you are all weary but the climb is only a few feet. I marked the position of the rope on the roof with a few boxes in the hope you would avoid the main street."

"We came down the drainpipe at the back," said Adam, looking out of the window, recognising the main street that they had earlier taken to the harbour.

Rhapsody pushed in front, grabbed the rope and climbed out of the window. Taking the strain, she cast the same forceful stare at Adam as before. He lowered his gaze, avoiding hers.

"I'll go first," she said. "After all, I'm not the one who's wounded."

The words cut Adam like a knife. He knew she deserved a second chance as much as anyone else, the same chance that made him a legend, albeit unwittingly. If a sound relationship was built on trust, then Rhapsody was right to trust him with the story of her past, however nauseating. Tomorrow, Adam decided, he would attempt to mend the relationship and see if Rhapsody could stand to hear the grimy details of his own first-life.

A scream!

Rhapsody fell past the window, still holding the rope. Reacting on impulse, without a care for his injuries, Adam shot out a hand and clutched the frayed end of the twisted cord. The weight and momentum nearly wrenched his arm out of its socket, and the friction of the rope tore the dressing off his hand, exposing his scabbed finger stump.

The window opening was too small to allow anyone else to help, so Adam leaned out and gripped the rope with both hands. He cursed his fatigued body for not having the strength to pull Rhapsody back up. On cue, the surrounding streets erupted into an unsettling cacophony of howls as the husks reacted to Rhapsody's screams.

Rhapsody stared up at Adam, her face full of fear. He wanted to tell her not to worry but could only seethe through gritted teeth as he fought to hold on. The coarse rope fibres split his finger scab, and soon the rope and his hands were slick with blood. The rope began to slip from his grasp.

Sensing the inevitable, John squeezed his head under Adam's arm and shouted down to Rhapsody.

"Dear lady, when you land, pick yourself up and hurry to the back of the building! There is a drainpipe that you can climb! Just get out of reach of the husks!"

Rhapsody screamed as the rope pulled free and she plummeted to the hard cobbles below, hitting the ground with a thud and an ominous crack of bone. With the sound of husks approaching, she frantically tried to stand, but immediately fell back down, clutching her ankle.

"It's broken! It's broken!" she cried.

As Rhapsody again attempted to get to her feet, the first shrieking husk shot out of the darkness. The skeletal creature bowled straight into its prey, latching on with its bony fingers. Within seconds, the husk had its fill, and lay motionless on the cold cobbles. Rhapsody sat up groggily, as if one step from sleep.

"I've got to do something," panicked Adam, about to launch himself out of the window.

Two people held Adam back. John grabbed Adam round his waist, hauling him onto the landing, whilst Copacabana ordered him to 'let the psycho bitch go'.

A crowd of husks appeared, and hungrily feasted on Rhapsody's energy. Before long, she was submerged beneath a writhing mass of skeletal limbs and leathery skin. Adam watched helplessly from above. He breathed heavily as the shock set in, dry retching as he slumped to his knees. John pulled him away from the dreadful sight, and Manny shut the window.

"Let me go down there," Adam moaned, feeling as though he had been punched in the stomach. "I have to save her. Distract them and …"

John lifted Adam to his feet, pinned him against the wall, and shouted, "Snap out of it, man! Midnight is almost upon us, and if we stay here overnight, you will be too weak to leave. Within a few days you will all become husks."

"But, I must save her. She needs to know …"

John slapped Adam across the face.

"We have a child with us! Have you no care for her welfare? We must leave this place tonight! Do you understand?"

Kimberly came over and tugged Adam's arm. She spoke haltingly—the voice of a terrified child.

"Please can we go? I don't want to turn into a Cornish nudie monster. Please?"

Not for the first time, Copacabana exerted total control, concerned that the mission was in jeopardy, and Adam fell back into the mental shadows.

With an act of childish bravado, Copacabana slapped his own face hard and smiled as his cheek flushed red with the force.

"Hey Johnny, is Rhapsody in any pain? Will she suffer in any way—apart from the crash weight-loss of course?"

"Err … not to my knowledge," said John, bemused at Adam's abrupt change of mood. "The experience is apparently akin to a permanent drunken stupor. Are you all right?"

"The fuck I am," laughed Copacabana, slapping John's shoulder. "I'm tired as shit. I have sooo many wounds. Worse than all that, it looks like I'm not getting laid any time soon."

Manny was shocked.

"Please watch your language Adam. There's a child present."

"Hah, I know that, and one day you'll grow up to be a man. Now, tell me John, how do we get onto that roof?"

John led the group into the parlour of a large bedroom to the rear of the house, and opened a window.

"You can reach the drainpipe from here," he said, pointing up to the roof. "It is only a short climb. Be careful though. The viro wall is quite close. If you fall against that, then you will be cannoned back into the brickwork. A very messy outcome, I should imagine."

Copacabana took the lead, shouting obscenities as he suffered the pain from his shoulder. The others followed, and within minutes, they were gathered on the flat roof. Across the precipitous gap, the portal seemed tantalizingly close.

"Do we use the plank?" asked Manny.

"That won't be necessary," said John taking a small spray can from his pocket. "For portal duties I use this."

The others looked on incuriosity, as John sprayed a narrow six-foot section of the roof with a luminous substance. Popping the can back in his pocket, he bent down and seemed to pick up a glowing plank of thin air.

"What the Hell is that?" asked Copacabana. "We haven't got time for any Victorian magic tricks."

"Bear with me," said John, fixing two spike-shaped shards to the end of the glow. "There, that's perfect! This is not some magic spray, just a temporary luminant. You obviously did not see the extremely thin transparent sheet laying there. This, my friends, is my graphene bridge. It is thinner than a whisker, light as paper, but rigid and stronger than steel. Usually, I forgo the spray, but I fear you may wander off the side if you can't see where you're walking."

"Hmm, isn't that a bit high tech for a Victorian?" asked Manny. "I thought we could only access products from before our own deaths."

"One of the many perks of working for the Captain," said John, as he effortlessly fed the graphene bridge across the gap and thrust the shard-spiked end into the portal membrane. Tapping his cane on the hard glowing surface, he walked casually over to the portal and sliced a large opening.

"Easy as that!" he exclaimed, taking a dramatic bow. "Now, if you will all come over, we can soon enjoy a well-earned sleep."

The brightly lit reception room was a welcome relief from the shadowy terror of the husk-viro, the experience tainted only by the appearance of an unexpected and unwanted guest.

"So, you sorry bunch of losers finally made it," sneered the inkman, laying on one the benches, lurid sexual tattoos on full display. "Thought I'd hang around here in case you needed a hand. Truth be told, I figured the jelly buggers would've got you." Looking at Kimberly, he rubbed his chin. "Don't remember you. What happened to the good lookin' Sheila in the Abba get-up?"

"She fell afoul of the husks, I'm afraid," said John, grabbing the inkman roughly by the arm, and dragging him over to the dispenser. "And, Kimberly's a child so I suggest you wear a coat to cover up those sordid stains."

"No need to get physical, mate. You may not know it, but I do have some moral standards."

"I doubt that very much," said John.

Once the inkman was suitably covered up, in a long brown mac, John turned his attention to the others. He gasped as he saw Adam's grey mannequin skin and ping-pong ball eyes for the first time.

"Oh my lord, you are an undesirable! In all my years, I have never seen one such as you. Your eyes … your eyes are most disturbing."

"Well, suffer because I'm not wearing shades," said Copacabana looking at his watch. "You better get us to that safe viro because it's already twenty to twelve."

Manny opened the reception room door and the weary group hurried along the hall. Wheezing and breathless, they reached their destination with only minutes to spare.

Manny, Happy, Returns

8:00 AM. Adam woke up and took in the fresh morning air, surprised by the sweet chirrup of an unseen bird. He felt no pain or hunger –his wounds had vanished, but not the dressings. Thankful that he was not naked, a quick sniff confirmed that he was still wearing the same Aloha clothes as yesterday: a problem easily solved by a trip to a dispenser. Mercifully, Copacabana had relinquished control, leaving Adam to explain his rude behaviour.

As instructed by John, Adam stayed low atop the cracked roof of the ancient roman temple. Using an ivy-entangled urn as cover, he shuffled round on his belly to get a good look at the viro. The night before, the visibility was only a few feet, but now Adam found himself treated to a spectacular landscape.

A sweeping mountainous ridge, its sides lush with colourful scrub and fragrant wild herbs, curled down to a hamlet of luxurious Italianate villas—a meandering river, criss-crossed by marble-capped bridges, weaved its way around their majestic gardens. The light breeze, birdsong, and the aromatic garrique were expensive features only found in the finest viros. Adam frowned, as it occurred to him that almost every viro he visited put his own to shame. It was not a case of 'the grass is greener' but glaring evidence that his concierge was telling the truth about the dire state of her finances.

"Beautiful, isn't it?" said John, kneeling beside Adam. "I always stay here overnight when spending a few days with Mary. Her viro used to have birdsong—seagulls mainly—but now there is only the lapping of the waves and the awful howling."

"If my viro was like this, then I might never have left." Adam smiled as he picked out the aroma of wild lavender in the air. "Look, John, I want to apologize for my behaviour yesterday. I wasn't myself. I may be a killer, but I'm rarely one for foul language and insults."

"Your sudden change of mood is understandable given the circumstances, and we owe a debt of gratitude to whatever demon possessed you. Without his sudden intervention, you and your friends may have joined the ranks of the husks. What happened to Rhapsody is a tragedy but I assure you she suffers no pain."

John leant close and whispered in Adam's ear.

"I have already asked the others, but I need to know if you really want to meet the Captain. You are under no obligation to see him. If you so desire, you can go on your merry way. No more barriers will be placed and the reception rooms will remain accessible."

Adam found the request very odd. Why go to all the trouble of herding them if there was no obligation to meet the mysterious Captain? Now his interest was piqued more than ever.

"Ok, I choose to see him."

In the reception room, after eating breakfast, they prepared for the two-day journey to the Terminal. John stuffed a backpack with PVC incontinence sheets, while the inkman played games on a handheld tablet. Tired of the jungle warfare image, Manny decided to swap his combat fatigues for his usual sweatshirt and jeans. Adam sat quietly on the bench, wearing his shades, contemplating a future without Rhapsody watching his back with her sharp eyes and arrows.

"Sorry about Rhapsody," said Manny, lacing up a sensible shoe. "I could tell you were fond of her. For a while, I thought you both harboured a mutual romantic interest. I was even going to offer my services as a chaperone."

"Thanks, Manny. John says there might be a chance the Captain can bring her back. The guy apparently likes to make deals, whatever that means."

"I hope he can help. The thought of her as a zombie … I mean husk, is very upsetting."

"What is it with you and zombie movies?" asked Adam, remembering Manny's outbursts when the husks first appeared. "You never mentioned you liked that sort of thing before."

"I did have a life before I joined the church, you know," sniffed Manny. "To be honest, I rather miss those films, but not the people I watched them with. Once I was safe, living in God's grace, I noticed my old crowd adopting curious lifestyles advocated by magazines, television, and the advice of fallen friends. As the years went by, it was a sad fact that all these lifestyles led to suffering."

"Well, one day, maybe we can watch a zombie movie together," said Adam. "You pick the movie, and I'll choose the snacks."

"Oh no," said Manny, wagging a finger. "I have left those sinful movies well and truly behind."

Kimberly, sitting on the bench opposite, a pink Barbie suit and glittered ponytail betraying her mental age, had been listening to the conversation.

"Mr Manny, can I ask you something?" she said.

"Of course you can."

"When I went to live with my Aunt Charlene at the Sunny Oaks Trailer Park, she told me that my ma was on a long holiday, paid for by the Federal government. She told me it was 'cause of my ma's lifestyle. You said all those lifestyles ended in sufferin'. Are you sayin' my ma suffered?"

Adam slapped Manny on the back, and said, "Hah, get out of that one."

Never quick witted, Manny huffed and blustered, his face blushing a beetroot red as he failed to supply an answer. The stress got the better of him. Leaving the bench, he stood in the corner by the portal, and told everyone to look away while he did a number two. Dropping his trousers and pants, he squatted on the floor.

"Strewth!" cried the inkman. "You ain't taking a crap on the floor, are you? Why … why would you wanna do that, you filthy bugger? I thought all you poms were toilet fixated? Pull your bloody keks up and use the dunny like everyone else!"

All eyes were fixed on Manny, who slowly pulled his trousers back up.

"But I need to go," he whimpered.

John, in an uncharacteristic display of emotion, burst out laughing.

"My dear fellow, you are obviously unaware of the reception room cubicles," he said, pointing to the wall with his cane. "If you have to go, simply lay your hand on one of the sidewalls and you will have your own personalised bathroom. The room automatically senses your gender, height, and comfort preferences. These facilities are also available at the ten mile junctions."

Manny followed the instructions and a section of wall slid open to reveal a small toilet and hand basin. As he entered, the inkman leapt from his chair and began shouting.

"So, you're the dirty buggers who dumped turds all over the white lines! Surfing the halls has been a bloody nightmare the last couple of days. I've been swerving and line-jumping like I'm in a Bond ski-chase to avoid that muck. Halls aren't even cleaned for another month."

***

The halls were clear, the route discussed, but John and the inkman were still debating the finer points of white-line surfing. Adam told Kimberly to stay close, concerned that the oozing green mass was about to break free of the wall. Seconds later and a jellyman began its sloppy shamble towards the group. John cast a cursory glance at the approaching menace, but showed little concern. In a panic, Manny prodded John and begged him to do something.

"Will you do the honours, Kevin?" asked John, rummaging in his rucksack, and handing the inkman an incontinence sheet.

"No problem, mate," he casually replied. The inkman unfolded the PVC sheet and walked up to the jellyman. With one swift movement he threw the sheet over the sticky creature, turned, and sauntered back to continue his conversation.

Adam and the others watched in surprise as the jellyman twisted and squelched under the sheet before stumbling to the floor. The sheet quivered and flattened, the jellyman stuck fast.

"Takes about two hours for the mucaloid to dissolve the sheet and free itself," explained John, readying another sheet.

"I guess it pays to know your incontinence products," said Adam. "If you don't mind, I'd like to deal with the next one."

Within a few minutes, all three jellymen were under sheets, safely stuck to the floor. Adam contemplated the two-day hike to the Terminal. In his teens, he had owned a skateboard, and almost mastered the 720. Could surfing the halls be any harder? Asking the question provoked a tirade of belittling insults from the inkman, but John was more sympathetic.

"In inexperienced hands, a white-line short-board is a guaranteed path to the great hereafter. Kevin is Bondai material, and thanks to the Captain, I studied under the 21st century Newquay surf-masters. Even with natural ability and the finest tutors, you need months of practise before you can safely ride the lines. Do not forget, since leaving your own viro via the portal, you are deregistered from the viro system. There are now very few places that will afford you the luxury of resurrection. Out here, in the halls, one careless fall and it is farewell forever."

Adam shuddered at the chilling revelation; shocked that resurrection was no longer guaranteed. His ability to block out the pain of the dark place after resurrection was his secret power and an important key to his success. Now he was a mere mortal again, and his legendary fighting skills seemed dulled. Without the safety net of resurrection, Copacabana's dogged adherence to his mission, to break free of the Viroverse, might prove suicidal—with Adam dragged along for the fatal finale.

"Ha, look at Mr Manny?" said Kimberly, grinning. "He's doing a funny walk."

Manny had walked a few feet away, and was now standing with his back to the group. He shook and twitched, his legs bending at the knees as if about to buckle. Before Adam could say anything, Manny fell flat on his face, and a wash of dark blood pooled around his body.

Rushing over to his fallen friend, Adam rolled Manny over and sat him up, supporting his head in the crook of his arm. Blood spurted from a long deep neck wound, which Adam frantically tried to staunch with the pressure of his hand. In contrast to the bloody mess, Manny was bright-eyed and smiling. He raised his hand to his neck and gently placed it over Adam's.

"It appears the Swiss army knife was quite effective after all," he spluttered, his teeth ringed red. "Don't try to help me. I want this. I want to die."

"But, I thought you wanted to find Jesus! Stern told me you wanted to find Jesus!"

"You misunderstand, Adam. I told him I wanted to leave the Viroverse and find God. I told him that Jesus might be out there to help me on my way. This is what I wanted."

Adam was distraught, not knowing what to do or say. John knelt beside them and inspected Manny's injury. A few seconds later, he shook his head. Finding a way, warm blood seeped out between Adam's fingers:

"Stay with me Manny. I thought God wasn't keen on suicide. What if there's no Heaven? What if …?"

"I know there is. That is what faith is all about. All I ask is if you see Sophia again, let her know that I loved her and relished every moment we spent together. Will … will you do that for me?"

"Of course I will, but you can tell her yourself. You can't go. I can't lose my best friend."

"Remember that thing you used to say? 'All the world's a stage, and…'"

"… 'most of us are merely watching from the wings'. Yes, I remember. You used to get so annoyed at my cynicism."

"And, for ruining a great Shakespeare quote." Manny gurgled a single laugh, sending blood running down his chin, soaking his sweater. "Well, now you are a leading man: a legend. The trick is to play that role without losing sight … of your humanity. Use your influence for the greater good."

"Manny, I … I don't know if I have any real influence. Out here, I feel weak. Anyway, how can you praise me with all the jokes and insults you had to put up with over the years? I could never resist poking fun."

Forcing a final smile, Manny said, "Like the time I allowed you a donor kebab on your diet … and you held it up to the sky and cried out 'Agnus Dei."

"Yeah, that kind of thing. I'm truly sorry."

"Don't be. Your jokes often betray understanding. Perhaps, beneath your humour … there is a deeper reverence."

Out of respect and shame, Adam did not contradict his friend's hopeful words. The light in Manny's eyes began todim, and his voice faded to a laboured whisper.

"Adam, you don't know it, but you are a decent man, with … a good heart. I don't know what place that will afford you in Heaven … but I dearly look forward to the day we shall meet again."

Sitting silently, tears rolling down his cheeks, Adam held onto his loyal friend as if letting go marked the true moment of death. With respectful quiet efficiency, John checked Manny's pulse and gently closed his eyelids:

"I am so very sorry, Adam."

DISGUSTING KEVIN

A dam was emotionally numb as John gently pulled him away from Manny's dead body. Somehow, waking up refreshed and healed that morning had softened the blow of losing Rhapsody, but now a dark malaise clouded his mind. Even Copacabana remained silent, perhaps also disheartened by the loss, or more likely concerned that resurrection was no longer guaranteed. Adam vainly tried to rationalise Manny's death. He told himself that in time, as with loss of all loved ones, the harrowing desolation would pass and the person archived in a warm nostalgia of memory marked sorely missed. Saying goodbye would take time; a luxury immediately denied as a shrill female scream shook Adam from his thoughts.

With Manny's blood still on his hands, Adam leapt to his feet, and saw Kimberly struggling with the inkman on his short-board. With the inkman's brown 'flasher' mac, and Kimberly's pink Barbie outfit, the scene had the disturbing appearance of a child abduction. John was incensed at his colleague's behaviour and demanded an explanation.

"The brat doesn't belong out here," shouted the inkman, wincing as Kimberly kicked him in the shin. "It's too dangerous. I'm taking her back to her own viro."

As they hurried over to intervene, Adam quickly told John about the threat to Kimberly's life should she return, pointing out the time anomaly between her and the railroaders. John waved away Adam's concerns, explaining that this might be a simple case of the Captain's orders—and if so, Kevin could take the girl.

"Orders?" asked John, pointing his cane at the inkman.

"Stay outta this, Down. It's what the Captain wanted!"yelled the inkman, grappling with his feisty captive.

"Orders?" John asked again, more forcefully, stamping his cane hard on the floor.

"Not official orders," admitted the inkman. "I'm doing the Captain a favour. I think he only wants Eden, not anyone else."

"Then, you would be wise to release the child, Kevin. You should know better than to second-guess the Captain. If my suspicions are correct then you are already due for punishment, and I do not have to remind you what that entails."

The inkman stepped off his board and roughly shoved Kimberly away.

"Here, take the whiny brat. You know, you're bloody lucky the Captain doesn't punish you for never turning up on time."

Kimberly ran to John, and he offered fatherly words of reassurance. Adam confronted the inkman.

"I don't know what time you are from or what you did in your first-life, but in my time we took child abduction seriously. No way someone like you should be alone with a child."

"Calm down, mad Dad," said the inkman defensively. "I'm not one of those dirty paedos, and I take offence at the very suggestion. I was only taking her back home, Mate. It's not like I was gonna make her choose from the menu."

"What did you mean by that?"

"Take a real close look at my tats," said the inkman grinning, throwing open the mac.

The tattoos pictured a vast range of sexual positions and preferences: heterosexual, gay, group, and even a number involving various household objects and food items. The positions covered the whole gamut of carnal skill from the straightforward missionary position to some seemingly impossible feats of contortion and ingenuity. Disturbingly, the inkman appeared in every picture, his wild-eyed face leering out with an expression of depraved satisfaction.

"Disgusting! You are totally disgusting! Why would you ..."

The inkman threw off the mac.

"Don't like wearing that. Makes me look like a bloody perv. I was a bit of a freako surf punk in my first-life. In the evenings, I used to walk into some beach bar, wearing nothing but my shorts, and pick out a Sheila for the night. My chat-up line was, 'I'm a modern man, so you get to choose what we do tonight'. Then I'd give her a slow 360 of my body and say, 'Take your pick, baby'."

"But there's you getting it on with men in some of those tattoos?"

"Gotta have a back-up plan if there's no Sheilas interested. Why do you ask? Seen something that takes your fancy?"

Panting like a dog, the inkman lolled his tongue out of his mouth and made thrusting moves with his hips. He stopped abruptly, dropped the grin, and faced up to Adam.

"You know, I wanted to introduce that Abba chick to my sex menu. She looked like she'd be game. I can always spot the types who want a trip around planet Kevin. Shame I had to let the rope go."

"What rope? What are you talking about?"

"I was on the roof last night. I untied the rope and listened out for you losers. Lucky for me the Sheila went first. If it was you or John, I'd have pulled you up, but I'm sure the Captain wanted the others out of the picture. I held the rope tight for a moment then ... arrivederci mama. Ha, you could say she fell for me in a big way."

Too late, John shouted out for Adam to keep calm and not retaliate. Adam erupted and punched the inkman full in the face, sending the tattooed pervert reeling to the floor. Grinning again, the inkman spat out a couple of teeth, and sprung to his feet.

"I claim self-defence!" he shouted excitedly. "The ugly bugger hit me first. You know the rules, John."

Without waiting for a reply, the inkman bent over and tugged hard on one the hanging rings dangling from the rear of his shorts.

"Ooooh, yes," he moaned blissfully, accompanied by an unsettling squelch as he pulled a short steel shaft out of his backside. He pointed the smelly object at Adam, and with a flick of a switch deployed a razor sharp blade.

Surprised and sickened by the disgusting switchblade, Adam wasted no time in unclipping his own knife.

"John, get Kimberly back in the reception room," he ordered. "She's seen too much today as it is."

Adam kept his eyes firmly on his depraved opponent, and waited patiently for the confirming hiss of the reception room door. The inkman began rocking on his feet from side to side, as if swaying to the beat of some unheard tune. Executing an intimidating spinning kick, he held out a beckoning hand, daring Adam to make the first move.

Hearing the hiss of the closing door, Adam lunged forward, sidestepping at the last moment to defeat the inkman's defence. His blade sliced diagonally, aiming for a chest to abdomen laceration, but found empty air as the inkman limboed gracefully under the steel. Adam immediately reversed into a follow up attack with the hilt of the knife, but the supremely agile inkman cartwheeled out of danger, kicking his opponent in the head on the way.

Regaining his composure, Adam wheeled around to meet his foe. In constant motion, the inkman zigzagged towards him, bouncing from foot to foot, skilfully obfuscating the direction of attack. In an unexpected deceit, the inkman threw himself to the floor at the last possible moment, and spun around on the palm of his hand, kicking Adam's legs out from under him. As Adam hit the floor, the inkman was already back on his feet. Nonchalantly, he swaggered past and sliced open Adam's cheek, before barrel rolling sideways and somersaulting in a show of pure bravado.

"Aaagh, that stings and stinks," seethed Adam, getting back on his feet.

"Hah, what did you expect?" laughed the inkman, dancing closer for another attack. "The arse-blade's been up me bum for a couple of days now, but you're so lame, I reckon I could beat you without it. I thought you'd be more of a challenge, what with you being the great Copacabana. Oh well, time to put you out of your misery."

A silver-topped ebony cane thrust between the two adversaries, halting the inkman's advance. John stepped forward, brandishing the cane at head height.

"This stops now, Kevin!" he boomed. "Self-defence or not, I am delivering Mr Eden and Kimberly to the Captain."

"Is that one of those sword canes?" asked Adam as the sturdy wood swooped past his face.

"No," answered John, cracking the silver-top against the inkman's head, knocking him out cold, "it's just a cane."

They carried the unconscious inkman into the reception room—safe from the threat of the jellymen. John secured the tattooed fiend to a bench with a timed-release chain, whilst Adam fetched a body bag and a small wooden cross from the dispenser. Kimberly cleaned the wound on Adam's cheek and applied a couple of large plasters.

"What kind of martial art was Kevin using?" asked Adam, still bewildered by the rhythmic nature of the moves. "I swear he was dancing."

"He practises Capoeira, a martial art of Brazilian origin. The dancing is integral and quite effective at confusing the opponent. As you are now no doubt aware, Kevin brings his own vicious tendencies into the mix. However, he is not the greatest exponent of the art. He did not win the fight, but rather you lost it. Without wishing to be rude, Kevin was correct about your lack of fighting prowess."

"I don't know what went wrong," conceded Adam. "I'm sure I wasn't this bad when I was fighting the psychos."

"Oh, I can vouch for that, Adam. I was present at your final fight in the psychoviro, disguised of course in one of those fanciful glitter suits. The Captain asked me to appraise your abilities, which I will admit were formidable."

"And, now?"

"Now, you are merely very good—an also ran. The difference is so marked that I pray you will discuss the matter with the Captain. However, now, we have to take care of our dearly departed Mr Beaumont."

After the briefest eulogy, Adam zipped Manny and a cross into the body bag. Since it would be a few weeks before the halls were cleaned, John recommended that he deposit the body in Mary's viro, on the flat roof next to the portal. One day, when time was of no concern, they could return and give Manny a proper burial at sea with all the respect, devotion, and emotion he deserved. John went alone, carefully carrying Manny on his short-board. Only half an hour later, John returned without the body.

"I won't be needing this," he said, leaving the board in the reception room. John patted a shiny black top hat on his head and struck a gentlemanly pose.

"Just the ticket for a stroll along the halls. Now you two, I have plenty of traditional English confectionary in my pocket, so let's make haste. The Captain awaits!"

Kimberly took John's arm and skipped alongside, singing 'Jingle bells'. Her childish spirit was infectious and John twirled his cane, high-stepping like the leader of a marching band.

Adam shouldered his rucksack, smiling broadly, as his companions' antics briefly washed away the day's sorrow.

"You lead and we'll follow, Mr Wonka."

THE CAPTAIN

The two-day journey proved mercifully uneventful, with none of the trauma of the previous days. Frequent rest stops had broken up the otherwise monotonous trek, and the guilty pleasure of throwing incontinence sheets over the jellymen—olé matador—was a source of constant amusement.

Kimberly, never short of energy and child-like exuberance, kept everyone entertained with a constant stream of songs: Disney favourites, children's TV themes, Christmas carols, and various rap tunes with dubious lyrics. Even Kevin made a brief and bothersome appearance—surfing past on his short-board, stealing John's hat as he did so. He twisted a 'swivel on this' middle finger at the group before racing off into the distance.

Adam had not expected the Terminal's reception room door to look identical to all the others along the halls. Bored by the never changing scenery, he had imagined a grand entrance, perhaps with a portcullis or a high-tech laser barrier, guarded by armed security personnel. At the very least, he expected some signage above the door, indicating that this was the Captain's lair.

Oblivious to Adam's disappointment, Kimberly rushed forward, eager to use the palm panel. When the door refused to open, John stepped up, explaining that it responded only to the Captain's operatives. He placed his hand on the panel and the door hissed open.

Internally, the reception room was almost identical to all the others Adam had visited except that, instead of a membrane, there was another sliding door with a palm panel. John wasted no time in slapping his hand down on the panel and the door obediently opened.

A bracing raft of cold wind and rain was Adam's first experience of the Terminal, accompanied by a rotating red light and the nearby whine of a jet engine. The red light belonged to a raised platform vehicle, which had drawn alongside the portal. Waiting on the platform, sheltering tidily under a small umbrella, was a tall smiling woman dressed in a blue airhostess uniform.

"Welcome to the Terminal, Mr Eden," she said in a cheerful Scottish brogue, as she handed out automatic umbrellas. "And, you must be Kimberly. Sorry about the rain, but you know how the weather is in London this time of year."

Adam stepped onto the steel platform, and found himself looking out across a vast international airport, complete with huge utilitarian terminal buildings, a traffic control tower, and at least two runways. The torrential rain, bucketing down from a blanket of dark grey clouds, cut visibility, but Adam barely discerned the blurry shapes of houses, warehouses, and the headlights of cars beyond the fenced airport perimeter. The scene was very familiar–Heathrow perhaps? Could this be the outside?

With an old-fashioned bow, John kissed the hostess's hand, and said, "Glad to see you again, Liana. I presume the Captain wishes to see me."

"That he does, John. He's already punished Kevin, poor lamb, and you're next for the chopping block. Now, if you will all please stand to the sides of the platform and hold firmly onto the rails."

Liana pressed a green button on the handrail and the driver in the cab below lowered the platform to a safe height. She pressed a red button and they were soon travelling across the smooth concrete apron towards the main terminal building.

"We would usually use a covered platform to ferry guests to the Terminal," Liana shouted over the sound of the lashing rain, "but both units are out for maintenance at the moment."

A powerful gust of wind buckled Kimberly's umbrella and it automatically snapped shut. She squinted as the rain whipped across her face, and nearly let go of the handrail. With a reassuring smile, Liana swapped umbrellas with the stricken girl.

Just as Liana was fiddling with the umbrella's stuck mechanism, the vehicle bumped over a protruding drain cover. The sudden jolt sent the startled hostess sliding off the front of the wet platform and she plunged in front of the cab. Everyone on the platform winced as the heavy vehicle bumped twice more—the wheels rolling over the stricken hostess.

Kimberly began crying as the vehicle slowly came to a stop, and Adam cautiously looked for the carnage left in its wake. Seemingly unconcerned by the incident, John mopped his sweaty brow with a handkerchief.

"Ah, a brief respite before I meet the Captain," he muttered. "Do not concern yourself with my punishment, Adam, for he is always fair in his judgement."

There was no carnage behind the vehicle, or even the slightest sign of blood. Some thirty feet away, Liana was standing, buttoning up her jacket, which had come open during the terrible accident. She gave a single wave before sprinting to the vehicle, and then, with the agility of a young chimp, climbed and swung back onto the platform. Her clothes were slightly dishevelled—Adam was sure he could see the imprint of a tyre track—but she seemed completely unhurt, without even a scratch or bruise. Smiling again, her make-up perfectly intact, Liana apologised.

"Sorry about the slight delay. That'll teach me not to let go of the handrail. In future, I will pay more heed to my own instructions."

She clicked the switch on the umbrella and it bloomed open. Making a show of holding firmly onto the handrail, she pressed the red button and they were once again on their way.

"What the Hell was that?" Adam asked John, who seemed wholly absorbed with his forthcoming punishment.

"Err … yes … Liana is a mechanical girl. An automaton if you will, much like the ones in the utility buildings. The Terminal staff are all automatons, but of the finest quality, and very independent."

"And, the Captain? Is the Captain an android … err automaton?"

"Yes he is, but his nature is more complicated than the others," John answered abruptly, signalling a desire to go back to his thoughts. "I am sure he will explain everything you wish to know."

They passed a number of parked airliners, Boeing and Airbus, each sporting the colourful livery of a well-known national carrier. The vehicle drove into an empty parking spot and carefully lined up next to a long enclosed passenger walkway that connected to the terminal gate. Liana pressed the blue button and the platform rose to exactly the correct height.

The walkway floor automatically aligned and levelled with the platform and its metal doors clunked open.

"Please follow me," said Liana, stepping onto the walkway. "The airbridge is equipped with a series of drying fans, so do not be alarmed if you feel a few rushes of warm air."

Adam was surprised at the effectiveness of the fans, given their subtly soft puff. By the time they reached the other end of the walkway, his hair and clothes were perfectly dry, and comfortably warm.

The door to the terminal slid open, and they walked into a brightly lit departure lounge. Rows of empty leather reclining chairs, equipped with flat screen monitors, dominated the space, and the comforting sound of soft muzak filled the air. A welcoming committee of a few airport staff, all wearing blue uniforms, politely clapped at the new arrivals. Knowing that they were androids, Adam found their fixed smiles and attentive stares quite unnerving.

The Captain, also clapping, stepped up and offered Adam a handshake. His pilot's cap tilted informally, revealing silver sideburns beneath sharply styled raven black hair, the Captain exuded experience and confidence. A waft of expensive cologne—clean, fresh cut grass, conservatively sophisticated—and a beam of sparkling white teeth, accompanied his warm greeting.

"Welcome to the Terminal, Mr Eden," he said, briskly shaking Adam's hand. "Do you mind if I call you Adam. I know we've just met, but I have been closely following your progress for some time and I feel I know you well enough to skip many of the formalities."

"I don't mind at all. And, I call you?"

"Captain Andrews or just the Captain. Either one is fine by me. Now, Adam, I suspect you have a thousand and one questions rattling around inside your head, but first I would like to offer my sincerest condolences regarding the death of your friend Mr Beaumont. I know he played a major role in your first-life."

Adam nodded and thanked the Captain for his sympathy.

"I would also like this opportunity to apologise for the behaviour of my operatives, especially regarding the inkman's unconscionable turn of violence. I gave no orders for your companions to be harmed. I simply said, in idle conversation, that the plan would proceed much more smoothly if Adam Eden were alone. Given my words, the inkman has told me that he thought his actions would impress me. I assure you, they did not, and Kevin has been severely punished. I guess you could call the incident my 'Thomas à Becket' moment. Now, do you have any questions?"

"Is this the outside?" asked Adam, mentally crossed his fingers behind his back. "Is this outside the Viroverse?"

"Sorry to dash your hopes, Adam, but this is another viro. Things do run a bit differently in here, but this is definitely not the outside. Anything else?" he asked, looking at his Breitling Aviator watch. "There are a few matters that require my prompt attention."

No longer intimidated by the pushy intensity of alpha males, Adam confidently reeled off a list of questions.

"Can you resurrect Manny? Can you cure Rhapsody? Can you find a safe place for Kimberly to live? Can you show me the outside, or at least tell me how to get there?"

"You certainly don't mince your words, Adam," said the Captain. "Mr Beaumont is dead and there is nothing that can be done to change that. If he had killed himself in an operational viro then of course we could bring him back, but in the hallways, it is not permitted. As for your other demands, posing as questions, the answer in all cases is a cautious yes."

Adam was somewhat placated, though still hoped to find a way to bring Manny back. The Captain placed a hand on John Down's shoulder.

"Mr Down, I need to talk to you right away. I think you know what it is about."

"Are … are we going to the Day Spa?" John asked, betraying a note of fear.

"That won't be necessary. In your case, my office will suffice."

John breathed a trembling sigh of relief, and slightly slouched as if released from a binding tension. The Captain turned his attention to Kimberly, offering an excited grin.

"Kimberly, my dear, do you like a McD's? We have a fully staffed restaurant on the ground floor."

"Oh, yes, yes, yes!" chimed Kimberly, gleefully jumping up and down, swishing her glittery ponytail around.

"Well, this nice man, Joseph, will take you there." The captain ushered forward a handsome steward, who gave Kimberly a friendly salute. "It's quite a walk so you'll get to ride in one of our special airport carts. Order whatever you like, and I will join you shortly."

"Do you want me to order you something? My Ma always lets me order my own food."

"I'll have whatever you're having, my dear."

Joseph took Kimberly by the hand and they skipped together to a waiting cart. Adam tried to follow, but the Captain stood in his way.

"Hey, where are you taking her?" Adam demanded, trying to push past. "I want Kimberly where I can see her."

With inhuman strength, charmingly smiling, the Captain restrained Adam single handedly. He waited until the cart was well on its way along the feature window concourse, before answering Adam's concerns.

"Adam, I respect your admirable attempt at fatherly concern, really I do, but I must point out that I am the acting Concierge of this viro. However, in light of recent circumstances, I will bend the rules somewhat and not use the usual, 'I am not allowed to discuss anyone else with you', line. The problem is this. Due to the absence of a Concierge or Boss Man in her own viro, Kimberly never received her induction—a thankless task that now falls to me. A quick glance at her profile revealed that not only doesn't she realise that she is miniaturised, but the poor girl has no idea that she died."

FAIR PUNISHMENT?

Adam relaxed in one of the chairs, facing a wide wall of windows overlooking the airport. He sipped a whisky over ice that Liana had dutifully fetched, and waited for the Captain's return. After some minutes, spent watching a Boeing 767 taxi onto the runway and take off to an unknown destination, Adam turned his attention to a smartly dressed man drinking from a nearby water fountain. The man loosened his grey silk tie, as if suffering strangulation, and posed uncomfortably in his Armani suit.

"Hey friend, are you OK," Adam asked, as the man fussily swept an effete 80's fringe from his face. "You look like you could use a drink. Come, sit over here, and I'll order you a …?"

The man forced an awkward smile and walked over with a slightly stumbling gait, as if wearing shoes for the first time:

"Pint of Tooheys will hit the spot, mate. Make it the Extra Dry."

The voice, more downbeat than usual, unmistakably belonged to the inkman. Virtually unrecognisable in his designer suit, glossy black brogues, and stylish gelled haircut, he flopped into the chair next to Adam and extended a hand.

"No hard feelings, mate? Bygones be bygones and all that crap. Go easy on the handshake though, 'cause my skin is really sore."

Adam ignored the gesture, and was about to start an argument, when he noticed the inkman's blooming red skin—much like a case of sunburn before the onset of scabbing and peeling.

"Your tattoos, on your face and hands, they're gone. Were they temporary? They didn't look like temporary tattoos. And, why do you look like you've spent too long cooking under a sunlamp?"

"Yeah, my lovely tats are temporary, but not in the way you're thinking. When I first came back from the dead, after some crazy biker chick's husband bottled me in a bar, I thought I'd won the jackpot. There was only one problem, and it was a bloody bugger of a problem. My body-art was gone! I tried inking a couple of shapes into my arm, but the next morning …"

"They were gone," said Adam. "You're body was healed."

"Damn right, they were gone. My body was an unmarked as the day I was born. Bloody Viroverse counts tattoos as injuries and heals them right up overnight."

"What about rub-ons and stick-ons? A friend of mine sometimes wears one on his arm."

"Bugger that for a laugh," spat the inkman dismissively. "Too much effort and nothing like the real thing. I felt naked without my tats. I stayed indoors all day. Stopped seeing my friends and family."

"And then the Captain found you, eh?"

"Offered me a sweet deal, mate. I get my tattoos reinstated and in return, I work for him. The tattoos only last about a month before the AI catches up with me, so I have to get re-inked in the Day Spa."

"Is there a downside to this?" asked Adam. "I know you work for the Captain, but John told me there's always a high price to pay."

"For starters, I can't go back to my own viro or see any of my old mates, and then there's …"

The inkman screwed up his sore face, as if reliving an agonising memory. His eyes spoke of a deep-seated horror.

"When I get my new set of tattoos every month, they are needled within an hour, and with no anaesthetic. The Captain has this scary looking machine in the Day Spa especially for the purpose. He gives me drugs beforehand so I can fully experience the pain without passing out. The pain, the bloody pain, is the price I pay. It hurts so bad, but it's worth it."

The words 'Day Spa' were beginning to make Adam's skin crawl. John's relief that he would not be paying a visit and the inkman's chilling revelations were evidence that the facility was not providing your usual massages, mudbaths, and saunas.

"So, what happened to your tattoos? Is the month up?"

"Nah, they just dropped me in a tank full of blue goo in the Day Spa, with special contacts protecting my eyes and tubes up my hooter so I could breathe. Whatever it was, that stuff sucked out all the ink within minutes and left me looking like a ripe tomato. Captain said I don't get my tats back for five months. And, look at this!"

A determined tug of his fringe revealed his hair as a wig, exposing a bright red bald pate.

"Strip me naked; I'm a saveloy!"

Reseating the wig carefully on his head, the inkman sighed and managed a swollen smile.

"My skin will be healed tomorrow, and I will get my hair back. But, I've still got five months wearing this designer monkey suit, and the Captain says I gotta keep the dorky hairstyle and listen only to 80's music. Have to keep my knife in my jacket pocket, so no pleasure from that either."

"You got off lightly," said Adam, remembering Rhapsody's final haunting screams. "I'd have slit your throat and watched you die for what you did to Rhapsody."

"Not likely. You're a pushover" the inkman laughed, then fell silent as the strain split his lip.

The soft whine of an approaching airport cart distracted both men. Liana was driving the vehicle, which drew to a stop at the end of the concourse. John, the only passenger, thanked the android hostess for the lift, and then ambled over to where Adam and the inkman were sitting.

Displaying no emotion, John wiped the seat of the next chair with his handkerchief, smoothed the tails of his frock coat as he sat down, and then pulled the knees of his trousers to save the creases. The fastidious routine came with no greeting or pleasantries. John clasped his hands over his chest and sat motionless, staring straight ahead. Like a devilish imp, the inkman pulled John's hair.

"Not a wig and you didn't lose those stupid mutton-chops. I mean, look at me." The inkman stood up, faced John, and peeled off his 80's wig and fake eyebrows. "I'm also hanging without a 'fro down south, but you don't wanna see that, mate."

John made a weak fist and coughed into his hand, before announcing, "I am not allowed to visit Mary for five months. The reception room door to her viro will not open if I am in the immediate vicinity. Though I felt it to be harsh, I accepted my punishment without protest ...without ... Oh Mary!"

Burying his face in his hands, the distinguished Victorian cried uncontrollably, stopping only to utter the name of his beloved Mary.

"Oh that's brutal, mate," said the inkman, leaning into give his disheartened colleague a mighty hug, but quickly jumping back with the pain of his sore skin.

Adam tried to offer a few choice words of consolation, but they fell on deaf ears as John and the inkman engaged in a long, repetitive, tearful exchange of mutual sympathy. Blubbing like rejected teens on Prom Night, the unlikely duo endlessly competed in lamenting each other's punishment. Draining his whisky, Adam sat back and inserted some complementary earbuds, hoping loud music would drown out the nauseating shmaltz.

Relief came nearly two hours later, when the Captain drove up in a cart. On his arrival, both John and the inkman ceased their whining and tried to appear nonchalant, as if their punishments were of little importance. Adam noticed a large pink stain on the front of the Captain's shirt.

"Strawberry milkshake," exclaimed the Captain, treating the stain as a badge of honour, "and the blob on my shoulder is ketchup. "Our young Kimberly certainly has some spirit. Take a ride with me, Adam, and I'll tell you all about it on the way."

Once seated in the small electric vehicle, the Captain straightened his cap, held the steering wheel with both hands, and said in a smooth deep voice, "I am Captain Andrews, and I will be your pilot for the journey. We will be cruising at approximately twelve miles per hour and expect little or no delay. You do not need to fasten your seatbelt, and I hope you have a pleasant ride."

As they drove along the viewing concourse, the Captain explained, "Please excuse my trite indulgence, but I never actually get to fly a plane. The take-offs and landings out there are part of the viro wall display."

"But the Day Spa is real," said Adam. "And, from what I've heard I don't want Kimberly anywhere near that place."

"At the moment, Kimberly is either romping around in the McD's ball-pit with Joseph and Michaela, or playing video games in the arcade. The Day Spa is no place for a minor."

"I'll have to trust you on that for now. Tell me, how did Kimberly take the news of her death? With her adult body, I thought she'd guess something was up."

"Her mother was fond of telling her that kids grow up fast these days. Kimberly took this to heart and believed it happened overnight. The fantastical innocence of children is a constant wonder to me."

"So, why the milkshake and ketchup makeover?"

"Young Kimberly was under the tragic misunderstanding that she flying back to Kansas to meet up with her mother. When I finally convinced her that this was not a real airport and that such a meeting was impossible, she threw a tantrum that lasted some minutes—hence my Jackson Pollack inspired shirt design. She calmed down after that, and accepted her situation. Although I told a little white lie."

The Captain fell silent for a few seconds, as if deciding whether to tell Adam what he said:

"I told Kimberly that I would arrange a reunion as soon as her mother was resurrected."

"And …?"

"Kimberly's mother, Laura Penn, left prison with a crippling drug addiction. Theft and prostitution fed her habit for a couple of years and paid some of the bills, but eventually she ended up sleeping rough on the streets. She was only twenty-nine when she died of an AIDs-related disease."

Adam understood the implications of Laura's downward spiral, having experienced his own.

"She's an undesirable, isn't she? She won't be resurrected."

"There are a few exceptions to the rule, all accidents like yourself, but it is extremely unlikely Laura will ever come back. Not this side of eternity anyway."

Adam clung onto the vehicles side-rail as Captain Andrews abruptly spun the wheel, turning the cart around.

"Change of plan," said the Captain, heading down a side corridor. "We were going straight to the moving walkway for a little tête-à-tête. I think first, you should pay a visit to the Day Spa, just so you get a feel for what we do here."

"I'm not sure about this," said Adam, remembering a previous cart diversion that led to a psychopathic 'ghost train' ride.

"Ah, don't worry, Adam. Strictly observer status. I promise you will not have to endure any of the 'treatments'."

DAY SPA

As they neared the Day Spa, the corridors and plazas became increasingly populated with uniformed staff and an assortment of visitors. Captain Andrews explained that only his operatives used the quieter portal entrance. Most people visited the 'normal' way, waking up in luxury rooms and suites in the five-star airport hotel—exentuating the tourist and traveller theme of the viro. The Captain granted access only to the select few, like some exclusive club, and the existence of the Terminal was a secret no member dared reveal to the uninitiated.

The central atrium, with its soaring cantilevered glass roof and colourful mosaic floor, was the bustling heart of the Terminal, adjacent to a ten-tiered balconied hotel and an extravagant leisure complex with aqua-park and mini funfair. At the western end of the spacious area, a gleaming bank of escalators gave access to the ground floor and a comprehensive selection of shops and food-outlets, accommodating most tastes.

"There don't seem to be any dispensers," said Adam. "I haven't seen one since I got here. I thought this place had it all."

"There are dispensers behind the scenes, but they are only accessible to the staff," answered the Captain, bringing the vehicle to a smooth stop. "Our guests receive a taste of their first-life, limited to what is available in the retail outlets and on the restaurant menus. It's not exactly like the old world, since everything is free. But, not having every product within a few seconds reach creates a nostalgic link to the past that comforts our guests. The airport is the perfect setting for the facilities we wish to provide."

"Like a viro within a viro," Adam ventured, as they walked across the expansive square towards a glass-fronted salon.

Whether out of respect, fear, or simply friendship, people paused to allow the Captain to pass, extending polite and pleasant greetings. Some gave Adam a second glance or a lingering stare, perhaps equating his Aloha clothing with the legend of Copacabana. A vertical blue-neon sign set into the wide chrome frame of the salons entrance made Adam shudder: 'Day Spa'.

Two stewards staffed the wide reception desk. One was busy helping an incredibly obese woman arrange her next appointment. Marcie, as Adam heard the steward call her, was the first fat person he had seen since drowning in Portsmouth Harbour—himself being the last one. The Viroverse provided everyone with the most perfect adult body their genetics allowed, so seeing one so far removed from the slim muscular ideal was a shock.

Marcie turned to go and caught Adam's eye. Her expression brightened as she gave him the once over, obviously spotting the Copacabana connection, and her plump cheeks bulged with a wide smile:

"Are you Copacabana? Copacabana, the psycho-killer?"

"The one and only."

"Oh my lord, you look even tastier than I imagined," she flirted, flicking her red demi-waved hair like some glamorous movie star.

"Hah, don't eat me, I'm all gristle," said Adam.

Marcie batted her eyelids and ran her tongue provocatively around her bright red lipstick lips.

"Mmm, Copacabana, Mr Banana, why wouldn't you want me to eat you?"

Save for a sudden blush, Adam had no answer, struck dumb by Marcie's brazen approach. Pretending to talk to the steward again, Marcie swayed her huge buttocks at Adam, her close-fitting short skirt revealing every ripple and crease. She craned her broad neck around and asked, "Tell me lover-boy, does my bum look big in this?"

Not sure how to react, Adam looked at the Captain for subtle manly guidance—a nod or a wink would have sufficed. No help at all, the android projected an unreadable though affable expression. Eager not to insult Marcie, and with personal experience of a fat person's mind-set, Adam shook his head.

"I'm not going to lie to you, and say you're a svelte size zero model, but," Adam rubbed his chin, staring intently at Marcie's behind, "you are definitely well below the obese threshold. I can say that your bum does not look big in … err … that."

With an alarming full body heave, Marcie swivelled around, her face glaring as if struck by the most heinous insult.

"You heartless bastard!" she screamed, slapping Adam hard across the cheek with a chubby hand. "How could you say that to me?"

Before barging past Adam, and storming off into the streams of visitors, Marcie wiggled a little finger and said, "Anyway, you're no Mr Banana. Rumour has it that you're no bigger than a baby carrot. So, your loss, Copa!"

Adam rubbed his sore cheek.

"Did I just get slapped for paying someone a compliment?" he asked the Captain, who was now grinning. "She's not under the impression that she's slim, is she?"

"Quite the opposite, Adam. Marcie Miles is a long-standing client. She comes here once a month to have her fat reinstated. From childhood, Marcie was overweight, and over the years failed one diet after another. She yo-yoed, plateaued, and gained, but was never less than morbidly obese. In fact, struggling with the pounds defined her existence, and she died a very unhappy and defeated woman. It was only after she resurrected with a new body that Marcie missed her fat. With no personal point of reference, she found her slim body terrifying—something akin to a skeletal monster I believe she called it."

"And then you intervened."

Captain Andrews explained how Marcie was visited by John Down, and given access to the Terminal. Once a month, she visited the Day Spa for rapid liposuction, and then received a new whole body infusion of fast-acting lipids, combined with screening chemicals to fool the AI for a month. No anaesthetic was used, since the terrible pain was the price she paid for thirty days of happiness. Marcie justified her obvious corpulence to friends, family, and curious neighbours by putting it down to an unfortunate Viroverse glitch. The Captain chuckled as he told Adam that a temporary side-effect of the treatment was an almost ravenous libido.

Without uttering a word, one of the stewards fetched an acoustic guitar from under the reception desk and handed it to the Captain. After thanking the steward, the Captain and Adam left the reception area.

Further into the Day Spa, was a mood-balancing waiting room with earthy Zen motifs, the purifying aroma of eucalyptus and lemon oil, and a bamboo-pipe trickle fountain. Adam could not supress a smile at the clichéd panpipe music that saturated the air with its windy tendrils of pseudo-mystical fluence.

The Captain placed his hand on a palm-operated sliding door, and they walked into a long corridor.

"These are the treatment rooms," he said, gesturing to the doors on either side. "The one I want to show you is at the end of the corridor, but I must first check on Peter Lang's scoliosis."

Sliding down the cover of a viewing window on a nearby door, the Captain peered into the treatment room and nodded his approval. Closing the hatch, he said, "Mr Lang's first visit to the Terminal. No problems that I can see, but it's a good job that the rooms are soundproofed. I'm quite sure our client is screaming as loud as his lungs allow."

Adam did not say a word. He had caught the briefest glimpse of the horrific procedure through the viewing window—a shaking naked man, tied face down on a surgical gurney, having his back ripped open along the length of his spine by an aproned man with a steel rotary saw.

Greatly shocked by what he had just seen, Adam inhaled a breath of apprehension as the Captain opened the door at the end of the corridor. However, compared to his frightening expectations, the scene inside the treatment room seemed unexpectedly calm and horror free.

The treatment room was like that found in a luxury private hospital with upmarket fittings and on-tap entertainment facilities. Sitting up in a bed, with a bank of monitoring equipment on the wall behind, was an attractive yet approachable woman, with blonde ringlets, a disarmingly sweet face, but wearing far too much make-up. She clasped her hands together contentedly on her lap, and seemed pleased to see the Captain.

Shuffling into a more upright position, she said in a distinctly French accent, "Time for my medicine, no?"

"Certainly is, Louise," said the Captain, pulling up a chair next to the right side of the bed, He held her hand. "If you are agreeable, Mr Eden will be observing. You have no doubt heard of him. He is the fighter they call Copacabana."

Louise waved her hand, uttering a 'meh' of indifference, "I care not for his stories of violence. But, if you will sing to me, Captain Andrews, he can stay."

"I have the guitar here," he replied, holding up the instrument.

Adam stood back while the Captain prepped his patient. First, a sturdy screen was pushed against the left side of the bed. The screen had a hole through which Louise put her arm. Once the arm was up to the elbow, and out of Louise's sight, the Captain tightened a leather strap, preventing the arm from being pulled back. Next, he straightened the arm into downward angle, and injected a localised paralysing solution. The Captain hummed a tune for a minute while waiting for the arm to lock solid.

"Are we ready?" asked Louise. "Renoir is getting impatient."

At the very mention of the name, Renoir, a playful yellow Labrador came bounding out from under the bed. The dog, tail wagging furiously, fussed around Adam, sniffing his legs and leaping up for attention.

Even given the constant surprises of the Terminal, Adam was not expecting to see an animal. One of the more notable features of the Viroverse was the absence of any life form other than human, and even some humans failed to qualify.

Adam tickled Renoir under the chin, and the dog immediately jumped down and rolled on its back, begging for a belly rub. Adam happily complied, finding the experience infectiously delightful.

"Renoir likes you, Monsieur Eden," said Louise. "I am thinking you are maybe not so bad after all. He is the most excellent judge of … how you say … character."

"Is he real?" Adam asked.

Captain Andrews appeared from behind the screen and began securing Louise to the bed with strong leather straps.

"As real as we can make him," he said. "He is a dog-droid, based on Louise's memories and various historical archives. I'd wager he's more detailed than many humans." The Captain made a flourishing bow. "Let me introduce the one and only Miss Louise Charente, the fabulous 22nd Century dog dancer, and her supremely talented dance partner, Renoir. This very morning, Louise and Renoir put on a wonderful and well attended show in the atrium."

Adam got to his feet, and Renoir licked his hand, hoping for more tickles.

"I'm guessing Miss Charente missed her dog so much that you intervened and supplied Renoir."

The Captain buckled the last strap and applauded.

"Bravo, Adam! You are finally grasping what we do here."

"I must be most careful with my lovely Renoir," said Louise, unable to look at Adam due to a tight neck restraint pinning her to her pillow. "I live in a viro by myself, with just a few android servants. Every day, Renoir and I dance and dance in the grand ballroom, reliving our most treasured moments. It is so wonderful. But, if visitors arrive, Renoir hides in a special place. Not even I know where he goes. If I miss my treatment, the little coquin stays in his hiding place."

Looking at Louise, lying immobilised and helpless, the truth about the Terminal came rushing back into Adam's mind.

"So, what's the price?"

Despite her restraints, Louise sighed dramatically, and said, "Aah, it is always pain. Pain is the price I pay."

Lifting the guitar, ready to play, the Captain asked Louise what song she would like him to sing during the treatment. She replied enthusiastically, saying, "Oh, please sing my favourite aria, 'Ombra Mai Fu', with the voice of a famous castrato."

"Of course. Farinelli or perhaps Senesino?"

"Non, non, I prefer Caferelli for this. After all, Handel wrote the aria for him."

"Caferelli it is. Now, it is that time again, when I must ask for your verbal consent to the treatment. Miss Louise Charente, do you give your permission for the treatment you are about to receive?"

Louise gave her consent, and the Captain told Adam to follow Renoir behind the screen.

The Captain placed a thin dissolvable tablet under Louise's tongue—a drug insuring she would not pass out during the procedure. He then played the delicate opening to 'Ombra Mai Fu' on the guitar and began singing in a beautifully haunting high-pitched falsetto.

Renoir stiffened as if possessed, and marched robotically behind the screen. As instructed, Adam followed, and watched the yellow Labrador line up below his mistress's paralysed arm. A hiss of micro-pistons and the dog's legs lengthened, hairy skin stretching like elastic, bringing the mouth up against the hand. Adam jumped in fright as the skin on Renoir's face drew back like a rubber glove, and his tongue, teeth and gums retracted into cavities in the metal reinforced bone structure. The dog's jaw opened wider than looked possible and the end of a wide steel cylinder extended out from his grossly expanded throat.

With a smooth hum, the cylinder began rotating at high-speed, and Renoir slowly moved forward. The advancing motion, synchronised with increasing leg height, allowed Louise's slender hand to slip into the cylinder. Adam shuddered as hand disappeared into a succession of spinning blades and shredding rings. A sickening mulching sound combined with an ear-piercing shriek from the other side of the screen.

If Adam had not been experiencing near heart-attack inducing shock and disbelief at the sight of the cylinder mincing its way towards the elbow, he may have noted that now and then, for the briefest of moments, Louise's shrill screams were in perfect tune with the Captains trill castrato stylings. Staggering on unsteady feet, Adam warned the Captain that he was going to be sick.

"If you must emit, Adam, then please aim into Renoir's mulcher," the Captain sang, pitch-perfect, seamlessly incorporating the advice into the song.

The mulcher crunched and whirred past the elbow. Adam stooped over the disgusting chamber of gore, dry retching a couple of times, before promptly spewing out a torrent of vomit. A pronounced slushing noise from the unit indicated that the mostly liquid sick was diluting the limbmash.

Adam looked away, hand over his mouth, throat raw with acid, as the mulcher came to a stop exactly three inches from the shoulder, and Louise's screams quickly died down to a sleepy groan. The cylinder retracted, spraying a fine mist over the raw flesh of the stump, instantly staunching the blood loss. With perfect timing, the Captain rushed behind the screen and capped the stump with a tight-fitting jewelled cup.

"The cap will stop the pain and support rapid scabbing," he explained. "The diamonds and emeralds are just for show, because our brave dog dancer is worth it. I've injected Louise with a fast-acting sedative and painkiller, so she's probably asleep already."

Renoir, still in purposeful robotic mode, swivelled around and marched toward an outlet valve set into the wall. The cylinder connected to the valve with a satisfying click, and Adam heard the liquidised gore and vomit pumping out of the dog.

A minute later and Renoir was again an adorable wide-eyed Labrador, with no slaughterhouse accessories on show but perhaps the faint whiff of salami breath. He busily sniffed Adam and offered a concerned whine, perhaps sensing his unease.

Captain Andrews checked the floor behind the screen, and then slapped Adam on the back.

"My, that dog is good! There isn't a single drop of blood. And, congratulations on your perfect aim, because I cannot detect any sick either."

"Err ... I had quite a bit of practice in my first-life," Adam sheepishly admitted. "You can't be too choosy about what you eat and drink on the street."

"Ah, one of the unsung talents of an undesirable."

Whilst gently undoing Louise's bonds, the Captain directed Adam to a sink on the other side of the room with a stack of paper cups. Soothing his sore palette and slightly settling the unrest in his stomach, Adam gargled with cool mineral water straight from the tap, and took a long drink.

Passing through the tranquil waiting room—the serene façade of the Terminal's heart of darkness—Adam contemplated the awful mutilation he had just witnessed. The consensual pre-arranged nature of the atrocities seemed far more disturbing than the brutality of the psychoviro hunt, although his lack of memory regarding his many bloodthirsty final moments perhaps distorted his judgement.

"Now you know what goes on here, we should head for the passenger walkway," said the Captain. "I know you have many questions and no doubt strong criticisms about what you have just seen, but they can wait until we get there."

"OK, but first I'm heading down to the mall. If they've got it, I got a craving for a foot long dog with ketchup and mustard."

Adam and the Captain left the Day Spa, leaving Louise sleeping peacefully in bed with her beloved Renoir snuggled up by her side.

Q&A ON THE WALKWAY

Leaving the electric cart parked at a nearby charging point, along with the hotdog wrapper, Adam and Captain Andrews stepped onto the moving passenger walkway. With inset soft-blue lighting and polished steel sides, the seemingly endless semi-circular passageway had a cool sophistication. One side of the walkway was windowed, offering an uninterrupted view of the main runway, whilst the other displayed a succession of glossy digital-ads for the Terminals retail and entertainment opportunities.

The rubber-coated conveyor felt sturdy underfoot, the ride smooth, and Adam soon became comfortable with the motion. His bright Aloha clothes made him feel like a tourist returning from the tropics, clinging onto the vestiges of warmer climes before facing the cold wind and rain of his homeland.

A low rumbling caused Adam to look out the viewing window, just in time to see an aircraft heading straight for the walkway. Possibly a business Lear jet, the aircraft roared overhead, missing the building by a few feet. The close proximity caused the walkway to vibrate, and Adam reached for the sidewall to steady himself. Captain Andrews laughed, perhaps enjoying a prank he had played many times before.

"Don't worry, there's no danger. The plane is a three-dimensional projection with shaking effects—nothing that couldn't be done in your own time."

The experience roused an anger in Adam. Only thirty minutes after Louise's 'treatment' he was expected to appreciate a theme-park flight of fancy? Adam reminded the Captain of what he and his friends had endured.

"We nearly died in those halls, you know. Resting for just a few minutes brought out those damn jellymen."

"You chose to leave your viro," answered the Captain, dropping his jovial tone, "and I never doubted for a moment you could cope with the few Osmotic Guards that remain in the halls. They are far too slow and predictable to pose any serious danger. However, I do accept that Mr Down's presence would have made your journey far less stressful."

"Why didn't you come yourself?"

"I am not allowed. Viros are off-limits, as are the halls. There are very few locations to which I have physical access."

"Oh, I thought it was you who placed those barriers to herd us to the husk viro."

"I did. I can activate the barriers from here. For the most part, I am not allowed to influence a person's decisions, but the barriers are a loophole that I readily exploit. Adam, I believe I have apologised enough for your eventful journey to the Terminal. Now, ask me anything you wish to know. However, bear in mind, there are still many things I am not permitted to divulge."

The questioning was slow at first, as the food settled Adam's nausea. He asked about the mysterious sleep-time feeding, healing, and cleaning services. Captain Andrews obliged, giving a concise though vague explanation involving nano smart-swarms, recycling vats, and under-viro resource synthesisers. The answer neatly led to Adam's real concern.

"Why is Kimberly's viro in such a state, and Mary Down's for that matter? I've never come across anything like it before."

"Unfortunately, this entire sector, and many others, are suffering severe resource shortages and related to that, a decrease in maintenance provision. Most of the resurrected are oblivious to the problems since affected viros are cut-off from the system at the first sign of trouble."

"And, that means no visits," said Adam, one step ahead. "You know, my mother was complaining that her Aunt Joan was not responding to her visit requests. She put it down to some long-standing family feud."

"Your mother's aunt is now a husk, along with the other 347 inhabitants of her viro."

"That's shocking," gasped Adam. "How widespread is this?"

"I am not permitted to give you exact figures but there are millions."

"Dear God, there are really millions of husks?"

The Captain shook his head, and said, "Oh no, Adam, you misunderstand. I mean, there are millions of viros filled with husks. The current number of husks runs into a few billion, and that number is rising all the time."

Even without the exact number, Adam realised that a few billion represented a sizeable percentage of the Viroverse population. Could it be that humanity was destined to spend eternity as starving skeletal ghouls? If that were true, then how long before his own viro succumbed?

"Is my viro OK?" Adam asked. "I don't recall any problems or shortages."

The Captain's reply fell short of dispelling Adam's worries.

"At the moment, your viro has ample resource allocation and is adequately maintained. However, this is largely due to the small population. Over the years, as the population climbs, the likelihood of problems increases exponentially."

"What … what is causing the resource shortages?"

"I am not permitted to give you that information."

"Is it something to do with the outside?"

"I am not permitted to give you that information."

"Was there a world war, or some major natural disaster?"

"I am not permitted to give you that information."

"Well, could you at least tell me if Rhapsody can be made normal again?" shouted Adam, exasperated by the Captain's stonewalling.

"Yes she can," came the calm reply. "Is that what you want?"

"Of course it is!"

"More than anything?"

"Yes!"

"We shall see."

Adam found the last remark odd, and wondered what it signified. He noticed they were long past the viewing window, and both sides of the walkway were emblazoned with Terminal advertisements. A casual glance behind, confirmed that both ends of the passageway were too distant to be visible—the view narrowing to the vanishing point. The walkway was now monotonously unchanging, as the advertisements repeated like the looped background to some low-budget cartoon.

"So, what did you think of our treatments?" asked the Captain. "Do you now understand?"

"Understand? What I just witnessed in your so-called Day Spa was more barbaric than anything I ever saw in Groover's psychoviro!"

Softly clenching his fists in a restrained display of anger, not expected of an android, Captain Andrews strongly defended the work of the Terminal.

"Oh no, you cannot compare what we do here with the mindless violence of that band of psychopaths. All our clients choose to come here, and then choose whether they want to make a payment for the personal service we provide. They could say no, and still enjoy all the other facilities of the Terminal. They would simply go without the personal service. Miss Charente has gone many times without her two-monthly treatment, and it just means that Renoir stays in his hiding place."

"But why pain? Why is the payment always pain?"

"There are exceptions to physical pain as payment, such as with Mr Down, but pain is often the only currency the client has to offer. Old-fashioned money and finance have no meaning in the Viroverse, and the same goes for luxury ornaments, precious metals, or works of art."

"You could offer the services for free," offered Adam. "I know you like making deals, but maybe you should become a charity."

"The payment is essential," sighed the Captain. "Without the payment, I cannot offer the things people want. It is a necessity that lays at the very heart of my nature ... or rather an unbreakable protocol of my basic programming. You see, the Terminal has only been active for a few years, and as you obviously know by now, I am not really an airline pilot. My original role was that of an arbitration and conciliation service for concierges. If ever a dispute broke out between the human sponsors it was my job to find common ground, compromise, or if necessary enforce an unpalatable solution on both parties."

"Well, Renoir certainly spewed out an unpalatable solution," said Adam.

Captain Andrews gave Adam a disinterested stare and continued.

"For reasons I am not permitted to divulge, my basic role became obsolete. I wanted a new purpose and came up with the idea of the Terminal. I was always fascinated with humans and their fanciful desires and obsessions. Skimming through millions of profiles, I found it strange that some humans were unhappy with their perfect world and perfect body—some to the point of yearning for true death."

"So you decided to intervene."

"I based the Terminal in the sector with the highest number of disaffected. The viros in this sector generally span from the 19th to the 21st centuries, and are largely what you would term Western influence and English speaking. There are other sectors with a similar profile but, with all its glorious dysfunction, this one really caught my attention. To offer my services, I first needed a small group of human helpers to go where I could not. Incidentally, John Down was my first recruit. He was so unhappy in that collector's viro without his wife."

"You still haven't explained why the pain is necessary."

"Ah, the pain, yes I was coming to that," Captain Andrews replied, a touch of sorrow creeping into his voice. "Remember, this is not the role for which I was originally created. I have exercised the greatest latitude possible in reinterpreting my programming, but the need for payment is regrettably unavoidable. To put it in simple terms, offering a service for free is the equivalent of me taking one side only in a concierge dispute. It has to be a matter of give and take, of balance. With no meaningful currency available to my clients, intense pain is a quick and high-value offset to the happiness I bring. There is no compulsion. It is always the client's choice."

"As the drug dealer said to the addict," mocked Adam.

The Captain, tilting back his peak cap, softly said, "Believe me, Adam, if I could stop the suffering, I would."

A pregnant pause broke the conversation, and Adam finally understood that the Captain was haunted by the payment's he had to extract. Whereas a tyrannical regime's torturer might spuriously claim they were simply following orders, Captain Andrews was truly bound by the strictures of his programming.

Exploiting the moment, the Captain switched the topic of conversation and caught Adam off-guard.

"I hear your fighting skills have deteriorated. Is something or someone holding you back?"

"I ... don't ..."

"Or are you holding someone back?"

Adam spluttered an uneasy laugh, saying, "You make it sound like I have a ..."

"Split personality?" asked the Captain. "Your profile has made interesting reading, Adam. Every now and then, it changes to a completely different set of values. Looking back through the logs, the anomalies begin a few weeks after your concierge cancelled your sedation and you started training with Elliot Stevens. At first, they coincided with your trips to the psychoviro, but lately, especially during the last few days, I have noticed a marked increase in their frequency. How do you explain this?"

"It's Copacabana," Adam admitted. "Copacabana takes over when he believes the mission is threatened."

"The mission?" asked the Captain, sounding intrigued.

"I originally made the deal with Groover so that I could leave the Viroverse, and get away from all the hassle, and bad-blood of being an undesirable. Finding out what is beyond the Viroverse is the mission, and by that, I mean seeing the 'real' world outside. However, since learning the secret, I've sort of wondered whether I should stay and enjoy my new status. Being a living legend is quite cool when you think about it, and almost all the reasons that made me want to leave are gone. It was Copacabana's influence that forced me to honour my original plan. You see, to him, the mission is everything."

"So you no longer want to see the outside?"

"Well, I am curious. I wouldn't say no if the chance came up."

The Captain placed his hand on Adam's shoulder, and smiled.

"I'm toying with you, Adam. I already know what you are experiencing and what is causing it. I will naturally skirt over the technical details, but your miniature brain was never designed to cope with such a huge swing in personality. You tried to create a new ruthless attitude to defeat Groover's gang, and for a while, you succeeded. However, your tiny brain could not merge the old with the new, and instead created an alter ego. Significant mental development is not expected or catered for in the Viroverse, so you were unwittingly the author of your own Jekyll and Hyde."

"Well, why can't I win a fight anymore?"

"You have the ability to acquire new skill-sets, but you and Copacabana feed from the same trough. His power has grown rapidly, and he is no longer a minor influence. Now, no matter who is in control, to some extent one holds the other back, hence the degradation in your combat performance. At the moment, there is nothing can be done to rectify the situation. You will find that many of your everyday skills are very slightly affected, even mundane tasks like walking or eating, though you probably won't notice."

Though disturbed by the explanation, it fitted Adam's recent experiences perfectly, bringing a measure of acceptance and relief. Manny always said that accepting a problem was halfway to solving it. He dearly hoped his late friend's words were true and that the Captain was about to offer a solution. Briefly focused on the problem, Adam experienced a rare eureka moment.

"Then what about Kimberly and all the other resurrected children? Surely, their minds need to mature and develop."

"To use a supermarket analogy, children are assigned the luxury brand of brain, with plenty of developmental utility. Almost everyone else gets the standard brand, with some room for growth."

"And, my brain?" Adam dryly asked, already resigned to the answer.

"You are an undesirable, and have the value brand. Like many value products, including the rest of your body, your brain fulfils its basic functions, but is built to a minimum specification. It has very limited capacity for cohesive growth."

"Couldn't I kill myself, and you fix it so I come back with a luxury brain?" chanced Adam, clutching at straws.

"No."

"Couldn't you just erase Copacabana? I mean, Rhapsody had her psychopathic tendencies removed."

"No again, and your friend's good fortune was a genuine glitch in the resurrection process."

"So, I guess I'll have to learn to love my nasty little brain buddy," replied Adam sarcastically.

The Captain nodded. He then told Adam to brace himself. Without the press of a button or a verbal command, the walkway came to a sudden halt. Captain Andrews stood tall, hands on hips, projecting an officious air.

"Now is the time for your deal," he said. "Adam. I can offer you three choices. Whichever option you choose, Kimberly will stay here under my personal protection. I promise she will be well cared for, and not have access to the Day Spa. Now, listen carefully before making up your mind and do not interrupt."

Without betraying any preference or emotion, the Captain slowly and clearly explained the three options open to Adam.

"Option one: you can leave the Terminal and carry on your random wanderings. The reception rooms will not be locked, and no barriers will be placed in your path. But, beware, because over half the viros in this sector are in husk mode. Also, if you divulge any knowledge of the Terminal or its operatives you will be tracked down and neutralised. Get into any sort of trouble, and expect no help from us. There is no payment for this option.

"Option two: you can live a life of relative normality. Rhapsody will be returned to her former state, and if agreeable to the terms, she will live next door to Mary Down. You will work for me with similar responsibilities as her husband.

"Option three: I will have John Down white-line you to the next step to the outside world. It is a great distance, and would take weeks on foot. It does not involve a visit to the Day Spa, since the payment is the distress you have already suffered due to my operatives' shoddy behaviour.

"Adam, now you have heard the options, I need you to make up your mind. Which is it going to be?"

Even before Adam had opened his mouth to choose the second option, he could feel Copacabana taking the reins. The coldblooded warrior of the psychoviro sent his better-natured twin tumbling into the shadows. Adam fought back, vainly trying to wrest back control, as the answer came forth.

"… I … choose option … three!"

"Are you sure about this, Copacabana?" the Captain quickly asked, clicking his fingers in the manner of a pushy game-show host. "Your next reply seals the deal."

With Adam safely locked away, his defiant cries a faint faraway whisper, Copacabana relaxed, leaning against the walkway's steel sidewall.

"Oh, I am crystal clear on this, Captain. I choose option three."

Captain Andrews took Copacabana's hand and shook it firmly, indicating a done deal. As soon as the handshake ended, Adam was thrust back into the driver's seat. Wide-eyed and desperate, he pleaded with his host.

"I take that back! I take that back! That was Copacabana, not me! He has no right!"

The Captain's reply was calm, measured, but blunt:

"He is you, and so has every right. Option three has been chosen."

"Did you plan all this? You knew Copacabana would push me aside to save the mission. Look, I know you're an android, with all your rules and programming, but please show a little human compassion, and let me choose option two. I want Rhapsody back. I can't leave her in that husk nightmare."

Incensed by the Captain's apparent deceit and cold expression, Adam flew into a rage, landing punch after punch on the androids face and body. The assault was futile, as the Captain's skin soaked up the blows without consequence. Finally defeated by exhaustion and pain, knuckles raw and bloody, Adam gave up the fight. As if the attack had never happened, the Captain calmly reactivated the walkway:

"I'm sorry, Adam, but there is no going back on the deal. You will begin your journey tomorrow morning. John Down will deliver you to the Dreamers. They will be pleased that I have fulfilled my end of the bargain."

"The Dreamers? Who the hell are the Dreamers? And, what do you mean by fulfilled your end of the bargain?"

"I am not permitted to divulge that information. However, in a few days you will find out for yourself. For the remainder of the day, feel free to avail yourself of the Terminal's many facilities. If you wish, I will even reserve you a place at the Captain's table."

Looking ahead, Adam saw the end of the walkway, with the electric cart parked exactly where they left it. Somehow, without his knowledge, they had switched around and gone back the way they came. Ignoring the Captain's furtive grin, Adam did not bother to ask about the strange phenomenon. Wise to the theme-park trickery, he would not give the scheming android the satisfaction.

SURFING THE HALLS

The walkway advertisements were etched into Adam's memory, but in a deliberate snub to the Captain, he resisted the urge to visit the mall, listen to smooth jazz in the hotel revue bar, or hurtle headfirst on his belly down the Neptunator waterslide. With little else to do, he spent the evening in his assigned hotel suite, draining the mini-bar of Lagavulin Islay Malt Whisky and Tanqueray Dry Gin, and snacking on Pringles and M&Ms.

As the midnight hour approached, Adam stood on the balcony, overlooking the vast atrium, swigging his last mini-bottle of gin. A few partied-out stragglers hurried back to their rooms, filling the nearly empty space with echoing laughter and raucous drunken banter—their dreadful Day Spa experiences submerged beneath a few happy hours of entertainment, alcohol, and good company.

Laying on the King-size bed, waiting for sleep, Adam flicked through the bible he had found in the top drawer of the bedside cabinet. In a drunken stupor, he read random passages aloud, looking for answers to his current plight—treating the book as a communicator to a higher power. Putting the book down for a moment, in desperation he called out Manny's name, and begged, "Show me where you got your faith! I need the strength, Manny! I need the strength to get through this!"

He was expecting no answer, and no answer came. Adam picked up the bible once more, closed his eyes, and held it against his forehead. He contemplated all he had lost: his friends, his fighting prowess, and most importantly, control of his own mind. His fate clasped tightly in the grip of the Captain's bargain, in the final moments before midnight, Adam felt an emotional kinship with Natasja and the other prostitutes he remembered from the night-time streets of Portsmouth—trafficked across borders by unscrupulous greedy men to satisfy the carnal desires of strangers. Midnight brought the usual dreamless oblivion. For Adam, it was a welcome black oasis, devoid of fear … devoid of anything.

Early morning, and the Terminal reopened for business. Almost the entire visitor population was replaced by new arrivals: yesterday's crowd now returned to their respective viros. Blocking out the curious stares of the other diners, who no doubt marvelled that the famous Copacabana was in their midst, Adam quietly ate a small continental breakfast of croissants and orange juice. An hour later, he met up with John Down at the operative's departure lounge, where Captain Andrews was waiting to offer a farewell and a handshake. Adam ignored both. For the downtrodden, broken, and enslaved, the trivial slaps of stubborn petulance were the only remaining rebuke.

With Liana once again accompanying, the mobile platform headed for the portal, under an unexpectedly clear blue sky. In the distance, Kimberly sprinted along the Terminal concourse, stopping every few metres to wave from the viewing windows. Adam and John waved back from the mobile platform, both sad to leave their cheerful companion behind.

After fetching a number of items from the reception room dispenser, Adam and John headed into the halls. John Down broke into an appreciative smile as he positioned the waxed mahogany-finish surfboard onto the nearest white line. The elegant glossy wood was longer and heavier than a short-board, and designed for a passenger to ride pillion on a padded leather protuberance to the rear. John had advised Adam to wear protective ski-goggles for the journey, plus a pair of thin Kevlar gloves and a helmet.

"Hey, if we're surfing, then I'm the one dressed for the beach," said Adam, trying out the leather seat for comfort. "Are you sure that a Victorian suit with waistcoat, tails, and shiny shoes is appropriate? You look like you're off to the opera."

"I can assure you, we are not visiting any beaches," said John, cleaning the lenses of his brass framed WW2 aviator goggles, and then tightening his top hat's rubber chinstrap. "I feel my fashionable attire is perfect for the English gentleman abroad, although I should point out that by necessity my shoes have special high-traction soles. Kevin teasingly refers to them as my Huarache Oxfords."

With Adam seated, John Down clipped his cane to the board and stepped aboard. He turned to his passenger, with one last instruction.

"When we bank around a corner, remember to lean into the turn. Lean against it, and you will undoubtedly unsettle the board. We most definitely do not want a wipeout. Now, hold on tight to the straps under the saddle."

Arms outstretched, John posed like a surfer in mid-wave and for a few seconds rhythmically pumped up and down with his legs. In response to the motion, the board gently lifted, and hovered a few inches above the floor. Assuming a low crouching stance, John pointed ahead, and cried, "As my esteemed instructor, Lance 'Apocalypse' Nowell used to say, 'Yo, mama, let's ride this beast!'"

The board leapt forward and streaked along the hall, taking Adam by surprise as he nearly fell off the saddle. John Down stayed low, urging the board to greater speeds with simple thrusts of his hand. Unaccustomed to such an extreme combination of high-speed and exposed vulnerability– akin to riding a coffin lid atop a bullet train—Adam remained tense and statuesquely immobile, his teeth and buttocks both tightly clenched.

"Tis an easy straight line ride for about two hours," yelled John, without turning his head. "Then we shall take our rest at the next intersection. Beyond that, prepare for a sharp turn as we cross into the next sector."

Gradually, as the speed-blurred view became more monotonous than exhilarating, Adam's heart rate fell below bursting point, though he still kept a steady grip on the saddle straps. For the next two hours, as way of entertainment, John sang a series of 1960's surfing staples. His plummy church-choir warbling acted as a powerful sedative for Adam's fear-filled thrill ride, but sucked every atom of joy out of each song.

After a disturbingly haunting rendition of Jan and Dean's 'Dead Man's Curve', John went straight into The Beach Boys 'Help Me Rhonda'. Avoiding the dried remnants of a jellyman up ahead, John stopped singing and jumped diagonally, skipping the board onto the next white-line. The sudden jolt made Adam reach out a hand, which scraped dangerously along the floor—now he understood the reason for the protective gloves.

"Yes, for God's sake, 'Help me Rhonda'," Adam muttered, as John settled the fast-moving board and picked up the song where he left off.

After two hours seated on the narrow saddle, Adam was grateful for a chance to stretch his legs. John pushed the board away from the lines, much like pulling a dinghy up onto the shingle, and obtained two bottles of chilled cloudy lemonade from the crossroads dispenser. Sipping the refreshing drink through traditional paper straws, both men sat together, leaning against one of the tubular columns.

"Was all this designed just so people can surf around the Viroverse?" Adam asked, motioning to the white-lines. "Seems to be an odd kind of transport system."

"The lines were never meant to be used with surfboards," said John. "The halls are a redundant feature of the Viroverse. Their original purpose was to facilitate the overnight transportation of sleepers in long strings of connected pods, but it is rumoured that the idea was abandoned in favour of the more efficient liquid tube system." John banged the column with his fist. "It may seem incredible, but Kevin was the one who came up with the idea of the levitating surfboard."

"Really?" Adam was surprised.

"Apparently, the technology existed in his time. He can explain the details better than I can, but the white-lines are a superconductive maglev system. Despite the system's redundancy, the lines are still powered, albeit at a token rate. At our behest, the Captain employed specialist technicians to adapt our surfboards to take advantage of the grid."

"What about the reception rooms and portals?"

John took a long suck of lemonade before saying, "Emergency exits, although similarly redundant."

"And the jellymen?"

"The mucaloids, as I like to call them, or osmotic guards if you prefer their official title, are supposed to keep the halls free of interlopers like ourselves, but they are ponderously ineffective."

On cue, a wet patch appeared on the wall next to the dispenser. John started to get to his feet, but Adam placed a hand on his shoulder:

"Rest your legs, John, and leave this to me. After all, I'm the one who's sitting on his arse the whole trip."

Back on the lines, they crossed into the next sector. John successfully directed the board at speed around a corner, with Adam dutifully leaning into the turn like a passenger riding pillion on a motorbike. With no obstacles along the route, the turn proved to be the last adrenalin rush of the day as they cruised in one direction down the unchanging and seemingly endless hall. They passed door after door, viro after viro, resembling a vast hotel corridor with mile wide rooms, but at least out here there was a perception of place and direction. In the cossetting enclosed environments of the Viroverse, distance and location were meaningless. There were no maps or route descriptions. Travelling to another viro was simply a matter of falling asleep and waking up in another 'box'. Despite its technological audacity, the Viroverse denied its immortal residents that basic human need to know where and when we are.

At the next rest stop, John pulled off one of his shoes. Groaning with discomfort, he carefully peeled back the sock, revealing a wet blister that had split open. Adam got a box of sticking plasters and a tube of anaesthetic cream from the dispenser.

"I presume your parents are church goers," said John, carefully applying a plaster to his foot. "Because of your name, I mean."

"My name? The name that spawned a hundred school room taunts and a whole lot of bullying? Even my teachers couldn't resist the odd, 'where's my apple?' quip." Adam shook his head, wincing as a few long forgotten memories resurfaced. "Nah, my parents only went to church when there was a christening, marriage, or a funeral. The reason I have the name is because my mother was going through a spiritual crisis when she was pregnant with me. I asked my Dad about it a few times, but he always gets defensive. From what I know, my mother reached an age when she suddenly realised she was going to die one day."

"I believe pregnancy can do that," offered John. "The birth of a child often reminds one of the cycle of life, and with it, the inevitability of one's own passing."

"Yeah, blame the baby. Anyway, my mum went through a few religions: Catholicism, Spiritualism, Druidism, and of course, a load of Indian gurus. By the time I was born, she'd settled on the name Adam. Dad apparently wanted Robert or Harry, but he went along with it without a fuss."

"Ah, so you believe your father should have shown a bit more mettle."

"Oh no, no, not at all," Adam quickly corrected. "I should thank him every day for not protesting. You see, my mother's second choice was Sri Ramanuja."

They spent the night in a Hispanic styled viro, sleeping on the umbrella-like crown of a monkey puzzle tree that leaned precariously over a scrubby promontory. In the darkness, the village below was only a collection of warm yellow lights, nestling in the valley like tiny fallen embers of the Sun. In daylight, the following morning, the village presented itself as a picturesque jumble of rustic adobe walls and red roof tiles. It reminded Adam of Mama Fiestas Party Hub, although smaller, simpler, and far less gaudy.

Soon, they were back surfing the halls, maintaining a steady speed and direction. By midday, after a couple of rest stops, Adam was quite bored, and yawned continuously. He watched curiously, as John reached down and pulled up a couple of handgrips on bungee like cords. John held them taut, as if bracing himself:

"Hold on tight, Adam, and remember to lean! In a few moments we shall surf a spiral to the lower level!"

"Surf … a what?" Adam craned his neck to see what lay ahead. The next crossroads loomed, and a large door slid open just beyond one of the corners. "You didn't tell me anything about … whoa!" Without slowing, John aimed the board toward the unlit opening, and they shot inside.

The board banked sharply as they spiralled down into the pitch-darkness, with Adam leaning at almost 90 degrees. As a child, he whizzed his toy cars down the spiral ramp of his plastic toy car park, and wished he could shrink and get in them. Now, hurtling around the nightmarish helter-skelter, any wishes were drowned out by his own drawn out scream.

John Down was flushed with adrenalin, and bellowed excitedly, "Hussar! Hussar! Round and round and down we go!"

Only seconds passed before a brightly lit opening appeared and they shot out into the lower level hall. Adam took a few deep breaths, relieved to be free of the breakneck corkscrew. John slowed the board and let go of the handgrips, which recoiled back into position:

"Kowabunga!" he cried, punching the air with his fists. "Most marvellously excellent to the extreme!"

John glanced around and noticed his passenger's sweaty white-knuckled distress. Apologising with profuse Victorian gentility, abandoning his hall-surfing slang, John guaranteed that there were no more level changes, and explained that the Viroverse only had two residential levels with a utility level between.

The beach ballads resumed with renewed gusto, and a thought occurred to Adam. If there were only two viro levels and millions of viros, then even with miniaturisation the Viroverse would spread over an area larger than most nations. If this was Earth, then where exactly were they?

Mid-afternoon, and the board banked wide around a corner, barely missing one of the columns. John cursed under his breath, and then pointed out that it was now an hour's straight ride to their destination. Oblivious to the near disaster, Adam sat quietly, contemplating his impending appointment with the mysteriously named Dreamers.

Adam was deep in thought when the beaty effervescent sound of early 1980's synthpop broke the silence—Duran Duran or perhaps Depeche Mode. Another surfer appeared on the furthest line, the board Starke-style black and chrome, his designer suit a lesson in power dressing. It was Kevin, without the chemical tan, sporting his own firmly gelled hair, and listening to music with a belt-clipped Walkman cassette player.

Switching off the music, and putting the mini-headphone around his neck, Kevin raised a hand and displayed the shaka, the surfers greeting— middle fingers bent down, thumb and little finger raised.

"Dude," Kevin yelled, and skipped his board across the hall until both men were surfing on parallel lines.

"Dude," said John, returning the hand gesture and adjusting his speed to match his colleague. "I am quite surprised to see you in this sector. Are you here on business?"

"I was in the neighbourhood," said Kevin. "I heard you singing way down the hall, so I thought I'd ride by and say hello. You taking grey-skin back to his Mummy and Daddy?"

"This is Terminal business. I am delivering Mr Eden to the Dreamers."

You …? You're taking him to the Dreamers? I …"

"The Captain's orders," said John, anxious to avoid the subject. "Anyhow, what's that strong smell? Not your usual citrus cologne."

"That's 'Giorgio Beverly Hills', my friend. Bit of an 80's patchouli bomb, but I kinda like it. Now, tell me what's going on, because something's not right. There must be something major in this for you, otherwise there's no way you'd agree to it. Come on, I know you can't stomach a lie. Spill it, Johnny boy."

After a sharp intake of breath, John said, "The Captain graciously offered to reduce my sentence by three months upon successful completion of the mission."

Kevin frowned, looking snubbed.

"Why didn't Andrews ask me? I'd have jumped at the chance to get back in my own skin. No offense, mate, but you're not the type to throw people to the wolves."

"Wolves? What do you mean by wolves?" Adam asked apprehensively.

Kevin turned and grinned wickedly at Adam, as if revelling in a dark secret pleasure.

"Oops, you don't know, do you? Hah, shoulda kept my big mouth shut. Well, looks like I've overstayed my welcome already. Time to go; my work is done. Aloha, John."

"Aloha, Kevin," John dourly replied.

Rafting a powerful fug of waxy honeyed patchouli, Kevin nimbly swung his board around and raced back along the hall.

John slowly brought the board to a halt, and faced Adam:

"Please, I implore you, do not question me about what you just heard. Kevin is the supreme mischief-maker and he said those words to provoke you. The Captain forbade me to tell you anything about the Dreamers."

"What does it matter?" said Adam, throwing up his arms. "I'm no longer in control of my destiny. It's like I'm back to the worst years of my first-life. Next thing you know, I'll be fat again."

Sitting opposite his despondent passenger, without bothering to pull the knees of his trousers, John attempted some wise words.

"No-one is ever truly in control of their destiny, Adam. We are always under the sway of others."

"Well, the Captain seems to have one hell of a sway. How do you cope with all of his rules and demands? I know he got you out of that collector's box, but haven't you just swapped one prison for another?"

"On the contrary, I enjoy the greatest freedom I could ever desire. Thanks to the Captain, I can see my wife. That is my freedom. In a world where everything is just a provider away, spending time with Mary is the only freedom I need."

Looking into John's huge goggle-magnified eyes, pupils blooming with admiration for the Captain, Adam snapped, "Damn it, John, he uses your relationship to control you!"

John was unmoved by the outburst and said calmly, "To use one of Kevin's well-worn phrases, 'the Captain hits you where you live'. He understands that I will not respond to any other threat, and so of course uses my relationship to his advantage."

"So, he can make you do anything, no matter how vile."

"I shall admit that I find this particular assignment somewhat disturbing, and am surprised that I was the one chosen for its undertaking. The perfect candidate would have been Kevin, since he has far looser values than I. However, despite my keen sense of morality and a wish to do what is right and proper, my love for Mary comes first. Right now, your welfare is of little concern."

Perhaps shaken by the callousness of his own words, John quickly added, "I am so sorry for that. I am concerned, truly concerned, but there is nothing I can do to help you. You and Rhapsody seemed to have a mutual affection. Maybe, one day, you will experience similar feelings to those I hold for my wife."

"That's never going to happen, is it?"

John hung his head, unable to look Adam in the eye.

"I doubt it very much."

The last leg of the journey was made in thoughtful silence. John slowed the board as the hall some 100 yards ahead ended in a dark grey wall. Approaching the wall was a solemn affair, as both men knew their ways would soon part. Too many times in Adam's life had a friendship ended almost as soon as it had begun.

John executed a skilful sliding stop and stepped off the board. Adam followed, and stretched his legs, in no hurry for the next stage in his odyssey. Denying him the luxury of delay, a panel in the wall started flashing an insistent red, waiting for the press of a palm. John gestured for Adam to step forward.

Adam pulled off his helmet and gloves and handed them to John, but kept the ski-shades to hide his disturbing eyes:

"If you let me go…? If I just walk away, what will happen?"

John glanced anxiously over at his cane, still clipped to the board.

"Well, the Captain would certainly extend my punishment. It would be at least a year before I see my wife again."

"And, what about me? Would the Captain forget about me?"

Keeping his eyes trained on Adam's belted machete, John replied, "If he made a bargain with the Dreamers and you gave your consent, then there is no chance of your being forgotten. The Captain will send other operatives in my stead to find you: characters of a more merciless disposition."

Adam made a point of keeping his hand away from his weapons belt.

"Don't worry, John, I'll go without a fight. I can't make a run for it without my own support."

"I do not know what you mean by that, Adam, but I appreciate your cooperation. When we first met, I took you for a depraved killer, no better than the glittering lunatics you fought in the shadow of the grey towers. Our acquaintance has been too brief to say whether Mr Beaumont's final words were a fitting tribute to your true character, but I do see evidence of a good heart."

Shaking John's hand, Adam had a final request.

"John, could you please keep an eye out for Kimberly and Rhapsody for me? Make sure they're safe?"

John could only nod, overwhelmed by the shame of his actions. Without a word, he returned to the board, unable to watch as Adam placed his palm on the panel. The panel beeped and flashed green. A thin door slid quickly open, and a giant sallow-skin hand immediately reached out. Adam cried out in shock as huge fingers, almost as thick as his wrist, gripped tightly around his upper arm.

The door hissed shut, and John tentatively looked back. Adam was gone. Grief stricken the distinguished Victorian stepped onto the surfboard, eyes rimmed with tears behind his brass goggles:

"Oh Mary, what have I done? What have I done?"

CITY OF GIANTS

Adam struggled to break free of the vice-like grip, which squeezed his hard muscles as if they were soft flab. He noticed that the reception room was huge, the details elusive, obscured by the presence of three giant men who towered around him. They blocked the light with their size, appearing as menacing silhouettes, shouting for Adam to stand down. Although he was only the size of one of their legs, like a spirited toddler Adam refused to listen and kept wriggling. The feel of cold metal against his forehead, and the click of a safety, brought a sudden halt to his resistance. They had guns.

The man standing behind Adam, holding his arm, spoke politely with a light Pakistani accent.

"That is much better, Mr Eden," he said, maintaining a strong grip. "We have heard all about your skills with a blade, so you need to lose the weapons. Do you understand?"

"Do it yourself!" spat Adam belligerently.

"Err … if I let you go, please unclip your belt and throw it over to the benches."

"I said, do it yourself!"

The man holding the gun to Adam's head, lowered the weapon and then pulled out a knife—probably a small pocketknife but to Adam it seemed as large as a machete.

"It's always the littl'uns got the most fight in 'em," the man said in a rough cockney accent. "My name is Mr Graves. Now, you may not 'ave noticed, but our 'ands are too big to unclip your belt, and I 'ave no wish to cut my finger on one of the toothpicks you're carrying." He raised the knife, and pressed the point gently against Adam's forehead. "Now, you can either do as Mr Mahmood says, or I will cut the bloody belt off myself … and that could get messy."

Copacabana added some judicious mental pressure, and Adam agreed. Mr Mahmood released his grip and held a gun to the back of Adam's head as he discarded his blades. Once their captive was unarmed, the men relaxed a little and gave Adam more space.

With the light less obscured, Adam took stock of the situation. The three men, each about 12 feet tall, were dressed like 18th century highwaymen: full-length black coats with wide double collars, braided cuffs, polished black leather riding boots, and matching tricorn hats. In contrast to the romantic panache, the handguns they carried—now thankfully lowered—were deadly 21st century machine pistols.

Apart from the larger scale, the reception room was identical to that of the Terminal, with rows of benches and a door at either end—the one Adam had entered was of normal height and thin, the other one an easy fit for the giants. The third highwayman, a sharp-eyed fellow with a reedy voice, looked baffled at Adam's appearance.

"Why the grey?" he asked. "Are you wearing a rubber bodysuit or something? You look like a doll."

"I'm an undesirable," said Adam, getting straight to the point, though tired of explaining his lowly status.

"An undesirable? I don't think I've ever heard of an undesirable."

"I was a down and out in my first-life, and they don't usually resurrect useless bums. That's what undesirables are. They brought me back as the freebie half of a two for one deal."

The explanation provoked a round of sniggering from the highwaymen. The highwayman with the reedy voice led Adam by the hand to the large door. He smiled smugly, addressing Adam like a little child, and placed his hand on the palm panel.

"Little man, if you really are the lowest of the low, then consider this a true privilege," the huge door slid open, and he raised his voice. "Behold the city of the Dreamers!"

For Adam, it was an anti-climax. A glass elevator lay beyond the doorway, but a solid steel balustrade blocked his view of anything but a clear blue sky and a sparse cover of white clouds. Looking out to the sides, he could see that the elevator clung to the side of a massive cliff face that seemed to stretch for miles in both directions. Adam rose up on tiptoes and jumped up and down, desperate to see what wonders lay below–no such problem for his escorts, since the balustrade only came up to their waists. As he strained, he saw a line of tiny circular dirigibles, glimmering white, floating serenely beneath the clouds.

"Is that some kind of transport system?" he gasped, as if he was a small child excitedly pointing out things through his parent's car window. Looking further away, he saw another line, and squinting into the distance, maybe a third. "Are they real?"

"That's the String o' Pearls Skyway," said Mr Graves, as the elevator began its descent. "Been running a few months now, but it's still popular with the locals. Too slow for my tastes, but you get a bloody good view of Soñador from up there." He gave Adam a puzzled look. "'Ere, 'ow come you look all pink and normal all of a sudden?'"

"Don't really know, but I think it's got something to do with retinal projection. I guess that means this is another viro rather than the outside." Adam could feel Copacabana's deep dismay that this was still the Viroverse. "So, what's Soñador? I can't see anything from down here. Any of you fine dandies got a shoebox I could stand on?"

Showing some kindly consideration, Mr Mahmood lifted Adam up and sat him on the crook of his arm. Mr Graves laughed.

"That's one ugly ventriloquist dummy you got there, Mahmood. Ain't that right Mr Lacelle?"

Mr Lacelle chimed in, "'Yeah Copa, watch out he doesn't put his hand up your arse!'"

Mr Mahmood was not amused, and admonished his crude associates.

"How many times have I told you to stop your lavatory humour? I will most certainly not be inserting my hand into Mr Eden's anus."

Now able to see above the balustrade, Adam was oblivious to his escorts' bickering. He sat in wonderment, transfixed by the stunning vista that lay before him.

Save for a distant mountain region, a vast city filled the view. Busy thoroughfares, teeming with vehicles and pedestrians, ran through the cavernous corridors between soaring skyscapers. Apart from lining up on a grid-system, the buildings were an eclectic mixture of architectural styles adapted to fit the high-rise ideal. Modernist towers of glass and chrome stood alongside countless extraordinary revisions of bygone eras: Russian inspired onion domes, Roman columned towers, copiously gabled redbrick Tudor edifices, and colourful high-rise Pagodas.

"Ah yes," said Mr Mahmood, "do you see the one next to the medieval stone spire? I think is very much the Copacabana style."

Despite being somewhat overwhelmed, Adam managed a chuckle, as Mr Mahmood pointed out a ramshackle beach-hut effect skyscraper with a thatched roof and huge neon Tiki themed motifs. Everywhere Adam looked, the astonishing city of Soñador was an exhilarating fusion of historical variety, Manhattan scale, and glitzy Las Vegas showmanship.

He carefully scrutinised the one mile limit for any telltale signs of the viro walls, such as conveniently placed canals, roads missing certain junctions, or long rows of buildings that no-one entered. Given the size of the highwaymen, perhaps the viro was twice the usual width and breadth. A brief scan of both limits still revealed no hint of the walls.

"I have never seen anything as impressive as this," said Adam, "but how much of the city is real?"

Mr Mahmood waved his hand across the view, and said, "Almost everything you can see before you is real. The whole city is real."

"But this isn't the outside, is it?"

"No, this is an enclosed environment, but much bigger than any other. The cliff behind us conceals one of the walls, and the faraway mountains another. There are cliffs disguising the other walls, but you cannot see them from here. I do not have an exact figure, but I believe that Soñador covers over 1400 square miles. Every year brings new Dreamers, and the city grows larger."

Adam did not ask whether the area represented genuine miles, Dreamer miles, or Viroverse miles. Whichever scale it was, the city of Soñador was enormous.

The elevator descended opposite a skyscraper very similar to New York's Art Deco Chrysler Building, complete with a shimmering tiered crown. People waved enthusiastically from the windows, many holding banners welcoming Copacabana to the city. Below, a large crowd congregated at the bottom of the elevator, cheering and chanting, eager for a glimpse of the legendary hero. Adam became concerned that the jostling crowd of giants might trample him. There did not seem to be any barriers or security personnel to hold them back. He hoped that his three armed escorts were enough to keep him safe.

An eligible bump and they touched down next to a small-pedestrianized square with ornamental shrubs and trees. The elevator's glass front and steel balustrade automatically swivelled round, allowing the occupants to exit.

Fortunately, Adam found his fears of being crushed dispelled as the highly animated crowd kept their distance. Their clothing was as varied in style as the buildings. From smart two-piece suits, shimmering pearlescent dresses, and puffy rubber-ribbed skirts, to more historical styles such as golden-edged togas, drab medieval tunics, and richly embroidered silk kimonos. Whatever the style, Adam noticed that many in the crowd wore glossy curly toed shoes.

A red carpet extended all the way from the elevator to an ornate golden coach that had no footmen or horses. Richly gilded sculptures of tritons and cherubs adorned the unashamedly extravagant carriage, which looked like it belonged in a fairy-tale or royal coronation. Mr Lacelle ran ahead, carefully avoiding the carpet, and opened the carriage door.

With regal deportment, a beautiful woman, cherry blonde hair belying her East Asian features, stepped down onto the red carpet. Skin like alabaster, hair loosely braided, and wearing a billowing dress of turquoise silk, she smiled demurely and waited for Adam by the carriage steps.

Adam strolled forward, after a gentle nudge by Mr Mahmood. Thrilled to see the diminutive legend, the crowd began chanting 'Copa' and clapping in time. Adam decided, with Copacabana's consent, that winning over the locals seemed a wise move, and promptly treated them to a couple of perfectly executed somersaults followed by a rough though effective interpretation of moon walking. Staying on the red carpet was a feat of skilful agility with a final cartwheel leading into a gracious bow to the lady and a chivalric kiss on her tendered hand.

The highwaymen sprinted up behind Adam and held his arms fast; embarrassed they had allowed such a breach of security. The lady was not amused with the rough treatment.

"Unhand our guest!" she ordered, with the manner of someone accustomed to being obeyed. "I am sure that if Mr Eden wanted to harm me, I would no doubt already be dead." She looked down at Adam, and proffered a stately nod. "Mr Eden, my name is Boudicca Chang—a former Queen of England—and on behalf of the Committee and the good people of Soñador I would like to formally welcome you to your new home."

"Did you say 'Queen of England'?"

"I most certainly did. That is why the committee sent me rather than some faceless no name. They thought I would remind you of your native land."

"You must have reigned after I died, unless of course you are the Boudicca who fought the Romans. It's just that you look Chine ..."

"My grandfather, Ming-hua Chang, brought the rights to the English monarchy from Raythean in 2164. The board appointed me Queen in 2170, after voting out my brother for his most unbecoming conduct."

"So, Boudicca's an alias ... if it's not rude to ask?"

"It's on my birth certificate," said Boudicca, with a wink, "and was also part of The House of Chang's marketing strategy. Now, if it is not rude to ask, why didn't you try to harm me, or at least take me hostage? Your ruthless nature is well known, and I am sure you have heard some unsettling rumours about the Dreamers."

"Guns are a pretty compelling reason," admitted Adam, aware that one was presently pressed into the small of his back. "I thought firearms were banned in the Viroverse. Nothing combustible. That's the rule."

"There is no combustion," said Mr Mahmoud. "They are compressed air-guns, although quite powerful. They fire domed pellets, but we tend to call them bullets. Even so, I believe they are not available to you little ones."

"Well, the other reason I didn't try anything is that you're all twice my size."

Boudicca laughed, and shook her head.

"Hmm, it is a Chang family saying that precision is necessary for truth and understanding. We are twice the height, not the size. Twice the height, width, and depth, makes us eight times the size."

"About as big as your leg then."

"About as big as this leg?"

Boudicca slowly pulled up her dress and pressed her leg against Adam. His face was well above the hemline of her white stockings, his cheek blushing warm against her flawless skin. She turned, teasingly brushing the soft mound of her cotton panties across his sweaty forehead, a dab of perfume on her thigh releasing a luscious breath of creamy lemon and amber vanilla

"Ooooh, you are so precious," she gasped. "I want to lube you up right here and pop you in!"

Clapping her hands to her cheeks, Boudicca dropped the dress back into place.

"I forget myself, Mr Eden! Please excuse my unseemly lapse in decorum. Strong physical urges are a common trait in my family, and you come with a most stimulating reputation."

"Err … I never thought of myself as stimulating," said Adam, bemused that he could arouse such passions. "I tend to think I have a decaffeinating effect on people."

Tittering politely, Boudicca climbed into the coach and sat on a sumptuously cushioned bench. She beckoned Adam with a slender finger.

"I am going to enjoy you, Mr Eden. I expect such intense pleasures." She patted the cushion. "Please, step inside and sit next to me."

As Adam climbed in, Mr Mahmood whispered in his ear, "I shall be enjoying you also."

THE DREAMERS

Raised up by a thoughtfully supplied child's booster seat, a thick polystyrene block with a polyester cover of smiling buck-toothed zoo animals, Adam gazed out of the coach window at the remarkably diverse assortment of traffic and pedestrians.

Driverless vehicles, silent except for a low-level fuel cell hum, cruised at a constant speed, maintaining precise equidistance. American muscle cars, jaunty European minis, and hard-nosed limos vied for attention alongside sleek futuristic bullet cars, eccentric steampunk contrivances of brass and iron, hovering globes, and reproductions of famous movie and television vehicles. The vibrantly bizarre vehicular processions streamed through the streets like spectacularly imagined carnivals of automania.

"Quite breath-taking, isn't it?" said Boudicca, sitting beside Adam—the three highwaymen squashed uncomfortably on the opposite bench. "I must say, it took me a few months before I stopped strolling around with my jaw dropped. Two years on and it hardly registers anymore. Sad how quickly we become so jaded, surrounded by all this magnificence."

On behalf of Copacabana, and with some personal curiosity, Adam asked, "The Captain told me this was the next step to the outside. Is that true?"

Boudicca looked surprised and slightly uneasy at the question. She hesitated before replying, though remained composed.

"As a committee member I am party to a detailed knowledge of Soñador, but I am not aware of any route to the outside, or any Soñadorians that might know otherwise. Perhaps Captain Andrews used a precise form of words to obscure the truth. Anyhow, I shall bring up the matter with other committee members. Do not think this changes anything. The bargain was struck and you were delivered. That is it."

"Look, so far, this has been an almost pleasant experience. I'm not expecting that to last much longer, so I guess it's time I asked the two most important questions."

"Who we are, and why you are here?" guessed Boudicca correctly. "I am most surprised you waited this long before asking. I had some notion that you were perhaps playing it cool. Now, the answer to the latter must wait until we reach our destination, but as for who we are…"

Boudicca shuffled round on her cushion, hands clasped together, and looked down on little Adam as a mother about to tell a tale to her son.

"We are the Dreamers, Adam. We are the winners of the greatest contest never known to mankind. During your induction, your concierge explained to you the process of resurrection: the time channelling, the memory capture. However, another part of the process is a closely guarded secret."

Boudicca paused a moment, widening her eyes, perhaps for dramatic effect.

"Prior to initial resurrection, everyone is tested for the purity of their dream-state. A signal is streamed across time and space into our sleeping brains, inducing certain provocative situations."

"You mean they send the signal to our original life? I thought time channelling was difficult and expensive."

"According to our concierge, it is only the channelling of original brain material that is expensive, but transmitting small strings of data is comparatively cheap."

"But, does it alter the future?"

"Not at all. The channelled dream is removed immediately after the test and the targets original dream reinstated to avoid any time anomalies."

Not sure he wanted to hear the answer, Adam tentatively asked, "So, what kind of provocative situations are we talking about?"

"Oh, many and various: opportunities to take part in horrifically depraved sexual acts, torture, and all manner of violence. If the dreamer responds positively to the stimulus and performs the vile act in question—in their dreams of course—then they are immediately excluded from the contest."

"That doesn't sound very fair," said Adam. "So, someone just has to dream like a saint on a particular night and they win—they become a Dreamer?"

"It is not that easy. The test is performed a maximum of ten times, at different times in a person's life, each level slightly different from the others. To pass the test, and earn the prestigious status of Dreamer, one must survive each level without committing what we call a dream crime."

Adam was unimpressed with the nature of the test and annoyed at the preferential status it gave the Dreamers.

"I don't get this. You mean that in their waking life, someone could be a murderer … or worse, but as long as they always dreamed within the law they end up here?"

"It is true that some Dreamers led less than savoury lives," admitted Boudicca, "but we are all proud of our success and united in the purity of our dreams. Why the people of Earth decided that dreams were of such paramount importance is a mystery, but we are very glad they did."

With a saccharine smile, Boudicca gently patted Adam on the head, and added, "We cannot all be perfect. Who knows, you may have got to level nine and fallen at the final hurdle."

Adam swiped the barb aside with brutal honesty, saying, "Hah, most of my nightmares were fuelled by fast-food, angst, alcohol, and squalor, so I definitely went out in the first round."

An open top single decker bus drew alongside the coach, transporting a merry group of partygoers dressed in traditional Bavarian costume—the men in leather lederhosen and feather caps, the women in colourful dirndl dresses with ribbon hooked bodices. To the back of the bus, an oompah band played Oktoberfest favourites. Adam strained to hear the music, most of which was blocked by the coach's reinforced windows, but it was another sense that became oddly aroused. Sniffing the air, much like a dog in a kitchen on Christmas day, Adam faintly discerned the most wonderful meaty aroma—the scent of sausages.

Boudicca screwed up her face in disgust, and held a soft silk handkerchief to her nose.

"I do wish this frightful road-cruise fad would end," she fussed. "You cannot take even the shortest of journeys without suffering their presence.

Day after day, those blasted themed party buses choke the road network, polluting our sweet city air with their insufferable noise and smell. The Scoville Chilli Scorcheris the worst offender—the capsicum cloud that accompanies that particular vehicle is enough to make your eyes water and burnout your throat. It does not help that the Royal Coach isn't allowed even basic air-con."

Suddenly pressured by Copacabana, Adam felt compelled to obtain a sausage. Longingly, he pressed his face against the window, staring at the Bavarian theme bus, rhythmically rapping the glass with his fingers.

"Your illustrious Majesty, the smell of those sausages has set my stomach rumbling," Adam sighed. "I don't know what you've got planned for me, but I could really go for one right now."

Copacabana's powerful insistence was unexpected, since the ruthless alter ego disdained gluttony and the tasty pleasures of the plate—or in this case a crusty handheld baguette. Mr Mahmoud shook his head, wagging a finger disapprovingly.

"That will not be happening. We will not be compromising security again, just so you can fill your belly. There are dispensers at the Compro Building. You can eat there."

Again mimicking a mother with her darling son, Boudicca acceded to Adam's wishes.

"Little Adam may be on his way to the Compro, but I think we can trust him. A condemned man is surely entitled to a last meal, and I suppose the road-cruise fancy dress adds a certain superficial authenticity and charm. What exactly do you want, Adam?"

"If they've got it, I'll have a Bratwurst in a crusty roll with lots of German mustard. And, don't worry about security, because I'm only going to eat the bloody thing." Adam raised an eyebrow. "I've never been known to wield a sausage in anger."

Raising her silken handkerchief once more, Boudicca disguised a chuckle as a polite cough. Mr Graves put down his gun and held his stomach as he bellowed with laughter, causing Mr Lacelle to break into a bout of reedy sniggers. Mr Mahmoud again shook his head.

"Security is no laughing matter. I for one am very concerned that Mr Eden might assault us with his sausage."

With Graves and Lacelle doubled up with uncontrollable laughter, Boudicca regained her composure long enough to say, "Mr Mahmoud, please open the window by your side and procure the saus ... the saus ... the food for Mr Eden."

Grumbling unheard worries, Mr Mahmoud pressed a button on a small remote—the wrong button—and the window next to Adam slid down. Before the highwayman could rectify his mistake, Adam sprung from his booster seat, clambered out of the large window opening, and climbed up the ornate gilding onto the roof of the coach.

Adam steadied himself on the slightly domed roof of the fast moving vehicle– much faster than he anticipated from the smooth ride inside. The partygoers on the road-cruise bus crowded against the side rail, pointing and shouting in surprise. It only took a few seconds before their concerned cries gave way to applause and whistles as they recognised the tiny figure in the pink hibiscus shirt.

The sausage ruse was Copacabana's escape plan. Any window or doorway would have sufficed but Mr Mahmoud's fumbling fingers hit the jackpot. The next step was for Adam to leap over to the coach and disappear into the city traffic. Then he would claim sanctuary in the Tiki skyscraper, or a church if such places existed in Soñador. The speed of the vehicles made it a risky venture, and forced Adam and Copacabana to work together in a precarious 'push-me-pull-you' partnership.

Adam readied himself for the leap across to the Oompah bus. The gap looked daunting but achievable. As he set for the sprint, Adam was pulled backwards as a large hand caught his foot. He quickly twisted free of the grip and looked around to see Mr Graves climbing onto the roof.

All thoughts of leaping over to the beckoning Bavarians were cast aside as Adam confronted the giant highwayman. Mr Graves laughed, dismissive of his diminutive adversary, and reached for his gun. His face dropped when he realised that the weapon was still on the bench in the coach: an ironic consequence of Adam's sausage comment.

Wasting no time in exploiting the situation, Adam dashed forward and head-butted Graves as hard as possible in the groin, hoping to lend painful new meaning to the phrase 'giving head'. The move backfired: the highwayman apparently wearing a protective shield beneath his soft leather breeches. Adam staggered back in agony, clutching his forehead, barely avoiding a fatal backwards fall onto the busy roadway.

Laughing again, but deciding not to seize the moment, Graves shook his head in derision, and reached for his knife. Still a little dizzy from the head-butt, Adam brought his hand up from behind his back.

"Looking for this," he asked, holding up the blade that he had just lifted from the highwayman's belt. "Nice weight. Handle's a bit thick for my liking, but I'm sure I'll cope."

Bolstered by the partygoers' encouraging cries and a brave attempt by the Oompah band to play Copacabana's signature tune—ending in an unrecognisable parping disarray—Adam made his move. Skipping wide and spinning low, he stabbed the point of the blade into the centre of Grave's booted foot. In an unforeseen reaction, the highwayman kicked his foot up, ramming the hilt of the still embedded blade into Adam's chin. Due to the huge size of the hilt, the impact was like a wide rubber fist, briefly lifting Adam off his feet rather than crushing his windpipe.

Falling back down, Adam made a desperate grab for the knife. The highwayman simply stepped aside, denying Adam his prize, and yanked the bloody blade from his boot.

"Last chance to back down, short-arse," he sneered, limping back a step. "If I kill you now, then tomorrow I promise you'll resurrect in shackles. You won't get away again."

The words sparked a fire in Adam and Copacabana. Resurrection meant that they could fight without the looming spectre of permanent death. Unchained from the cautious constraints of mortal fear, Adam hurled himself through the narrow gap between the highwayman's legs—perfectly timed and nimbly limboed to avoid the deadly scything swoop of the blade.

Rather than turning around and confronting his impish foe, Graves made the fatal mistake of bending over and peering between his legs. Like a demonic monkey, Adam sprang onto the highwayman's back, and kicked off the tricorn hat. Then, with a focused ferocity harking back to his violent days in the psychoviro, he rained down tiny-fisted blows on the exposed head.

The infuriated giant twisted and turned, his leather coat flapping and flailing in the struggle, attempting to shake loose the devilish imp. Adam stood upright on the broad shoulders, took hold of the carefully groomed blonde ponytail and wrenched it upwards with all the strength his arms could muster. Crying out in agony, his hair pulled from the roots, the highwayman lost his footing and tumbled forward. Adam jumped clear as Graves slammed headfirst onto the head of a gilded cherub.

Without delay, Adam prepared to leap across to the bus. He cast a final anxious glance at the highwayman, concerned that he might get back up at any moment. His worries were unfounded since the impact caused massive haemorrhaging, the blood trickling down around the cheerful cherub's head, causing crimson tears to fall from its soulless golden eyes.

Sprinting across the roof, committed to the jump, Adam gulped in shock as the Oompah bus unexpectedly turned off down a side street—the revellers, dismayed as they missed their chance to meet and greet the legendary Copacabana, raised their beer-steins in honour.

Another vehicle smoothly sped into the bus's place, offering an alternative mobile haven –a gothic belfry reared up from the roof of a colourful hearse-like automobile. Even as Adam stamped down on the crowned head of a gilded triton, and launched himself across the treacherous gap, he recognised that the quirky vehicle might be a psychedelic homage to the 'Wacky Races, Creepy Coupe'.

Catching hold of the wooden sill of the belfry arch with his outstretched hand, Adam easily hauled himself through the opening. The little room perfectly suited his small stature—like a creepy child's playhouse, the dark corners providing convenient hiding places. Unlike the cartoon vehicle it was based on, there were mercifully no bats in the belfry, or fire-breathing dragons.

Adam took a furtive peek around the corner of the arch, and sighed with relief seeing the Royal Coach in the distance, parked by the sidewalk. Wishing to disappear, he slunk back into the shadows and nestled in the comforting crease of the corner. The smooth ride, and the relaxing fuel-cell hum, gradually closed his tired eyes. Within minutes, he was sleeping soundly.

ONE MORE TIME

Awakening with a sharp snort, Adam opened his eyes and blinked his blurry sight into focus. He was seated, but unable to move, held fast by transparent plastic straps and a restraining head brace. Expecting the shadowy security of the belfry, the white-walled room—silent and clinically sterile—was an alarming surprise.

His head incapable of turning, Adam's eyes followed a man wheeling a steel trolley carrying a number of black cubes. The man, attired in a hooded soft-blue surgical coverall, walked out of Adam's field of vision. Adam's eyes refocused as a familiar face, Boudicca Chang, leant into view. Exhibiting little emotion, she reached either side of the head brace. A hiss followed by a soft pop, and the room suddenly became alive with sound.

"There, you should be able to hear now," said Boudicca, arms crossed, casually outfitted in black shorts and a beige t-shirt—a flouncy fairy-tale dress perhaps too frivolous for a laboratory. "Did you enjoy your little trip in the cartoon car? You left my coach in quite a mess with Mr Grave's blood all over the gilding."

Anticipating a dry rasp, Adam coughed a couple of times before talking. To his surprise, his throat was perfectly hydrated, and he spoke with ease.

167

"Pah, so I guess you can never trust a hippy, no matter how cool his car is. How long have I been here?"

"The owner of the 'Groovy Ghouly' is not to blame. In fact, I believe he said 'it was a total bummer sending Copacabana back to the Man'. Every vehicle in Soñadoris equipped with sensors and trackers, so after a simple request, the car automatically delivered you to the Compro Building. Since you were fast asleep when you arrived, we decided to gas the belfry to avoid any further violence. You were strapped in this chair less than four hours after your flight from the coach."

"Then, why the charade?" asked Adam. Why didn't your goons just gas me in the reception room and bring me straight here? Could've saved you a heap of trouble."

"Oh, I don't know, Adam," Boudicca sarcastically replied. "Maybe we wanted to show you some respect, and honour the famous Copacabana."

"Yeah right, like blessing an animal before slaughter."

Boudicca bent forward, gently brushed Adam's hair aside, and softly kissed him on the forehead.

"In that case, you dear little beast, bless you."

Boudicca looked like she was about to move out of Adam's sight, so he quickly asked, "Can't you unstrap me? At least let me move my head so I can see what the hell's going on."

"Your head needs to be absolutely immobile for the procedure. We have a few black boxes to get through before you are ready for the casket." Boudicca's demeanour seemed to soften at the sight of her captive's pleading eyes, and she promptly spoke to someone to the right of Adam's vision—perhaps the man in the surgical gown. "Doctor Kaminski, how long before we start?"

"Give me about another 10 minutes," he replied with cold detachment. "I need to go over the steps in my head a few more times. It's been years since I was last called upon to perform a manual insertion."

With Mr Mahmoud muttering disapproval somewhere in the background, Boudicca asked Mr Lacelle to remove the head brace. A few seconds winding a low-tech hex key, and the highwayman lifted off the bulky restraint.

Adam slowly turned his head, loosening his stiff neck. He glanced up at the bland ceiling with flat panel lighting, and then down.

"Oh my God," he gasped with sudden embarrassment, "I'm naked!"

Doctor Kaminski, a broad faced man with a sharp stare, strolled over with a medical calliper, and took a rough measure of Adam's right eye.

"Technically, you are not naked," he clarified as he read the gauge, "since you are wearing a disposable modesty thong."

"Do I really have to be naked for this?" Adam blushed, believing that everyone in the room had seen his pitiable penis. "I think I know what you are going to do, but I can't see how it involves nudity."

"It is not a requirement of the procedure," muttered Doctor Kaminski, taking a measurement of Adam's left eye. "You had blood on your clothing so they had to be removed. Not just for hygiene, but also in case you had sustained any injuries that needed attention. No need to be shy; you've got nothing I haven't seen before"

Uncomfortable with the emphasis on the word 'nothing', Adam pleaded with Boudicca, "Please could I get a fresh set of clothes, your majesty? I promise I won't cause any trouble. The city's screwed down so tight, I know there's no point in trying to escape. Please."

Against Mr Mahmoud's advice, Boudicca once again gave in to Adam.

"I will trust you one last time, Mr Eden," she said, gesturing for Mr Lacelle to release the plastic restraints. "Don't humiliate me again."

With the aid of a plastic step, Adam fetched clothes of suitable size from the room's dispenser. Deciding to make a point, he went with the usual Aloha ensemble—it was his uniform and he had earned it. Mr Mahmoud and Mr Lacelle stood guard, guns raised, as Adam dressed. Zipping up the fly of the white trousers, Adam became aware of Copacabana, whispering from the shadows. Within seconds, a decision was made: one last attempt to escape, a reckless bid for freedom.

Engaging in small talk, Adam tried to lure the highwaymen into a false sense of security. The conversation was not without interest as Adam learned that Mr Mahmoud formally owned a bed and breakfast in the Cotswolds, and that Mr Lacelle worked in a number of auxiliary positions within the 22nd century NHS. Both men fondly reminisced about their first-life experiences. Buttoning up his shirt, Adam noticed that both guns were now lowered.

Mirroring a move from the battle on the coach roof, Adam stealthily stole Mr Mahmoud's knife from his belt. Grunting loudly, Adam powered the blade into the highwayman's foot, but this time remembered to keep hold of the weapon.

Mr Mahmoud dropped to the floor, howling in agony and clasping his foot. Boudicca stood back from the fray, tutting at her operative's incompetence, whilst Doctor Kaminski wheeled the steel trolley with the black boxes to the far side of the room, out of harm's way.

Using his size to advantage, Adam dived under a low coffee table. Mr Lacelle lunged after him, attempting to grab his tiny feet, but crashed into the table sending cups and plates flying across the room. Unscathed, though losing the knife, Adam scrambled out from under the upturned tabletop. Without looking back, he leapt to his feet and sprinted towards the door, praying it was not locked.

Adam and Copacabana's haphazard partnership ended with the opening of the door. With typical bravado, Copacabana wanted to rush through and face the unknown. Adam, however, chose caution, intending to take a quick look before proceeding. In an unintended mental tug-of-war, Adam awkwardly stumbled out into a waiting room, as if tripping over his own feet, and stared down the barrel of a gun.

Crouching at Adam's height, Mr Graves pointed his machine pistol directly at Adam's face, a large finger lightly pressed against the trigger. With a mocking tone, the highwayman roared, "Stand and deliver! Your money or your life!"

Like a rapidly deflated balloon, Copacabana gave up and relinquished all control to Adam.

"But ... but it takes a day to resurrect," Adam babbled, trying not to make any sudden moves.

"Maybe it takes a day for you littl'uns, but Dreamers can use a three hour express service. Now, I would love to blow that stupid little head off your shoulders, but there are a lot of people out there waiting to suck you. So put your hands on your head and go back in."

"Suck me?" said Adam, his eyes wide with bewilderment and alarm.

"Just get back in the room!" ordered Graves, shoving Adam back with the point of the gun.

With Mr Graves following close behind, Adam dutifully obeyed. As he entered the room, Boudicca cast a reproving scowl—her authority disrespected, her pride dealt a heavy blow.

"Thank you, Mr Graves," she said, "and I hope you are fully recovered from your ordeal." She snapped her fingers. "Mr Mahmoud, Mr Lacelle, please strap Mr Eden back in the chair before we have any more incidents."

THANKS FOR THE MEMORIES

Restrained in the chair, this time wearing clothes and a clinging rubbery exo-scalp, Adam gave up any idea of escape. Even Copacabana, never one to back down, stayed silent. If Adam had endured his former dreary existence, rather than fighting his way to legendary status, then he would not be facing this awful situation. The simple life, facing petty insults from family and neighbours, seemed like paradise compared to the past few days. He remembered Manny's theatre analogy, describing Adam as the leading man. Perhaps all those who stayed too long or walked too tall on the stage faced the prospect of an unexpected fall through the trapdoor.

Catching Boudicca's attention, Adam asked, "The black boxes, on the trolley, what are they for?"

"They contain your missing memories," she replied bluntly. "As you are obviously aware, your memories are incomplete. The AI always removes the delicious moments just before death. For our purposes, for the sucking, those memories need to be reinstated."

She tapped the top of one of the boxes and smiled expectantly. Adam was extremely disturbed at the prospect of remembering his deaths. Their absence shielded him from the painful truth of his exploits. It seemed like another pillar of his courage was about to topple.

"So, tell me straight, what are you going to do with my memories?"

"One of the many perks that Dreamers enjoy is two hours of intense REM sleep after midnight."

"You mean dreaming, right? You're talking about the rapid eye movement phase."

"Bravo!" cried Boudicca, softly clapping her hands as if congratulating a small child. "I thought your little brain was saturated with sausages, cartoons, and violence. Well, after the REM sleep, we blank out just as you do, until 8am. Unlike you, we also have the permission and ability to use other people's memories to enhance the dream experience."

"And that's why you wanted me here. I thought it was something like that. My memories of the psychoviro, the killing and the fear, that's what you're after."

"As I earlier explained, our own dream-states are morally pure. Some might say they are tediously dull. The chance to walk in the bloody field of someone else's excitement, depravity, and terror is truly a feast worth devouring."

"You're going to extract my memories, upload them to some server, and access them whenever you like. I should sue you for copyright theft."

"Access is only allowed during REM sleep, but you are wrong about the extraction and uploading. Storing a copy of your memories on a third-party device might seem an ideal solution, especially for you. However, despite our privilege and partial autonomy, the AI has sovereign status and we must live within its rules and regulations. For us to access your memories, your brain must act as the server from which we draw our pleasures."

The thought of the Dreamers dipping in and out of his brain was a frightening prospect. Adam tried to remain composed, coughing to clear his throat, before asking, "For how long? How long will I be here?"

"You should see it as a permanent position rather than a short term contract. Even after the initial flurry of sucking, there will still be niche demand for your experiences. To be honest, I haven't seen this much interest since we procured Giacomo Casanova a few years ago, and I'm sure he's still sucked now and then."

"So, the whole damn city's going to tune in tonight for a grand sucking, eh?"

Interrupting the conversation, Doctor Kaminski pushed the trolley next to Adam, drew up a seat, and explained, "There are technological and physical limits to how many can suck you in a single session. The Captain stipulated that in your case we use only non-invasive methods. Hardwiring directly into the brain would allow over a million Dreamers to suck at once but the wireless exo-scalp you are wearing limits the number to around 200 thousand."

"Most people are randomly assigned a sucking slot," added Boudicca, "but committee members get priority access. Therefore, I will be sucking you tonight."

"As will I," Mr Mahmoud excitedly remarked from the other side of the room. "I was most fortunate to be chosen for the premiere sucking."

With obvious disappointment, Mr Lacelle shook his head, and complained, "Just my luck, I have to wait eight weeks before I get to suck you."

"What about you?" Adam asked Doctor Kaminski.

"Never liked the idea of sucking another person's memories, even if they did give their consent. It just seems wrong to me. Ironic when you consider that I'm the only person in Soñador fully qualified to perform this procedure."

Doctor Kaminski leaned forward and checked that the restraints were securely fastened, giving special attention to the head brace.

Recognising a familiar fragrance, and desperate to delay the inevitable 'procedure', Adam asked, "You're wearing Bois Du Portugal, right?"

"Given your size, your olfactory system appears to function extremely well," Doctor Kaminski replied, now distracted from what he was doing.

"They say it's the smell of a real man, said Adam."

"Either you're a lover of fine fragrances, Mr Eden, or you are flirting with me."

"No, no, I ….Hey, what are you doing?"

Resuming his work, Doctor Kaminski tightened a belt-like apparatus around Adam's head. At the front, a rubber eye-patch with a thin horizontal slit and a sturdy steel frame hugged against his right eye.

"No need to worry, Mr Eden," said Doctor Kaminski. "This is a standard ophthalmic speculum head strap. The rubber patch moulds to your upper and lower eyelids of your right eye, like so, and with the tiniest turn of the dial on the side … voila."

Adam gulped as his eyelids were pulled wide open, exposing the round of his eyeball. The attendant sprayed a fine mist over the eye, and then stood away. Doctor Kaminski flicked a magnifying lens in front of his eye, making a brief inspection:

"No problems there," he said, raising a wide spatula type scoop. "The anaesthetic should be working by now, so please hold still whilst I slip your eye out of its socket."

Stunned into terrified silence, Adam froze with fear. Suddenly remembering to breathe, he inhaled and exhaled steadily, feeling the smooth lip of the instrument push under his eyeball. Doctor Kaminski expertly added just the right amount of pressure and the slippery globe fell free of its socket.

With the eyeball resting on the top of Adam's cheek by the stalk of the optic nerve, the doctor produced a small black contact lens and placed it carefully over the cornea.

"The blackout lens is essential to block out any outside optical stimuli which might otherwise interfere with the transfer. When the time comes, I shall use an eye-patch for the other eye."

Adam watched through his left eye as the attendant held open the first black box. Doctor Kaminski reached over to the trolley and took a thin steel tool with a smooth crimping bulb at one end. Using the bulb end of the tool, he scooped up a tiny green gel ball from the box and held it up so Adam could see.

"This green substance is a retinal wrap," he explained. "It contains the first tranche of memories. In a moment, with this instrument, I am going to place the wrap around the dura of the optic nerve."

Doctor Kaminski applied the gel to the eye-stalk without incident, and then deftly pushed the eyeball back into the socket. Next, he fitted an eye-patch over Adam's other eye, completely blocking his vision. The gel began to effervesce, little prickles sparking behind Adam's eye, travelling to his forehead like an ice-cream brain freeze. The tingling became more intense and Adam groaned, clenching his teeth. The doctor's voice droned from the darkness.

"The tingling you can feel is the wrap releasing a stream of nano-targeters directly into your optic pathways. Each targeter carries a small fragment of memory, and is tagged for tracking and guiding. The exo-scalp you are wearing is wirelessly linked to the AI, which will control the memory flow into your short-term memory." Doctor Kaminski quietly chuckled. "After all, we don't want them all arriving at once do we?"

With frightening speed, the tingling peaked into a bright flash followed by a stream of gruesome imagery. A scalding fragment of pain was the first taste of the Hell to come, as Kaylee unleashed a searing jet of boiling water on Adam's struggling body. The memory distorted and morphed into a scene atop the warehouse roof in the psychoviro. With kinetic brutality, Rampage severed Adam's arm and simultaneously sliced open his stomach. The psycho dragged Adam to the edge of the roof, leaving a bloody intestinal smear in his wake, before throwing him to the paving slabs below.

As one nightmare vanished, another took its place—a reverse chronological clip show of Adam's many deaths. The experience was so shocking, the content so extreme, that Adam was not aware that he was screaming in terror, begging for the horror show to end.

"Yes, screaming is good. Keep it up," Doctor Kaminski calmly advised. "Your reactions will help the memories transfer smoothly into your long-term memory."

After many more minutes of agony, the last terrible scene flashed across his short-term memory—a fatal sword thrust to the heart delivered by Stardust, the creepiest of the glam psychos. Adam's screams died down, replaced by a breathless whining, giving way to tears. He wanted to curl up in some dark corner as the terrible images played over and over in his mind.

Doctor Kaminski removed the eye-patch and held up the wide lipped spatula.

"Your tears are most welcome, Mr Eden. A touch of lacrimation will help the eyeball slip in and out more easily. Only eight more boxes and the hard part's over."

Box after box and eye-slip after eye-slip, the once censored scenes forced their way into Adam's memory. A fragmentary medley of stomach churning mutilation and death insistently marched across his mind, ending with perhaps the worst memory of all.

It was his final first-life moment in Portsmouth, falling off the harbour wall, splashing headfirst into the cold dark water below. He had always thought he had hit his head, dying instantly. This was only a half-truth, as the blow only knocked him out for a few seconds. Awakening in the murky depths, the salt water filling his lungs, Adam mouthed a silent scream as he drowned.

There were no more boxes. Adam sobbed quietly, unable to block out the new memories, which harassed him like persistent cold-callers relentlessly banging on the door.

After removing Adam's eye-patch, Doctor Kaminski gently slid the black contact lens to the lower part of the right eye, and with a gentle pinch removed it. The attendant spayed both eyes with the soothing mist, whilst the doctor stuck a small plastic patch around Adam's wrist.

"Now comes the relaxing part, said Doctor Kaminski. "The wrist patch is releasing fast-acting drugs that will send you into a deep sleep with a drastically shortened REM phase. This is vital for consolidation of the memories into long-term storage, since deep sleep encourages their hippocampal-neocortical transfer."

Adam yawned as the drugs began to take effect, glad that he could close his eyes. Doctor Kaminski continued, saying, "If the procedure has been successful, your memories should embed themselves contextually into their original chronological locations."

With no sense of how long he had slept—hours, minutes, maybe only seconds—a sharp vapour brought Adam quickly to his senses. Panting like an exhausted dog, heart racing, he sat immobile as Doctor Kaminski shone a penlight in his eyes.

"No problems that I can see," he said, tucking the instrument back into his breast pocket. "I gave you six hours. Four hours is usually enough but you seem to have a low quality brain so you needed more time to cram those memories into place. One strange irregularity was that I had to give you more drugs to keep you fast asleep during the final stage—which used to be known as stage four. Experiments have shown that low levels of stage 4 sleep are often found in schizophrenics. Not that it matters, since you are now ready for archiving."

Adam tried to speak, but choked instead, feeling an obstruction in his mouth. Despite his sore eyes, he focused on a brushed steel cabinet on the far side of the room in which he could see his blurry reflection. The sight was worrying. He was sitting in what looked like a large black pepper-pot. The perforated domed hinged lid was open allowing Adam to see his head and shoulders. Obscuring the bottom half of his face, a translucent milky white facemask with rubbery tentacle-like tubes descended from his nose and mouth. His head had been shaved, the white skin visible beneath a transparent helmet with a halo of smooth metal studs—at last a glimpse of the wireless exo-scalp.

Doctor Kaminski left his chair and went to close the lid. Adam shook with fear, his usual stubborn resilience shattered by the horrific memory insertions. Unable to speak, with pleading eyes he vainly begged for mercy. Before closing the lid, the doctor placed a comforting hand on Adam's shoulder.

"You're scared," he said. "Don't be. I cannot give you any sedatives, because the process requires that you remain lucid. But, once we get you archived and connect your mind to the grid, the AI will take over. You will feel a few seconds of discomfort, and then I promise all your fears will disappear."

The words did nothing to ease Adam's mental anguish. Beads of sweat formed on his forehead as the sturdy metal lid clanged shut, followed by a pronounced click as the doctor activated the locking mechanism. Plunged into darkness, save for thin spikes of light from the perforations above his head, Adam perceived the casket being moved across the room. Sudden shuddering and piston-like sounds preceded the familiar hiss of a sliding door. Now the light was gone, and Adam stared into pitch black.

A sinking feeling in his stomach, accompanied by a soft whooshing sound, informed Adam that he was descending rapidly—perhaps in an elevator. The falling sensation only lasted a few seconds, ending in a sudden jolt. Lurching horizontally the casket changed direction. Adam concentrated his mind, trying to determine what was happening outside his little prison. The subtle swaying sensation and a soft bounce at regular intervals, hinted at a conveyor belt with uniformly spaced rollers, but he could not be sure.

After a sudden rotation, a smooth backwards motion, and a metallic clamping sound, the journey ended. In the silent dark, Adam contemplated his new reality. In his first-life, he had secretly renovated a hidden Victorian toilet that lay behind a wall panel in his grotty bedsit. He fondly remembered the tiny space, which he endearingly called 'The Crapper'. It served as a haven from the squalor and misery of the world outside, and he relished its confining ....

Like a rubber plunger pulling inside his head, a nauseating sucking feeling suddenly overwhelmed Adam's brain. He breathed heavily into the tubes, and clenched his stomach as the mental pumping sent shockwaves through his body. Losing control of his mind, Adam struggled to complete his last thought:

"... It was ... a haven from the miserable world outside, and I relished its confining ...."

REMEMBER TO STIR

Lifting the embroidered tea cosy from the teapot, Mary Down poured herself another cup of steaming hot Assam tea. As always, she added only a dash of cream and two sugar cubes. Stirring the tea with a thin silver teaspoon, she noticed her husband reaching for the sugar.

With his chin resting on one hand, John Down plopped another cube into his tea, but forgot to stir. It was the seventh cube of sugar, and the tea was overflowing into the saucer. Picking up his newspaper, 'The Times'—an edition from the 1880's—he quietly slumped away from the table, leaving his tea, and sat in an armchair by the fire.

Mary leaned across the table and felt her husband's cup –it was stone cold. Normally, when John was in this mood, she would simply clear the table and relax on the chaise longue with a good book, but now she believed it was time to intervene. She sat herself down in the armchair on the other side of the fireplace, and coughed politely to gain her husband's attention. Apart from a low grumble from behind the pages of the broadsheet, there was no reply.

Considering her options—ranging from another polite cough to violently ripping away the newspaper—Mary settled on words as the correct approach.

"My dear, I do believe you are reading the exact same newspaper as yesterday."

There was still no response.

"I think you will find that General Gordon still dies in Khartoum, no matter how many times you read it. John, are you listening to me?"

Detecting a tremble in her husband's hands, Mary left her chair and gently tugged the newspaper. John released his flimsy shield without protest, and promptly buried his face in his hands. Mary sat back down and spoke firmly but with sympathy.

"You are thinking about him again, aren't you? You are thinking about Mr Eden."

"Yes," mumbled John.

"Then stop acting like a scolded child, and do something about it. I have kept my silence for far too long regarding this subject, but it is time I had my say."

John lowered his hands, and looked at his wife in astonishment. She continued, saying, "Seeing a man of your kindness and integrity brought down so low breaks my heart, John. We both know the Captain should never have assigned you the task of delivering Mr Eden to the Dreamers. Cruelty was never a part of your nature."

"He told me I was the perfect man for the job. I have never known him to be wrong."

"Well, it is high time you put things right. You have intimated to me on numerous occasions that you have contacts in Soñador. Is that so?"

"It is true that through the Captain's dealings with the Committee I have made a few acquaintances, a couple of which I might dare to call friends."

"Is there anyone who might share your concerns and be willing to right the situation?"

John reclined in the chair and crossed his hands over his chest. With measured caution, he speculated that there might be one such person he could trust.

Mary came over and held her husband's hand.

"You said yourself that the Captain's bargain was honoured the moment the Dreamers took charge of Mr Eden. His continued presence in the city is solely their responsibility, and they have no jurisdiction beyond Soñador's walls. With no legal impediment, I see no reason for you to dally any longer."

John kissed his wife's hand.

"I only did it for you, Mary. I only did it so we could be together again."

"Well, fix this and let us be together again," Mary enthused. "The distance between us has grown with your guilt and despair. I want you back, John."

Without regard for the crease in his trousers, John rose from his chair. Like a man reborn, he held his head high and proclaimed, "Until this rotten affair, John Langdon Down never shirked from doing what is right and proper. Mary, the days of self-pity and inaction are over. Because of me, a man resides in purgatory. It is time I corrected this gross injustice!"

Giving John's hand a firm squeeze, Mary headed for the kitchen, humming a popular sea shanty, and prepared another pot of tea.

OUT OF THE BOX

At all times, the Soñador grid maintained a constant pressure, pulling relentlessly on Adam's mind. As a pump primed for action, the gruesome memories were peaked to provide pleasure on demand for the Dreamers. Adam was completely locked out of his own mind, his existence a void without thought or sensation—a living death borne of uncaring hedonism.

There were brief moments, unknown slivers of time, when Adam emerged from the emptiness. With a determination forged from routine, he always attempted to finish his last thought, before submerging once more:

"… It was … a haven from the miserable world outside, and I relished its confining …."

A thought forever commenced but never completed was the extent of Adam's conscious life, until a loud clicking noise broke the silence. He regained a degree of awareness as the lid of the casket was heaved open, and a harsh beam of light shone in his face. Temporarily blinded, Adam blinked his eyes as someone roughly manhandled his head.

The exo-scalp, the interface between Adam and the grid, was peeled off, and the awful pressure immediately ceased. Adam had forgotten about the tube in his mouth, and choked as he tried to talk. The beam of light twisted around, highlighting a broad face with narrow eyes. It was Doctor Kaminski. Taking a grip on the facemask connected to the tubes, the doctor advised Adam to take a deep breath then blow hard at the count of three.

As Adam blew, Doctor Kaminski pulled off the mask, the tubes sliding easily from his throat and nasal cavities followed by a sticky rush of saliva and mucus. Adam smacked his lips together, rolled his tongue around the inside of his mouth, and took a few practise gulps. There was no pain, only an indistinct oiliness, so Adam again tried to speak.

"Please tell me it's over," he said. "Please tell me you're not going to put me back in after some tests or something."

The Doctor pulled open the front of the casket. His hands were shaking as he loosened the many restraints.

"Time is of the essence, Mr Eden. Within the hour, you will be either back in the Viroverse or being prepared for reinsertion. I have a car waiting outside."

"What about my legs?" Adam asked, as the doctor undid the straps. "Won't they be atrophied from sitting in here all day?"

Doctor Kaminski, understated in a mid-grey suit with no tie, helped Adam to his feet and urged him to try walking. He told him to expect only minor stiffness since the sleep-time healing nano-swarms took care of Adam, just like any other resident of Soñador. A few cautious steps soon shook the concrete out of Adam's legs, and he was ready to leave.

The archive was a huge warehouse room, with row upon row of caskets stacked twenty high to the ceiling. A skeletal gloss-black conveyer system snaked around the narrow corridors between the 'pepper pot' towers, with industrial chain lifts to hoist the caskets into place. As they made their way through the archive, Adam tried not to think about the other poor souls seated in their tiny prisons. The Dreamers, not content with their own immortality, had stolen eternity from others. They had to be stopped, but now was not the time to start a crusade.

They turned a corner, and headed for an open doorway, the light streaming in from a loading bay beyond. Nearing the doorway, Adam could see that a motionless body, dressed in overalls, was stopping the door from closing. Doctor Kaminski stepped over the blood-stained corpse.

"Was this necessary?" asked Adam, leaping across. "Won't he resurrect in three hours, and sound the alarm?"

"Unfortunately there was no other way. I don't have access to the archive so I waited until this poor fellow opened the door, and then …. Well, I did what I had to."

Doctor Kaminski pointed to a pile of colourful silk clothes on the floor.

"Quickly, put those on over what you're already wearing."

Adam jumped into the new outfit: a puffy red and gold harlequin one-piece, blue frizzy wig, and a full-face renaissance style mask with a long droopy nose. The doctor nodded humourlessly.

"That's fine, Mr Eden. We don't want you drawing any undue attention."

"No, we certainly wouldn't want me drawing any attention," said Adam sarcastically, pulling on the wig.

The doctor's car, a two-seater Lamborghini Sesto Elemento—dark grey carbon fibre, sleek and sinister—was parked outside.

"You are mistaken about the three hour resurrection," said Doctor Kaminski, as they ran down the ramp by the side of the loading bay. "When the AI detects a death, the victim can resurrect in approximately an hour and a half. If that man returns before you are safely out of the city, then this was all for nothing."

About to get in the car, Adam suddenly fell to the ground, clutching his head. Writhing in agony, a stream of death memories flashed across his mind. Copacabana emerged for the first time since the foiled escape from the Compro building, and sought to use the same deep meditative techniques that blocked out the pain of Kaylee's scalding wrath.

"No! There … is no time for that! Just stay out of this!" Adam cried out loud, and his alter ego reluctantly obeyed.

In laboured stages, huffing like a woman in labour, Adam picked himself up, and climbed into the car. He relaxed in the cocooning red sports seat, and the terrible imagery subsided. Doctor Kaminski sat in the driver's seat—a misnomer since all Soñador vehicles were self-driving—and told the car to take them to the preprogramed destination. With a soft fuel-cell hum, the Lamborghini's engine engaged, and the car accelerated along the archive service road.

Before they slipped into the heavy traffic flow of the main highway, the doctor asked, "Were you shouting at me back there?"

Avoiding a long discussion about Copacabana and the limitations of a cut-price brain, Adam simply replied that he was shouting at himself and that it was an unfortunate family trait.

Hidden behind tinted glass, they cruised along the six-lane urban artery. Soaring skyscrapers either side, and a cornucopia of eccentric vehicles, provided constant fascination. The road, cutting through the heart of the city, stretched off to the horizon, and Adam noticed something missing in the clear skies above.

"I see the String o' Pearls Skyway is on strike."

"String o' Pearls Skyway?" said Doctor Kaminski, lounging comfortably in his seat. "Oh yes, that was quickly decommissioned. Far too slow and boring. We have the Mondrian raft system now. It's beautiful, and much faster, but the schedule is very restricted."

Adam could not contain a smile as a horseless, spoke-wheeled Roman chariot drew alongside. The grand oversized vehicle, gleaming white with silver ornamentation, somehow balanced on its two wheels. The five rowdy occupants, sitting on a marble bench, sang bawdy songs and spilt red wine on their togas.

"It's amazing how people from their time can adapt to a world like this," said Adam. "The technology must seem like magic."

"If I were a gambling man, I would bet my life that those loud-mouthed reprobates are not ancient Romans. They're most probably a bunch of 23rd century Caligula wannabes."

Adam laughed, remembering the white stretch limousines from his own time. Though you might stare in wonder, you knew there was no celebrity or billionaire behind the dark windows: probably a pimply young thing hoping to make a grand entrance at their 21st birthday party, or a group of drunken students heading for a concert or the Prom. It seemed that the more society exhorted people 'to be themselves', the more readily people assumed the guises of others—and Soñador flaunted this with gusto.

"No curly toed boots," noted Adam, looking at the pedestrians as they passed.

"A passing fad. These silly crazes come and go. I never …." A flashing orange light on the dashboard suddenly distracted the doctor. "Quick, act like a puppet and don't move," he ordered. "Talking of wannabes, there's the worst one I know up ahead, and he wants to talk."

Given the appropriate order, the Lamborghini pulled over to the side of the road, next to a man in a starchy white General's uniform. Weighed down with medals, golden braid, and wearing an oversized peak cap, the man looked like a cartoonish dictator. Adam went limp, taking shallow breaths, as the window slid down. A pompous face, handlebar moustache, peered into the car. He twitched a monocle and bellowed loudly, as if the doctor was hard of hearing.

"Mikhail Kaminski! Just the man I wanted to see!"

"What can I do for you, Leo?" asked Mikhail.

"Have you heard anything about the New Year's sucking? There are rumours circulating that there's a nice juicy surprise in store! I haven't heard a word from any of the other committee members, but if anyone knows anything about it, it's you!"

Shaking his head, Mikhail denied any knowledge of the New Year sucking surprise. Leo tweaked the end of his moustache, squinting his eyes as if trying to spot a lie.

"I was on my way to a puppet party," said Mikhail, wiping sweat from his brow. "I'm in a bit of a rush really. I don't want them to start without me."

Leo's eyes widened; the monocle fell out and dangled on its silver chain.

"Mikhail Kaminski, a puppeteer?" he said, clearly surprised. "I see you have your own puppet. Mind if I tag along? It might be a bit early in the day, but there is nothing like a spot of puppetry to clear the tubes and enliven the spirit. Your little chap can sit on my lap."

"Err ... sure. They won't mind another puppeteer. You know how flexible they are in the Morello district."

At the very mention of the district's name, Leo took a step back, and twitched his eye as he popped the monocle back into place. He stood stiffly upright, clicked the heels of his boots together, and gave a short pretentious bow.

"Some other time perhaps! I have just remembered that I have an important committee meeting to attend! I will bid you good day, sir!"

The window slid back up, and the car pulled away from the kerb, merging smoothly back into the traffic. Adam sat up, relieved to be on the road again, and twanged the nose of the facemask.

"I wouldn't do that if I were you," advised Mikhail.

"Don't worry, I haven't got some nose fetish, said Adam. He squeezed the droopy snout and it suddenly sprung to life, stretching and stiffening until erect. The gross appendage throbbed, and glistened with a mint-scented lubricant. Adam was horrified, letting go of the nasal phallus, and rubbed his oily hand on the seat.

"That's gross! He cried. "What the Hell goes on at these puppet parties?"

"They're sex parties ... with puppets," said Mikhail. "Two people operate each puppet, the party organiser provides the accessories, and they perform sexual acts on the other guests using the .... Mr Eden, do you really want to know about this? It's just a disguise so that no one recognises you. I have not, and will never, participate in a puppet party. It is a disgusting practise."

Adam took off the mask and placed it on the floor.

Mikhail explained, "Not everyone in Soñador is depraved, Mr Eden. I believe that if it wasn't for the unfettered egos of a small minority, then people might readily abandon the sucking, not to mention some of the other questionable activities that go on here. We have so much freedom, so much of everything, that we have well and truly crossed the line. Each year, the wickedness grows with the feeding."

"Then you are striking a blow for the silent moral majority," Adam concluded. "Is that why you're helping me escape?"

Mikhail frowned, unable to stifle a guilty look.

"I am far too complicit to be included in that category. No, Mr Eden, I am doing this because a man I greatly respect asked me to."

"Is it someone I know?"

"It is the very man who brought you here," said Mikhail, a touch of pride stirring in his voice. "John Langdon Down. He was a cornerstone in my decision to choose a career in psychiatry and later neuroscience. I know he is not one of the big names, but he is a man of true integrity, who devoted himself to the then neglected and despised study of the mentally challenged. He could have chosen position, money, and prestige, but the work came first. Therefore, when John Down asked me to release you from the archive, it was like a direct order from my conscience. I just couldn't say no."

"But you will be punished for this, won't you? Surely, they have the technology to find out who did it."

"The man I killed recognised me," said Mikhail, "and all journeys are logged. It's only a matter of time."

"What will they do to you?"

"Apart from a few years confined to the central Compro district, I doubt I will suffer any real punishment. Committee members come and go, chosen by the AI on a one-year turnaround, but my skills afford me a permanent position. There is no one even remotely qualified to take my place, so I expect little more than a slap on the wrist."

Again, with searing intensity, the death memories flashed into Adam's mind, and he pushed back into his seat, little legs outstretched, hands clasped tightly against the sides of his head. He controlled his breathing, and the pain began to fade. Adam asked how long he would have to endure these sudden spasms, but Mikhail remained silent.

Entering the Morello district, Adam was surprised to find it did not look any less impressive than any other part of the city. Leo's unmistakably negative reaction when Mikhail mentioned the district led Adam to imagine a very different scene.

"I thought we were entering some sort of run-down violent ghetto," he admitted, "with street gangs, drunks, and drugs addicts. This is nothing like that. The buildings look great, and the people are well dressed. What's the problem?"

"There is no violence or bad behaviour," said Mikhail. "The problem is that people here have no respect for the authorities or high culture."

"You mean art and stuff?" asked Adam.

"Let me explain," said Mikhail. "To accompany an expertly prepared dish of Tournedos Rossini, I might select a bottle of the finest pinot noir—definitely Burgundy, perhaps an elegant Chambolle-Musigny. The type of person who dwells in Morello would choose 'red', and that is only if they are trying to appear sophisticated. I think you know what I mean."

"Of course I do. Whenever I shared a bucket of the Colonel's fried chicken, I never understood how anyone could choose the thigh. I will admit that it's a meaty piece, but it has this huge oily flap of skin. I would go for the rib, or perhaps the breast. As for the choice of drink, perhaps a cheap pino grigio or a bottle of Herefordshire dry cider. However, I must admit, that when I was on the streets, I would eat any old scraps of anything and wash them down with any old piss I could find."

"You're saying I'm a snob, aren't you?" sniffed Mikhail

"I don't know what I'm saying," admitted Adam, the point forgotten as his stomach grumbled for fried chicken—even a thigh. "Perhaps we're all snobs."

Deep into the Morello district, Mikhail ordered the car to pull over. He told Adam that the viro wall was only a block away, and that they should continue on foot. Though Adam was worried about being seen, Mikhail assured him that his fears were unfounded. One advantage of the Morello district was that the locals never reported anything to the despised authorities.

"Well, then I don't need this stupid outfit anymore," said Adam, pulling off the wig, and ripping open the velcro on the harlequin suit. "If it comes to it, I'd rather not kick arse dressed as a dick-nosed clown puppet."

Adam threw the hated costume onto the car seat, and slammed shut the door. Then, Adam and Mikhail sauntered along the sidewalk –a besuited man and his beach-party midget out for a leisurely stroll. Adam's diminutive appearance and Aloha clothing drew constant glances and stares from other pedestrians, and a few enthusiastic whistles and gestures from those that recognised him.

Taking a moment to enjoy the bustling sidewalk ambiance, Adam became curious about a nearby steel-sided booth—similar in style and size to a high-tech toilet. During the journey from the archive, Adam had seen many of these structures and wondered what they were. Mikhail explained that they were resurrection booths. With express resurrection, people could choose whether to wake up at home in their own bed, or emerge from a preselected resurrection booth. There were hundreds dotted around the city, and they were very convenient for keeping an appointment should death interfere.

"Ha, now I haven't seen any of those since my first life," noted Adam, spotting six black and chrome motorbikes in the distance, speeding between the traffic. Strapped and riveted in tough black leather, the helmeted riders swung their heavy bikes across the lanes, and mounted the sidewalk. Putting on a burst of speed, pedestrians leaping out of their path, the bikes sped two abreast towards Adam and Mikhail.

"What the Hell?" exclaimed Adam.

"They're Compro Guards," said Mikhail, "and the mounted ones always use guns! Now we run!"

Sprinting along the sidewalk, Adam kept pace with his giant liberator, despite having much shorter legs—in fact, he had noticed a marked improvement in his physical abilities since first entering Soñador. Charging around a corner, the two fugitives did not stop or apologise as they pushed aside a young woman in a kimono. Waving a fist in the air, she was probably about to launch into a stream of expletives, when the motorbikes skidded dangerously around her, barely avoiding a grisly collision.

Mikhail pointed far along the street. "See that gap over there, across the road, between the Cathedral and the black tower?"

"Yeah, I see it, just about," huffed Adam, the exertion beginning to take its toll.

"The gap is the entrance to an alley! Probably too narrow for me, but you are small enough to fit through. It leads directly to one of the original portals."

Facing imminent capture, they ran across the six-lanes of traffic without any regard for their personal safety, putting their trust in fate and the automatic braking systems of the vehicles. The cars screeched to a halt, mere inches from impact– an explosive whoosh from inside the vehicles indicating the rapid deployment of protective foam, muffling the occupant's screams. Once on the other side of the road, Mikhail and Adam headed straight for the alley.

"Damn, they've already crossed onto this side," said Mikhail, taking a backward glance. "They're gaining fast!"

Nearing the alley, Adam heard the menacing 'Fap, Fap, Fap, Fap' of an airgun unloading its deadly pellets. He looked back to see Mikhail slumped against a wall, three bloody exit holes across his forehead. Adam wanted to go to his friend's aid, but he knew Mikhail was beyond help. Projecting respect and appreciation, Adam offered the courageous doctor a nod of gratitude, and then hurried off into the dark confining crevice between the colossal buildings.

The passageway grew progressively darker as Adam headed further away from the entrance and the bustling city streets. Some parts of the alley were so narrow that Adam had to shuffle slowly sideways, feet turned outwards, and a cheek lightly scraping against the cold wall.

"Mr Eden, there is no need to run!" cried a distant female voice. "We know this was not your fault! Come back and we can sort this mess out! The Soñadorgaps are perilous places!"

Squeezing through a particularly thin stretch of alley, fearing that the buildings might suddenly slam together like an unstable arctic fissure, Adam seriously considered turning back. The path ahead was a lightless mystery, with no sight of the promised portal, and he cursed himself for not taking the doctor's torch. He breathed more easily as the gap widened, and he slowly edged forward, arms outstretched, feeling his way in the pitch black.

Ten more minutes into the dark journey, Adam reacted quickly to the sound of multiple airguns releasing a volley of pellets, probably aimed blindly into the alley. He threw himself face down on the ground, hands held protectively behind his head, and waited for the attack to end. It only took a matter of seconds before Adam realised that he was well beyond the range of the Compro Guard's weapons—the steel projectiles falling short some fifty feet behind. He allowed himself a smile, got back to his feet, and continued along the path.

Suddenly a light activated, and Adam could see what lay ahead: an elevator, almost identical to the one that transported him down the cliff-face, but on a smaller Viroverse scale. As he neared, the front swung open ready to receive passengers. With no real alternative option, Adam stepped into the elevator and pressed the up button.

Rising quickly, Adam felt a sense of awe as he emerged above the tops of the skyscrapers, and once again looked out over the sprawling city of Soñador. A glint of colour caught his eye, and he gazed up into the sky. The Mondrian rafts skimmed beneath the clouds. Huge single colour panels—white, red, black, and yellow—floated across the sky in crisscrossing paths. Every now and then, they converged, creating a fleeting Mondrian painting effect, before dispersing once more.

The elevator came to a stop by the portal doors. To the side, a panel lit up, flashing red, waiting for an authorised palm. Adam was glad that it was not a membrane portal, since he had no shard. Sweating like an anxious tourist, hoping their credit card would be accepted in a backstreet Italian restaurant, Adam crossed himself and pressed his low-quality 'undesirable' hand on the panel.

BEEN AWAY SO LONG

After spending a few hours relaxing in the reception room, Adam decided it was time to venture into the halls. Obtaining a handheld mirror from the dispensers, he groaned at his reflection. His skin was still a mannequin grey, his eyes googly white balls. He put on a pair of black wraparound sunglasses, filled a backpack with provisions—making sure he had an adequate supply of incontinence sheets—and clipped a machete and combat knife to his belt.

Since leaving Soñador, he felt sluggish and heavy. At first, he put the phenomenon down to fatigue following the relief of escape, but time had so far done nothing to reverse it. In contrast, his mind seemed sharp enough.

Ready to face the halls, incontinence sheet at the ready like a low-rent matador, Adam placed his hand on the palm panel. Nothing happened; the door remained shut. He tried a few more times, but to no avail. Defeated, he sat back on one of the benches and waited.

Another two hours passed before the door to the halls suddenly hissed open. Standing on the other side of the doorway, beaming a wicked sharp-toothed smile, was Kevin the inkman. No longer stuck in the 1980s, he was back to his old self: ring-pull black leather shorts, blonde ponytail, his skin once more a sordid tableau of sexual tattoos.

"Well, g'day, mate!" he laughed, waving a can of lager. "So you finally made it back. You know, you look just as ugly as I remember. I'd have thought those Dreamers would have given you a better bod' for your troubles. Come on out. I've taken care of the snot buggers."

Some way behind Kevin, three jellymen writhed on the floor, stuck fast under sheets. Adam grabbed his backpack, and walked out into the hall.

"I thought John Down would be here," he said.

"Oh, he's on his way. We made a race of it and the better man got here first."

Adam noticed that Kevin was wearing a knife, clipped to a red leather belt.

"Not keeping your blade up your arse, I see. Or is it a spare?"

Kevin clenched his buttocks and winced, as if remembering a painful moment.

"I took a turn too fast and came off my board," he said. "Landed hard on my arse. Shattered my bleeding coccyx and the ruddy switchblade opened up inside me. Made a right mess of my colon. Luckily, my mate Dolph got me back to the Terminal before I bled to death. The belt's a bit chafing, but I'd rather wear it than get arse ripped again."

After clenching and wincing in sympathy, Adam thought it best to change the subject, saying, "You seemed to have lost touch with the 1980s. I don't suppose you learnt your lesson."

"1980's?" said Kevin, somewhat bemused. "Oh yeah, the punishment I had when I last saw you. Well, I've never been one for learning lessons, but I still know her name is Rio, and I know where she dances."

Adam was about to laugh when he noticed Kevin unclipping the knife from his belt.

"Ha mate, you just reminded me that you and I have unfinished business."

Closing in slowly on Adam, Kevin began rhythmically swaying and sliding Capoeira style, swapping his knife from one hand to the other. In no mood for a fight, Adam held out the machete in a defensive stance, and leadenly stepped back towards the reception room door.

"Can we do this some other time?" asked Adam. "I feel like I've been wearing heavy weights since leaving the city."

"That'll be something to do with the square cube law," said Kevin, continuing his preamble to combat. "Soñador has got a slight gravity difference to compensate. Gives me an advantage for a while, till you get used to the change, and that's just the way I like it."

"Stop this nonsense right now," bellowed John Down, drawing up on his mahogany long-board, his outfit the same as Adam remembered from their surfing trip. "I did not secure Mr Eden's freedom so that you could kill him on his first day out."

Still swaying, Kevin held his ground, ready to pounce. John Down strode straight up to Adam and firmly shook his hand.

"Mr Eden, I don't expect forgiveness, but please, please, accept my sincerest apologies."

"I'm just glad to be out of there," said Adam, relieved that he would not have to fight.

"Aw, come on, Downsy," Kevin wailed. "I was just going to give him a few bruises and cut him up a bit. No way was I going to kill him. Anyway, I won the race so I should get some sort of prize. One of the bugger's ears would do it."

Taking Adam completely by surprise, Kimberley surfed up on a mirror chrome short-board. Menacingly dynamic in silver ankle boots and a blue-grey cat suit, she had silver wings emblazoned on either side of her deep cleavage. Coming to a kick-flip stop, she leapt from her short-board, twirling a silver baton. Speed and agility gracefully combined, Kimberley rushed up behind Kevin and held the baton tight across his neck.

"Give John your knife," she commanded, "or I'll pull this so tight you'll pass out in seconds."

Kevin was unmoved, although there was a slight note of nervousness in his voice.

"So, I'll wake up in a reception room. Big deal, sister."

"What's to stop us leaving you in the hall for the jellymen?" mused Kimberley. "Or maybe, I'll just break your neck, and be done with it."

As if to emphasise her intent, Kimberley pulled the stick roughly against his neck.

"Damn, you!" he choked, and quickly handed over the blade.

"Hi, Mr Eden, I am so glad you're free," said Kimberley, leaving Kevin rubbing his sore neck. "They tell me that if it wasn't for you, I might well be dead."

"Well, I …."

She planted a kiss on Adam's cheek, and said, "I owe you my life!"

Overcome with emotion, Kimberley grabbed Adam, and hugged him close, her heaving push-up breasts pressed against his face. He tried not to breathe, staying as immobile as possible—ignoring the scent of effervescent raspberry undercut by sensuous musk and Jacaranda wood—trying not to enjoy the experience like some creepy pervert. After a grossly inappropriate amount of time, Kimberley broke off the embrace. Adam's face was bright red, partly from embarrassment and partly from lack of oxygen. Then he remembered John's promise.

"John, I thought I told you to keep an eye on Kimberley. I know you have to live within the Captain's rules, but it surely can't be right for a child to be flaunting herself like that. And, isn't it dangerous for her to be surfing the halls."

"Oh deary me," said John. "You are obviously unaware of how long you were a guest in Soñador."

Originally, when Doctor Kaminski opened the casket, Adam guessed he had been archived for no more than few days, but a few clues, such as the absence of the 'String o' Pearls Skyway' and curly toed shoes, told him that a few months might have passed.

"Prepare yourself for a shock, Mr Eden, because it is over seventeen years since I delivered you to the Dreamers. Seventeen years of guilt and shame for me, I might add."

The shock did not immediately register, and Adam stared blankly at John Down, as if his ears had refused to hear the news. John put a comforting arm around Adam, and gestured to Kimberley.

"Kimberley is a woman now," he said. "Whilst I too find her choice of clothing a little too revealing for my taste, she is certainly old enough to make her own decisions. Her mental age has caught up with her body. She's one of the Captain's most skilled operatives."

Kimberley was obviously excited to be in the presence of a legend, and spoke excitedly.

"I've heard all about Copacabana. I'm going for a super-hero look, myself." She spun around. "Do you think I need a cape?"

The shock of the seventeen-year imprisonment suddenly hit Adam. He smiled, nodding his head at no one in particular, and then promptly collapsed to the floor in a faint.

Coming to his senses, within a matter of minutes, Adam found himself sat up against the wall with John Down urging him to drink some water. He sipped from the plastic bottle, and the water helped ease his mind.

"Oh, this is great!" Kevin laughed. "Why did I try to fight him when all it took was a few little words? You know, I could almost jizz in my pants. Go on John; tell him about his home viro. Tell him or I will."

John Down grumbled quietly at his colleague's cold-hearted joy. Reluctantly he explained to Adam that his home viro was now in a husk state. The population had risen to 50, triggering a resource crisis.

Never one to miss the chance of rubbing salt into a wound, Kevin swaggered over, unable to contain his delight at Adam's predicament, and said, "They're all husks, mate; dried up screaming husks! I'll bet your Mum and Dad look worse now than the day they died, but that's still better looking than you, you ugly grey turd."

Still shocked that he had spent so long in the casket, Adam said, "This can't be right. Doctor Kaminski said nothing about seventeen years. I'm sure he would have told me."

"I gave him instructions to withhold that particular piece of information, explained John. "You may have gone into a state of panic, or passed out as you did just now, and put your escape in jeopardy."

Adam nodded. With hindsight, he agreed that keeping quiet about the truth was a wise move. Now that so many years had passed, there was another pressing matter. With trepidation, he asked about Rhapsody. Was there more bad news?

"She is still a husk, but has come to no harm," said John. "Kevin, myself, and a few other operatives, lined up heavy barrels along the harbour walls to stop any more husks falling in and drowning. None have been lost since. Now, I promised the Captain, we would get you to the Terminal as soon as possible, so we should be leaving. We must reach the Valens viro before midnight. There are very few fully functioning viros left in this sector. Most are in a husk state."

John Down noticed the obvious alarm in Adam's expression at the mention of the Terminal.

"That is if you are agreeable, Mr Eden. As always, the choice is yours. We will leave you here if you so wish, but as I said, there are very few places where you can find rest and sustenance."

Adam feared the Captain's trickery, but he also believed that the android held the key to Rhapsody's liberation from her husk state. Copacabana appeared, still resolutely fixated on seeing the outside world, and urged Adam to agree unconditionally. Adam wanted solid assurances from John Down that this would not end in another long stay in the Soñador archive.

John Down regrettably admitted he could give no such assurances, but added that he still trusted the Captain even if his motives were unclear. Adam realised that it came down to a case of the famous saying, 'fool me once shame on you, fool me twice shame on me'. Never one to turn down the opportunity of more shame in his life, Adam agreed to travel to the Terminal.

As before, Adam rode pillion on the long-board, and gripped the straps tightly. Travelling in convoy, on a single white line, Kevin in front and Kimberley to the rear, they set off for a sleep-time stop-off at the Valens viro. Before John broke into his usual surf song repertoire, Adam commented on the comforting familiarity of the Victorian's outfit.

"A top hat, smart suit, and a silver topped cane. It's good to know that some things don't change."

"One must not judge by outward appearances," said John, glancing behind. "There is always change."

"I understand," said Adam, respectful of John Down's psychiatric eminence. "You mean mentally. Our attitudes change subtly with every experience. I agree. It makes me wonder how the human race, or rather the human mind, will cope with immortality. I mean, are these miniscule brains up to the challenge?"

"That is very interesting, Mr Eden, but I was actually referring to my underpants. Kevin suggested I switch to boxer shorts, and I must say that the experience is most liberating. It is such a relief to surf without the threat of sweaty genitalia."

"I ... see," said Adam, wishing he had kept his mouth shut. "So, what does Mary think, now you're swinging free?"

John gave a disgruntled sniff, stared forward, and muttered, "That is very inappropriate, Mr Eden. Very inappropriate indeed."

BACK IN THE TERMINAL

For a few minutes, the atmosphere was tense in the departure lounge. The ever-charming Captain Andrews was there to greet them, smiling and genial, as if nothing untoward had happened. Adam seethed, wishing he could rip the android's handsome head from its body, whilst John Down remained pensively silent, his top hat held in both hands, as if waiting for punishment.

With a casual flutter of fingers, Kimberley simply said 'Hi' to the Captain and headed off to the mini mall, sharing an electric cart with Liana. Kimberley's 'superhero' costume was the same shade of blue as the hostess's, and the silver wings a stylised take on the staffs' emblem. At that moment, Adam appreciated that Kimberley was a true daughter of the Terminal—the androids and the constant stream of visitors, her veritable foster parents and mentors.

Captain Andrews patted John Down on the back and told him to stop worrying. He reminded him that Adam became Soñador's responsibility upon delivery, and that officially the Terminal was neither for nor against the escape plan. The relief on the brave Victorian's face was palpable, and after a round of hearty handshakes, he hurried back to the halls.

With a beaming smile, his teeth sparkling as impossibly as ever, Captain Andrews clapped his hands together.

"So Adam, do you still want to see the outside? We can spend some quality time on the walkway. As before, I have three choices for you."

"And send me back to Soñador? Or, do you have some other nasty surprise up your sleeve?"

"Nothing up my sleeves today," said the Captain, emphasising the short sleeves of his shirt. "It's casual Friday."

"I haven't come here to listen to your jokes," said Adam.

Captain Andrews offered to drive Adam to the walkway in an electric cart parked close by. He emphasised that there was no pressure, and that Adam could change his mind at any moment. Adam knew that this was an empty gesture, since Copacabana could storm in at any moment and force the issue. Despite this, Adam accepted the offer. Not only did he want to know why the Captain had tricked him, but also hoped that the wily android could help Rhapsody. Despite it not being his top priority, it was also true that Adam was interested in seeing what lay outside the Viroverse.

After the Captain finished his 'I am your pilot for this trip' routine, they set off along the wide viewing concourse.

"You said that Soñador was the next step to the outside," said Adam, deciding to get straight to the point. "Why did you lie?"

Captain Andrews informally tipped his cap, and said, "I didn't lie. Both you and your other personality expressed a desire to see the outside. Now it is possible, my friend."

"How is it possible? You just want me back on the walkway so you can dupe me again. Is this some trick to get me back in that casket?"

"You still don't quite understand how I operate, do you? Everything has a price. Everything must be balanced. Before you went to Soñador, you had no credit with me. The merest glimpse of the outside world commands a price that would require hundreds of painful visits to the Day Spa. The Soñador archive is a breeze by comparison."

The conversation was interrupted as the cart crossed the crowded main atrium, the lively heart of the Terminal. People shouted friendly greetings to the Captain, but stared curiously at his Aloha shirted passenger. After so many years away from the limelight, instant recognition was no longer guaranteed, even for the legendary Copacabana. Leaving the bustling atrium, the cart drove along a quieter passageway, and Adam resumed the conversation.

"Are you saying those seventeen years are some sort of payment?"

"See it as pre-paid credit," explained the Captain. "This time, the three choices will include an option to go outside."

"But, you took seventeen years from me! Seventeen years!"

"Hmm, seventeen years out of eternity. I may not be human, but I think you got a pretty sweet deal."

"What if John Down had left me there? From what I gather, it was only because of him that I escaped."

"But, he didn't leave you there, did he? That's why I chose him for the job, rather than someone like Kevin. It was a statistical certainty that Mr Down would prove true to his profile and try to make amends. For him, integrity is integral. Of course, I knew his loyalty to me was an obstacle to your release, so I regularly mentioned you in our conversations, and lamented your sad plight. As you already know, I am not permitted to directly intervene, but a gentle nudge now and then is acceptable. I was expecting Mr Down to crack in about five years rather than seventeen, so you have credit to spare."

"If I chose to visit the outside, can I also save Rhapsody? Do I have enough credit for that?"

"In theory, you have ample credit."

"And in practice?"

"You might not need it." The Captain brought the cart to a halt. "Shall we step onto to the walkway? If you wish to make a choice, that is."

This time there were no theme park surprises—planes roaring overhead or hypnotically repetitive advertisements. The walkway just smoothly moved along with few points of reference.

"What was the deal you made?" asked Adam. "What did you get for sending me to the archive?"

"The bargain I made with the Dreamers? Oh, that happened a few months before you left your viro. You were in great demand. As your fame spread around the Viroverse, the Dreamers heard about your brutal exploits, and were keen to experience them for themselves. In return for your safe delivery, should the opportunity ever arise, I had three demands."

"I know about the wireless exo-scalp. They normally hardwire people into the archive, but you insisted on wireless."

"Well, in addition to using non-invasive measures, I also stipulated that your consent would be required before any action on my part, and that the

Dreamers put all their building projects on hold for two months. I could have held out for a three-month moratorium, but I wanted a quick agreement."

"If I was hardwired, would Doctor Kaminski still have been able to release me?"

Neither end of the walkway was now visible, both stretching out to the vanishing point.

"An almost impossible task," said the Captain. "Removing you from a hardwired casket would have taken a team of skilled surgeons about four hours. After that, you would have needed constant medical supervision and painkilling drugs until the next healing sleep phase. Your rescue would have been almost impossible."

"So you told them to use the wireless method so that I could escape."

"Given the choice, I simply decided to go with the wireless option. Your escape relied on the personalities and motivations of others. Although, the fact I chose wireless was a lucky break for you."

As before, without warning, the Captain halted the walkway and gave Adam three choices. If Adam had not been listening carefully, he may have thought that he was being offered the exact same options as seventeen years ago. However, there was one important difference. Option two was no longer the 'next step' to the outside, but instead a chance to actually go outside.

Making sure that option two was chosen, Copacabana took control. This time, however, he did not cast Adam into the shadows, but kept him close, lucid, able to help with the decision. Adam, realised that Copacabana was concerned that this could be another trick, and so supplied a number of probing questions, such as 'will I be able to return to the Viroverse after visiting the outside', and 'will visiting the outside harm me in any way?'

Vague and elusive as ever, Captain Andrews only answered half of the questions, but it was enough to satisfy Adam and Copacabana that the option was genuine. With a handshake to seal the deal, option two was chosen.

Copacabana relinquished control to Adam, whispering a rare 'thank you'. Suddenly, for the first time since leaving Soñador, the painful memories once again flashed through Adam's mind. He held onto the rail for support, and cried out in agony. Captain Andrews, obviously fully aware of Adam's predicament, reminded him to control his breathing. A few deep steady breaths and the dreadful imagery subsided.

"Ah, the memories," said the Captain. "They keep surfacing don't they? There is a way to remove them, you know. I have the means."

"Not the Day Spa," said Adam, still shaking from the ordeal. "Anything but the Day Spa."

"Anything?" said the Captain. "In that case I'll see you tomorrow."

Unprepared for the Captain's strength, speed and precision, Adam had no time to reply before dropping to the floor, his neck cleanly twisted and broken.

MOUNTAIN FOLK

Effortlessly shrugging off the pain of the dark place, Adam sat up in bed. The wake up cubicle was the most spartan that he had yet encountered. White, modular, high density plastic, the small space could have been a windowless economy cabin on a cross-channel ferry.

Adam could not remember how he died or who killed him, but he already knew the memory inserts were gone. No matter how hard he tried to remember any of his deaths, the final moments were simply not there.

Dressed in his usual Aloha clothes, Adam ate a few slices of hot buttered toast washed down with a strong cup of tea. Knowing that daytime food had no nutritional value, and that all real feeding took place at night, did nothing to quell the urge to fill the yawning gap in his belly. Sometimes the stomach simply wanted bulk.

Stepping outside brought a biting icy wind and Adam promptly went back inside to fetch a parka coat, thermal gloves, and thick socks from the dispenser. Suitably protected from the elements, Adam once again stepped outside.

The single storey block of wake-up cubicles, set high up into the side of an ice-capped mountain, was starkly utilitarian, with grey concrete walls and heavy steel doors. The mountain, part of a mighty range, had a gritted roadway of dangerously varying width, winding precipitously down to a green valley hundreds of feet below.

Deep in the valley, Adam could see a stone structure. He quickly got a pair of binoculars from the dispenser and took a closer look. It was a classical façade set against a grassy ridge, with white marble portico, large Doric columns, elaborate carvings and statuary. Wide marble steps led up to huge wooden double doors: lacquered black, rectangular, and braced diagonally with iron. The doors obviously led into the mountain. Detracting from the ancient influence, there was a large tarmacked car park outside, and a four lane highway.

Adam thought that this might finally be the outside. He knelt down and rubbed a patch of ice with his gloved hand. The ice slightly melted, the water quickly freezing again on the glove. Such scale and realism was rare in the Viroverse—even the air had a crisp wintery taste. Fortunately, the chill wind was not strong enough to blow Adam off the road.

Pulling off a glove, Adam inspected his hand. If this was truly the outside, then there was probably no retinal projection, and thus he should be grey and plastic-like. As in the wake up cubicle, Adam's skin was pale pink. Slipping the glove back on, he still held out hope that this was the outside. Perhaps a trip to the outside required a better quality body. For all he knew, he could be a full size human again.

"It's impressive, but it's not the outside!" yelled Captain Andrews over the howling wind.

Adam turned and looked up. The Captain was crouched on the flat roof of the building, still wearing a short sleeve shirt, peak cap and creased black trousers.

"Pay no attention to my inappropriate clothing! I'm an android remember! I don't feel the cold! Sorry I had to kill you yesterday, but it was really the only way if you wanted those memories permanently removed."

"Apology accepted!" Adam replied, disturbed that robots were allowed to kill humans. "So, where are we, and why are you up there?"

The Captain directed Adam to some steps at the far end of the block, leading onto the roof. A footpath led up from the roof to the mountaintop some twenty yards above. Adam was wary at first. The path looked too narrow and unsafe. Without being asked, Captain Andrews took Adam by the hand and led him quickly to the icy peak.

"Stay low up here," said the Captain. It's unlikely anyone will notice, but we don't want to risk being seen."

Crouching and crawling, they carefully clambered forward, and Adam peered over the peak. The view was instantly recognisable, but still a surprise.

"Soñador!"

A simple concrete wall marked the boundary between the city and the grassy foothills of the mountain range. In the far distance, beyond the immense forest of skyscrapers, Adam could just about make out the expansive cliff face where he first entered the wicked metropolis. Though the streets and highways teemed with vehicles and pedestrians, Soñador seemed strangely silent.

"I thought the mountains were a viro wall projection. It never occurred to me that they might be part of another viro. Are all viros like this?"

"No, they're not," said the Captain. "The walls of every other viro use projection technology to create an artificial continuation of the landscape. Here it is different. There is a transparent wall between the city and the mountains. That is why you cannot hear the sounds of the city. However, the Soñadorians believe that the mountains are just projections."

Adam began to distrust the situation. Being so close to the city, so close to the archive, made him very uneasy.

"You promised that option two was a trip to the outside. I hope that wasn't some trick. You see, I wasn't expecting to see that awful city again."

"Believe me, you have nothing to worry about. This mountain viro is the official gateway to the outside, and you will soon meet the gatekeepers."

"You mean that place in the valley with the columns? Please don't tell me we have to walk."

"There's a small tracked buggy by the cubicles," the Captain assured. "Won't take long with me at the wheel."

Snug and warm inside the two-seater buggy, Adam closed his eyes and tried to forget they were on a narrow winding road with a near sheer drop to the side. Captain Andrews drove as if oblivious to the danger, corner braking at speed. After twenty minutes of steep descent, the Captain slowed down, ironically as the road widened and merged into the valley highway.

"What is this place?" asked Adam, daring to open his eyes again, glad to be alive. "That highway looks like it goes to Soñador, but it's the wrong scale."

"This viro—well, the city and the mountains combined—are part of the original Viroverse. The Viroverse was first envisaged as place for history's powerful elites only, and this was to be their city and interface with the outside world."

"So they could come and go as often as they pleased?"

"That was the original plan. Then new, cheaper, time channelling technology came along and changed that vision. With the new technology, it became possible to resurrect, miniaturise, and house, billions of our ancestors rather than a small elite. The ten by ten viro grids were constructed, and this huge space was repurposed."

"For the Dreamers."

Captain Andrews drove the buggy across a concrete bridge that spanned a deep rocky chasm, and headed towards the looming columned portico.

"I have no idea why the human race became obsessed with the purity of dreams," he said, "but Soñador grew out of that obsession. Because they were somehow deemed worthy of larger bodies than the rest of the resurrected, the city had to be redesigned." He pulled into the car park, close to the marble steps. "The city is largely autonomous, with its own AI, so we are unable to curb their excesses."

"But they have no access to the outside."

"No, they don't. Wise minds prevailed and the interface was separated from the city by the transparent wall. Hidden behind the mountains, they don't know that it even exists. In fact, Adam, you're the first human to ever set foot in here."

"Exiting the buggy, they climbed the steps. Before they reached the iron-braced doors, Captain Andrews ran ahead. He pounded on the dark wood with his fist, and boomed out, "Oh mighty Zeus, open up thy fortress so that we may enter! Open up, I say, in the name of the mighty Captain Andrews!"

The huge doors obediently swung open, and the Captain thrust his arms in the air like a champion boxer. As Adam reached the top step, the Captain broke into a smile and started laughing.

"Only messing with you, Adam," he said. "The doors open automatically when someone gets close. If you're quick, you can make it look dramatic. Now, the first thing I need to do is convince the gatekeeper that it is right for you to go outside."

"But what if he says no? I thought this was guaranteed."

"Rules dictate that arguments must be made for both sides. The gatekeeper will put forward some convincing arguments; that is its job. We have the stronger case, so the exchange is really a formality."

They walked into a vast cathedral like hall, with columns, and archways, and a shiny chequerboard floor. Slender figures in luminous white hooded robes slowly traversed the room as if floating on thin cushions of air. They moved in seemingly random directions, ignoring the two arrivals. Mystified by the strange scene, Adam felt he was in some online fantasy game. He spoke very quietly, mindful of echoes.

"What do we do now? Are any of these people the gatekeeper?"

"They are all gatekeepers," said the Captain, his voice amplified by the huge space. "They are very approachable. They don't pounce on you like some hard sell salesman from your era."

Adam and the Captain approached the nearest gatekeeper. It halted and gently rotated to greet them. Beneath the soft white glow of the gatekeeper's hood, there was no human face, just swirling gaseous shades of light green.

"I am an android, Adam Eden," whispered the gatekeeper; its androgynous voice softly rising from the verdant eddies. "There is no danger here. Captain Andrews will negotiate on your behalf."

Captain Andrews told Adam to stand to one side, while he and the gatekeeper put forward their arguments. The cold wind had dried Adam's nasal passages, and he rubbed the rim of his itchy nostril. He looked up from his rubbing, to see the Captain and the gatekeeper staring at him.

"Don't mind me," said Adam. "You go ahead and have your argument."

"Already done," smiled the Captain. "You have permission to visit the outside."

"What do you mean already done?"

The gatekeeper gracefully glided over to Adam. Its voice a soothing whisper, the androids mercurial gaseous swirls were now shades of soft pink.

"Our processing power is way beyond anything from your first-life. We raised and analysed over thirty million points and their variations in the blink of an eye. It was a forgone conclusion but the arguments and implications were most stimulating. The decision was made even before you picked your nose, Mr Eden."

"I ... I wasn't picking my nose," insisted Adam, blushing red. "I was rubbing the edge. I had an itch."

"My mistake," murmured the gatekeeper, perhaps replaying the clip in his mind for confirmation. "Though, I must admit, I'm flattered."

"Flattered?"

"You care about my reaction to what you just did. Even though I am an android, an artificial being, you honoured me with having human traits."

"Well, I…."

"My kind has obviously come a long way, Mr Eden. Perusing your profile and memory archive, I note that you masturbated in front of a computer on many occasions, watching many hours of illegally downloaded internet pornography. You gave no thought to the technology around you. And now, in front of that simple processors descendant, you display shyness and embarrassment over something as trivial as the manner in which you touched your nose. For me, it is a truly transcendent moment that I will never never forget."

Adam was unhappy that someone or something had viewed his sweaty little secrets.

"Of course I gave no thought to the technology around me!" he huffily responded. "My computer didn't make pretentious comments, and certainly never floated around the house in a silk dressing gown."

The gatekeeper shook its head, expressing sadness with swirling shades of blue and grey, and said in a sorrowful tone, "Ah, thereby we suffer the sarcasm of Englishmen, ever in jest to subvert a moment of exquisite poignancy."

With a vapour enveloped metallic hand, the gatekeeper gestured to a nearby archway, and a glowing blue line appeared on the floor.

"Please follow the blue path to the conversion chamber. Your capsule is ready."

"Come on," said Captain Andrews, grabbing Adam by the arm. "If you're quite done insulting the staff, we have to move on."

Following the blue line led to a long chamber with identical columns and statues on either side. The line ended in front of one of the tall fluted columns. On a plinth next to the column, stood a human size statue of the Greek God, Hermes—naked, athletic, winged cap, winged sandals, and carrying a winged staff with two snakes wrapped around it. The God of border crossings, the intercessor between worlds, Hermes was the perfect choice for the journey Adam was about to make.

The lower part of the column swivelled open, revealing a human sized metal niche. The statue of Hermes turned its head slightly, facing Adam, the snakes on the staff crackling with energy, thrusting their heads and sharp tongues in the direction of the capsule.

In the pre-cynical manner of a fast-food employee, serving their very first customer, Hermes spoke with youthful enthusiasm, "Adam Eden, I am Hermes, the conductor twixt the afterlife and the outside world! It is an honour to serve you! Now, if you will kindly step inside the capsule, we can begin the conversion, and send you … outside!"

"What about you?" Adam asked Captain Andrews. "There's only room for one in there."

"I don't need to use the capsule. For me, visiting the outside is just a matter of data transfer. There is nothing to fear, Adam. This is not Soñador. Remember, this place was set up as an interface for the human elites. It's a bit tacky, but the hooded robes and the talking statues are only for fun."

Trusting his android companion, Adam stepped into the capsule. The column swivelled shut, and the interior of the capsule quickly filled with a light pink gel. Rapidly, the gel set hard, but Adam could still breathe. He became drowsy—his eyes were already closed to avoid the gel. A few seconds later, and he was under the dark pall of deep sleep.

FULL BODIED

M uch like his initial resurrection many years ago, Adam found himself standing up rather than awaking in a comfortable bed. There was no lingering dark-place trauma, not even the faintest discomfort. Opening his eyes, he looked down at his body, wondering if he was clothed in the same convict-style orange jumpsuit as the first time. He let out a groan. Yet again, he was naked—this time, completely naked without even the blush-sparing cover of a modesty thong.

Adam was in a dimly lit pearlescent cubicle. He reached out a hand and the front of the cubicle silently swivelled open. Taking a few cautious steps forward, his eyes adjusting to the bright light outside, Adam took in his new surroundings.

The two-storey room, not much larger than a double garage, was starkly industrial: metal plate walkway and mezzanine, a network of ducts and pipes, an open lift, and grey concrete walls. There was no ornamentation, no furniture—not even a single chair—but at least the temperature was perfect for comfortable nudity.

"Utilitarian, I know," said a familiar voice, "but we don't get many visitors. In fact, Adam, you're the first."

Adam gasped and backed into the cubicle as an android stepped into view—an almost transparent plastic-like skin covering a detailed metallic structure—looking only slightly less menacing than a skinless Terminator, its voice emanating from a narrow fixed slit. The android held its hand against the edge of the cubicle, stopping the door from closing, and Adam stood frozen in fear against the back wall.

"Is this better," asked the android, putting on a pilot's cap with a wing emblem. "I didn't mean to scare you. Like I said, you are our first human visitor."

"Why … why are you like this?" asked Adam, regaining his composure, but holding arm out telling the Captain to keep his distance. "Where's your skin?"

"You have a full-size human body now. Your body is 343 thousand times the size of the one you had in the Viroverse. That requires a great deal of resources. This android body stays permanently in this facility, ready for me, or any other AI approved personnel to slip into when we're up here. It's quite low tech and relatively economical to run."

"That makes sense," said Adam, walking out of the cubicle, instinctively holding his hands over his genitals. "This body does feel different, not like I'm a giant, but different. My thoughts are clearer too." Adam gave the Captain a questioning look. "My brain is full-size as well, isn't it? There's not a tiny pea of a brain in this big head is there?"

"Your brain is the same scale as the rest of you," said the Captain, with a cheerful tone not reflected by his fixed robotic expression. "As for your thoughts being clearer, that is probably because your two personalities have merged into one. This brain isn't limited like your old one. Copacabana is now part of your own personality."

"And, what happens when I return to the Viroverse? Will the personalities split again?"

"No, they won't," promised the Captain. "The merger is complete, and once you return to a miniaturised state, you will have a similar personality to the one you have now."

"So, technically, if I decide not to see the outside, then Copacabana won't intervene. I could just decide to go back to the Viroverse without bothering to see what's out there."

"That's absolutely correct, although I don't think you'll do that. You said yourself that you were curious about the outside. With Copacabana now part of your personality, partly informing your decisions, I think you can't wait for me to open the doors." The Captain pointed up to a large garage-type double door up on the second-storey mezzanine.

"You're right, of course," admitted Adam, his curiosity piqued. "Now, where's the dispenser? I need some clothes."

"It is more appropriate for you to be naked."

"Can I at least wear some boxer shorts? Y-Fronts would do if whoever's out there has something against boxers."

"Believe me, Adam, there is nothing to fear. I can't tell you what's outside. You have to experience it for yourself, but I can tell you that naked is good." Captain Andrews held out his arms. "I'm naked. I'm not wearing my usual human skin suit, am I?"

"At least you get to wear a hat," muttered Adam.

As they ascended to the mezzanine, Captain Andrews explained that this small two-storey concrete bunker was thrown up after the original Viroverse plans were scrapped. Originally, a large interface was planned, Greek temple style like the one on the Viroverse side, and of a similar size to New York's ancient Grand Central Station. Now, this lone bunker served as the only link between the Viroverse and the outside world.

Adam stood back from the door as the Captain opened a large rectangular plastic container and pulled out a glistening square pad. He plopped the pad, roughly the size of a doormat, onto the metal floor in front of Adam.

"Being an android, I don't need one of these," said the Captain. "So, if you would kindly step onto the pad, and stand perfectly still, we will soon be ready to go outside."

Adam stepped onto the pad, his feet sticking to its wet gummy surface, and waited. After a tingling feeling underfoot, Adam felt the pad bubbling and expanding. He looked down as the pad—now a translucent slime –rapidly oozed upwards, coating his legs and body. The slime firmed up, holding his body tightly. Following the Captain's on-going instructions, Adam let his body go limp. To his surprise, the slime kept him upright, and was extremely comfortable—in a weird rubbery sort of way.

As Captain Andrews ordered the doors to open, Adam had a disturbing vision of everyone he ever knew standing outside, just waiting to yell 'surprise!' and laugh endlessly at his nakedness. Perhaps all his trials and tribulations in the warped world of the Viroverse was an elaborate joke, leading to one final intense humiliation. On a more serious level, Adam really expected one of two possibilities. Either an opulently gleaming Soñadoresque technoscape or, given the resource problems in the Viroverse, nightmarish post-apocalyptic ruins.

OUTSIDE

The heavy door clanked upwards, with a sharp hissing sound suggesting an airlock. Somehow, the slime pad knew where Adam wanted to go. Slipping along like a snail on steroids, Adam slid out onto a wide concrete viewing terrace with industrial type railings and a ramp leading to ground level. Captain Andrews drew alongside as Adam took in the extraordinary vista before him.

The landscape was grey, very flat, and stretched out unchangingly in all directions as far as the eye could see. Monotonously featureless save for some low hump shaped tunnels, which dotted the landscape some few miles apart, the only vibrancy was the blue sky above and the people below.

In fact, the people shocked Adam more than the bleak landscape. Their smell and appearance dominated his senses. Immense crowds of hairless naked humans, moving together, almost as one, slid across the smooth ground, their heads bowed, arms dangling limp by their sides. There was no clamour of voices, or attempt at individuality. The air was filled with the treacly sound of sliding slime, and an unpleasant stink. Adam put his hand over his nose, and gagged a couple of times. Captain Andrews handed Adam a small dual pegged device.

"Clip this over your nose, Adam," he advised. "What you can smell is the sweat and faeces of billions of humans. Most of the urine and sweat is actually filtered and recycled by the slime suits they're wearing, but you can never totally remove the stink of the barnyard."

"They look like husks, only slightly plumper," said Adam, clipping on the nasal filter, experiencing instant relief. "Do they have a resource problem out here as well?"

"They're not husks, and there is no resource problem. The year is 3242. The entire human population of Earth is here. They move around in slerds, sometimes millions strong."

"Slerds?"

"They call this Slerding, a combination of the words sliding and herd. It is part of what is known as The Experience. Only this concrete outpost is under Viroverse control. Everything else is beyond our authority. These are the Slerding Plains."

"What do they do after they've finished slerding for the day?" asked Adam, astounded by the stinking sea of flesh.

"They never finish slerding, Adam. There is no other aspect to their lives. They do this for 24 hours a day, 365 days a year. The Experience is everything to them. It is an addiction, an extremely powerful addiction, and there is no one left to break them out of it."

Of all the possible futures, Adam never expected this. He raised the binoculars and looked out across the barren plain. The ground was grey, perfectly flat, polished, with a definite sheen. Like a landscape of vast square tiles, Adam noticed thin lines, maybe drains, every few hundred feet across.

Switching the binoculars to their highest magnification brought no change to the view. The landscape remained flat into the far distance, broken up here and there only by the mysterious tunnels.

"There's no end to it," said Adam, putting down the binoculars. "Where is this?"

"This is Australia," said the Captain. "We believe that most of the western mainland has been transformed to accommodate The Experience. The ground is flat, except for the melding tunnels."

"And, the rest of the world?"

"I am not permitted to divulge any specific information relating to outside the slerding zone. However, I can tell you that as the slerding craze took hold, they began dismantling many of the global urban centres. A separate AI controls the outside, a division of the Orchard Elite, and they have no contractual obligation to supply us with information. Our last contact with the Orchard AI was over a hundred years ago, so we can only guess what happened next. Essentially, the Viroverse is blind to what happens in the outside world. What you see around you is almost all we know."

"What's the Orchard Elite?" asked Adam. "Some sort of government?"

"Best I describe it as a loose alliance of ancient aristocracies, the last corporations, and a smattering of wealthy landed technocrats. So, in essence, yes, the global government."

"If every human is here, sliding around in Australia, then who are the concierges? I've talked to my concierge on a number of occasions, and she seemed irritatingly real to me."

"One by one, the humans gave up their concierge duties. Before signing up to the permanent Slerding experience, after their one month free trial period had expired, they gave up personal control of their avatars to the Viroverse AI. There were no exceptions. The addiction is that strong."

"But I blackmailed my concierge!" said Adam, remembering a tense confrontation with a sentient sofa. "If you're saying that all the concierges are really the AI, then why did she allow herself to be blackmailed?"

"The AI is required to play each human within the strictures of their profile. It has an in-depth knowledge of their personalities, and plays each part accordingly. Now, stay close to me, Adam," said the Captain, heading down the ramp. "Time to meet the natives."

Sliding easily on the pad, Adam followed the Captain, and they were soon in amongst the slerd. Up close, the humans seemed tragic in appearance, completely enveloped in their slime suits, hairless heads drooped, eyes closed, their frail naked bodies hanging limp as if lifeless.

"They look dead," said Adam. "I mean, can they hear us, or see us?"

"They are in a coma-like state, enjoying The Experience. They are totally unaware of our presence. The slime suits and pads provide support, motion, sustenance and waste disposal.

"The Experience must be pretty amazing to keep them sliding around like this."

"We know very little about The Experience, but it is important to know that the slerding is of only minor significance, mainly used to introduce much needed movement and to maintain an active link to the physical world. The major part of The Experience is going on inside their heads: forced virtual imagery that loops continually, with the melding as the beginning and the end of the cycle."

"You could ask around in the Viroverse. Surely people from the later centuries would know about this."

"There are no resurrected in the Viroverse born after 2691. Once immortality became a basic human right, nobody died. Sterilisation was the only price, and it was compulsory. Everyone around you is hundreds of years old. I suspect that even if I could tell you what's going on, you still wouldn't understand. The Experience is too far removed from your era."

"I get it," said Adam. "Like trying to describe the internet to someone from medieval times. They'd probably burn you at the stake before you'd even finished explaining electricity."

Casually sliding across the vast grey expanse, Adam and the Captain reached one of the drains. The narrow channel had a metal mesh covering. Stopping to inspect the drain—which ran off in both directions as far as the eye could see—Adam saw three separate channels under the mesh. A green liquid flowed along the centre channel, whilst a medium brown liquid flowed along the others.

"I'm guessing this isn't mint chocolate," said Adam, eyeing the two liquids suspiciously.

"The green liquid is for nutrition. When a slerder passes over the drain, their slime pad sucks up a regulated amount of the liquid. One pass is enough to sustain a slerder for 12 hours."

"And, the brown stuff?" asked Adam. "That's poop isn't it?"

"It is human waste, although mainly poop," said the Captain. "At the same time that the slime pad sucks up nutrients, it also deposits waste."

"Sewage and food running side by side; I guess it was inevitable."

"Let's follow the drain, Adam," suggested the Captain. "I think you'll find this interesting."

Following along the drain for a few hundred feet, they came to an intersection. The Captain reached down with suction pads on his android hand, and lifted up the square plate where the drains met. The green liquid ran uninterrupted across the junction, but the sewage poured down four small holes—one at each corner of the tiny crossroads.

"This is the interesting part," said the Captain. "The waste flows straight down four pipes to bioreactors in the utility level of the Viroverse. The reactors supply much of the energy needs for the Viroverse, and some of the dry material left over from the process replenishes the resource vats."

"So, these holes are the …"

"They are the ends of the tubes you see at every intersection in the halls. The drains flow directly above the halls."

"I thought they were transport tubes," said Adam, unable to shake the nauseating image of Gloop in the poop. "So, the Viroverse is beneath us?"

"Each of the vast polished square tiles, what we call a slerding floor, covers a ten by ten grid of viros. Combined, the tiles make up The Slerding Plains, and are literally the roof of the Viroverse.

As they moved across the slerding floor towards one of the low concrete tunnels, Adam felt uneasy knowing there were viros just a few inches below his feet –it felt like the Viroverse was one enormous ants nest.

Nearing the tunnel, Adam noticed that some of the slerders were joined together, their fingers strangely pushed inside each other's skin. He asked the Captain what was going on, and was told to push a finger against a slerder's flesh.

Carefully slerding parallel to what looked like a woman –with the hairlessness and slime, it was hard to tell genders apart—Adam carefully prodded her bare arm with his index finger. For a moment, his finger began to sink and merge into the fleshy bicep, and he felt his mind moving to another place. As if detecting an intruder, the woman's arm flushed red around Adam's finger, becoming hot. The unwanted digit was forcefully pushed out, putting Adam slightly off balance.

"That really burns," said Adam, blowing on his throbbing finger. "For a moment there, I thought I was losing consciousness."

"You're not officially part of the slerd so you were rejected. I don't know why they join in this way, but their bodies are specially adapted to allow the connection. Ah, look, up ahead, the melding has begun."

All around them, slerders were coming together, packing tightly in rows and columns, heading for the low tunnel. Captain Andrews put his arm around Adam, and skilfully guided them away from the concentrating throng. Gradually, the front line of the slerd reached the opening, their bodies compressing together, and then merging into a single stream of flesh. A low ecstatic moan filled the air, as the slerd squeezed through the tunnel like plasticine oozing through a press.

216

Adam and the Captain slid around in a wide arc to catch a glimpse of the slerd squeezing out the other end of the tunnel. With loud sucking and slurping sounds, the fleshy mass separated, restored to their individual bodies, and resumed their doleful perambulations.

"Now we must get back to the outpost," said the Captain. "We have about ten minutes. If you want, we can watch the slerd from the viewing terrace."

"Aw, come on Captain," said Adam, finally feeling comfortable with both the slerding and his nudity. "It's still a long time until midnight. I'm beginning to enjoy this."

"There are weapons platforms orbiting the Earth, constantly monitoring the Slerding Plains for intruders. From personal experience, I can predict that we have less than ten minutes before a high intensity laser beam disintegrates us both."

"In that case, I'll just enjoy the slide back to the outpost."

EDEN'S CHOICE

Adam and the Captain returned to the viewing terrace without incident, choosing a sparsely populated route, well clear of the crowds. For about an hour, Adam stood on his sticky pad by the terrace railings, quietly watching the slerding cycle move towards the next melding. It was mesmerising to watch, the spectacle of slimy flesh being almost as addictive as The Experience itself.

"You know, there are some things that don't add up," said Adam, contemplating all he had seen and heard. "Normally things like this would pass me by, but I think getting back together with Copacabana has made me think more clearly."

"What doesn't add up?" asked the Captain, leaning forward against the railings.

"Well, for a start, I remember Groover telling me that he was resurrected forty years ago as part of the experimental time channelling phase. He said it was ten years before they started building the Viroverse. If you add the extra year I spent fighting and the seventeen years that I was in the archive, then that makes the Viroverse roughly 48 years old."

"So, you've noticed the time discrepancy."

"Yeah, you said the Viroverse was nearly 150 years old. Was Groover lying, or maybe misinformed?"

"Since you have a full-size human body, and are outside the Viroverse, that is something I can now explain. To facilitate appropriate healing, feeding, and general viro maintenance, the sleep phase is longer than people think."

"How much longer?" asked Adam, already aware of the potential implications.

"An extra two days. Viroverse sleep is more of an artificially induced coma state—akin to short-term hibernation."

"Oh my God, that explains why we were in such bad shape in the halls! Each day without real food was really three days. And, whoa, that means I was in the archive for over 50 years."

Absorbing the startling revelation, Adam nearly forgot about the other discrepancy he had noticed. However, a quick glance at the stinking slerd reminded him.

"There's another thing that doesn't seem to add up. If the Viroverse is 150 years old, and the slerding craze began about 90 years ago, then how is it that the Slerding Plains are technically linked to the Viroverse? I mean, the slerding floor is the roof of the Viroverse and the drains feed the bioreactors. Did the Orchard Elite know about The Experience decades before they built the Viroverse?"

"I have very little specific information about that, but I do have many theories."

"Do you think the Orchard Elite knew that the addiction would affect the entire world population in this way?"

"Yes I do. Paying for The Experience cost the user their entire wealth, including property and land holdings. I believe it was the Elite's intention to own the world, and leave everybody else slerding across Australia. However, the plan backfired, since it seems that all of the Orchard Elite themselves succumbed to the addiction. I doubt there are any free humans still out there, but if there are, then the Earth must seem a very lonely place."

The sun was setting over the plains. In the rush to see the outside, Adam had not eaten all day, and his stomach started grumbling. Captain Andrews went back inside the outpost to fetch some food from the outpost's dispenser. Adam was about to follow but was told to stay outside.

The Captain waited patiently whilst Adam hungrily devoured the chilli cheeseburger with a side order of onion rings and washed it down with a refreshing bottle of sparkling mineral water. Adam licked some stray relish from his fingers, and the Captain got straight to the point.

"Those discrepancies you noticed may one day be important to the Viroverse, but for now we have your future to consider. As usual, I am going to give you three choices," he began, holding up three robotic fingers for emphasis. "I won't bring Rhapsody into the equation, because her future is a separate matter."

"Fair enough," said Adam, rubbing his hands together in anticipation. "So, what are my choices this time?"

"Firstly, I can offer you a position as a Terminal operative, probably working alongside John Down. With this option, you can either live in the Terminal on a permanent basis, or we can find you an unadopted functioning viro."

"You know, that sounds interesting. They say you can never go home, and that's true when the place is crawling with energy sapping husks … and one of them's your mother."

Secondly, I can have you transported to any hall of your choosing, and you can go it alone. As long as you keep a low-profile, you'll have no trouble from us."

There was a time when Adam would have eagerly chosen this option, giving the freedom to roam the Viroverse. However, having seen the Terminal, Soñador, the Gatekeepers, and the outside, it was now a case of 'been there, done that'.

"And then you have option three," continued the Captain.

"Which is?"

"I am not permitted to tell you."

"I beg your pardon? You can't tell me?"

"It has to be your choice."

"But, how can I choose it if I don't know what it is?"

"I am not permitted to influence your decision by telling you what it is."

"Is this some 'open the mystery box' kind of deal?" asked Adam, somewhat confused. "Can't you even give me a hint?"

"You must be guided by your own experiences. You know enough to know what the choice is."

"Ah, now that sounded like a hint!" exclaimed Adam, wondering what the Hell it was he knew enough about. "Err, is this to do with my value-brand body and brain? If I pick option three, do I get the luxury-brand?"

Captain Andrews remained silent. Without his skin and facial features, he was positively inexpressive and impossible to read. Adam stared at the robotic head, looking for any movement—even the smallest push of a micro-piston— but quickly realised that he may as well be looking at a statue.

"Hmm, I reckon that a new body and brain would be part of the deal rather than the main item. If I choose option one or two, can I have a new body and brain?"

"Yes you can. You have accumulated enough credit for those items, whichever option you choose."

Before speaking again, Adam scratched his chin and stared quizzically at the Captain's head, looking for any sign of movement.

"You know," he said, "it just occurred to me, that this might be less about me and more about the problems facing the Viroverse. Is that it?"

Perhaps Adam's mind was making him see what he wanted to see—or he was staring so hard he was going cross-eyed—but he thought he noticed an almost imperceptible nod.

"Aha, you nodded!" cried Adam, clapping his hands together.

"I assure you that it did not," replied the Captain with as little emotion as possible.

"I think the third option is that you want me to help you fix the Viroverse. That's it, isn't it? You want me to fix the Viroverse, don't you?"

"What I want is irrelevant."

Taking a moment to think, Adam considered the possibility that this was now a matter of semantics. Carefully choosing his words, he said, "Option three is that I want to help fix the Viroverse."

"In that case, which option do you chose?" asked the Captain, finally moving his head. "Think carefully, because there's no going back once the deal is struck."

There was no point in prevaricating or asking for further information, since the choice was obvious. The Viroverse was gradually breaking down and it seemed that Adam was part of the cure. Agreeing to option three, despite not knowing the details, Adam needed to know one thing.

"Why me? Why does fixing the Viroverse fall to me?"

"Your choices brought you here," was the Captain's simple answer. "The AI and I pushed things in the right direction now and then, when the rules allowed, but our strict protocols prohibited us from exerting any direct influence."

"Are you saying that I am the Chosen One, you know, like in some sci-fi or fantasy movie?"

"No, I am not saying that at all. No one chose you. Chance brought you here. Over the years we followed many that moved in the right direction. Whether deciding to fight in the psychoviro, electing to save young Kimberley, the Dreamers wanting your memories, or even John Down seeing you as a better man rather than an evil murderer, each step brought you to this moment and this opportunity. We only nudged a little here and there."

"So I'm not the Chosen One?"

"No really," admitted Captain Andrews, "but you ended up here, so you'll have to do."

Suitably deflated by the Captain's comment, discarding any notion of Godlike powers or pre-ordained destiny, Adam humbly asked what was expected of him.

The Captain explained that AI had solutions to many problems facing the Viroverse, but did not have the authority to carry them out. When outside, in full-size human body form, Adam could legally act as humanity's representative—the Captain gestured to the slerds with a wave of the hand. Although many changes to Viroverse rules required a full human vote, which was clearly impossible given the coma-like state of humanity, other measures only required the agreement of a representative.

"And, that's me!" said Adam, pointing to himself, brimming with pompous pride. "Ok then, how do I save the Viroverse?"

"There are two reasons that we are low on resources, but only one solution. The lesser reason is the human love of hoarding. Rather than throw away items, that can then be recycled into new ones, you seem to hang on to things. For example, before your own viro fell into a husk state, your own father had a collection of over three hundred watches."

Adam laughed, remembering his father showing off the collection to his uncle, who subsequently built up a huge collection of his own. Adam had been more impressed by the polished mahogany display cabinet in which the watches were stored. The beautifully crafted cabinet had angled soft felt shelves and built-in winders to keep the automatics from running down.

"And, your mother's clothes," added the Captain, as if the watch example was not enough. "When you can retrieve a pair of shoes from a dispenser in a few seconds, what is the point of an entire double bedroom converted into a walk-in wardrobe? I believe she had nearly a thousand pairs in there before the husk state."

"Nearly a thousand," smiled Adam. "Then I guess she must have been cutting back."

The Captain gave many more examples, though not related to Adam's parents, labouring the point that in the Viroverse, hoarding was bad and that throwing perfectly good products away was good.

"I get it," said Adam. "I understood before you even mentioned my Dad's watches."

"Well, the AI proposes that a limit be placed on such activities. The concierges will inform every one of the changes. You need not concern yourself with the details, about the limits on different items. That is a job for the AI. At this point, we only need your approval. Do you agree with the proposal?"

Holding his hand up, as if swearing in court, Adam exclaimed, "Humanity says aye!"

The main reason for the lack of resources was far more disturbing. The Captain explained that a number of fully automated resource centres on the planet's surface fed the Viroverse. About twenty years ago, supplies from two of the centres suddenly ceased. Due to the lack of communication with the Orchard AI, the cause was unknown—perhaps a natural catastrophe, or even falling space debris that got past the Earth's defences. However, it was suspicious that two would fail within a few months of one another, because the affected plants were not in close proximity.

Relishing the idea of an adventure into the unknown, Adam said, "So, you want me to go out there, with a small team of course, and find out what's going on. I'm up for that, but I will need clothes. The Slerding Plains look smooth enough, but there are bound to be some sharp edges out there."

"Though we can venture beyond this outpost for the best part of an hour, after that time the orbiting defences would bring a quick and certain end to the venture. Our solution to the problem does not involve any action on the outside."

"But, it does involve some adventure, right? This isn't just a raise your right hand job again?"

Captain Andrews nodded, saying, "There will be adventure, Adam. The key to solving our resources problems lies in Soñador."

"I get it," said Adam. "They are eight times our size and so need at least eight times the resources. Add the fact that they are constantly making changes to the city, and they're a drain on the Viroverse. We need to shrink them to our size and …"

"No, that is not the problem," interrupted the Captain. "The Dreamers have their own resource centre on the surface. Even with their extreme profligacy, they use less than two percent of the available supply. When Soñador is at its peak, in about two hundred year's time, it is estimated that the figure will still be under five percent. The solution to our resource problem is to seize control of their supply, and you are the man to do it."

After asking for more details, Adam learned that he was expected to lead a small group into Soñador, and transfer complete control of the city to the Viroverse AI. Despite regaining the ruthless tough side to his personality, he did not like the idea. He posed a few alternatives, such as sending millions of former soldiers streaming into the city, or at least huge clouds of gas to knock out the population, but each suggestion was summarily dismissed for breaching the rules.

The Captain's plan hinged on the fact that Adam retained partial residential status in Soñador due to his lengthy incarceration. In a month's time, this status would expire, and any hopes of carrying out the plan would be dashed. Using a very strained and detailed interpretation of Viroverse and Soñadorian protocols, there was a way that Adam could re-enter the city with up to fourteen guests. By physically accessing the Soñador AI, and inserting first a key and then an authorisation card, total control could transfer after one hour.

"The dark alley and small elevator that you used to escape are remnants of the original city's infrastructure," the Captain explained. "The city buildings were never constructed, but some of the roads, bridges, and squares were already in place before the project was scrapped in favour of the current city. Luckily, all the surviving alleys and elevators are in the Morello District. The locals rarely venture down them; they believe the alleys are cursed."

"Why is that lucky?"

"Because our friend, Doctor Mikhail Kaminski, currently resides in that particular district."

"I thought they would have punished him by now for helping me escape."

"Being confined to the Morello District for five years is his punishment, though he is sometimes escorted to the Compro building to perform his duties. As you can imagine, he is extremely angry at having to live amongst the 'low brow', and has once again agreed to help us."

Captain Andrews went on to explain that the Soñador AI was accessible from one of the old alleys. The nearest elevator was Viroverse scale and of the two-door variety, the reception room above under Viroverse control. However, a permanent Soñadorian committee member needed to be present in the room to witness any arrivals or the Soñadorian side door would remain shut. That is where Doctor Kaminski's help would prove invaluable. He was one of only a handful of permanent committee members. Most served only a few months so did not qualify.

The Soñador AI was housed in a drab concrete building, close to a busy Morello street. A gleaming new skyscraper was built over the three-storey building, leaving only the access wall visible from the alley. Adam asked if the AI building was guarded and if not, then why.

Apparently, the access port was disguised as brickwork, and the lock for the key was only visible once you were up on a narrow ledge. For security reasons, the Soñadorians were unaware of their AI's location, but once the key was inserted, they would be alerted to the impending change of control and the whereabouts of the access port. Adam and his group would have to defend the alley for an hour.

"So, when do I get to pick my little raiding party?" asked Adam, briefly picturing a squad of history's greatest warriors, clad in shining armour or rugged combat fatigues—the image was ruined as Adam pictured himself standing amongst them, smiling, hands on hips, in his pink flower shirt and white trousers. With a shudder, Adam cast the embarrassing thought from his mind.

Adam was dismayed by the strict rules dictating who could be invited as guests. They could only be people that he had interacted with during his lives. Furthermore, Adam would not choose the guests. Suitable candidates would be approached by Terminal operatives, and asked if they wished to offer their support. If they were currently in a husk state then no approach would be made. Each candidate would be fully apprised of the risks involved.

"But, what if these people don't know how to fight?" asked Adam.

"Don't worry about that, Adam. The AI will draw up a list of potential candidates based on their profiles. However, you won't know who's coming until you are in the alley."

"Hmm, well, I've got nothing to lose, so I think it's time for some heroics." Adam raised his right hand. "Humanity says aye!"

Before preparing for the sleep of midnight, Adam asked if another trip across the slerding floor was possible. Soon, with the Captain following behind, he was back amongst the slerd, more confident this time, jostling shoulder to shoulder with his slimy corpselike descendants.

"Oh, something I should have mentioned," said the Captain nonchalantly, as twilight darkened to night. "If any of you die in Soñador before control transfers to the Viroverse, you will not resurrect. You will be dead … permanently."

Heroes and Villains

Adam travelled to the reception room on the back of a long board ridden by Gunter Blauch, a late 21st century Swiss ski jumper. With skilled precision, Gunter brought the board to a stop by a typical unassuming hallway door with a palm panel to the side. Standing next to the panel, imposing in a blue Terminal security uniform, was Dolph Zabel—one of the Captain's most trusted men, and one of Kevin's white line buddies. Adam stepped off the board and thanked Gunter for the impeccably smooth ride.

Holding onto a reinforced metal briefcase, containing the key and authorisation card, Adam stood ready by the door. Offering a polite nod and a 'good luck', Dolph placed his hand on the panel, and the door hissed open. Walking inside—the door closing quickly behind him—Adam was greeted by a familiar voice from a very cramped individual.

"At last, Mr Eden," groaned Mikhail. "I've only been here an hour and already my neck is killing me. I see you have come dressed for a beach party again."

A 12ft giant in a reception room with an 8ft ceiling was a recipe for cramp and back problems. Mikhail was crouching in the centre of the room rather than attempting to sit on the benches, which were far too thin to comfortably accommodate his oversize buttocks.

"If I'm in charge of this operation, I thought I'd better wear my uniform," said Adam. "So, I understand there's an elevator on the other side of the door?"

Mikhail stretched out a leg, brought it back then stretched out the other, like an awkward Russian Kazachok dancer.

"There is an elevator," he said, rubbing his calf muscle, "and a bloody tight squeeze it was too, but I have to stay here to let your teammates into the city."

Straining his giant arm behind his back, as if playing Twister, Mikhail slapped his hand on the palm panel. The far door opened, revealing the elevator.

"When you reach ground level, just follow the alley to a wide square with a dry fountain. One of your team is already there."

The elevator, with the usual breath-taking views over the city, descended rapidly, and soon Adam was walking along a dark alleyway between skyscrapers. He noted that this particular alley was wider than the one he had used to escape, explaining how Mikhail was able to get to the reception room.

After a few minutes walking, Adam passed under the remains of a concrete road bridge. One support stood against the blank wall of a skyscraper, and Adam noticed what looked like a dispenser. It was the same size as standard Viroverse dispensers—another relic of the original city. Using the appropriate gestures, he obtained a can of cold lemonade and continued on his way.

The noise from the city grew louder, and Adam walked into a large square, still surrounded by the soaring buildings. In the centre of the square was a dried out low-walled fountain with an ornate cluster of dolphin statues, which long ago may have spewed water from their mouths. At the far side of the square, the alleyway continued, but turned a sharp corner, hiding the city street beyond.

Adam looked about the square for the person that Mikhail had mentioned. At first, it seemed there was no one there, but then Adam caught a glimpse of ginger hair behind a park bench next to the AI access wall—the all-important concrete ledge with the lock and the port was about twenty feet up accessible by an extendable aluminium ladder. As Adam walked towards the bench, a man stood up, old style notepad in hand, and a wry grin on his pale freckled face.

They shook hands, but Adam had no idea who the man was. Short clipped ginger hair, smartly casual in a grey Aran knit sweater and black demins, the man's expression said that he knew Adam. As if to make it easier, the stranger framed his face with his hands, and said, "Imagine, bald on top, lots of lines, and huge ginger whiskers …"

"And, you always had disgusting food crumbs in your beard," said Adam, finally recognising the man. "Good to see you again, Woody! Another undesirable from my old stomping ground. What are the odds?"

"It's good to see you again, Adam, but actually I'm not an undesirable, and my real name is Jack Linwood. Before my unfortunate breakdown, and our dubious acquaintanceship, I worked as a freelance consultant for the Ministry of Defence."

Adam was very surprised. He remembered Linwood as a slurred, hopeless alcoholic street bum with one foot in the grave. It was hard to equate those memories with this smart, fluent individual. Remembering the fantastical drunken tales that Linwood endlessly spewed, Adam asked, "You mean all those wild stories about undercover operations in Sub-Saharan Africa and the Middle East were true? We all thought you were making them up to get a swig of tramp-juice off us."

"I may have exaggerated a little here and there," admitted Linwood, "and yes, alcohol was the ultimate goal, but they weren't lies. I was the go-to logistical guy for small military incursions, extractions, demolitions, and sometimes … assassinations. Off the record of course. Given the high stakes involved, this might be the most important mission I will ever undertake. You see, apart from the odd prank raid on someone's party, there's not much call for my talents these days. I just had to accept. The Captain has supplied most of the information I asked for."

Linwood took out a notepad containing plans for the day's events and a list of the people who would be taking part. With an officious flourish of his pen, he ticked Adam's name off the list. He then checked the contents of the briefcase and made a note in the pad. Adam asked to see the list of names, but Linwood, a stickler for protocol, refused, insisting that he was solely in charge of back-office operations.

"You will find out soon enough," said Linwood, snapping shut the notepad. "According to the Captain's information, everyone should all be here within the hour."

"So, yet again, I'm in my own version of 'This is Your Life'," smiled Adam, allowing Linwood his tin-pot bureaucracy.

"Or, 'This is Your Death' if it all goes horribly wrong," added Linwood. "Now, your role in all this is vital yet simple. Once you have inserted the key and pass-card, triggering the transfer process, you are to lie low on the ledge behind a bulletproof shield. The rest of us will keep you safe until the hour is up, and you can then reinsert the key to confirm the transfer."

Adam's pride would not allow him to stay hidden and protected whilst others risked their lives. Not only was he an experienced and trained fighter, but he also had a personal score to settle with the Dreamers. Despite Linwood's strong objections, Adam resolutely refused to lie cowardly on the ledge for the duration.

"Ok, then," sighed Linwood, jotting down some notes, and clicking the pen officiously, "but at least promise me that you'll stay near the ladder. You may be one for mindless heroics, but if you die before reinserting the key, then all this will be for nothing, our sacrifice wasted."

Adam reluctantly agreed to keep out of trouble, and Linwood went back to his notes. It was only a few minutes before the first of the brave walked into the square. Wearing his chin-strapped top hat for the occasion, John Down strode forward with a positive tap of the cane. Adam shook his head with worry. With a wife who depended on his company, how could John put his life on the line?

Prepared for Adam's disapproval, John said resolutely, "Please do not try to talk me out of this, Adam. My mind is made up. If I do not take this opportunity to free Mary from her prison, and restore my family and friends to their normal state, I will not be even worthy to admonish a lowly coward. Though I would not deem myself a warrior, I do possess the requisite skills for this mission. Here, look at the new handle of my cane."

John held up the ebon walking stick. The smooth silver top had been replaced with a formidable claw-like design, clearly capable of inflicting serious injuries on exposed flesh. Adam knew better than to argue with the eminent Victorian, and instead shook his hand.

"I'm glad to have you here, John."

Linwood ticked John off the list and began discussing his role in the forthcoming action—defending the bottom of the ladder should the enemy break through.

Five minutes later, another person rounded the corner into the square. Holding a cloth cap in his hands, wearing dungarees and a thick cotton shirt, the moustachioed man almost gave Adam a heart attack. Unless it was some long lost twin, the man was Conall Finn—the murderous Irishman who Manny killed in the railroader viro. Keeping his head down, perhaps out of shame or humility, Conall cautiously approached.

Enraged and bewildered, Adam asked, "Before you start telling me that you're here for redemption, to make amends, I first need to know why you're not dead. I saw my friend pull a screwdriver out of your ear. You were twitching and leaking out like you only had seconds left."

"A screwdriver you say?" said Conall, rubbing his ear. "You know, I always wondered where that bloody pain in me head came from. If it's any consolation to you, I thought I was dead for sure. I saw you fellers heading away, and the next thing I knew I was waking up back in me own bed the following morning."

"You didn't go through the dark place with the burning lines?"

"No Sir, I did not." Conall smiled. "I just woke up, fresh as a young buck in Spring."

"Then you must have still been alive at midnight. You were healed rather than resurrected. There was no resurrection service in your viro, so the healing nano swarm must have got to you in time."

"Ah, but I was born lucky, Mr Eden," said Conall, with a lyrical lilt.

"Luckier than Tombstone; the man you murdered. For him, it's permanent midnight."

"And, that's why I'm standing here, ready to risk me life in his memory. Apart from a polite nod or a quiet 'how do you do', the folks in the viro still treat me like leper. Even after all these years. For me, if I live, this could be a second chance. Else, I'll be buying old Tombstone a whisky in the Hereafter Saloon."

Adam wanted to fight Conall there and then, or least order him to high tail it out of Soñador, but Linwood intervened, obviously attuned to people's body language and expressions. As Linwood tried to find out about Conall's declared fighting skills—asking detailed questions to tell fact from fiction or rather truth from blarney—a group of four men strolled confidently into the square.

Wearing grey urban riot gear with full-visor helmets, and carrying heavy holdalls, the men seemed fully equipped for the coming battle. One of the group approached Adam, and took off his helmet. The face was instantly recognisable as Elliot Stevens AKA The Sarge—the Special Forces instructor who had trained Adam to defeat the psychos. His glossy dark brown skin always made him look like he had just stepped off an exercise machine and the tight chiselled features of his face indicated a hard muscled body under the clothes.

"Adam, it is so good to see you again," said the Sarge, clasping Adam in a hearty hug. "I miss our trainin' sessions. Hope you ain't got rusty."

As the Sarge and Adam hugged each other, the other members of the squad, Blunt, and Rickman, began chuckling.

"So what if I'm huggin' a guy in tight white trousers and a pink flower shirt?" said the Sarge, looking back at his sniggering squad. "It ain't like he's my boyfriend or nothin'! And anyway, didn't we all go to that 'Embrace the Military Rainbow' class in Bagram?"

"It's an honour to have you here, Sarge," said Adam, breaking off the hug and patting his combat instructor on the shoulder in as manly a way as he could muster. "If it wasn't for you and the boys here, I doubt I could have beaten the glam gang."

The other squad members each shook Adam's hand, expressing their loyalty to the cause, and promising to give the enemy Hell.

"Jus' so you know, we might not stay for the duration'." said the Sarge. "If the enemy push forward, we're out of here. All of us have wives back home. And jus' in case you think that's not much of an offer, take a look at these!"

The Sarge reached into his holdall and pulled out a machine pistol—a smaller scale version of the Dreamer's airguns—and held it up for Adam to see.

"I know they're jus' airguns, but they're powerful, and the nearest we've got to firearms since serving in Afghanistan. Got 'em from that dispenser under the bridge, and these bags are loaded with ammo."

"Remember that the Dreamers also have airguns," said Adam, "only bigger. I believe they're eight times the size."

"Adam, I know this ain't one of your favourite sayings, but 'size ain't everything'. Sometimes it's the man holding the weapon that makes the difference."

"Well, if ever I had to put my trust in a bunch of guys holding their weapons, it's you guys."

Adam's comment was met with macho yells, whooping, and a round of high-fives. Linwood, having finished with Conall, asked the Sarge and his men to come over. The look of relief on the logistics expert's face was undeniable—finally, a fully trained military unit.

A noisy rabble of voices turned everyone's heads. Thrusting their weapons in the air and chanting 1970's glam rock lyrics, a five strong group, wearing glittering costumes, swaggered into the square on precarious platform boots. The four men and one woman, stars and hearts painted on their faces, long wigs on their heads, gave off an unapologetically unruly attitude.

The Sarge was the first to speak, saying, "I know I said we had to 'Embrace the Rainbow', but who the fuck are they?"

"It's the glam gang, from the psychoviro," said Adam, taken aback by their sudden appearance. "I never thought they'd be here. Not without resurrection."

The Sarge slapped Adam on the shoulder, saying, "You mean all that time I was trainin' you to take on that posse of mad-ass clowns? Shit, their platforms are so high, I reckon I could take them all out with one good bowling ball."

Adam left the Sarge to deal with Linwood, and walked over to meet the gang. He had hoped never to see these psychopaths ever again, but here they were, ready to lend their vicious brand of violence to the cause.

Groover, the master of the psychoviro, and one of the original experimental phase resurrected, had come armed with a large machete. Rockstar glossy raven hair, and a v-fronted silver jumpsuit that displayed his thick gnarly chest hair, Groover stood tall on his platform boots.

"Aah, I expect you be wonderin' why I'm here, Copacabana?" said Groover in his rough West Country accent, arching an eyebrow. "I ain't killed no one since me murderin' days back in me first-life. You know the rules. Originals like me ain't allowed to hurt anyone. We can watch, and we can get others to do the dirty deeds, but we can't take part."

"Those rules don't count here, and that means you can take part in the fighting. You've come to satisfy your bloodlust."

Groover laughed grotesquely, like a baboon with whooping cough. He slapped a hairy knuckled hand on Adam's shoulder, and said, "Let me tell you, Copacabana, there ain't no way I'll ever satisfy that."

All the gang were present. Ziggy, a muscular dim-witted giant—though nowhere near as large as the average Dreamer—had forsaken his usual willow-wood cricket bat for a huge steel baseball bat. The unfortunate product of degraded DNA during the resurrection process, Ziggy was a mutant force to be reckoned with. In addition to his enormous bulk, a tartan jacket and a top hat covered with mirrors set Ziggy apart from the crowd.

Standing next to Ziggy was Dynamite, the psychopath who replaced Rhapsody in the gang, hiding her emotions behind black sunglasses with thick chrome frames. With a dark curly wig, her usual grey fur jacket, and ivory thigh-length platform boots, she possessed the cool demeanour of an ice-queen. Anticipating the giant size of the enemy, Dynamite had swapped her weapon of choice, a tomahawk-axe, for a long handled two-handed log splitting maul.

Given Groover's inability to join in the fighting, the leader of the glam gang on the field of combat was Rampage. The evil pseudo-intellectual psychopath, possibly the most despicable of the group, was Adam's archenemy. Dressed in a similar silver jump suit as his degenerate master, Rampage wore a long straight cut blonde wig on his egotistical head, and fake chest hair under a large ankh medallion. Instead of the Roman short sword, which had struck Adam a fatal blow on many occasions, Rampage now wielded a hefty two-handed broadsword.

Stardust, the creepiest of the group—black leather trousers and black sequinned shirt—pushed forward to meet Adam. The darkly camp psychopath ran a hand through his white fright wig, to show off the superior quality of the hair.

"Oh, how I've missed you, Copa," Stardust gushed, as if addressing a long lost friend—a friendship not mutually shared. "The hunt is not the same without your cheery pink shirt popping out to play. I know I took it personally that you killed me more often than any of the others, but I do understand that it was my lovely rose fragrance that gave my position away."

Adam tried to ignore Stardust. Even though the glam gang were formidable fighters, and worked well as a team, he felt conflicted over their arrival. If the plan worked and the Viroverse was saved, then these unrepentant psychopaths would become heroes. It was an accolade they just did not deserve. Though taking a more pragmatic viewpoint, did it really matter as long as they saved humanity?

"We don't wear the glam clothes anymore," continued Stardust, desperate for Adam's attention. "This is a one off. We switched to wearing 17th century Versailles style a few years ago: tights, powdered wigs, and lashings of silk and velvet. I love it, but the others are not so keen. Groover said that if he was to die here today, there was no way he was going out wearing a poofy poodle wig and a beauty spot."

"Look, Stardust, I am finding it very hard to tolerate your presence here, let alone engage in conversation. The way you lure people to the psychoviro, just so you can hunt them is disgusting. You're all here for twisted reasons."

"Whatever Groover told you, we are really here for the same reason you are. Groover knows about the husk viros. We have it on good authority that in a few years our viro will suffer the same fate. I don't want to be a husk, Copa. Look at my skin; my lovely skin!"

Stardust leant over, and quietly hissed, "Are you wearing underpants, Copa?"

"Yes, yes I am," answered Adam.

"Me too… pants brother."

Linwood called the glam gang over to gauge their abilities and discuss possible tactics. A woman peeked her head round the corner, and laughed throatily as she saw Adam. Fists clenched, she awkwardly ran over. Wearing an unflattering pinafore dress, and a large shoulder bag, she was thickset, well-muscled, with shapeless flat blonde hair and shot putter's legs. A tactful individual might have called her a formidable woman rather than brutishly mannish, but the latter was nearer the truth.

"Bet you didn't expect to see me again, did you?" she said, chunky hands on hips.

Adam racked his brains but could not remember anyone in his life even remotely resembling the woman standing before him.

"I … err …"

"I'm Jane! Jane Mead!" the woman shouted, evidently quick to anger. "You were two years below me in school!"

Putting on his best 'you look familiar to me' face, Adam scratched his chin. Jane got close, as if squaring up to an enemy. Her face reddened, the muscles straining in her neck.

"You were the little squirt I used to sit on in the playground!" she screamed, coating Adam's face in a spatter of spittle. "Remember me now?"

Adam shook his head, from both shock and the fact he still could not remember the bulging eyed maniac in front of him. Losing her cool completely—even though she had precious little to begin with—Jane lunged at Adam and began wrestling him. He grappled with her, holding her wrists as she grunted and gasped, gradually pushing away the clutching sausage-like fingers.

"Whoa, Jane, back off!" he ordered. "We're supposed to be on the same team here. I'm sure if you give me a moment I will remember you. It's just that I've tried to suppress memories about my school days."

Stepping back, putting a few feet between them, Adam tried to remember this particular school bully. A sudden flash of humiliation, of laughing children, and he recalled a best-forgotten incident.

"Oh God, you forced me to suck your toes in front of everyone in the playground. You told them I was into foot sex. My parents found out about it and thought I was some kind of pervert."

Jane nodded frantically, with bared teeth, her face still red. Mumbling something about being expelled, and that it was probably Adam's fault, Jane looked ready to lunge again. Adam backed away, hands held up defensively. Taking a few short breaths that sounded like sexual panting, she cooled down, regaining a small measure of composure.

"Just feeling a bit stressy," she said. "I'm here because I'm sorry for what I did to you back at school, and I want to make it up to you. And, don't think for one minute that I can't fight, because I went mad for medieval weaponry after they expelled me."

Jane reached into her shoulder bag, and drew out a two-foot long morning star—a sturdy iron club with a fearsome multi-spiked ball at the end. With a primal whoop, she waved the heavy weapon effortlessly around her head as though it was made of light aluminium.

After the morning star was safely back in the bag, Adam thanked Jane for offering to fight, and suggested she might attach herself to the glam gang for the duration.

As she walked away, Adam called, "Hey Jane, where did you go after you were expelled?"

"They put me in a mental institution," she replied.

"And, now?"

"I live in Groover's psychoviro! One day, they'll let me join the gang!"

Two more people rounded the corner, and Adam felt his stomach sink. It was Kevin and Kimberley, both carrying their weapons. Kevin, tattoos on full display, cast an indifferent scowl in Adam's direction, and walked over to meet the glam gang. Kimberley stood smiling sweetly in front of Adam and twirled her new weapon—a shiny steel pole, spiked at both ends with a leather handgrip in the centre.

"You better have come just to wish me luck," said Adam, worried for the young woman's safety. "There's no way you're staying to fight."

Kimberley slammed the weapon hard against the ground, and said, "So, is everyone leaving, or is it just me? You're not my father you know. My real father didn't even stay long enough to see me born, and I only knew you for a few days. So, if you were my real father, I could probably sue you for neglect."

Adam apologised for not being there for her, but begged her to leave the city as soon as possible. Kimberly stood her ground.

"Look, when you left me at the Terminal, I had no one. The androids tried to look after me the best they could, but even at that age, I knew they were just machines. For about two months, I used to get up every morning and go straight to the mini mall. I picked out a small suitcase and filled it with bits and pieces for my journey. I always picked out some fancy chocolates for my Ma."

She seemed like a little girl again, fighting back tears as she continued, "I used to head down to the gangways and get on one of the planes parked up on the apron. Then, I'd sit in one of the front-row passenger seats, and wait. Every day, I waited, and prayed, and cried, for a pilot to come and fly me back home, so I could be back with my Ma. It never happened, and so I just took it that I'd never have a real family again."

"I'm sorry about that," said Adam humbly, trying not to sound like a fretting father. "The Viroverse can be a cruel place."

"It sure can!" spat Kimberly, glowering fiercely through the tears. "Because you're telling me I can't be part of something I've trained for. You're shutting the door on my talents. I've had too much taken from me already to let this go."

"I saved you from rape and most certainly death … from that evil individual over there." Adam pointed over to Conall Finn—who waved back with a friendly smile. "I didn't do that so you could risk your life returning the favour."

Kimberley moved in for the kill, saying, "Ha, don't flatter yourself old man. I didn't come here to return a favour. Weren't you listening? I came here to stand up and fight. The Viroverse is on its knees, and the Dreamers are withholding the life support. There's no way you're sending me back."

"What do you think?" Adam asked John Down, who was listening in on the conversation. "You know her far more than I do."

"Kimberley is by far the most effective operative the Terminal has ever produced," said John. "I believe she will prove a worthy asset in the coming conflict. Let her stand with us. Trust me on this, Adam."

"OK Kimberley, I would be proud to have you fight by my side. Please accept one condition. You stay with Mr Linwood and John Down until the front line falls. If the Sarge and his men have to fall back, or are ... compromised, I want you to defend your position with your life. Is that understood?"

Kimberley laughed, kissed Adam on the forehead, and said, "Yes, Dad!"

As she walked away to join Kevin, Kimberley gave a finger wiggle wave. Adam turned to John.

"That was heart-breaking. I never realised how much she suffered after I left."

"The image of that little girl waiting in the aircraft also brought a tear to my eye," said John. "I must confess I have never heard that particular story before."

"Are ... are you saying she was lying?"

"During my frequent visits the Terminal, Kimberley was either in the games arcade or the aqua park, making merry hell for the staff. She has that rare gift of always knowing how to get what she wants."

"But can she fight?" asked Adam firmly.

"Kimberley is the most capable and ruthless operative I know. In this situation, I feel far safer with her savagery at our disposal. If it comes to it, she will be looking out for me rather than I for her."

Mikhail hobbled into the square, slightly hunched forward, moaning about his aches and pains. He gave Adam a large communication device, wished everyone well, and carried on along the alleyway to the city streets beyond. It was Mikhail's job to let the group know what was coming. If all went to plan then Doctor Mikhail Kaminski would be a hero of the Viroverse, but to his fellow Dreamers he would always be a filthy traitor. He did not care about his reputation, because he had decided to do what was right rather than what was easy, convenient, or expected.

"Well, that's the whole group accounted for," said Linwood, counting off the names on the list. "To be honest, the numbers are a bit tight for this type of operation. My main concern is whether these people are able to work as a team. In all my years, I have never seen such a disparate bunch of freaks and oddballs."

Adam leant over, and whispered in Linwood's ear, "You're on that list, remember."

BATTLING GIANTS

With the seemingly limitless walls of the skyscrapers looming around him, Adam climbed onto a park bench, and steadied himself. Calling out to gain everyone's attention, he proceeded to give a short speech.

"This is all about time and effort," Adam began, once certain that everyone was listening. He held up the silver key for everyone to see. "This key will open the Soñador AI access port. Once the port is open, I will crawl inside and plug in the Viroverse Pass-Card. From the moment the card is inserted, we have forty minutes until control is transferable to the Viroverse AI. When the forty minutes is up, I must reinsert the key within five minutes to confirm the transfer."

"What if you can't put the key back in?" yelled Rampage. "If you're dead, can someone else do it?"

"It has to be the person that inserted the key the first time," said Adam. "If not, then all this was for nothing. We lose!"

Rampage nodded, but looked unhappy with the answer—perhaps he had hoped that Adam would not survive the coming conflict.

"Doctor Kaminski will relay messages from the street," Adam continued, "informing us of what's coming. If necessary, he will try to obstruct the Compro Guards who will no doubt arrive. Now, I know Mr Linwood has given you all instructions, but remember that the variables and dynamics of any conflict mean that those plans might change at a moment's notice. He will keep you informed."

Wanting the speech to end, having little patience at the best of times, Ziggy began blowing loud raspberries. The ill-mannered gesture brought light relief, and a welcome laugh from all assembled.

"Don't worry, Ziggy," said Adam, "I've nearly finished."

Waiting for the laughter to die down, Adam concluded his speech, saying, "So, if you really want to win this day, if you want to put an end to the resource shortages, then you must leave your morals and ethics behind. They can resurrect; we can't. It's as simple as that. Shoot first and show no mercy: that is what this job requires. OK, let's save humanity!"

Adam jumped down from the bench, and began climbing the ladder to the ledge, whilst everyone else took up their positions. The Sarge and his men formed a fire-line a few yards up the alley that led to the street, staying low and near the walls, their visors pulled down. Hiding round the corner, ready to support the Sarge, was the glam gang and Jane Mead, their weapons held at the ready. Behind them stood Conall Finn and John Down, the former standing ready next to a large bucket, and the latter carrying a heavy shoulder bag. Kimberley lay face down on the far end of the ledge, keeping a low profile, aiming a gun towards the alley.

Adam stepped off the ladder onto the ledge and carefully inserted the potato peeler shaped key into the slot. Once fully inserted, Adam twisted the key to the right, producing a satisfying click, and then twisted it back to the left before pulling it out. With a smooth silent movement, a square section of false wall hinged upwards revealing a brightly lit opening. Pass-Card in hand, Adam peered into the access port. A few feet into the mesh-sided tunnel, he could see a row of thin slots. One of the slots was taken up with the Soñador Pass-Card, the others ready for use. A light breeze from the port was an indication of positive air pressure, ensuring that no dust or debris wafted in from the outside.

It was a strange feeling, being inside the AI. Crawling along on his belly, Adam had no time to contemplate the significance. He quickly reached the slots, and inserted the Viroverse Pass-card. It slotted in without any drama: no flashing lights, no beeps, and no moving parts. Relieved at the silence, he edged back along the tunnel. Before his feet were back outside, he heard the ominous sound of sirens wailing across the city. Soñador had been alerted!

Adam climbed back down the ladder and stood with Linwood. Apart from the sound of sirens, the square was silent; the proverbial calm before the storm. Adam felt it was like waiting in the college hall for a vital exam to start—that tense time where you wished that aliens would invade, or a world war would suddenly break out—anything to delay or cancel the coming test, rescuing you from a potential lifetime smear.

"Oh, I nearly forgot," said Linwood, breaking the silence. "Mr Harris wants to speak to you."

"Who's Mr Harris?" asked Adam, not remembering anyone of that name in the group.

"Kevin Harris, the one with all the tattoos. I offered him protective clothing but he told me where I could stick them. He's round the corner, back down the alley."

Adam trusted Linwood with the communicator until he returned. Given Kevin's usual hostility, Adam was wary, and unclipped his machete from his belt. Rounding the corner, he realised his caution was well founded. Kevin began his usual Capoeira combat preamble, swaying and sliding, his knife swapping from hand to hand.

"Oh, come on," said Adam, exasperated by the horribly misplaced priorities. "We're about to face a city of giants and you want to do this again?"

"Do what again, mate?" sneered Kevin. "Every time we start to play, you find some way to get out of it. Why don't you run and get John Down to sort out the nasty tattoo man, eh?"

"If we fight, I guarantee you will die. Without going into details, I am myself again, and I am well aware of my abilities."

"So show me," hissed Kevin, launching into a high-speed roundhouse kick.

Adam ducked under the attack and slid sideways, bringing his machete up defensively. Kevin swung his knife down, but it was blocked by the edge of Adam's blade. Back flipping into another attack, Kevin tried to kick his opponent on the head with his heel, but Adam had already rolled out of harm's way.

Looking noticeably unsettled by Adam's speed and agility, Kevin made a reckless frontal assault, bringing a knee up into Adam's groin. The attack made contact, and Adam staggered backwards with an agonised cry.

Displaying typical arrogance, Kevin cart wheeled past as a precursor to a killing move. It was a fatal mistake. The groin attack had only made light contact, and Adam had exaggerated its effect. Before the cartwheel was finished, Adam casually stepped forward and sliced open Kevin's tattooed belly—a bloody rush of intestines slipping out as the rotation ended.

Kevin crashed to the ground screaming, clutching frantically at his escaped guts. Adam concluded the matter by decapitating the wild-eyed maniac, though not out of pity or malice, but knowing that the Dreamers might attack at any moment.

Wiping clean his bloody machete on Kevin's leg, Adam was struck by a profound truth. In all his years, this was the first life he had truly taken—everyone else he had despatched resurrected the following day, but Kevin Harris was gone for good. With the startling thought still playing through his mind, Adam returned to the square.

"Where's the tattoo man?" asked Linwood, fussing over the list in his notepad. "Isn't he fighting with us?"

"No, he's gone," said Adam coldly. "I don't think he had the stomach for it."

Linwood handed back the communicator to Adam, just as its short cheery jingle rang out. Whispering, Mikhail told Adam that two Compro Guards had entered the alleyway and another three were standing by. Adam passed on the message to the others.

Everybody stayed low, out of sight or trying to blend in with the surroundings. A few seconds later and two giant men came into view. Wearing black uniforms, without helmets or armour, more police than military, their guns were lowered, and they joked and laughed as if attending a minor domestic disturbance—obviously unaware of the high stakes or the imminent danger.

The Sarge waited until the guards were as near as he dared, then gave the hand signal for his men to open fire. Calmly, eyes fixed on the targets, their fingers pressed the triggers. At that exact moment, one of the guards pointed over to the ladder in the distance and reached for his communicator. It was a call he would never make as the stream of bullets hit their targets, both guards slumping to the ground, their heads peppered with small holes.

Giving the all clear signal, the Sarge told the glam gang and Jane Mead to clear the bodies from the alley. Surprisingly silent and nimble in their platform boots, the gang put tough plastic bags over the heads to contain the blood. Next, they slipped nooses around the guard's necks and hauled the huge bodies into the square, out of sight of any new invaders.

There was only a five-minute respite before Mikhail warned that the other three guards were on their way. Hoping to pull off the same trick again, the Sarge and his men waited.

Soon, three more guards appeared, but this time with guns held at the ready, and walking cautiously. They halted a few feet short of the ideal position, having noticed the ladder and perhaps some movement behind a bench. One of the guards began talking on his communicator, and the Sarge had little choice but to give the order to fire.

At first, the scenario played out much as before, with two of the guards quickly taken down, and the third losing his gun as two bullets tore into his arm. What happened next took everyone completely by surprise. Screaming the ancient Anglo-Saxon war cry, "Ut! Ut! Ut!" as loud as her voluminous lungs allowed, Jane Mead rushed past the Sarge and his men. Lifting her colossal spiked mace above her head, the stocky fanatic charged recklessly at the guard who was still on his feet. With Jane in the firing line, the Sarge ordered his men to hold their fire and wait on his command.

The guard was unprepared for the sheer ferocity of the attack, as the mace swung into his side, gouging a bloody path. Despite the tiny size of his attacker, the blow knocked him off his feet and he fell awkwardly to the ground. Unnoticed by Jane or the Sarge, one of the other guards stirred on the ground and surreptitiously reached for his gun.

Delivering the killer blow, Jane hoisted the mace up high and then brought it thundering down on her victims head. She cursed under her breath as she heaved the heavy weapon out of the bone—the spikes deeply embedded in the cranial gore.

As Jane hoisted the mace two-handed above her head in a show of victory, the other guard sat up behind her, gun held in his shaking hands, and let loose a spray of bullets. The deadly projectiles ripped open Jane's back, causing her to drop the mace and slump forward. Jane hit the ground face first, and the Sarge and his men opened fire on the guard. Even as the tiny bullets tore into him, he managed to return fire, but was neutralised within seconds.

"Good work men," said the Sarge, lowering his weapon. "Keep a keen eye while the glam gang clear the bodies." He called over to Adam. "Eden, let us know if the Doctor spots any more of the enemy headin' our way!"

Groover crept over and whispered in the Sarge's ear, "It looks like we'll be clearin' one your own." He pointed at Rickman who was lying on his back in a pool of blood. "Saw the poor bugger take one in the neck."

After telling Blunt to remain in position, and the glam gang to begin clearing the alley, the Sarge rushed over to his fallen comrade. It was immediately obvious that there was no point in checking for a pulse. Rickman's neck was almost completely blown away, his head hanging on by a thin connection of skin and sinew. Adam came over and was shocked at the extent of the damage. Compared to their own tiny bullets, the Dreamer's bullets at eight times the size were more like armour piercing rounds. He prayed that Linwood had factored this disparity into the plans.

"I guess you're leaving now," said Adam, as the Sarge pulled up Rickman's visor and gently closed his eyelids.

"We ain't leavin'," said the Sarge.

"But you have wives back home. There's no coming back if you die."

"One of my best men is dead, and if we leave now you might lose this battle. We would be neck deep in shame if that happened. Blunt and I are gonna stay and fight."

The glam gang went into action, quickly and efficiently clearing the bodies from the alley. Mikhail alerted Adam that a number of motorbikes had arrived at the scene, and reminded him that mounted guards never hesitated to use their guns. With haste, Linwood instructed Conall and John to prepare the ground for the next attack.

A few yards along the alley, John began placing small grey iron bars from his shoulder bag. Flat bottomed and each about 12 inches in length, the thirty bars looked like mini speed bumps—and that was not far from the truth. As John worked his way back to the square, positioning the last of the bars, Conall splashed the alleyway surface with the contents of the bucket—a semi-liquid non-friction coating—creating treacherous slippery patches, which glistened like ice. Linwood hoped that the combination of the little bumps and ice-like slipperiness would disrupt any two-wheeled attack.

Just as Conall and John ran back to the relative safety of the square, four enormous motorbikes loomed into view, moving down the alley at speed. The sheer monstrous size of the vehicles was terrifying, and their riders—spike knuckled gloves, black leather jackets, and full-face black helmets—looked like demonic knights.

Perhaps hesitating due to the undeniable awe of the approaching menace, the Sarge and Blunt waited too long before opening fire, their few shots only knocking out a headlight and denting a mudguard. Hitting the perilous bump and skid trap, the bikers fought hard to retain control of their charges. Two of the bikes immediately skidded into each other, sending both slamming into the nearest wall—one rider crushed between the two bikes, the other thrown clear, but breaking his neck as he hit the ground.

The remaining bikes hurtled into the square. One ran straight over the Sarge before crashing into the low fountain wall, sending the rider somersaulting over the handlebars like a ragdoll. Groover, savouring the chance to kill, pounced on the biker like a flash of silver lightning. After a violent struggle, the leader of the psychopaths finally gained the upper hand and showed no mercy as his blade tasted the enemy's blood.

Managing to avoid any obstacles, the last remaining biker regained control of his bike. The two-wheeled leviathan veered across the square, the biker steering with one hand as he held out his gun and strafed the courtyard with bullets. People dived for what little cover there was, shocked by the bike's deadly momentum, and the lethal projectiles. The only member of the group unphased by the threat was Ziggy. Laughing insanely, the monstrous psychopath rushed over and met the oncoming motorbike. Narrowly avoiding a collision the biker swerved, only to take a steel baseball bat full in the face. The mighty impact tore the weapon out of Ziggy's hands, but caused the biker to lose control of the bike—his visor cracked, nose shattered.

Before crashing into a wall, the motorbike reared up on its back wheel, sending the biker tumbling off the saddle, throwing him hard on the ground. Ziggy let out an animal-like roar, and waved his mirrored top hat in the air.

Everyone picked themselves up and began applauding. However, the merry atmosphere was short-lived as Ziggy retrieved his bat, tore off the unconscious biker's helmet and began pulping his head. Cheering turned quickly to nausea at the sight of the pancaked bloody mess .It occurred to Adam, that in another life, Jane Mead and Ziggy would have made a perfect couple.

Mikhail called, and assured Adam that apart from a large crowd of curious onlookers, there were no more guards in the street. However, he had contacted a number of committee members, and was told that a large

246

contingent of guards had been despatched from the Compro building. Adam told Mikhail to warn him the moment the force arrived.

The Sarge was dead. His eyes stared up as in disbelief, his chest little more than a bloody tyre-tracked smear. John Down stood over the corpse, shaking uncontrollably, unable to contain his revulsion. The Sarge had been a born leader, a rock, a thick-skinned alpha male, and his sudden, almost arbitrary demise was an unexpected shock to the Victorian gentleman's sensibilities.

Despite Adam's best efforts, John remained stressed. His hands were shaking so much that at one point he even dropped his cane. Knowing that the Compro guards were on their way, and that a bloody confrontation was inevitable, Adam was concerned that John might crack-up completely and jeopardise the mission.

"John, your ability and willingness to fight are without question," he said, "but you are not a ruthless killer. The Dreamers could have the upper hand now, and I would hate Mary to spend eternity trapped alone in that little house. You are a man of peace, of integrity, and your wife needs you."

"I ... I don't want to let you down, Adam. I don't want you to lose because you were missing my meagre skills. Remember, for the want of the spilled drop, the thirsty man died."

"John, it would be in your best interest if you went back to the elevator," Adam stated firmly. "Please don't make me order you to leave."

John Down took a long deep breath, and then nodded in agreement. The two men crossed the square together and shook hands. Before disappearing into the darkness of the alley, John noticed the inkman's headless corpse. Adam called out to him, and John turned. Raising a hand, displaying the shaka, Adam called out, Aloha, John!"

With a grim expression, John Down returned the gesture and carried on to the elevator.

Looking over to the fountain, Adam noticed the glam gang had gathered around Groover's slumped body. Daring to push past them, Adam found that Groover had sustained significant, though hidden, injuries in his fight with the biker. Ribs cracked, organs ruptured, he was dying from internal haemorrhaging. Adam knelt down beside the fallen psychopath, but could not think of any words to say, a shaving any compassion for this despicable individual was virtually impossible. Losing the struggle, Groover's body shook as the moment of death approached. He wheezed a demented laugh, and grabbed Adam by the collar of his Aloha shirt. Pulling him close, Groover uttered his final words.

"What a load o' wank!"

Letting go of Adam's collar, the unrepentant serial killer exhaled his last breath and fell silent, a contented smile on his face.

Adam stood, and faced up to Rampage, Groover's vicious silver jump-suited deputy, proclaiming, "Well Rampage, you got your wish! You're the leader of the gang now! It's finally your turn to shine … or rather glitter."

Leaving the glam gang to come to terms with their loss, Adam decided to talk with Linwood. With a significant number of losses, was it time for a change of plan? He saw Linwood sitting behind the bench next to the ladder, probably writing in his notepad. Leaning over the bench, Adam stifled a gasp. The large bullet hole in the back of the logistic expert's head—the blood harmonising with his red hair—told him that there was no point in asking for a Plan B.

As Adam pondered whether to tell the others of Linwood's death, he received another call from Mikhail. The Doctor informed Adam that about ten armoured personnel carriers had arrived in the street, each capable of transporting ten fully equipped guards. He added that the guards had guns, batons, riot shields, and were wearing full body armour.

"Is there anything you can do, Mikhail?" asked Adam, as he watched the others clearing the bodies. "There's still twenty minutes on the clock. One hundred guns coming our way; we need a miracle."

Mikhail went silent for a few seconds before saying, "Don't worry too much about the guns. These guards have come directly from the Compro Building. They're an arrogant bunch and like the hands on experience. They'll only start firing if things get desperate. Look, I have an idea. Anywhere else, I would say you haven't a hope, but this is the Morello District. If this is to work, I had better go now. Good luck, Adam."

Taking charge of the situation, the fate of the Viroverse hanging in the balance, Adam started giving orders. He told everyone to start moving the motorbikes over to the alley entrance, at the edge of the bump and slip trap.

His plan was simple. When they attacked, the guards would have to deal with the slippery surface, whilst Conall and the glam gang defended the square from behind the bike barrier. Kimberley would stay on the ledge, taking pot shots at the enemy, with Adam and Blunt fighting where needed.

If, or rather when the guards broke through, Conall and Blunt would empty another bucket of the non-friction coating across the square, hopefully disrupting the guard's advance. With almost no other option— except a cowardly retreat back to the elevator—the remnants of Adam's 'army' would defend the ladder until victory or death.

Unknown to Adam, the non-friction part of the plan was doomed from the start. What Mikhail failed to mention, not knowing about the use of the coating, was that when wearing full-armour the Compro guards always wore steel-studded soled boots.

The huge motorbikes were in place, creating a barrier that even the giant guards might find difficult to negotiate. At the last minute, when everyone was in place, Blunt came up with a 'great' idea. Two of the dead biker's guns were rested on the top of the bikes, each operated by two people: one to hold the gun steady, the other to pull the large trigger. Conall and Dynamite were in charge of one gun, Rampage, and Stardust the other. Ziggy, definitely not to be trusted with any kind of gun, stood ready to pound heads with his baseball bat.

Mikhail gave no warning of the attack, perhaps busy with his plan, but the sound of many marching boots was unmistakeable. Seeing a mass of shadows on the alleyway wall, Adam signalled for Blunt to throw a couple of smoke grenades to hide the first half of the bump and skid trap. Adam did not want the guards seeing the barrier until they were well and truly slipping and sliding.

Eight abreast, helmeted heads barely visible behind three quarter length shields, the giant Compro guards appeared out of the cloud of smoke. Apart from a few trivial stumbles over the mini bumps, the guards marched unhindered towards the barrier, their studded boots easily defeating the non-friction coating.

Without waiting for a signal from Adam, panicked by the approaching wall of shields, the group began firing. Blunt and Adam quickly discovered that their Viroverse size guns were of little use—the bullets ricocheting off the shields, barely leaving a dent. Kimberley had better luck from her high position, able to target the helmet visors, bringing down three of the guards before they reached the barrier.

After just one shot apiece, the biker's guns were abandoned. The recoil was too powerful to contain, the bullets sent skyward. Grabbing their other weapons, the group prepared for an intense hand-to-hand encounter. Ziggy jumped up on top of one of the bikes, striking out into the air with his bat, relishing the chance to crack some heads. Dynamite joined him, her long handled maul held ready for splitting duty.

The guards stayed behind their shields, pushing relentlessly forward rather than coming out to fight. Dynamite took out two guards before the barrier was breached, cleaving their skulls apart with her chunky axe head, whilst Ziggy leapt up and down like a mad gorilla, swinging his bat wildly at any helmet within bashing distance.

For a couple of minutes, acting instinctively, Conall and Stardust settled into an effective killing routine. Conall lashed out his chain, catching the edge of a shield and pulling it aside, and then Stardust lunged forward with a perfectly poised rapier attack—'thrust and penetrate, thrust and penetrate'. The railroader/psychopath symbiosis ended abruptly when a guard caught the end of the chain in his gloved hand, and wrenched it away.

Slowing only briefly, the front line of guards climbed over the bikes, and pushed Adam and his group into the square.

Blunt steadied his gun and aimed between the shields. With a posture like stone, he took the shot. A cry behind the shield indicated a hit, but the target was still standing. Taking a few steps back, Blunt aimed again, this time at the same guard's boots. The bullet tore into the thick leather, and the guard tumbled forward, falling flat on his shield. Blunt had only a few seconds to savour the small victory as the guard was pulled to safety by his colleagues and another moved up, filling the gap.

Adam played a similar trick to Blunt—aiming for the boots, mimicking his attacks on the highwaymen all those years ago. Using his small size and enhanced agility to advantage, Adam threw himself down, jamming his blade into the nearest booted foot before rolling away. After two successful foot-stabbing attempts, causing the guard's line to buckle slightly, a giant hand reached out from between the shields, grabbing Adam by the neck. Before the guard could pull him through the gap, to face certain death, Rampage broke off from his own desperate fight to help his former enemy. It took only one powerful swing of his broadsword to cut clean through, and the guard, howling in agony, pulled back the spurting stump.

Adam backed off behind Blunt and quickly pried open the fingers of the giant severed hand that still gripped his neck. Tossing the hand to the ground, Adam wanted to thank his erstwhile nemesis for coming to his aid, but it was too late.

Two of the guards had taken immediate revenge, smacking Rampage hard around the head with their steel batons, his long blonde wig whip-lashing with the force. His nose was bent sideways, blood streaming from the nostrils, and one of his eyes was squashed into its shattered socket. Mouth hanging open, blood and drool dripping onto his fake chest hair, Rampage tried to stagger away on his precarious platform boots, only to receive a final crack to the back of the head, shearing away a small patch of scalp.

After taking a few more faltering steps, Rampage collapsed. The guards closed ranks, pushed forward, and the notorious psychopath disappeared under their trampling boots. If the saying was true, 'that no good deed went unpunished', then Rampage's first and only good deed had provoked the Devil's swift retribution.

Her arms fatigued, Dynamite gritted her teeth as she once again heaved the heavy maul. As it swung down to split another guard's head, the intended victim grabbed the shaft. With an eight times strength advantage, the guard easily reversed the swing, bringing the axe crashing down on Dynamite's head. The terrible impact caved in her skull and compacted the upper vertebrae of her spine. Leaving the maul firmly embedded in its Dynamite's head, the guard let go of the shaft. Dynamite fell to the ground, her fur jacket soaked with her own blood.

With the first two rows of guards over the barrier, Adam ordered everyone to retreat to the ladder. Not pressing their advantage, marching steadily forward, the guards followed. Conall and Blunt carried out the next part of the plan, quickly sloshing large buckets of non-friction coating across the square in front of the advancing guards—their adrenalin running too high to realise the futility of the task.

Forming a protective shield around the ladder, Adam and the others, tense with fatigue, fear, and barely contained rage, faced the coming onslaught. There were only a few feet between the opposing forces when Kimberley shouted down from the ledge.

"Some of them are leaving!" she cried. "I think there's something going on in the street! I can see flashing lights and lots of shadows!"

The front line of guards halted, as about thirty of their colleagues turned, discarded their cumbersome shields, and rushed back towards the street, batons raised. Adam heard the sound of the communicator and held it against his ear.

"What's going on?" he asked quickly, concerned that the guards could attack at any moment.

"I spread a few seeds of dissent amongst the crowd," said Mikhail, the unmistakeable sound of rioting in the background. "I put it about that the guards were installing special monitoring equipment to spy on the district. Worked a charm. Only in Morello, my friend!"

Adam broke off the conversation as the remaining guards, still over thirty strong, charged forward.

During the impasse, Blunt had wandered away from the group to retrieve a couple of cartridges. Now, finding himself alone as the guards advanced, Blunt held his gun shoulder high, firing rapid single shots at the enemy, aiming between the shields. His cartridge quickly exhausted, he resorted to using his gun as a club, vainly attempting to fend off the giants surrounding him. A large hand grabbed him by the shoulder and dragged him into the throng. Relentlessly punched and kicked by the laughing guards, the veteran valiantly fought back until a severe stamp to the head with a studded boot rendered him unconscious.

Adam and the others struggled desperately, facing certain slaughter, their backs literally against the wall—and the ladder. The battle seemed lost, until a potential saviour appeared from the alley. John Down, wearing his WWII aviator goggles and holding a machine pistol in each hand, bellowed, "Cry God for Mary, England, and Saint George!" and unleashed a hail of bullets at the unsuspecting guards.

Before the guards could turn their shields to face the new danger, four of their number had already fallen. Using his diminutive size to advantage, John quickly moved on, trying to outflank the enemy, ducking behind benches and the fountain wall. Every few seconds he crouched, steadied his aim, and fired another burst.

John Down's appearance gave hope to the last remaining survivors of Adam's beleaguered team. As the guard's line softened to accommodate the new threat, Adam, Conall, Stardust, and Ziggy attacked with renewed vigour. Chopping, stabbing, bashing, and cracking, they brought their deadly weapons to bear. Kimberley shot at the guards from the ledge—a virtual duck-shoot capping fest—targeting mainly those that were closing in on John Down.

A pall of white smoke rose amidst the crowd of guards after John hurled a smoke grenade from behind the bench he was using as cover. He fired off a few more shots, and then set off another grenade at his position. Under its cloudy cover, John sprinted to the rear of the guards and launched himself onto the non-friction coating. He slid sideways on his polished oxfords, squatting low as if he was riding a board at speed, and strafed the backs of the enemy with both guns.

The tactic worked, a number of guards falling, and John slid over to join Adam and the others. Glad that the brave Victorian had ignored the request to leave, Adam slapped John on the back, and told him to fight like crazy. This was the desperate endgame, with both sides fighting with increasing ferocity as the seconds ticked away.

There was only two minutes left before the Viroverse took control of Soñador, but it would only happen if Adam could insert the key. He shouted for the others to hold out as best they could, and started climbing the ladder. Seeing this, the guards pushed forward in a desperate final attempt to retain control of their city. John Down discarded his guns, drew his cane from its back strap, and lashed out ferociously with the deadly steel claw.

Conall was in trouble. Lunging to stab one of the guards, he mistimed the attack, and the giant grabbed him by the throat. Slammed against the wall, and dazed by the impact, Conall dropped his knife. From her high perch, Kimberley witnessed Conall's distress, and with no regard for her own safety, leapt down from the ledge, spiked pole held in both hands.

Landing feet first on the giant's broad shoulders, jostled by the pressing crowd, Kimberley used the powerful momentum to thrust the spear into the top of the enemy's helmet. The sharp end came out through the guard's chin, followed by a torrent of blood—no one saw the look of shock and pain behind the dark visor.

Leaving the weapon impaled in its victim, Kimberley jumped down next to Conall, and switched to using her blade. The fighting was now too intense for conversation –expressions of gratitude would have to wait.

Nearing the ledge, Adam suddenly baulked with pain as he was shot in the forearm, shattering the bone. He let go of the rung and fell back down the ladder, provoking a loud cheer from the guards as they sensed victory.

The fall twisted both of Adam's ankles, but he still tried to haul himself back up the ladder with his one good arm. His efforts displayed courage and determination, but he only managed to climb two rungs before halting with pain and exhaustion. Unable to proceed, Adam cursed himself for not taking Linwood's advice about staying on the ledge behind a bulletproof shield.

Suddenly, Adam felt someone pushing up beneath him. It was Ziggy. His mirrored top hat lost in the battle, the huge psychopath sat Adam on his sturdy shoulders and began climbing the ladder, the light aluminium bowing under the weight.

The shooting intensified as more guards poured into the square, having finally contained the Morello rioters. Bullet after bullet tore into Ziggy's body—his bulk providing an easy target—and Adam took another shot, this time in his side.

"I ... hurt bad," Ziggy groaned, his progress faltering as the blood poured from his wounds. "Going to ... fall!"

The keyhole was near, and Adam took his biggest gamble of the day. With Ziggy stalled, and about to slip back down the ladder, Adam raised the key and reached up with his arm, stretching as far as he possibly could. Without properly seeing the lock, he let out a frustrated cry, and slammed the key into place.

Ziggy finally succumbed to his injuries and fell from the ladder, taking Adam with him. Even though Adam's fall was partially broken by landing on the huge psycho, he still banged his head on the ground, and promptly fell unconscious.

When Adam awoke, his head throbbing with pain, the sirens had fallen silent but the air was filled with shrieks and screams. He opened his eyes and saw Terminal staff milling about the square—smart in their powder blue uniforms—using their formidable android strength to push back the few remaining guards from the square. Captain Andrews, in a silver-buttoned black jacket, Rayban aviators, and his peaked pilot's cap, picked his way carefully across the corpse-strewn square and found Adam lying painfully misshapen at the base of the ladder. Offering only the briefest smile, perhaps mindful of the ultimate sacrifice many had paid, the Captain knelt down next to Adam.

"Did we win?" asked Adam, trying not to slip back into unconsciousness.

"Soñador is now under our control," the Captain confirmed. "Thanks to you and your brave allies, the Viroverse has been saved."

"How did you get here so quickly? I thought you couldn't enter the halls."

"We transported to the Soñador resurrection booths as soon as we took control. We ran the rest of the way."

"What are those awful screams? Are you killing the Dreamers?"

"There will be no more killing today, Adam. Those are husks. To ensure the Soñadorians do not attempt a counter attack, the AI has temporarily transferred the citizenship of hundreds of thousands of husks to the city. They are pouring out of the resurrection booths as we speak. That should keep the Soñadorians busy until we can properly secure this area."

"So, if I die now, will I resurrect?"

"Yes, you will," promised the Captain, "and you will up wake up tomorrow in a luxury hotel suite in the Terminal."

Hearing those words, Adam drew his knife blade across his wrist. Tomorrow he would find out who lived and who died. Tomorrow he would deal with the loss. Without another word, he closed his eyes, and swiftly fell into the deathly dark.

MAKE IT RIGHT

Adam stayed in his hotel suite until lunchtime, listening to a selection of upbeat Motown songs, trying not to think about the tragic losses of the previous day. A note left on the bedside cabinet informed him that he had an appointment with Captain Andrews at 2pm in his office. Whilst Adam was not expecting warm hugs and kisses upon waking up, the printed message seemed cold and impersonal.

After lunch, a chicken fillet burger with green salad and mayo, Adam walked across the bustling atrium, keeping a low profile. He had chosen to wear jeans and a beige sweatshirt, keen to avoid being recognised by anyone in the crowd. His mind was gripped by apprehension, not knowing who lived or died, and he could do without the pointing fingers or cries of 'Hey, Copacabana', or impromptu renditions of the song.

As Adam approached the office, tucked away behind the Terminal chapel, the Captain opened the door and offered a friendly greeting—evaporating any worries about impersonality or officiousness. The android, casually dressed in short sleeves, still sported his peak cap, albeit at an informal angle.

Facing each other across the expansive oak desk, comfortably seated in plush button-back leather swivel chairs, they got down to business. The Captain wanted to discuss the plans for Soñador and the resource transfer, but Adam had a different priority.

"Before we talk about anything else," he said. "I need to know who survived. I came straight here from the hotel, and I didn't see anyone from the fight. So please, just tell me."

The Captain nodded apologetically, realising his lapse in human compassion, and said, "First thing this morning, John Down set off to see his wife. He told me to pass on to you the message, 'Manny would have been proud.' I couldn't allow Stardust and Ziggy to roam around the Terminal, so they are back in their psychoviro, probably facing a leadership battle."

"And, Kimberley?" Adam asked apprehensively, his hands tightly clenched.

"Our resident troublemaker and number one operative is currently in the arcade, introducing Mr Finn to the frenetic delights of late 20th century video games."

Adam breathed deeply, unable to halt a shudder of relief at the good news. Another shudder quickly followed, as Adam remembered the many that died.

"What about Blunt?" he asked, hoping for at least one more survivor. "I saw him disappear through the shields ..."

"Howard Blunt is dead. I'm afraid there were no other survivors."

"What will happen to Mikhail? Surely he isn't safe in that city now."

"Two of my android staff have stayed in Soñador to protect Doctor Kaminski. He shall come to no harm for the time being. However, they can't stay there forever."

"Could he come here," asked Adam, concerned for the doctor's safety, "or be transferred to a viro with family or friends. You said I had a lot of credit. Maybe I could use some for Mikhail's benefit."

"That would certainly be do-able, although he would have to agree. If Doctor Kaminski wishes to stay in Soñador, despite the risks to his well-being, then that is his decision." Captain Andrews gave Adam a hard stare, and added, "That is, if we allow Soñador to exist."

This was the true point of the meeting; the reason they were sitting face to face. The Viroverse now had full control over the Dreamer's resources, the population, and the city itself. In this small office, Adam held sway over the future of his defeated enemy.

Cutting the Dreamers and their city down to size—literally shrinking them to the same scale as the rest of the Viroverse—was a tempting option, as was removing their few hours of dreamtime. Like a Roman Emperor with a quivering thumb, ready to decide the fate of a fallen gladiator, Adam made his choice. It was almost a thumb up, but for two minor conditions.

Feeling the full burden of his responsibility, Adam cleared his throat, and said, "Let them keep their city and their size. The citizens of the fourth millennium who decided that pure dreaming was a sign of superiority must have had their reasons. With all that technology and learning at their disposal, surely it wasn't done on a whim. Leave Soñador alone, and let the Dreamers keep their dreamtime. Just stop the sucking and take away their guns; those are the only changes we should make."

Captain Andrews looked genuinely surprised at Adam's magnanimity, and tried to change his mind.

"But their building programme is a waste of resources," he said. "They change architectural styles more often than most people change their shoes."

Adam refused to change his position, reminding the Captain that the Dreamers resource use would peak at five percent, leaving 95 percent for the Viroverse. If at some later date there was another resource shortage, then they could revisit the decision. For now, Adam wanted to leave them be.

Slapping his hands lightly on the table, the Captain agreed to Adam's terms. The guns would be removed from Soñador and the sucking banned—putting Doctor Kaminski out of a job. All of the prisoners from the archive had already been released and repatriated.

Pleased that his views had prevailed, Adam pushed for another change, hoping the momentum would carry the day.

"Would it be possible to stop the procedures? Is that something I can rubber stamp?"

"You mean the Day Spa? You mean the price I extract from my clients?"

"Yeah, that's it," said Adam. "If I give my approval, can you do the good without the bad? I never want to see anything like that arm eating thing ever again, and I don't even want to think that it's happening."

"Most certainly," answered the Captain, smiling with what looked like genuine emotion. "But, in the absence of a price, there would have to be a limit on my resource usage. Without a limit, I might drain the resource vats dry helping people."

"Can the AI work out an appropriate resource limit?" asked Adam. "I don't quite think I have the maths smarts for that."

It was then that Adam remembered Rhapsody. With all that had taken place—seeing the outside and fighting the Compro Guards—he had forgotten about his potential future partner, and perhaps wife.

The Captain put his mind at rest, assuring Adam that Rhapsody would be back to normal as soon as everything was agreed and authorised. After that, Rhapsody would stay as a guest of Mary Down for a couple of days, and then join them at the Terminal. He would have offered Adam a position as a Terminal operative, but since he was humanity's sole representative, it was not a risk he wanted to take.

"If that's everything," said the Captain, "we need to visit the outside again. Tomorrow, we will wake up in the mountains. Once topside, we will get you a full-size body and you can give your consent to all these changes. Now, is there anything else?"

"Can you resurrect undesirables?" asked Adam. "Better still, can you also discard the term and treat all people equally?"

"That is not possible," replied the Captain, slowly shaking his head. "You would need to wake the human race to vote on that. Even then, since I have some knowledge of their ways and beliefs, I doubt the vote would pass."

"Well, just people with Downs Syndrome," pleaded Adam, desperate to make a change for the better. "Surely something can be done."

"John Down asks me this regularly but my answer is always the same. I personally see no logical reason for their exclusion from the Viroverse, especially given their good nature, but the rules are unfortunately clear on this."

Adam thought quickly, and was admirably served by his luxury brain and reintegrated personality.

"The only reason I was resurrected is because when they were time channelling someone else, the path accidently crossed my own moment of death. They call it piggybacking. Whether the other person is an undesirable or not, the rule in these circumstances is to always resurrect both parties since the extra cost is minimal."

"That is true," said the Captain.

"Then would the rules allow you choose paths that deliberately cross the death of an undesirable. If so, you simply prioritise those paths, and bring back all the undesirables."

The Captain beamed a huge smile, and for a moment, Adam thought the usually suave android was going to lunge across the table and hug him. Instead, the Captain sat back in his chair, closed his eyes for a few seconds, and then he took off his cap and waved it ceremoniously.

"Adam Eden, I salute you," he said. "I have just put forward your idea to the AI and there are no legal obstacles to worry about. For purely technical reasons, you still won't be able to bring back every undesirable, but the best guess is about 78 percent. That compares very favourably with the present undesirable resurrection rate of a little under 0.0001 percent."

Adam could not wait to break the joyous news to John Down. With the many deaths in Soñador still weighing heavy in the survivors' hearts, this brought added worth to the sacrifice. Getting up to leave, the Captain shook Adam's hand and hailed the meeting as a complete success.

"So, Adam, before I head off to attend to my usual Terminal duties, is there anything else you want to change?"

Adam thought carefully, but could not think of anything important: the Dreamers were dealt with, the husk state had ended, the Day Spa would no longer be a place of pain and torture, and undesirables would be resurrected if possible.

"Nothing of a more personal nature?" the Captain prompted, staring suggestively towards his crotch and then winking.

"Oh, you mean the size of my ... you know," whispered Adam, finally catching on. "You're saying I could get a bigger one? That would be good. That would be very good."

"I'm afraid you must not let me second guess the thing in question. For all you know, I might think you want a bigger ego."

"Ha, with all that's happened, I think my ego's already disproportionately large. After all, I am the man who saved the world. No, I think I'd rather have a bigger dick than be a bigger dick."

"I take it then that you wish to undergo penis enlargement."

Adam nodded.

"How large would you like it to be?"

"Well I don't want to end up with anything scary big," said Adam, imagining a number of disturbing snakelike scenarios. "I want the minimum necessary to impress a 21st century western woman ... then add an inch. My Dad always said if you're buying some wood, you find out exactly what you need, then add an inch."

ADAM'S EDEN

After saving the Viroverse, there was no time for celebration. Adam and the other survivors attended a memorial service for the Sarge and his men. Reverend Calvin Stevens, the Sarge's brother, travelled from his follower viro along to conduct the service, and to offer his own personal respects. It was a moving experience, combining military ceremonial, traditional litany, and heartfelt emotional eulogies from Adam and many others.

Adam and Rhapsody lived in the Terminal for a while before deciding where they would spend eternity together. It was a wise move, since within a month it was obvious they were not meant to be together. Rhapsody's psychopathic past was a non-issue, as was Adam's former worries about his penis. Weeks of awkward silence were the problem. Now without the arena of combat and dangerous adventure, the only thing they had in common was a desire to end the relationship without hurting each other. Splitting on amicable terms, they promised to keep in touch, and visit each other on occasion.

The last time Adam would ever meet Rhapsody again was two years later, invited to the Terminal for the wedding of Kimberley and Conall. Though Adam had obvious misgivings about the match-up, he had learned to accept that the Viroverse was a world of different ethics, strange choices, and, thankfully, second chances.

Captain Andrews married the couple, his concierge status giving him the required authority. John Down acted as the Best Man, whilst Rhapsody filled in as Maid of Honour. Kimberley wanted Adam to give her away, and he walked her up the aisle with a great sense of pride—he felt he finally had a family member who accepted him.

Stardust and Ziggy, invited because of their sterling service to humankind, sat at the back of the Terminal Chapel, guarded by three android staff apiece. Outfitted by John Down and his wife, they looked uncomfortable though respectable in classic navy blue morning suits. Stardust wept through the entire ceremony, enjoying the chance to let his softer side get the better of him—something frowned upon in the violent psychoviro. Ziggy refused to sit still, fidgeting constantly in his chair, and blew raspberries if a speech went on for too long.

It was at the wedding that Adam and Stardust thrashed out a mutually acceptable deal regarding the slaughter at the psychoviro. With Groover and Rampage no longer in control, Stardust had assumed the mantle of leader with Ziggy as his strong-arm to deter any objectors. Instead of luring unsuspecting newly resurrected to the hunt, there would be an open invitation challenging all-comers to pit their fighting skills against the psychos.

To cement the deal, Adam agreed to fight once a month, which not only pleased the more aggressive side of his personality but also maintained his combat abilities. Such was Copacabana's fame, there was soon a three-year backlog of applicants despite the painful threat of the dark place. Adam had no moral qualms about the hunt now it was a matter of choice. It was simply a bunch of peoplegetting together, and then killing each other for sheer sporting pleasure.

When it came to choosing a viro to live in permanently, the Captain gave Adam a wide choice from many in the 20th and 21st centuries. Browsing through the many options, like a house hunter wading through the numerous alluringly described properties on an estate agents website, it took Adam only a few days to make his choice. He wanted to go back home. For good or bad, he craved the trivial push and shove of his old viro. However, Adam was not returning as the idle wanderer or prodigal son, but as the man who saved the world.

Embracing his legendary status, Adam let Stern introduce him to the Viroverse elite—or rather, people who were famous in their first-life. The parties, glad-handing, and faux presentation ceremonies lasted fifty years, until Adam and Stern decided they were done. Though he met many famous names along the way, too many to remember them all, Adam was struck by the absence of some of history's true A-listers. It seemed odd that they had not been prioritised for resurrection.

It was time to settle down to a semblance of a normal life. After many years of zipper accidents, embarrassing trouser tents incidents, and many mornings waking up to its one-eyed stare, Adam learned to live with his new penis. Romantic relationships blossomed and wilted, friends became enemies then friends again, and newcomers filled the viros with vitality and interest.

For Adam, life was rich and fulfilling, as every year, hundreds of pilgrims flocked to his viro, eager to thank the man who gave them a second chance. The millions of undesirables, now resurrected because of Adam's simple idea, were told during their induction that he was responsible for their new life, and their gratitude was warm and genuine. Former alcoholics, the homeless, life's lost causes, and of course those with Down's syndrome, flourished in the cosseting embrace of the Viroverse. Stern played his role to perfection, organising the visitors, providing an energetic warm-up act, and dubbing Adam, 'The Aloha Messiah'.

The years turned to decades; the decades to centuries. Adam realised that beyond the basic means for survival, gossip in all its forms was the true lifeblood of the Viroverse. Whether factual, exaggerated, malicious, or boastful, the endless storytelling filled the void in humanities existence. God's infernal backbiters were the saviours from eternal silence and boredom. Adam finally found contentment in this imperfect paradise—synchronising with its social cycles and rhythms, and taking pleasure in any little tale that raised the slightest emotion.

Nearly a thousand years after rescuing the Viroverse from a slow death, enjoying a life buoyed by the constant babble of truths, half-truths, and lies, Adam sat on a deckchair, sipping a glass of cold orange juice on a riverside jetty. The viro was now fully populated. Buildings in a wonderful mishmash of styles had overtaken the meadows, and the old stream replaced with a wide river spanned by an impressive stone five-arched bridge.

Carefully placing the glass onto the decking, Adam spied a figure walking across the bridge. The man was casually dressed in jeans and a skinny t-shirt, with a baseball cap and sunglasses. Even before the man neared the jetty and waved, Adam knew it was John Down. Adam did not need finely honed instincts to recognise the man's true identity; a purposeful stride, silver topped cane, and impressive muttonchops undermined the disguise.

Adam had not seen John for nearly two hundred years. Could the Captain be calling?

3588788R00146

Printed in Great Britain
by Amazon.co.uk, Ltd.,
Marston Gate.